PIRA

At Ryan's touch Janielle stirred, raising huge violet eyes to him, relief flooding through her. But as the expression of arrogant superiority on his handsome face, she remembered that she loathed him.

He reached down to her, lifting her to her feet. Gaining her equilibrium, Janielle swayed against him, carefully steadying herself.

"Angry, love?" he taunted.

Furiously, Janielle brushed past him, moving quickly toward the door. Instantly, his hand reached out, preventing her. Janielle spun on him.

"You unspeakable jackanapes!" she stormed.

Ryan laughed down at her. "I am amazed at the refinement of Challey serving wenches."

"I am not—" Janielle started angrily.

"Not what, love?"

"Your reputation is well earned, *pirate—bastard—lord*!" she spat at him, ripping her arm free of his grasp.

His hand slashed across her face, hurling her across the bed. Then he was upon her, smothering her beneath his long, hard body. Even white teeth flashed down at her.

"You gave me no quarter with your words. Now I give you none!"

Also by Lynna Lawton:

GLORY'S MISTRESS

Under
Crimson Sails

LYNNA LAWTON

LEISURE BOOKS   NEW YORK CITY

For Art, and the Tall Ships

A LEISURE BOOK

Published by

Dorchester Publishing Co., Inc.
6 East 39th Street
New York, NY 10016

Printed in the United States of America

prologue

Crisp parchment, angrily hurled from the *Waverly*'s foredeck, winged steadily downward, its carefully tended lettering sliding, distorting, as it grazed the silver glittered wavelets below. A lone harbor gull, its curved, ocher-hued beak open in anticipation, swooped low, gathered the curled, sea-rinsed message into its beak and glided heavenward, out to the immense sea. For a moment the gull soared; then, realizing its curious mistake, it let the paper fall. Years of distance lay between the message floating seaward, and the captain who watched with wintry eyes as the words drifted out to sea.

Ryan Deverel, his lean, dark fingers gripping the rail of the *Waverly*'s main deck, listened to his ship's anchor groaning in protesting rhythm against its confinement to land. His stormy eyes traveled across the harbor to the nestling curve where sky met sea. A good voyage from London, a profitable one. For awhile the sea would have to wait for him. And it would.

part one
CHALLEY

---

chapter 1

"Easy, love," he breathed, his voice low and husky in the darkened shadows. Gentle fingers trembling with warm strength closed over her mouth. His tall form loomed above her, silhouetted by choked, murky light from the vine-cloaked window.

Daylight? No, it couldn't be, not this soon. Janielle fought the wavery clutches of slumber, her heart drumming a wild roll toward awakeness. How had he known she was here? Her weighted limbs began to struggle upward against him as his long arms pinned her to the day couch.

The masculine, sea-wild scent of him mingled with a faintness of bitter, rich brandy. The span of his wide shoulders, the encrusted gold buttons of his Surtout pressing against her, brought Janielle up sharply. Dark, crisp hair grazed her shoulder as he leaned across her, his mouth only inches from her own.

"A name, love, and an explanation as to your presence here—only if your voice is soft," he said, a mocking tone to the words.

What should she tell him—the truth? That she had delayed leaving Challey for a single glimpse of him? A vain, foolish decision, prompted by the fascinating tales whispered about him in the drawing rooms of

Charleston's landed gentry. Or that she had been his mother's companion for the last few weeks until her death? That she was John Patterson's daughter, and everyone along the Santee Sweep and in Charleston's aristocratic social circles was in awe of her family's esteem?

But he wouldn't be in awe. If she were to believe the fevered gossip about the rakish bastard heir of Challey, nothing save a woman's willing body would be of interest to him. Or, perhaps, the clinking of gold coin passed to him from pirate's plunder on the high seas.

Suddenly angry shudders surged through her. Wildly, she shook her head free from his large hand. Slowly, caressingly, his lean, sun-darkened fingers curled around her slim shoulders. She squirmed beneath the scalding, bold intensity of his gaze. His eyes bored down at her from ice-blue pools, a wintry, sea-swept pastel in a sunburnt face.

"You are hurting me, sir," Janielle managed.

Instantly the steel fingers relaxed their hold. A slow, lazy smile eased across his mouth. Janielle caught her breath, her tumbling, crazed thoughts groping for escape from the situation.

She would tell him nothing. Let him think what he will. Only a few hours remained until full light, and she could slip down the stairwell and out through the unused slave quarters, and find Micah. He'd fetch the field wagon and take her to Patterson Woods.

The immediate predicament was more pressing. Lord, a scandal like this would rock her prestigious father's career and doom her to spinsterhood. She must handle the situation with delicacy.

Thick tallow sputtered protestingly against the flaming tinder, yielding a spread of golden-hued, silky light. Janielle shielded her eyes from the sudden brightness; then, in a moment, she had her first full look at the man towering over her. She pulled in a sharp breath, not daring to move. It was all true.

7

Ryan Deverel felt a rocking jolt that reached down to his belly. Muted candlelight played across her white-gold hair, spread recklessly like a silvery gossamer fan across the pillow. Clear, honey-tinged skin caught the golden light of the candle flame. Her firm, delicately molded breasts thrust impudently up at him, straining against the low curve of her gown. Slim, tapered fingers clutched at the satin coverlet. Her huge violet eyes, flecked with hazy indigo, swallowed him.

Suddenly the forms of countless women swirled before him, blurred in a meaningless rush of cold memories. This small one, whoever she was, he would remember.

Slowly he straightened, though his steady, ice-blue eyes never left her. "Now, love," he said quietly.

Now what? Janielle thought wildly, a ripple of fresh panic snaking through her. She thought, I'll quickly explain with a pert remark and he'll leave. First, though, she must correct her vulnerable position. Rigidly Janielle sat up on the edge of the day couch, adjusting her loosened bodice and brushing wisps of white-gold hair from her face.

"Have you a name?" His voice was taunting.

Remember your resolve, Janielle cautioned herself silently. Aloud she said, "I—uh—was to have been dismissed before your arrival. Arrangements were scant after the burial." She spoke softly. Why did the words feel thick in her mouth?

"You lived at Challey?"

"Yes sir," she lied, almost pleased with her deception.

Ryan studied her intently, watching her eyes, glowing violet pools, dance in the candlelight. God, she was beautiful—serving wench or not. How she had come to stay at the decadent manor with his deranged mother was beyond his reason. Yet she appeared to know who he was.

The night had suddenly taken a full round turn. The long wet ride from Santee Point, crossing the churning, swollen waters of Dancer's Creek on a skittish roan, the invariable unwelcome of George Silas, the aged Challey house slave with his usual, "We are not receiving, suh," had shattered any measure of triumph Ryan felt on his long-awaited return to Challey. A cold repast of stringy river grouse and stale rice bread lay heavy in his belly. Finding a chipped decanter of Italian brandy had eased his ire long enough to make him willing to settle for the gloomy night in the manor.

Exploring the familiar pattern of Challey manor had provoked the scars on his wide back, stirring them to life, his flesh quivering again at the dreaded, haunting cadence of Charles Deverel's riding whip. Pain, long ago but never forgotten, never healed.

He had roamed the deserted manor, finding the front parlor closed and musty, with soiled shrouds draping the few pieces of furniture that remained. The sun porch, paralleling the verandah, was bare, with only a tottering wicker table sprawling awkwardly on three legs. He had snapped the bolt across the grime-encrusted French doors, his jack boots pounding the scattering chaff of crinkled leaves under the doorway, leaving a powdery path to settle with his passing.

The library had offered little more. Naked bookshelves glared down from their lofty stance, with only one mice-chewed volume of William de Braham's *Atlantic Pilot* still in evidence.

Christ, what a heritage! Enough of what should have been. Enough to survive the next few days until Morris Chapman arrived from Charleston, carrying the final estate papers. Ryan would sell Challey and use the money to buy a companion merchantman to his frigate the *Waverly*.

What had drawn him to the smooth, circular stairwell in the alcove behind the bookshelves? His mother's constant childhood scoldings that the stairwell was dangerous and that he was forbidden to play there? But he had.

9

Tonight, when he climbed the splintered wooden steps that ended in the dressing closet of his mother's sleeping parlor, he had been unexpectedly rewarded. Strange, though, that a servant should be quartered here.

Janielle's wide violet eyes flickered over him, an uneasy, cornered glance that he caught before she could hide it. Suddenly he reached down to her, scooping her up in his arms, dragging the satin embroidered coverlet with him. She felt soft, small, against him.

"Wh—where are you taking me?" Janielle gasped.

"It is chilly up here and the day couch is narrow, too short for my long legs." Ryan spoke evenly, nuzzling her white-gold hair.

Janielle twisted half around in his arms, feeling a rush of pure terror. "You can't do this," she stormed at him.

"I am doing it, madam." Ryan unlatched the rusted bolt, edging the door open with his boot. Janielle shoved with all her strength against him, struggling wildly to free herself. Ryan gripped her tight.

Quickly, Ryan closed the distance down to the dark upper floor, following the eerie path of shafted moonlight spilling through the hallway. He moved into the closed master wing, now gravely still and heavily draped. A choking smell of mildew and rotted mouse nests hovered in the darkness.

Pounding dread seeped through Janielle. She would explain, reason with him, and he would let her go. The whole situation was a confused mistake. Damn her curiosity!

Swallowing her fear, she said haughtily, "I am not what you believe, Master Deverel."

Ryan laughed softly, his dark profile outlined in the spidery light. "Few women are, love."

She knew where they were. Even in the darkness, the wide shape of the elaborate Renaissance bed that had belonged to Roland Devereaux—a piece Loranna Deverel had refused to sell—emerged from the dusky shadows. God, he wouldn't.

Ryan dropped her onto the massive bed, walked quickly back to the door, slid the over-door bolt, and turned the ornate key in the sculptured keyhole.

Janielle jammed a fist to her mouth as she watched him move to the shuttered window, thrusting it outward, heaving the heavy key outside onto the driveway. She heard the key clatter on the smooth granite steps below.

Scrambling to her feet, her eyes darted to the only other way out of the master wing—through the sleeping parlor. She doubted that she could outdistance him, for his long strides were more than a match for her. Try reasoning first.

"Master Deverel." She spoke quietly, trying to disguise the tremor in her voice. "It appears time to—"

"Indeed, love. It is time." Ryan smiled, bridging the distance between them.

Janielle stepped backward, feeling the edge of the bed against the bend of her knees. She pulled herself erect, still shadowed by his height.

"You mistake my position, sir. Surely you cannot think that I would—"

"I think, madam, exactly that."

"Then you err, sir!" Janielle shouted. "You cannot confine me here. I demand that you unlock the door!"

Ryan smiled insolently down at her, reaching to the buttons of his surtout, his lean fingers slowly rotating the buttons free. Shredded snowy light stole through the wide panes of the window. Wandering tendrils of river fog crept weavingly from the ground. Dawn fog.

Roughly he reached for her, pulling her into his arms, tilting her head up to him. She was tense, but he would remedy that. With his forefinger he touched her mouth, sliding his finger gently along her moist lips, parting them. His mouth followed, blazing down on hers, drawing, engulfing her, his tongue thrusting into her deep sweetness.

She fought him, excited him. His hand fastened in white-gold hair, cupping her head, holding it firm while he savored her. Relentlessly he kissed her, crushing her, sensing a vague limpness in her defense. He would have to hurry her. The day was almost upon them.

Suddenly the rapid bark of musket fire shattered through the approach. He released her so abruptly that Janielle sagged to the floor, struggling to regain the life's breath that he had pulled from her.

Ryan bolted to the window, his eyes searching the copse of sweet gum and live oak. The fog parted enough for him to catch a quick glimpse of a lone figure stalking between the chalky wisps. He spun to face Janielle.

"Stubborn British, or runaway slaves?" His voice was suddenly harsh, cold.

Janielle shook her head. Enough for now that he had released her. She couldn't survive that onslaught of passion.

Ryan jerked at the frayed swag along the velvet drapery, yanking it free, wrapping the braided coils around his hand. He advanced on her, dragging her to the cabriole leg of the bed. He knotted a ratline twist to one end, slipping a noose about the ivory stalk of her neck, drawing the other end down to her wrists. Janielle felt the tightening knot cords bite into her flesh as he secured her to the bed.

All in a matter of seconds, he was finished. Stunned, she tried to lift her head. The silken noose stretched taut.

"You forget, love, I also know of the other adjoining door. The first ten years of my life were spent in this damnable mausoleum. I shall return for you shortly."

Janielle swallowed a rising sob, choking to voice the words. Helplessly she watched Ryan slip through the small shuttered door, a dragoon pistol gripped familiarly in his large hand.

"Wait, please, Master Deverel. Don't leave me here like this." Janielle's anguished words faded against the slam of the door.

chapter 2

River fog spread milky curling wisps around Ryan as he reached the approach. Traces of crimson sunrise skirted the edge of the valley floor beyond the approach, thinning through the layers of fog.

Quickly Ryan checked the load, firing hammer and powder in his flintlock dragoon. He moved into the fog-cloaked path through the sweet gum and live oak copse, certain that the intruder, whatever his purpose, was headed in the direction of the manor. Nearing the orchard thicket Ryan paused, his senses alert to every waking daylight sound.

Soon, thudding hoofbeats threaded their way into the thicket, marking an unhurried, unsuspecting gait. Ryan waited until the shape of the horse cleared in the fog layer, then suddenly moved forward, grabbing at the bridle. Startled, the riderless horse swerved to the right, spinning around in the path.

Ryan eased the horse about. The sorrel was fresh, wearing an English saddle, certainly not a field horse, yet not outfitted in British harness. Running a hand along the sorrel's flank, Ryan felt for rowel marks. The scars were not markings from a British spur.

At a sudden sound behind him, Ryan wheeled, his dragoon leveled. A huge black moved across the path, his yellowed eyes wild in his dark face. He crumpled at Ryan's feet, shedding the aged musket and brace of rabbits he carried.

Ryan advanced on him, the dragoon barrel poised at the black's head. Roughly he grasped the man's shirt collar. A tiny circle was branded into the man's ebony neck—the mark of a Challey slave.

"Why are you permitted a weapon?" Ryan demanded, snatching the still warm barrel of the musket from the black.

The black man's mouth hung open. Slowly, he swallowed, gulping forth the words. "I—I fetch de game for breakfast," he managed.

Steadily Ryan regarded the man kneeling at his feet. The slave bore the weary expression of resignation that was too often the look of one of his kind. The expression had always unsettled Ryan. It still did.

"Get to your feet," he ordered sharply.

Awkwardly, the slave scrambled to his feet, gathering his crumpled red hat between his massive hands.

"What are you called?" Ryan demanded.

"I be Micah, suh."

"A Challey slave," Ryan mused softly, thinking that perhaps there were others on the land. "Are there other slaves quartered with you?"

"Yes, suh. My woman and two of mah seed."

"And the mount—a Challey horse?"

"No, suh. The sorrel belong to Masta Brandon."

Instantly, Ryan connected the name to the list that Morris Chapman had given him. Brandon Ord was the Challey overseer.

"Why were you not sold with the other slaves?" Ryan asked.

Micah fastened sorrowful eyes on Ryan. "Masta Charles give me de paper afore he died, but Challey is mah land."

14

Ryan shrugged indifferently. Loyalty among slaves turned out, more often than not, to be treachery. Pale sunlight glittered above the copse, burning away the swirling dawn fog.

"Are there other slaves living in the manor?" Ryan drawled, stamping the beading moisture from his jackboots.

"Only be Irene, de cook, and George Silas, the houseman, suh."

Ryan frowned into the sun. "Who is the lighthaired serving wench quartered in the gable room?"

Micah shook his head, confused. "Nobody lak that, suh."

Ryan swung about, leading the sorrel down the path toward the approach. Many things about Challey puzzled him. His mother, demented and a recluse, had died without sympathy or friends. The carefully worded message brought to him aboard the *Waverly*, summoning him to return to his birthplace, mentioned nothing of the condition of the manor or fields, leaving him to speculate as to its value. The scattering of slaves that remained on the land surprised him. Loranna Deverel had sold everything of value after the war.

The land had altered little since his childhood. The Challey lantern posts, marking the Challey boundary, still stood in sentinel position near the fork road, their rust-chewed lanterns dangling grotesquely from their once proud mountings. Everywhere the presence of decay accosted him.

At the rise of polished granite steps Ryan paused, turning to the slave who followed him. "I will prepare a list of supplies and you are to take the wagon to Pine Bluff and bring back what is needed. Tell the slave who cooks to prepare a meal for me and set water for a bath. Advise the overseer to join me in two hours—I wish to ride the fields."

Ryan hesitated, allowing the black to absorb his commands. Micah nodded understandingly, his wide lips parting in a weak smile.

"Glad yo' is home, masta, suh," he said, clamping his red hat on his head. "Powerful glad."

Ryan grappled at the dwindling sliver of tallow soap, running it across the dark furring on his wide chest. Despite the narrow space in the brass tub that forced his knees to his chin, the warm water had its soothing effect. Ryan smiled, remembering the sunken marble tub at Marie Cecile's sporting house in New Orleans. Space for his long body, even enough for his favorite *ramera*, Teresa, to join him. Some nights, he sampled her along with one of the New Orleans quadroons, provoking a mild scolding from Marie Cecile.

"Ah—monsieur, such a man. Two women a night for the pirate lord. Cannot one accommodate you?" Marie Cecile would tease, watching Ryan dress.

"A gift of your favors, love, and I should not be forced to such measures," Ryan would reply laughingly, reaching a hand to caress her reddish tresses.

"Ah, no, Monsieur Deverel. A young one for your taste. Always a young one."

Returning to his young mistress at Linden, Ryan was invariably disappointed in Carey's bland performance. Often he had thought of dismissing her after his stays in Charleston, but somehow the thought of her waiting for him at the cottage quarters she kept for him prevented it. He felt little attachment to her, but her innocent, worshipful surrender to him, regardless of his wanderings, somehow always brought him back.

Ryan eased from the tub, toweling himself with a patched flannel wrapping. He felt clean of the death-rot stench that clung to the manor. Even the meager breakfast of steeped blackberry leaves that passed for tea, and the gamey rabbit stew, thickened with pork side gravy, had been tasty this day, though he refused to subsist permanently on slave fare.

He pulled fawn-colored string breeches over his lean hips, reaching for a dark linen, boot cuff shirt. His newly cropped dark hair fell free about his face as he stamped his feet into his snug jackboots. Looking around the brick-walled room, he smiled. The French called such a room *salle de bains*, but here, at Challey, the honor fell to the cooking room.

There was much to be attended to this day. Bristling with anticipation at the new challenges before him, Ryan stalked from the room. The servant girl upstairs in the master bed chamber would be waiting for him to release her. She might prove more submissive by now, perhaps even glad to see him. He was anxious to know.

Janielle strained against the knotted swag cord, feeling some give to the silken bonds that secured her. Frustrated tears had long since dried on her cheeks, though the seething hatred for the arrogant Challey heir who had left her in such disregard, threatened to shatter her. Neither pillorying, nor gaoling, nothing short of the executioner's black noose would suffice for such an outrage. She would glory in his punishment.

Hot salt tears clouded her eyes as the sluggish moments dragged on. What if he returned to Charleston without releasing her? It would be agonizing days before she was found, if at all. Outcries were senseless. Irene stayed in the cooking shack set well apart from the manor; George Silas rarely ventured to the upper floors; and Brandon Ord had not set foot in the manor since Loranna Deverel's illness. No one knew Janielle had not returned to her home.

Panic snaked through her. How could she have done such a foolish thing? There had been no reason for her to remain at Challey after Loranna was buried, only a gnawing curiosity to see the most controversial man in

17

Charleston. In that she had succeeded. Of the outcome, she feared.

Janielle edged slowly around the leg of the bed frame, positioning herself against the frayed satin counterpane, pressing her flushed face into its coolness. How much time had elapsed—an hour, perhaps two? Finally, exhausted, she closed her tear-swollen eyes.

Ryan moved quietly through the shuttered, adjoining doorway to the master chamber, the key he had retrieved from the approach riding the narrow pocket of his breeches. He hadn't unlocked the center door yet. Let her wonder.

The room was still. For an instant he felt alarm. What if she—Hurriedly he glanced toward the massive bed, swallowing a sudden catch in his throat. In the screened sunlight filtering through the long window, her small form lay curled against the side of the bed, bathed in reverent illumination, her white-gold hair alive with shifting sunbeams.

A rush of alien emotion poured through him, a tug of tenderness pressing him. He stared down at her, baffled by his reaction. This could scarcely be called his usual style, restraining a servant wench until he was ready to use her.

Shrugging aside the unfamiliar sentiment that had momentarily gripped him, Ryan walked across the room and bent over her, freeing the large ratline knot at her wrists. The lesser knots loosened in quick succession. Deftly he slipped the silken noose off her head, smoothing her white-gold hair that tangled in it.

At his touch Janielle stirred, raising huge violet eyes to him, relief flooding through her. But at the expression of arrogant superiority on his handsome face, she remembered that she loathed him.

Ryan reached down to her, lifting her to her feet. Gaining her equilibrium, Janielle swayed against him, carefully steadying herself.

18

"Angry, love?" he taunted.

Furiously, Janielle brushed past him, moving quickly toward the door. Instantly, his hand reached out, preventing her. Janielle spun on him.

"You unspeakable jackanapes!" she stormed.

Ryan laughed down at her. "I am amazed at the refinement of Challey serving wenches."

"I am not—" Janielle started angrily.

"Not what, love?"

"Your reputation is well earned, *pirate—bastard— lord*!" she spat at him, ripping her arm free of his grasp.

His hand slashed across her face, hurling her across the bed. Then he was upon her, smothering her beneath his long, hard body. Even white teeth flashed down at her.

"You gave me no quarter with your words. Now I give you none!"

Janielle thrashed wildly against him as his mouth lowered to hers, searing her, bruising her. She clawed at the invading hands that ripped at her gown, freeing, loosening her bodice. Ryan's mouth found her breast, drawing the pink-tipped softness to him. Janielle felt a scorching sensation as Ryan's mouth teased her. Her fingers caught in his tousled hair, wrenching his head away, but it seemed only to intensify his hunger. His hand reached downward, searching, parting her, exquisite in its exploration.

Janielle was aflame. Rampant torrents of uncontrollable passion swept her, setting her adrift from herself, letting him seek her, urging ever forward to meet his questing hands.

Suddenly he stopped, was still. Janielle moaned, opening her eyes, her ragged breath catching in her throat. His form blurred above her, ice-blue eyes glazed with passion pierced her.

"Now, bitch, tell me you do not wish it," Ryan said hoarsely.

Janielle trembled, clutching at him. "No, please—I—"

19

Ryan laughed deep in his throat, the harsh lines in his face softening.

"A fitting name for a comely wench," he mocked, shifting above her. "Bitch!"

"My—my name is Janielle," she murmured haltingly against his wide shoulder.

Hands that were angry, rushed, became suddenly gentle, caressing her slowly, expertly, tracing the sensitive, warmly moist softness of her. His mouth moved in a quiet pattern along her cheekbones, kissing the curve of her throat, lowering, heightening the glowing flame that engulfed her. His fingers moved across her belly, readying himself. At the moment he raised above her, she knew, and yielded.

Ryan pressed boldly, deeply into her, tensing as he felt the natural obstruction to his piercing thrust. A sharp cry tore from her throat, stifled by his mouth upon hers.

Still he came, determined, relentless thrusts, parting her, splintering her with sweet agonizing warmth. Locking himself tightly to her, surging into her depths, a long deliberate shudder racked Ryan, and finally, blissfully, he was still.

For a space of eternity, he lingered above her, the gentle tugging inside her gradually receding, leaving her. Janielle lay stunned, silken tears sliding down her cheeks, finding their way to Ryan's shoulder. Somehow, the ending was hurtful, an aching loss she couldn't fully understand.

Abruptly he rolled away from her, swinging his long legs over the edge of the bed, running lean fingers through his dark hair. Through veiled eyes, Janielle watched the wide curve of his muscled back, wondering at the webbing of faint scars that stretched across it. Somewhere the pirate king had tasted of the whip.

Ryan eased his labored breathing, still shaken by the intensity of his swift climax, a practised routine, usually prolonged and always controlled. He felt neither satisfied nor victorious, only enraged.

He stood up, drawing his breeches together, fastening them away from her view. Sensing her eyes on him, he turned to her, feeling only the need to escape.

"Why did you not tell me you were a virgin?" he demanded.

"You did not ask," Janielle replied quietly.

Ryan's mouth set in a harsh, stubborn line, his crystal eyes cold and unreadable.

"You may remain at Challey to serve my needs until I return to Charleston, and draw your coin when you leave. Your awakening today will undoubtedly demand more of what I have given you." He paused, ignoring the dazed pain in her wide violet eyes.

Finally, Janielle found her voice, the words thin. "You—you raped me," she gasped.

"Hardly, love," Ryan sneered, hooking his thumbs in his belt. An easy, indifferent smile crossed his face as he gazed down at her.

"I suggest you rise slowly when you leave my bed. Virgins are often faint, afterward."

Janielle watched him swagger to the door and casually unlock it, leaving it standing wide open as he moved through it.

chapter 3

Morris Chapman eased back from his desk, stretching his long legs. He rose slowly, leaning his hands on the massive oak desk top. His gaze wandered out across the teeming Bay Street wharf, where a steady flow of cargo and ships elbowed for space. Talk of the canal connecting the Santee, Wateree, Broad, and Saluda Rivers with Charleston, was swelling the city's population as traders and speculators swarmed into the low country. A colonial barrister could do well in these prosperous times, though the tedium of reviewing the headright land system in South Carolina and the representation of the Charleston merchant oligarchy, wearied him. The work required that he spend most of his time in his clapboard office above the Coast Merchants' headquarters. Visits to his elegant home in McClellanville were rare now, though his work excused him from his wife's grinding social plans.

Morris sighed as he watched the spitting drizzle that had been falling since dawn. "Well, thank God," he thought solemnly, "the day Loranna Deverel was buried was one with sunshine." Lord, he missed her. Their times together had been spent in haste with scatterings of conversation about Challey or Ryan. But never once would she discuss Charles Deverel or her second marriage to Lord Phillip Coswelle.

Morris shrugged, thinking disgustedly about the rakish Lord Phillip, who had married Loranna to gain the wealth of Challey. Morris had made inquiries to a Royalist circle in Wilmington, who implied that the lordship, granted at Brighton-Chichester, was questionable, and Phillip Coswelle had been accepted in British circles primarily on the strength of his cousin, the Earl of Wellingborough. His marriage to Loranna had brought her only grief, for Charles Deverel's friends had shunned her due to their anti-British sentiments. Lord Phillip had immediately proved his motive for marriage by gambling away the Deverel money and spending the remainder on his string of mistresses in Charleston. Morris was vastly relieved when Lord Phillip fled the country, following the war. But Loranna had become a recluse at Challey, refusing to see anyone.

Morris could not recall a time when he hadn't loved Loranna Deverel. His first glimpse of her those many years past, descending the staircase at Challey, in her white gown with dark roses spilling across her flowing skirts, came to life again in his troubled thoughts. She had married Charles Deverel to gain Challey and he had wed the wealthy Editha Thompson to secure his barrister's education. They had attained their selfish ambitions, but had lost each other.

Morris strolled back to his desk, casually scanning the draft he was preparing to appoint an intendent and thirteen wardens to preserve order among the returning patriots. The visit to the City Chambers would have to wait until his business at Challey was completed. He and Editha were spending Thanksgiving at Patterson Woods, and he planned to journey to Challey to see Ryan and prepare the documents for sale.

The vision of Editha loomed in his mind as he pored over the petition. Editha! Even her name of late brought a sense of repugnance. No guilt remained with him after the long years spent with a wife he had never loved. Her faithful wifely duty, with her sharp tongue and incessant complaining as bed companions, left him limp, and only the thought of Loranna Deverel could call forth an adequate hardness. Edith's already expanding figure had broadened over the last few years and now the thought of caressing her huge, udder-like breasts repulsed him. The sour feeling in his delicate belly was gnawing again as the image of Editha, descending the portico with her waddle-like walk, the huge bodice of her gown covered with bright red strawberries, caused him to retch. The only time he had ever felt capable of loving her was when she nursed Johnathan at her breast and Morris had seen his son, the handsome result of his uninspired lovemaking.

Morris retreated back in thought to the night when he had responded to Loranna's desperate message summoning him to Challey. When he had arrived, young Ryan Deverel stood waiting on the granite steps, his small hand clutching a bulky valise. Sounds of shattering glass and incoherent curses reverberated from the manor, while the Challey servants clustered on the columned porch, their expressions reflecting various facets of terror and bewilderment.

Loranna Deverel had run from the manor, sobbing hysterically, the bodice of her gown torn, her disheveled hair falling across her bleeding mouth. She fled to Morris and buried her face in his shoulder.

"Morris, dearest," she gasped. "Please take Ryan away from Challey before Charles kills him. I told him when he kept hitting me. Oh, God! He knows, Morris, he knows!"

"Come with us," Morris had begged.

"No, I promised to stay with him if he'd spare Ryan. But he made me agree never to allow Ryan to return to Challey. He disclaimed him." Loranna choked on the words. "Charles is murderously drunk. Please go, quickly, Morris," she had pleaded.

Morris had ridden away, taking young Ryan with him.

They had spent the night in the flood shack on Dancer's Creek, where Morris tended the boy's back as well as he could, fighting the revulsion he felt when he saw the deep, bloody lash wounds. He had enrolled Ryan in Brocksburg School in Charleston, and through the years the boy had shown a remarkable degree of adaptability. His ciphering and reading marks were exceptional and Morris had goaded Donald Harkins, the commission agent for Coast Merchants, to take Ryan in apprenticeship. Miraculously, Ryan had earned the shrewd old merchant's favor. On occasion Morris had taken the boy to his home in McClellanville and Ryan and Johnathan had become friends. Editha had finally been persuaded to allow Johnathan to attend Brocksburg School with Ryan.

When Morris had business in Charleston he would take the boys to the docks, letting them roam and explore, learning what young boys can by adventuring on their own. When Editha learned of the weekend excursions, she balked.

"You are taking as much interest in that Deverel cast-off as you do in our own son. You cannot expect to raise gentlemen by allowing them to mingle with the dock rowdies. I won't abide it, Morris!" Editha had shrieked.

As the boys grew to manhood, their interests drifted in different paths. Ryan had remained steadfast in his determination to succeed as a merchant and Johnathan pursued a barrister's course at Oxford for a time. Both had advanced well into the world of position.

Morris licked his dry lips and painfully returned to the present. He reached in the top drawer of his desk and pulled out the yellowed clipping which he had read countless times. The aged notice from the *Charleston Gazette* stated briefly that Charles Deverel of Challey, member of Coast Merchants of Charleston, had succumbed to death after a fall from his horse, and would be entombed in the plantation cemetery at Challey. The

25

article added that Charles Deverel had died without heirs.

Morris refolded the clipping and placed it back in the drawer. For a time he had believed it possible for Loranna and him to rekindle the love they had once felt for each other. But Loranna had behaved foolishly after Charles' death.

A sharp rap on the door broke Morris' reminiscenses. Benjamin, his assistant, barged in energetically, excited as always when he had a message to deliver.

"Mr. Chapman, sir, Johnathan sent word he'll accompany you to Santee Point. He also wants to visit his friend, Ryan Deverel, at Challey. He said the Pattersons were expecting all of you for Thanksgiving feast." Benjamin smiled proudly at having accomplished his mission.

"Very well, Benjamin. I can imagine my young buck son is anxious to see his bride-to-be. Hand me my brief with the Deverel documents," Morris said wearily.

Benjamin charged across the room to help Morris slip into his greatcoat. He handed Morris the leather briefcase and held the door open for him. "The ride on the barge will be chilling today, with the mist," Benjamin offered.

"I know that," Morris replied irritably.

"I saw Ryan Deverel's mistress today," Benjamin said shyly.

"That is not your concern," Morris scolded.

"She is a beautiful woman, and dressed in the finest," Benjamin began.

"Expect my return in a week," Morris interrupted, turning back from the doorway. He tucked the brief under his arm and slowly descended the creaking wooden steps that led to the dock. He thought of the open rumors concerning Ryan Deverel's new mistress and wished that Ryan could be more discreet. His reckless affairs with women troubled Morris. Ryan must be nearing thirty now. "I wonder if he—" Morris closed off the thought that had presented itself, and slowly made his way across the wet dock.

chapter 4

Patterson Woods rose majestically from the jutting bluff overlooking the northwest sweep of the Santee, its Grecian roof and gleaming Ionic marble columns commanding a lofty span of the wide reddish-yellow river. The Yemassee Indians had used the site as a flourishing barter colony visited by French and English trappers who traded for their deerskins and furs. The enterprising Yemassee had constructed the impressive causeway down the sloping bluff to the landing jetty.

Heady fragrance from vermilion honeysuckle and flowering jasmine vines creeping along the causeway's base breathed an overpowering aura to assault the senses. Thickly clumped palmettos parted at the rise of the causeway, revealing the lush pathway to the manor. Towering magnolia grandifloras edged the path, their purple cones and pendent scarlet seedlings nodding quietly in the breeze.

From her corner window, Janielle watched swollen rain-laden clouds poised above the river, slumbering in the hushed twilight. Dimming sunlight lent a lavender shimmer to the peaceful waters below as the sun retreated upriver, taking imaginary flight from the undulating waters.

Janielle seated herself on the velvet dressing bench,

gazing deeply into violet pools that reflected back at her. Her wrapper fell aside, revealing her full, ripened breasts, a sensuous part of her that Ryan Deverel had known, caressed, savored. Lean, dark fingers had—

No! Janielle gasped inwardly, fighting the warm flush that invaded her. Throughout the day since Ryan had walked away from her, leaving her warm and moist after their lovemaking, she had battled against the raging emotions within her, recalling every moment with him, his words, his caresses and his cruelty.

How foolish she had been to follow a girlish curiosity. She had hidden in the gable room, hoping to observe him from a distance and then run home to safety, like some gawking schoolgirl. She had found him to be merely a man, intent on seducing a servant girl he discovered in his house. He had succeeded. He had won and she had lost all.

Hurrying down the stairway after he had left the room, her white-gold hair tangled, her gown mussed and wrinkled, she had encountered George Silas. The aged Challey house servant, his ebony face reflecting only mild surprise, lifted drooping eyes to her.

"Mornin,' Mis' Janielle," he said vacantly, brushing at his threadbare black uniform.

Janielle caught an uneasy breath. The dim-witted Challey slave, his mind still encamped in the vivid rose gardens of Challey's once affluent past, would be pressed to recall that she had not returned to Patterson Woods as planned.

"Mr. Ord come to say his condolence and he and the master took out for the fields. Been gone 'bout an hour," George Silas said absently, his heavy eyes fastening on her.

Janielle steadied herself. "Tell Micah to bring the wagon and fetch my trunk from upstairs. The things Mis' Loranna gave me need special crating and I haven't time now. And be quick about it; I am anxious to return home."

28

George Silas nodded obediently, shuffling through the library door. At the threshold he paused, casting a bewildered look at Janielle.

"Mis' Loranna ain' about any more," he said softly.

Janielle swallowed hard. "No, George, she isn't."

The wagon groaned through the stately lantern posts marking the Challey divide. Roland Devereaux had built the impressive entrance to Challey, rumored to be a close resemblance to his chalet near Nemours. The elder Devereaux had arrived in the British colonies under a cloud of scandal that caused him to flee his beloved France. The breath of disgrace linked to his name had vanished after his close association with the Pickney family. For a long time, Roland Devereaux had remained unmarried, his time devoted to the construction of Challey manor. It was whispered that the man was eccentric, preferring the company of slaves, and his French bondswoman, Adele, to visits from the other Santee planters. Challey had always maintained an aura of mystique, even after Roland Devereaux married Elise Hoskins, the daughter of a Charleston tanner. Elise had died in childbirth leaving only one heir, Charles Roland Devereaux. Charles had gone to live with the Pickney family after Roland Devereaux made a sudden decision to return to France. Challey had been left in the hands of an overseer and a young factor in Charleston named Morris Chapman.

Janielle could remember her father's commenting on how fortunate Charles Devereaux (who had shortened the family name to Deverel) had been in taking Loranna Simmons as a wife. Loranna was an incredibly beautiful, ambitious woman who had brought warmth and charm to Challey. Their joining was thought to be perfect. And so, for a time, it was.

After a few years, the black iron gates to the Challey approach were locked and Charles Deverel spent his time at the Charleston Planters' club or the Coast Merchants' quarters in Charleston. Loranna Deverel did not accompany him. A son had been born to them but his whereabouts were cloaked in whispers. Ryan. Ryan was that son—but Charles Deverel was not his father.

Janielle shuddered, gathering the shawl about her slim shoulders. The wagon lurched into the road paralleling Dancer's Creek. The languid creek, lying in the backwash arm of the Santee, was at full surge. The legend of the creek had always intrigued her. Childhood visions of Andre Danzier, the French trapper who had died in the low-running creek defending himself against the attack of two Cherokee Indians intent on stealing his furs, had always stirred her imagination. Danzier had fallen on his long hunting knife, his forefinger stiffly pointing to the wide Santee. Patterson slaves had found him in the grotesque death stance and her own grandfather had named the creek Danzier's Creek. But the British surveyor's plat and district map of 1778 had designated the site Dancer's Creek, and thus it stood.

Micah turned a sloe-eyed gaze on her. "You seems terrible jumpy dis mornin', Mis' Janielle," he said quietly.

Janielle shot him a withering look. "I'm tired, that's all," she snapped.

The sound of the wheels crackling over loose rock brought Minna out the front door of Patterson manor, her fat legs pumping up and down as she hurried down the wide curving steps to the approach. A growing smile lighted her black face as she began to twist and grasp at her long, starched-white apron. Janielle was irked watching Minna indulge in her favorite habit.

"Home to stay, Mis' Janielle, for sure," Minna called breathlessly, trotting alongside the wagon. "News, news. Folks comin' tomorrow. Mr. Johnathan and all his folk, and de' Mallens from McClellanville, even bringin' Mis' Kaylee."

Janielle climbed down from the wagon. "All of them, tomorrow?" she said weakly, following Minna into the manor.

"Yo' is lookin' peaked," Minna said worriedly, lumbering up the stairs behind Janielle.

Janielle cringed. As if the day hadn't been overwhelming enough thus far; now there was the dread of facing Johnathan and Kaylee's unnerving company. The rest of the conversation blurred as Janielle sought the comfort of her own room.

Darkness had fallen along the river land, the shortened days bringing a sense of stillness to the plantation. Janielle walked listlessly to the armoire, plucking distractedly at her gowns. Finally she chose a heavy cream satin accented with spilling auburn lace. The gown was a favorite, but tonight it did little to lift her spirits. Her father would be pouring his second Scotch by now, anxious to have dinner announced on schedule. He would ask endless questions about her lengthy stay at Challey with Loranna Deverel. And she would give him the careful answers he sought, how she had cared for Loranna, read to her and waited while Loranna slipped free from life. They would discuss the condition of the Challey fields and the possibility of his purchase of the land. And John Patterson would tell her of the constitutional session and his plans for the future of South Carolina.

Her sheltered life at Patterson Woods would resume. Johnathan would press her for an announcement of their forthcoming marriage. She would attend the winter soirées in Charleston and visit the Mallens over the Christmas holidays. The days would unroll in continual boredom as they had for the past year. And known only to her would be the interlude at Challey.

Sudden tears crept down her cheeks. Mocking blue-flint eyes flashed before her. She felt his warmth again, the closeness of his large body, his experienced hands touching her. But there was no shame. She had wanted him and he knew it.

Janielle brushed aside the tears as Minna blustered

31

into the room. "Your father is ragin' for his dinner! 'Fetch Janielle,' he say, 'retirin' early,' he say, 'folks comin,' he say. Lordy, child, and you sittin' there dreamin' of that handsome Mr. Johnathan."

Minna fumbled a dark hand into the pin bowl. "Yo' hair done look lak the sun lives in it. Yo' been goin' without yo' bonnet too much."

"I hate bonnets." Janielle sighed, piling her white-gold hair on top of her head. She wound two stray tendrils around her fingers, letting them fall in ringlets about her ears.

"Yo' is too skinny, too," Minna scolded, placing a pin in Janielle's hair. "A man lak a woman wid some meat on her bones."

Janielle smiled slowly. Ryan Deverel had not objected to her slimness. She cast a wicked look at Minna.

"How would you know that, Minna?"

"'Cause I know what mens lak," Minna said gruffly. "And I know what it's lak to miss a man. Lak yo' missin' Mr. Johnathan."

Janielle rose from the dressing bench and moved to the door. "I suppose it's like that," she said wistfully, moving out into the hall.

chapter 5

The Mallens arrived at Patterson Woods on Thanksgiving Day, displaying the fanfare for which they were noted. Two perfectly matched bays excitedly presented the gleaming red barouche that bore the Mallen crest on its step side. Harrelson Mallen wore his gentry tall hat and carried his walking stick with the enormous silver hammered knob, the two accessories that invariably identified him.

The barouche drew to a halt before the sprawling manor, carrying its beautifully attired and gaily waving guests. Aurora Mallen alighted at once, glancing about for her husband. She was considered by most of her prestigious circle to be a flighty, vain woman who continued to impress upon each and all the importance of her kinship with General Benjamin Lincoln. The repetitious telling of the family history rarely varied.

"Such a dark day," she would lament, "when dear Uncle Benjamin was forced, utterly forced, to surrender our beloved land to that dreadful Clinton. Why, poor uncle was fair exhausted with the fighting and that sultry May heat, and then his dear wife—" The final scene called forth the perfumed lace handkerchief to dab at the corner of her eye. Nevertheless, because Aurora Mallen was an extremely hospitable lady, her audience was usually willing to witness the familiar performance again.

John Patterson emerged from his glorious manor, bounding down the gleaming marble steps, overjoyed that his holiday guests had arrived. He had been obsessed of late with the constant need to entertain and, with Janielle home from Challey, the invitations could increase.

"Hail, and welcome to Patterson," John Patterson called across the approach way. Reaching the barouche, he extended his hand to assist Kaylee Mallen from the carriage.

"Ah, Kaylee," he said. "You are still the most beautiful green-eyed princess in all of South Carolina. We must find you a suitable prince." He chuckled as he bent to graze her cheek with a fatherly kiss.

"Daddy Patterson, you do say such sweet things," Kaylee replied coyly, taking his arm. The men clasped their arms about one another, laughing and talking in low tones. Kaylee waited for Janielle to approach, sensing the subtle dislike Janielle had for her. Then she extended her gloved hand.

"Dear Janielle," she said sweetly, "how are you? Mercy, it seems we're forever inviting you to McClellanville and you're forever declining."

"*En garde*," Janielle thought, as she heard Kaylee's barbed greeting. She forced a smile. "I have been needed at Challey the past few months. Your dress, it's Parisian cut, is it not?" She was adept at fencing with Kaylee, after numerous years of practice. Seeing the expression on Kaylee's face, she knew she had succeeded in creating a diversion.

"Mrs. Banks only finished it yesterday, but she bumbled the sleeves in her haste," Kaylee commented. She was already casting her eyes about to see whose arrival had preceded her own.

John Patterson rushed everyone inside, as the sun was

34

blinking bravely through heavy dark clouds and the river wind was rising in a cool, angry bluster. Once inside, the men retired to the library to sample John Patterson's new sour mash whiskey. Janielle longed to join them, even though it required listening to another recounting of the battle of Eutaw Springs, the outcome of which each man claimed was largely the result of his own heroism. The lengthy discussion of Tim O'Fallen's distillery would follow, then Harrelson Mallen's oration about his new shipyards would last until dinner.

Janielle quietly led Aurora and Kaylee Mallen to the formal parlor, showing them the new twin rosewood and green brocade swivel chairs and low stool, a grouping currently referred to as a "courting set." The circular table near the window was inlaid with marble birds whose eyes were blazing rubies. Aurora Mallen gave a cry of delight when she saw it. Kaylee studied herself in the gold-leaf mirror that hung over the Egyptian marble fireplace, watching Janielle pass a silver tray filled with tea cakes, apées, macaroons and rusks.

"I must say, Janielle," Aurora Mallen said, licking her fingers, "these macaroons are tasty. Your mother's recipe?"

"Yes, Aurora. Cook Bertha still makes them," Janielle replied wearily, dreading the forced conversation that lay ahead. Kaylee regarded her warily as she settled into the chair by the window.

An hour past noontime, Morris and Johnathan Chapman arrived at the causeway, ahead of the threatening storm that was moving inland. Janielle jumped when she heard the landing bell, and excused herself from the watchful company of the Mallen women. She slipped a woolen shawl about her shoulders and rushed down the causeway to meet the visitors.

In two long strides Johnathan Chapman was embracing her, his tall body pressing her close as he bent his blond head to kiss her. Janielle felt the cold damp of his

35

greatcoat against her body, the smell of the river wind clinging to it, his warm breath on her face. She was immeasurably glad to see him.

Morris Chapman gloried in the sight of his tall, ruggedly handsome son as he held Janielle. They made a striking twosome and he felt enormously proud of his son's selection of a wife. Janielle broke free from Johnathan to clasp Morris' hand.

"Welcome again to Patterson," she murmured against Johnathan's cheek.

Morris Chapman smiled, gripping his windswept cloak about him. "Janielle, you're beautiful as always. Maybe a trifle thinner. Have you been pining for Johnathan?" he teased.

Johnathan had temporarily had his fill of Janielle's mouth, and found his voice. "God, Janielle, I've missed you." He held her at arm's length and his eyes roamed her body. "Let's get married today. I'm not a patient man," he said softly. "I want you now."

The three of them climbed the causeway, the men sheltering Janielle from the chilly gusts that swept across the river. The gloom she had been feeling gradually lifted as she walked between Johnathan and his father. Now everything would be as before, almost.

Ryan Deverel and Brandon Ord rode at an easy canter along the road that led to Patterson Woods, following in the wheel ruts made earlier by the Mallen barouche. Brandon glanced at the profile of his companion, feeling almost a kinship with him. The role of the overseer was usually held by a man of common birth, but not so with Brandon Ord.

He had been born on the Santee sweep, the son of a wealthy Englishman who, through reckless investments and failure to pay the Crown for his grant, had lost all. Brandon's parents had succumbed to yellow fever after a short stay in New Orleans, leaving Brandon and his sister alone and penniless. Felicia had returned, heartbroken, to Liverpool, begging Brandon to accompany her. He refused, returning instead to the Santee country. Among his father's friends John Patterson had been the most highly esteemed, and Brandon sought his help in finding suitable employment.

John Patterson had suggested to Loranna Deverel that young Brandon would well fit the need for an overseer at Challey. Within a short time Brandon found himself quartered in the overseer's small cottage on the Challey land, eager and determined to prove the confidence placed in him.

Brandon had been deeply troubled during Loranna Deverel's illness, knowing that if she died Ryan Deverel might return to Challey and he would be forced to leave. The smatterings of rumor he had heard concerning the bastard heir related that Ryan had been banished from the plantation during a family quarrel, while he was just a lad of ten. One of the field hands had told Brandon that Ryan had been educated at Brocksburg School in Charleston, apprenticed with Donald Harkins of the Charleston Coast Merchants, and now owned his own merchant vessel, the *Waverly*. Brandon still felt a twinge of envy when he thought of Ryan Deverel's success, for at times he imagined himself master of Challey.

Much apprehension had vanished upon meeting the mysterious new master, for he immediately approved of the tall, forceful man when he had come to introduce himself. They had ridden the land together during the last two days, and Brandon's initial impression was proving correct.

They had been in the study earlier in the day when the rider from Patterson Woods had been announced. George Silas handed the envelope bearing the red waxen seal, "J. P." to Ryan, scowling his displeasure at the intruder from Patterson. Ryan read it carefully, then handed it to Brandon.

37

"What's this about, Ord? It's a supper invitation from John Patterson." His reluctance to accept was apparent.

"It would seem, sir, that John Patterson includes most of the planters in his invitations these days. He has been a sad, miserable man since Mrs. Patterson and his eldest daughter died during the epidemic, and he is entertaining lavishly and often now. On numerous occasions I have accepted his hospitality. My father spoke highly of him, and of course my presence here is due to his kindness." Brandon stretched his long legs from under his chair and reached for his pipe.

Ryan listened intently as Brandon commented on the invitation. Then he said, "I believe that John Patterson is a friend to Morris Chapman, my barrister. I attended Brocksburg with his son, Johnathan, and they mentioned the Pattersons. Chapman was due at Challey today, but I suppose the winds on the river delayed him. I heard that Johnathan has his own merchant office in Savannah now and is under consideration to join the Coast Merchants."

Brandon Ord declined further conversation and they turned their attention again to the warrants of survey and surveyor's plats on the table.

Earlier in the day, after a tour of the Challey lands, Ryan had thundered back into the house, a worried but determined overseer close on his heels.

"God Almighty!" Ryan had roared. "Has nothing been done here the past year? The fields show deplorable waste! The fallows should have been planted. Two years, you said, it has been?" He glared at Brandon. "How in God's name has there been any coin from this plantation? The whole south side of the valley should be in tobacco. Even an inexperienced planter such as I can see that!" Ryan paused in his ravings.

"It was your mother's wish that—" Brandon began.

Ryan paced the long room, whirling suddenly on Brandon.

"Patterson slaves have been working here. By whose

design was that? I'll have no debt to John Patterson! Perhaps the invitation tonight is for an accounting."

"I think not, sir," Brandon said.

"Then is he of such a generous nature that he farms out his slaves to the unfortunate?"

"Mr. Patterson felt compassion for your mother's misfortune," Brandon said slowly, watching the harsh expression on Ryan's face.

"A state of her own choosing," Ryan snapped, leaning across his desk. He pulled a long sheet of parchment before him and reached for the quill. "I wish you to list the number of slaves borrowed and the length of time they worked Challey land. I accept charity from no one. It has been my thought to sell Challey, but I expect a good return. After viewing the fields it is apparent that one is not forthcoming. It will take time to set them in yield. Also the manor is in dire need of repair and a thorough cleaning," Ryan concluded.

Brandon nodded, relieved that his position had not been further threatened. The remainder of the day had been spent in studying the outdated surveyor's plats and estimating the cost of seedlings for the cotton and tobacco. Ryan had suggested that a sluice be run from the spring house creek to the orchard thicket, giving the parched tree roots a continual feed until they spread.

"Fruit is valuable cargo aboard ship," Ryan had commented. "Even the stingy British cry for it." He turned back to Brandon. "You are a man who knows Challey land. What say you of my plans?"

"They are your plans, Master Deverel," Brandon said.

Ryan got up and leaned against the mantlepiece, his eyes scanning the faded canvas that swung crookedly above it. The pigments were streaked with age.

"Where did this monstrosity come from?" he asked irritably.

"A gift to her ladyship from Lord Phillip," Brandon said quietly.

Swiftly, Ryan reached for it, pulled it from its hanging, hurled it into the fire. "A fitting end to Lord Phillip's gifts."

Brandon watched impassively, not alarmed at any of the actions of the new master of Challey. Ryan Deverel was his own man; that much had been clear from the outset.

After an uncomfortable silence, Brandon rose to leave. "Do you wish to attend the dinner at Patterson Woods?" Ryan asked as Brandon reached the door.

"Patterson Woods boasts of being the social focus of the Santee sweep," Brandon replied.

Ryan's laugh was brittle. "Do you imply that I need a glimpse of social life?"

"John Patterson would be offended if you did not accept," Brandon said.

Ryan nodded, turning back to the hearth. "Inform the messenger that we will be in attendance, then," Ryan said, glancing up at the mantle clock as it loudly chimed the hour of three.

chapter 6

Tiny diamondlike prisms danced across the gleaming crystal goblets placed in proud display on the stark white dinner cloth. Huge candelabra glowed above the wide bowls of freshly cut roses and carnations. Marble urns, brimming with cypress vine and flowering jasmine, stood at selected stations behind the guest chairs, creating an atmosphere to soothe all the senses. The late arrival of two accomplished musicians, borrowed from Thunder Oaks plantation, completed the lavish preparations, and the soft strains of beautifully tuned violins floated melodiously through the dinner room.

John Patterson, attired in a dove-grey velvet dinner coat, with a rich red brocade waistcoat and soft white britches, casually adjusted his cravat, listening to the men discussing the rumor that the capital of Charleston was to be relocated to a newly appointed site called Columbia.

"Hell, it's those settlers moving into the Piedmont who are causing all the ruckus. Charleston has always been the leader in South Carolina and will continue to be," fumed Harrelson Mallen.

"Perhaps," Morris Chapman commented dryly. "However, the Scotch-Irish moving into the new up country are rapidly gaining support and demand that control be more evenly distributed."

"Charleston is and has always been the economic basis

of the state, and there's no argument as to its cultural and intellectual leadership. Now, with John in the Constitutional Congress, he can put an end to this nonsense," Harrelson Mallen reiterated.

John Patterson was pleased to see his new blend of whiskey being approvingly consumed. He glanced at the group of splendidly attired men, particularly young Deverel, and felt a sense of fatherly pride at his selection of guests. Brandon Ord, the Challey overseer, wore a burgundy evening coat with which his white ruffled shirt contrasted becomingly. And, he mused, Janielle will be elated when she sees Johnathan in his wheat-colored velvet coat, the color matching the sun-streaked shade of his hair. Morris Chapman continued to wear somber tones—probably through Editha's influence.

Patterson frowned as he watched Morris Chapman refill his glass. The strained relationship between Morris and Editha Chapman still puzzled him. The post arriving earlier in the day was from Editha, stating her intention of remaining in McClellanville with her sister. Morris had seemed visibly relieved. Only the Mallens appeared disappointed. John Patterson's eyes fell upon Harrelson Mallen, whose cane was tapping at intervals, coinciding with the emphasis of his viewpoints.

John Patterson's gaze moved toward the window, where the tallest of his guests stood looking out at the black, windswept night. Ryan Deverel had been a complete surprise to him. There was an aloofness about him, yet his friendly smile and charming manner made him welcome in the group. His wit was sharp and his humor quick and natural, and Patterson had cordially welcomed young Deverel to his home. The sea-green velvet dinner coat that Deverel wore fit snugly to his broad shoulders, yet moved smoothly as he turned. His white ruffled shirt reached below the sleeve cuffs of his coat and one low ruffle traced the ridge of Deverel's lean

42

brown knuckles.

"Now that's a new sleeve cut," John Patterson thought admiringly. "I must ask him who does his tailoring." As he watched him, Ryan Deverel's ice-blue eyes met his own, and he smiled.

The chatter coming from the hallway indicated that the ladies were moving downstairs. "Finally," John Patterson thought, relieved that dinner would be served on schedule. He led the way to the foot of the wide stairway, anxious to make the formal introductions.

Kaylee Mallen floated down the staircase, proud as every head turned in her direction. "Pretty Kaylee," she was always called, with her gleaming dark hair, deep green eyes and fair skin. Her gown was a vibrant red and she carried a fur boa over her arm. John Patterson took her hand and brought her to Ryan Deverel. The impact was electric.

"This is Kaylee Mallen, Mr. Deverel. Watch she doesn't trample your heart." John Patterson chuckled as he presented her.

"Rest assured, sir, I shall watch at all times," Ryan coolly replied, raising Kaylee's soft hand to his lips.

Johnathan Chapman moved up the stairs to assist Janielle, who had stopped halfway down to adjust the trailing drape of her lavender satin gown. She looked radiant in the soft candlelight, her white-gold hair catching the glints from the tapers as she turned. Her bodice was cut daringly deep, exposing the upper fullness of her beautifully formed breasts. Johnathan felt a tingling in his groin as he neared her. "God, I want her," he thought as she reached for his arm.

Slowly they descended the wide curving stairs. Janielle started to tell Johnathan how much she liked the shade of his coat, her eyes sweeping absentmindedly over the waiting guests below. Suddenly she froze. The broad shoulders towering above the others, the dark hair, the arrogant stance—no, it couldn't be. What in God's name would he be doing here? She had to fight the urge to run back up the stairs.

Too late; her father was taking her arm and leading her across the hallway to Kaylee Mallen and Ryan Deverel.

"Janielle, dear," her father began apologetically, "this is Ryan Deverel. I forgot to inform you that I had sent an invitation to Challey today." Turning to Ryan, he said proudly, "This is my beautiful daughter Janielle."

Ryan disengaged his arm from Kaylee's and stepped gracefully foward. "I am honored once again, Miss Patterson." He lifted her cold hand to his mouth, looking mockingly into her huge violet eyes. His eyes held hers as he addressed himself to John Patterson.

"Miss Patterson and I met briefly at Challey, when I arrived." Ryan's voice was low and gentle. "Much too briefly, I assure you, sir."

Janielle stood silently, staring up into Ryan's cool blue eyes; she didn't trust herself to speak. Johnathan, sensing the tension of the moment, moved quickly to her and gently placed his arm about her waist, while John Patterson finished the introductions and led his guests into the dinner room.

Janielle was vaguely aware of performing the functions of a perfect hostess. The first course consisted of Eulalia Patterson's famous turtle soup, its thickness attributed to the leg of beef simmered with it, seasoned with cloves, cayenne pepper and mace. The final touch was a pint of Madeira wine. Every guest who had visited before expected the tureen of turtle soup on the Patterson winter supper table.

Janielle accepted a small portion of chicken a la Tartare and Ashley rice bread, as the elaborate platter was offered to her. She made motions of eating but was just rearranging the food on her plate, her ice-cold hand shaking as she held her fork. The room felt uncomfortably warm despite the howling wind outside, and she signaled for the house servant to start the *punkah* above the table.

Ryan Deverel sat directly across the table from her, with Kaylee seated next to him. Ryan gazed boldly at Janielle as he listened to Kaylee's witty conversation. The men were discussing the proposed Santee river system, while Aurora Mallen had engaged Brandon Ord with her tale of Uncle Benjamin's surrender to General Clinton. Brandon responded attentively, suppressing a smile when Aurora Mallen reached for her lace handkerchief, indicating that the performance had ended.

The fluffy cheese okra casserole was passed at Janielle's elbow. She tapped her wine glass with her spoon, requesting another refill of claret. She caught the surprised look on her father's face as she quickly downed the purplish red wine.

"I don't care if he disapproves," she thought rebelliously. "I need it to get through this evening." She cast a withering look at Ryan Deverel as his cold blue eyes mocked her from across the table. "What if he tells Johnathan," she thought wildly. "Or father—what if he tells father? I wish I could vanish," she agonized, as Kaylee's silvery laughter drifted across to her. "Maybe he's forgotten it happened," Janielle tried to reassure herself. But a quick glance across at him as his eyes raked her told her he hadn't.

Johnathan was pensive as he watched Janielle, who was sitting next to him. Her beautiful breasts, thrust forward from the bodice of her gown, seemed to be rising and falling more rapidly than usual tonight. The diamond-and-pearl necklace he had given her this afternoon sparkled brilliantly against her smooth, slender neck. She had seemed upset when he told her of his pending voyage to London next week, even though he had assured her he would return before Christmas. He had to go, he told her. The new accounts had to be secured and his father trusted no one else to handle the matter

45

properly. Johnathan had held Janielle close in the circle of his arms, pleading with her.

"Set the wedding date, Janielle—early spring or summer, as you wish. I'll divide my time between here and Savannah, but I am determined to continue my business. I don't know if I'll be a good planter, but I *am* a good merchant." His eyes had searched hers. "I want you, Janielle. I want to be the only one ever to have you. I want you to bear my children. I love you, Janielle."

Janielle's violet eyes had brimmed with tears, and Johnathan had gently kissed them away. Her voice was low. "I miss you so, Johnathan, when you're away. Only I need some time here, after staying at Challey for so long. The strain of Loranna's illness and the last few months at Challey have proved exhausting."

Johnathan's hands were softly caressing her silken breasts, his blond head lowering to their fullness.

"No, Johnathan, please," Janielle had gasped. "We'll be married soon, and then—"

Kaylee Mallen's enchanting laughter brought Johnathan abruptly back to the moment. Her green eyes smiled at him. "God, she is a challenge to any man," Johnathan thought, watching her across the table. Kaylee seemed to be openly infatuated with Ryan Deverel—but then, with Kaylee, nothing was certain.

John Patterson was ordering the final course to be served. The chilled almond ice, blanc mange and Charlotte Russe, served in silver goblets, brought a gasp of surprise from the dinner guests. There were few meals in the Santee sweep that could compare with those served at Patterson Woods.

Janielle breathed a sigh of relief, knowing that the lavish meal was nearing a close. The wine had had its effect, numbing the tension she had felt thoughout the dinner. She cast one long look at Ryan Deverel as he leaned toward Kaylee, feeling pure hatred at the attentive way he listened to her chatter. Kaylee was obviously enthralled with the Challey heir and was using her every wile to keep him amused.

As the sumptuous dinner drew to an end, John Patterson rose from his chair. "Gentlemen, a game of cards in the library follows, and after-dinner cordials, if you desire. Ladies, your charm has lent itself most generously to our dinner and we bid you good night. I am informed the weather has turned even worse, as you can hear by the rising gale. It is my hope that each of you will remain as my guest overnight, or until the weather improves." John Patterson bowed to his guests and led the way from the dinner room.

chapter 7

Venting its unleashed wrath against the soft river land, the winter storm roared inland, the swollen black clouds writhing within their masses as they lowered to spill their store of icy, pelting rain. The howling attack sparred with its formidable brick opponent, emitting an anguished moan as it traveled the wings of Patterson Woods manor.

Janielle stirred from her restless slumber, mildly alert to the intermittent thumping sound below her corner room. Accustomed to the usual shifting wind from the river bluff that rattled her window, she turned on her side, willing the repeated noise below to cease. Closing her eyes, she lay quietly, anticipating the noise again. Not hearing it, she settled to sleep, but was suddenly startled when a loud thump resounded from below. Throwing back her satin quilt, she rose, donning her green fleece wrapper and matching cloth slippers, thinking that the noisy culprit was probably the loose shutter in the library. Its hinge had rusted months ago and rarely stayed secure, even in a mild wind.

The dim hallway was silent when she stepped from her room, casting a wary glance down the corridor to determine if the recurrent noise had awakened the Mallens. Their door remained closed, as did Kaylee's at the end of the hall.

The heavy fragrance of rose petals pervaded the lower rooms as Janielle walked through the darkened interior of the spacious manor. She angrily shoved from her mind the distressing evening, Ryan Deverel's gloating face when he was introduced to her, Kaylee's affectations, and Johnathan's brooding manner all evening. Only her father's apparent happiness at entertaining his chosen guests had made the evening bearable. John Patterson's years immersed in grief over the loss of his wife and older daughter during the epidemic had ended with his election to the Constitutional Congress, which seemed to be largely the result of Morris Chapman's influence in the low country. Now Patterson Woods was gradually claiming the social leadership in the high Santee sweep.

The banging grew louder as Janielle neared the closed double doors to the library. The room was in darkness with the only illumination coming from the red-gray ashes of the wasted fire. She shivered as she made her way to the window, feeling for the table and chair that stood close by. She located the loose shutter, dangling by only the lower hinge, feeling the moist coldness of the windowpane as her hand brushed against it. She pulled the shutter aside, securing it against the wall until it could be repaired.

Stifling a yawn, she moved carefully in the darkness, threading her way back across the library. "I should have brought the candle tray," she thought, inching her way along in the dark.

Her soft slipper suddenly nudged against something warm and it yielded. Janielle stumbled backward, sick with fear. She groped along the mantlepiece for a tinder and flint, running her hand along its length. It was bare.

The dim embers of the fire cast a ghostly outline along the side of the sofa to a long arm, dangling lifelessly, the slim fingers slightly curled on the rug below. A broad naked back sprawled belly down, the head buried under a loose dark velvet cushion.

Janielle forced her feet forward, the sound of her own heartbeat roaring in her ears. She had to know.

Suddenly the long arm reached upward, gripping her about the waist, pulling her roughly down to the sofa. She squeezed her eyes against the assault, her breath coming in gulps. She was being pressed into the wide, hard chest, her face brushing the light furring across the center.

The strong arms slackened their hold. "Were you seeking me, Janielle?" Ryan Deverel's low mocking laughter rang in her ears.

Janielle let her breath go in a rush. "Oh, Ryan, you gave me such a fright."

Ryan's laugh was muffled against her hair. Then he moved his head away and smoothed her white-gold hair with his hand.

"Why are you sleeping in here?" Janielle asked incredulously.

"I have an aversion of late to sleeping alone," he confessed mockingly, "so I make a cozy pallet by the fire to ease my loneliness."

"But it is chilled in here and very dark," Janielle said, shivering.

"Not any longer," Ryan said, winding a tendril of her white-gold hair around his lean finger. His breath was warm against her face. "You stared at me all through dinner, Janielle. I was indeed flattered that the prestigious statesman's daughter found me so attractive," Ryan accused, laughingly.

"Twas you, sir, who stared," Janielle retorted furiously, remembering the discomfort of Ryan's blue eyes devouring her.

"Your role as parlor wench at Challey appeared more befitting." Ryan's tone was suddenly caustic.

Janielle jerked free, nearly unseating herself on the floor before Ryan's arm caught her. Simultaneously they heard a screeching rip from the cushion beneath them as they struggled. Ryan felt along the sofa's edge, allowing the fast spilling feathers from the cushion to fill his hand. He trickled them over Janielle, letting them drift slowly downward across her hair and face. She brushed them away frantically as Ryan scooped another handful, raining them over her.

They began to laugh in hushed tones; then, giving way to the ridiculousness of the situation, they joined in peals of merriment, until they lay back, breathless, exhausted.

"My beautiful white dove has shed all her feathers, I fear. Perhaps forever," Ryan said lazily, as they contented themselves with an occasional delayed burst of laughter.

"Some unclothed dove wanders about in the windy winter night," Janielle said lightly, relaxing in Ryan's arms.

Unexpectedly, the sagging shutter broke free from its rusted hinge, crashing to the floor as a powerful gust of wind rocked the window. Startled, Janielle bolted upright. Ryan threw his long legs across the sofa, grumbling as he walked over to the window.

"It's cold as a tomb in here," he complained. "God, the wind sounds like a blow at sea."

Janielle watched his arms and his wide back work in a fluid, graceful motion as he placed fresh logs on the hearth. She remembered the morning at Challey when she had traced her fingertips across the raised scars on his back, wondering idly about their cause. Ryan felt his way across the darkened room, closed the library doors, slid the bolt and set the chain in the overhead groove.

The brightened firelight gradually illuminated the room and Ryan caught her worried glance before she could hide it. She trembled nervously, drawing her knees close to her chest, pulling her wrapper protectively around her. Her white-gold hair spilled across her arms when she bent to rest her head on her knees.

Ryan leaned against the mantlepiece, warming his back at the fire. He watched Janielle's feigned composure. So she was John Patterson's young daughter. He had

51

concealed his astonishment at that news well, having a slight forewarning when she descended the stairs on Johnathan Chapman's arm. He had unwittingly felt a twinge of jealousy when her father brought her to him for introductions. Still, he did not regret his treatment of her at Challey. He had found long ago that where women were concerned he had no conscience.

Janielle was shivering openly, whether from the ebbing chill or the strange situation, Ryan couldn't determine. He moved quickly to her, lifting her by her slim wrists and gathering her in his arms.

"The little dove is cold without her feathers to warm her," he whispered, nuzzling her white-gold hair.

Janielle's voice was low. "Ryan, I am betrothed to Johnathan."

"I know that. Why are you here with me?"

No answer was forthcoming as Ryan's mouth closed on hers, searching, demanding, his large hands caressing her trim back. His hands circled about her waist, which fit securely within. His long fingers traveled her ribs, sliding inside her wrapper. His mouth seared her throat, her eyes. His warm, swollen manhood probed against her thigh before he lifted her in his arms, taking her to the sofa and covering her with his long, hard body.

Deftly his fingers worked open the tiny pearl buttons of her sleeping gown, drawing her breasts together, hungrily sampling the full, pink-tinted peaks that thrust forward to entice him. He savored their sweetness, hearing soft moans of rapture escape her lips. He kissed her mouth again, tasting the saltiness of her tears.

"You'll hurt me, like before," Janielle gasped.

"No, my love. I promise you will only know pleasure this night."

Ryan's warm fingers moved gently into a soft opening, lingering, searching. Her need was uncontrollable now, reaching the urgency of his. She felt a rush of warmness enter her, shaping, dividing, uniting as it sought its path.

White flashes of bursting light exploded behind her closed eyes as she lent herself fully to the surging power within her. His rhythmic thrusts matched her own, gaining in intensity as they explored. She arched forward to him in one long moment, while he waited, certain of her fulfillment. The tides of their passion rode the undulating wave, hesitated, throbbed, then quietly diminished. Janielle's slender arms clung to him, refusing to finish the perfection of the moment.

Ryan shifted above her, smiling warmly into her wide, contented eyes. He had given her the taste of completion, the awakening of her total womanhood. He rolled onto his side, letting Janielle snuggle peacefully against his chest.

He reached down, tilting her face up to his. "I expected you to be at Challey when I returned from viewing the fields. My women usually wait," he scolded gently.

Janielle only nodded sleepily, nestled back into his shoulder and was instantly asleep. He let her sleep for awhile, then moved gently away and began to dress. The milky wash of dawn was filling the sky as he unlocked the library doors.

Then he walked back over to the sofa, gazing down at her. She seemed very young and very small as she slept. He rearranged her night clothing, then reached for the knitted coverlet on the window seat and wrapped it snugly about her. He gathered her up in his arms, glancing toward the window at the oncoming dawn. The manor was still as he stepped outside the door, though he detected a trace of quiet activity from the kitchen wing.

Muffling his footsteps as best he could, he climbed the carpeted staircase, pausing at the top to determine which room was hers. The doors up and down the hallway were closed. He moved quietly to the end, noticing one door slightly ajar. He pushed it open with his shoulder, then recognized Janielle's lavender dinner gown spread across a velvet chair.

He laid her gently on her canopied bed, piling the satin quilt over her. She sighed, smiling, as he straightened above her. There was a fleeting desire to hold her again as he bent down, kissing her lightly on the forehead.

"Rest well, Janielle," he breathed softly. Smiling broadly, he quickly left her room and went seeking his own.

chapter 8

Hordes of invaders swarmed the premises of Challey, filing in somber procession through the bleak interior of the impoverished manor. Their horses, hitched to the empty freight wagons in the approach, swished their tails impatiently in the muggy afternoon air, occasionally pricking their ears to the sounds of rousing activity inside the manor.

A harsh bellow from within, issuing emphatic orders, preceded the shuddering crash of a wall collapsing on the upper floor. The teams shifted uneasily in their traces while the cloud of plaster dust from above settled to the ground.

"Who the hell are you going to hire who can undertake such a chore?" Brandon Ord's angry voice resounded across the approach.

"You are paid for management of the Challey fields, and from what I've observed you're not earning your money!" Ryan's voice boomed.

"First the fields and orchards, then the manor," Brandon shouted.

"By God, I will not live in a barren pigsty! I am master here and I say it will be accomplished!"

Brandon's boots sounded heavily along the bare hallway as he stormed from the manor. He jerked his sorrel loose from the post rail, mounted angrily and galloped away, riding for the north pasture.

"Stubborn son of a bitch," Ryan muttered, scanning the sketches laid before him.

"Masta Ryan, I brung de women to clean, like you tole me." Micah spoke hesitatingly.

"I delegate the cleaning chores to you, Micah. But stay in the lower rooms. The walls upstairs are being moved," Ryan snapped.

The original intricate design of Challey had proved challenging to Ryan's knowledge of construction. Roland Alexis Devereaux, Ryan's claimed grandfather, had planned the grilled scrollwork and delicately laced iron balconies after his elaborate home in Paris, forgetting that the humid climate of the low river country would erode the dainty metal work. Most of the adornments had long ago rusted from their attachments, requiring new outside surfaces to which to affix the deteriorated grills.

Ryan frowned, considering the magnitude of his project. He and Brandon had been arguing ever since the evening at Patterson Woods when Ryan, pricked with envy over the magnificence of Patterson manor, had impulsively decided to restore Challey. The disagreement today over the arrival of a testy little man from Charleston, who claimed the honor of having restored the ravaged Plantation home of Thomas Pickney, further inflamed Brandon.

"How in God's name can you waste your money in this manner?" Brandon had asked bitterly.

"My finances are well able to stand the expenditure. There will be ample for the new seed and purchase of extra field hands for your use," Ryan answered.

"And is it still your intention to finish this madness before Christmas?" Brandon had asked incredulously.

"Exactly!" Ryan had insisted, though his own doubts weighed heavily.

Now the sound of a high screeching voice issued from

56

the front parlor. "You'll destroy that chair before you clean it," Daniel Lisot wailed.

Ryan grinned. Lisot and Micah had been at odds all day over the treatment of the few aged pieces of furniture from Alexis Devereaux's collection that remained at Challey. Only Ryan could maintain peace between the temperamental Frenchman and the fiercely loyal black slave. Ryan had presented a staggering list of duties to each man.

"Impossible! Utterly impossible!" Lisot lamented as he read the schedule, then scurried away to see the chores completed. The only plan that did not bring a cry of anguish from Lisot was the complete redesign of the master wing, which could contain a sunken marble bathtub, cut by a master stone cutter from Charleston, and placed in an adjoining room off the master suite.

"That, Master Deverel," Lisot commented excitedly, "will be a challenge to my talents."

Ryan found the pressing demands on his time increasing as the work on Challey manor proceeded almost to his requirements. He was everywhere, as was his overseer, Brandon Ord. Forgetting their initial disagreements, they shared the noon meal in the kitchen of the manor, exchanging ideas and discussing the soundness of their many plans for Challey.

"I'd flood the east section and plant it in rice," Brandon suggested, lighting his pipe.

"Not this year," Ryan said firmly. "Only cotton for now. The market in Europe is high and I can transport the bales aboard the *Waverly*."

Brandon nodded his approval. "The river barge brought the blacksmith from Santee Point. He is forging the grills," Brandon remarked, sipping the cool tea that Irene had served.

"The barge also brought a post from my Scottish captain, Wyler McGee." Ryan laughed, reaching for the letter. He read it aloud.

To: Ryan Paul Deverel, Challey Plantation.
Me ass has grown barnacles awaitin' yer
return to Charleston. Cargo is aboard and me
feet aches for the sea beneath them. For God's
sake, me man, what be yer delay?
                    Captain Wyler McGee
                    Waverly, Charleston Harbor

Brandon roared with laughter as Ryan folded the letter. Ryan had penned an immediate reply, instructing Wyler to sail for Liverpool at once. He trusted the thrifty Scottish sea master to turn a fair profit on all of the *Waverly*'s voyages.

The sound of hammers and saws echoing throughout the manor brought a sense of exhilaration to Ryan as he climbed the curved stairway. The armoire sat in the hallway, surrounded by piles of freshly cut lumber. He kicked the rolled Turkish carpet aside and opened the lower drawer of the armoire. Shucking the soiled shirt he wore, he selected a freshly laundered indigo homespun. He wandered slowly back down the staircase, struggling to fit his wide shoulders into the shirt. Then he pulled the snug shirt halfway down across his dark chest, pausing as he glanced down toward the open front portal.

Kaylee Mallen stood among the curled wood shavings and deep sawdust, a vision of beauty in her emerald green riding dress. She smiled entranced, as she watched Ryan Deverel descend the stairs, fitting the dark shirt close about his waist, tucking it inside his narrow breeches.

Ryan's surprised expression was cloaked by his warm, easy smile. "Miss Kaylee, a pleasure," he bowed politely. "You are my first guest at Challey since the restoration began. As you can see, we are far from completion."

"Challey is the talk of the Santee." Kaylee smiled warmly, her green eyes flashing up at Ryan. "All I have heard are rumors. I saw Brandon at the fork and he directed me here. I intend to have a thorough look."

A whiff of breeze lifted the powdery accumulated dust across the hallway, enveloping them. Ryan took Kaylee's arm, steering her to the verandah. George Silas stood forlornly on the granite steps, methodically brushing the dust particles from his dark servant's coat.

"Tell Irene to fetch a beverage," Ryan ordered, fluffing the cushions on the worn wicker sofa.

A river dove cooed softly from the spreading branches of the magnolia grandiflora overhanging the long verandah. Kaylee settled herself comfortably on the low wicker sofa, arranging her wide velvet riding skirt about her legs.

Ryan peered up, frowning against the afternoon sunlight. "I thought I heard a laughing gull this morning," he commented, his gaze falling downward across Kaylee. "Made me restless to return to sea."

"They seldom come this far upriver," Kaylee said. "But perhaps one followed you to Challey."

Ryan chuckled, handing Kaylee a glass of the iced lemonade that Irene had brusquely served. The servants were not yet accustomed to visitors at Challey.

Kaylee daintily sipped from her glass, her green eyes encompassing the awesome view of the Challey land. "It's beautiful here, Ryan," she said.

"You're beautiful, Kaylee." Ryan spoke softly.

Her eyes flickered emerald green. "Being beautiful has some advantages," she replied coyly.

"Particularly from where I sit," Ryan agreed. His ice-blue eyes regarded her critically, thinking of the first mention of her name that had come to his attention. Morris Chapman had warned him against entanglements with wealthy young Carolina girls, stating in his barrister's manner the example of Evan Reed, who had courted the green-eyed heiress. Evan Reed, an aspiring ship's surgeon, assigned to a British man-o-war, the *Dover*, had resigned his royal commission and purchased a river tract near Pine Bluff in anticipation of his marriage to the heiress he had courted for a year. Kaylee Mallen had promptly ended their courtship, declaring her preference for living in McClellanville or Charleston. Ryan recalled having seen Evan Reed recently on the docks at Charleston, unkempt and noticeably drunk at midday.

Later he had mentioned the encounter to Morris Chapman, who had nodded sympathetically. "Evan Reed was a fine surgeon, even attended the Queen's minister before his naval commission. Seldom do I find him sober when he's in the city. His British pounds were negotiated through my office for the purchase of his land. As it appears, he built only a rough cabin which he shares with an old Yemassee medicine man he calls "I too." Poor lad truly loved the Mallen girl, but she loves mostly herself. Wasteful indeed," Morris had concluded dryly.

As if reading his thoughts, Kaylee cast a quizzical glance up at Ryan.

"Why have you come to Challey, Kaylee?" Ryan asked quietly.

Kaylee flashed her brilliant smile at him. "Never, never inquire into a woman's whims, Ryan. However, since you ask, Patterson Woods is incredibly dreary with everyone gone. Johnathan left three days ago and Daddy Patterson is at the Congress. I suppose I should have returned with my parents to Charleston. Janielle is so boringly involved with seeing to the plantation, I am bored beyond belief!"

"We must remedy your boredom," Ryan offered teasingly. "Do you know the use of a hammer, or perhaps a saw?"

Kaylee wrinkled her nose in distaste. "Brandon Ord asked if I would care to see the natural waterfall on Dancer's Creek," Kaylee pouted. "Do you think I should ride with him?"

Ryan winced, knowing full well Brandon's intentions, judging by his own. "The waterfall is truly a memorable display," he commented dryly.

"I suppose you are too occupied with your 'restoration' to go anywhere," Kaylee said sarcastically. Ryan weighed her obvious invitation carefully, controlling the urge to teach Kaylee a well-deserved lesson from a man thoroughly experienced with women. "She sorely tempts a man," Ryan thought warily, his eyes raking her full breasts.

"I am presently occupied in absorbing your breathtaking beauty," he offered gallantly, hiding his real thoughts.

Kaylee looked imploringly at him. "I am leaving within the week. I promised Mother I would attend her soirée for Editha Chapman and her sister."

"And you came here for ease from your—ah—boredom until you leave." Ryan's eyes were suddenly stormy.

Kaylee squirmed under his sharp gaze. She was uncertain how to proceed with this ruthless giant of a man. His reputation with women was open talk in Charleston circles, and his doubtful parentage added to the aura of rakishness he presented. Ryan Deverel played few gentleman's games with women.

"I must go, Ryan," Kaylee said uncomfortably, rising to leave.

Ryan laughed softly at her discomfort, sensing inwardly his effect on her. "I have to ride to the flood shack for some supplies," he said. "Would you care to ride with me?"

Kaylee raised uncertain eyes to his. "I'll see Challey when it's complete," she said softly, following him across the approach.

The flood shack, built by Alexis Devereaux for surveillance during the heavy rain season, commanded a wide view of the Santee at the lower bend, at a point which flood waters would choose should they escape their banks. The long stem of pipe used as a flood gauge still bore the faded red markings that the elder Devereaux had left upon it.

The deserted shack stood in a heavy copse of oak and

61

birch trees, so carefully concealed that only one knowing of its whereabouts could find it. A small stone fireplace protruded from one side of the cabin, now used for storage. Fresh water trickled over a mound of gray-pocked rocks behind the abandoned shack, sitting securely in its sentinel position.

Ryan dismounted, moving to assist Kaylee from her sidesaddle perch. She rode well for a woman, probably the result of having had a costly riding master, Ryan reflected.

"May I go inside?" Kaylee asked curiously.

"It's merely a rough cabin; certainly not what you're accustomed to," he snapped, thinking irritably of Evan Reed and his cabin at Pine Bluff.

Kaylee chose to ignore his sarcasm. She pushed at the sagging plank door until it yielded, swaying on one lower hinge. Her wide green eyes reflected terror.

Ryan laughed heartily. "No ghosts here, milady," he teased, seeing the frightened expression on her beautiful face. He walked to the inner room, brushing the dust from the shelves until he located the oversize nails that Lisot had requested.

Kaylee sat down on the rough log table, her green eyes following his movements. He came close to her, reaching to help her to her feet.

Kaylee's slim fingers touched his arm, traveling caressingly up to his wide shoulders, groping her way until she locked both arms about his neck. She lifted her mouth to his, kissing him wantonly, pressing her full ripe breasts against him, moving them softly across his rough homespun shirt.

"No, Kaylee," Ryan breathed, setting her a space away.

Kaylee's green eyes flared with surprise. Determinedly she sought his mouth again, flinging herself wildly into his arms.

"Love me, Ryan," she breathed against his mouth.

"No, Kaylee." His voice was low, even.

Kaylee stepped back quickly, her eyes blazing with fury. Angrily she raised a gloved hand to strike him. He caught her wrist, holding her firmly.

"No one refuses me! No one!" she spat, jerking her wrist free.

"I just have," he replied calmly.

Kaylee stood glaring at him while he strolled to the sagging door, holding it open for her. She stormed through the doorway, waiting for his assistance in mounting her black Arabian horse.

Ryan caught the horse's bridle, steadying the nervous gelding. Kaylee tossed her head angrily, refusing to meet his hard blue eyes. He forcefully tilted her face up to his.

"I'm not a man who is easily had, Kaylee. It is well you remember that."

He lifted her to her saddle, fitting her knee around the horn. Kaylee brought the riding crop down hard against the gelding's flank, causing the startled horse to rear. Ryan stepped aside as the flailing hooves beat the air, watching as the horse pitched forward, setting a gallop through the thick copse of birch trees.

Watching Kaylee disappear into the thicket, he smiled lazily, wonderingly, at his own restraint.

chapter 9

Janielle toyed absently with a long feathered quill,
watching the brilliant morning sunlight cast a row of long
bright bars across the scrolled warrior dragons on the rich
Chinese carpet. The weighty events of the morning had
brought her to her father's massive tulipwood desk,
seeking solitude amid the packets of unanswered mail and
legislative journals.

Idly she lifted from the stack a yellowed official
envelope bearing the British Crown seal, curious as to its
sender. Charles Pickney had posted the letter to her father
from his British prison ship in Charleston harbor before
his exchange and departure for Philadelphia. The letter
contained an outline of proposed legislative reforms, of
little interest to Janielle on this particular day.

Her eyes fell upon the mahogony sofa across the room,
its center cushion neatly repaired after the night she and
Ryan had spent alone in the library. She smiled wistfully,
remembering her surprise at finding the crinkled white
envelope beneath her bed pillow later in the morning.
Eagerly she had ripped it open, laughing as the soft pile of
white feathers drifted into her hand. She had flown to the
armoire, selecting a tangerine morning dress and
hurriedly tying a matching velvet ribbon about her neck.

Then she had rushed downstairs, hopeful of finding Ryan at breakfast with the other guests.

Jebba, the house man, had soberly informed her that Mr. Deverel and Mr. Ord had breakfasted earlier and departed for Challey. Veiling her disappointment, Janielle had joined Johnathan and the others for the morning repast, though the aching emptiness she felt had persisted. Even Johnathan's clever attempts to cheer her could not salvage the ruined day. He attributed the cause of her distress to his forthcoming voyage to Europe.

So Ryan had appeared in his usual fleeting manner, then quickly gone, after an interlude she found difficult to forget. His charm was almost an illusion, murky and troubled, then clear and incredibly tender, then vanishing to emptiness.

The crunch of wheels turning in the approach abruptly jarred her from her musings. She walked to the window, recognizing Micah pulling the team to a halt. Brandon Ord rode the seat beside him. For an instant her heart leaped, thinking it might be Ryan.

"Good day, Miss Janielle," Brandon greeted her as she stepped through the doorway to the columned porch.

"Brandon," Janielle acknowledged, descending the marble steps.

"Micah needed a potion from one of your midwives for an ailing black woman at Challey. No need to disturb yourself, I can wait while he sees to it," Brandon spoke respectfully, his dark eyes roaming Janielle's trim figure.

"Nonsense, Brandon. Step inside out of the wind." Janielle smiled warmly.

Brandon followed her into the palatial hallway, uncertain as to how to proceed with his errand. Ryan's harsh words still rang in his ears.

"Give her the note and bring her," he had ordered.

"And if she refuses?" Brandon had asked.

"By God, I said bring her!"

Brandon felt for the envelope in his pocket while

65

Janielle ordered tea to be served. He settled into a large French chair facing her, absorbing the elegance of the Patterson formal chamber.

He cleared his throat. "Is Miss Kaylee still visiting?" he asked quietly.

"She left yesterday on the river barge. She was terribly bored with the routine life at Patterson," Janielle said distractedly, still puzzling over Kaylee's erratic behavior since her ride to Dancer's Creek a few days before. Always shrewish and spoiled when there were no men about, Kaylee's manner had been intolerable after the impulsive ride that afternoon.

Finally Brandon could postpone his errand no longer. Micah had returned and was waiting outside by the wagon. He handed the envelope to Janielle.

"Mr. Deverel requested that I give you this." Brandon spoke formally. He watched as Janielle studied the old Devereaux seal, firmly stamped in red wax, before she opened the flap.

Janielle's eyes flashed across the polite words.

> *Dear Miss Paterson:*
> *There are matters at Challey that require a gentlewoman's decision. I ask that you return with Brandon today. I shall see you escorted back to Patterson before dusk.*
> *Ryan Paul Deverel*

Janielle reread the note, mildly curious, but peeved at the tone of command the words conveyed. She was aware of Brandon's eyes watching her guardedly.

"What matters would he be referring to?" she asked.

"There were certain possessions belonging to his mother that she intended for you," Brandon replied smoothly. "Ryan has completely refurnished and restored Challey manor; you might enjoy seeing the changes," he added.

66

"I think not," Janielle said coolly, feeling an invisible knife twisting inside her.

Brandon stared down at his dark lean hands, groping for adequate words to persuade her. If he were unsuccessful, Ryan would undoubtedly come back and fetch her if he had to abduct her.

"Miss Loranna would wish you to select what you wanted from Challey," he offered uncertainly.

"My stay at Challey was out of fondness for her, not for any reward." Janielle's violet eyes were stormy.

"True, Miss Janielle," Brandon urged softly. "But you should consider her last wishes."

His honest words pricked at her conscience as she glanced down at the envelope on which Ryan had carefully penned her name. His face seemed to leap up at her. She wanted to see him again and somehow he knew it.

"If you'll wait, I'll change to a warmer dress," she said, rising from her chair, smiling at the expression of obvious relief on Brandon's handsome face. He was older than Ryan, and bore himself well, in the stately British manner. Suddenly she understood how difficult his errand for Ryan must have been for him and realized that, as usual, Ryan had achieved his purpose.

Janielle shivered with excitement as Brandon swung the wagon into the Challey approach. Even from a distance she could see the new marble pilasters, heightened by Corinthian capitals and ornately carved with acanthus leaves, glistening in the full morning sunlight. The entire brick facade and wooden exterior of the manor, washed with fresh white paint, dazzled her eyes. The delicate scrollwork, balconies and window appointments were smooth and tinted in a vivid shade of gamboge. She was scarcely prepared for the vast transformation of Challey.

Brandon lifted her from the wagon seat, setting her gently on her feet. He smiled down at her.

"Ryan has ordered a new barouche from Richmond. My apologies for the discomfort of the field wagon."

Janielle stared dazedly up at him, her mind still reeling from the outward appearance of Challey. "It is unimportant," she mumbled, glancing down at the freshly scrubbed and polished granite steps leading to the new fan-carved entrance.

Brandon took her arm, leading her into the hallway. She lifted her violet eyes to the Irish glass chandelier hanging from the smooth hallway ceiling. The crystal pieces clinked softly as they passed underneath. Brandon was shouting for Ryan when George Silas shuffled from the front parlor.

"Masta Ryan be down shortly. He be seein' to de pond upstairs," George Silas muttered, smiling at Janielle.

"The pond?" Janielle asked incredulously, turning to Brandon.

Brandon laughed softly. "Ryan has different tastes than most, as you will see. I would stay to enjoy your surprise but there are tasks to tend in the fields. Enjoy your day, Janielle." He tipped his straw field hat to her.

Janielle smiled uncertainly, watching him leave. George Silas left too, wandering down the long hallway to the kitchen, leaving her standing alone in the entrance way. Suddenly she felt apprehensive. She shouldn't have come here, especially alone. She should have brought Minna with her. What madness had possessed her? If she hurried she could catch Brandon before he rode to the fields, and ask him to take her home. She moved toward the door.

"Janielle—" Ryan's voice halted her. She turned slowly to see him bounding down the stairs, fastening the buttons at his ruffled shirt cuff. His ice-blue eyes held hers a moment, reflecting genuine warmth and welcome. He flashed a wide smile as he neared her.

"I am honored you came," he said softly, reaching for her hand, raising it to his mouth.

Janielle felt the familiar tremor at his warm touch. Determinedly, she stepped back. "Brandon said there were things of your mother's that I was to see to." She spoke crisply.

"Yes, but later, Janielle. Let me show you some of the new Challey," Ryan said lightly, taking her by the arm.

"The change on the outside is sweeping enough," she replied tartly.

He laughed, oblivious to her stiff manner. "The whim of an irritable perfectionist from Charleston," he explained. "Do you approve?"

"I don't know," she reflected thoughtfully, following him into the formal parlor. Her eyes swept the new wallpaper, hand painted in tempra, the style a variation of the rococo elements of Chippendale mode. A new red bay table stood in the center of the room. She ran her hand across the beautiful polished wood rays, noting the matching side chairs, carved with acanthus leaves on their cabriole legs. A new brocade Queen Anne sofa sat in front of the wide window, its graceful lines exuding comfort and elegance.

"It's beautiful, Ryan," Janielle said.

"A sofa is an important purchase for any manor."

She felt suddenly flushed and stepped back into the hallway. He steered her toward the library, pushing open the double doors.

Janielle gasped. The naked bookshelves were filled with new bound volumes. Her eyes roamed the gleaming bombe secretary desk, richly ornamented with rococo and classical elements. A Newport gaming table with French scroll feet stood beneath the window, the gaudy cards arranged for a hand of 100. A pair of elegantly carved easy chairs decorated each side of the fireplace, with an octagonal cellarette sitting by the hearth.

She raised surprised eyes to Ryan. He laughed softly,

lifting the top of the cellarette to display the fine choices of wine.

"The wine would warm before George Silas could fetch it from the dinner room, so I moved the butler in here. Now the ice chunks melt before he can deliver them," Ryan joked, watching Janielle's reaction.

She smiled knowingly, recalling her own irritation at the incredible slowness of the aged Challey house servant.

"I have purchased other pieces, but they have not yet come from upriver," Ryan explained, leading her from the room.

"Are all the rooms restored?" she asked quietly.

"Only one other, upstairs." They climbed the stairway, now spread with a vibrant carpet runner. The aroma of cleaning oils and beeswax permeated the long hallway of the upstairs floor.

Ryan paused before the door of Loranna Deverel's former sleeping parlour. He turned to Janielle, his expression impassive.

"It is strange," he remarked. "I could not touch this room. It is as she left it. The list for you is inside, as are all the items I could locate. Micah will help with the crating and wrapping. I'll be downstairs," he said hurriedly, striding away down the long hall.

"Ryan—" she called after him. He turned at the top of the stairway, his eyes studying her calmly.

"The newness of Challey is beautiful," she spoke softly.

He smiled, nodding, then continued downstairs. She watched him disappear, feeling a familiar uneasiness as she opened the door of Loranna Deverel's bed chamber. Ryan's reasons for asking her to Challey were suddenly clear. Something deeply troubled him about his beautiful mother, and he wanted all reminders of her taken away. Simple enough, Janielle decided, looking about the eerie room.

She seated herself on the caned daybed, running her hand along the familiar Flemish scrolls, a habit she had acquired when reading for long hours to Loranna. The list Ryan had mentioned lay on a nearby upholstered stool. Wandering about the room, she selected the French porcelain clock, a silver-plated Argand lamp and the Dutch chocolate pot, setting them on the cherry dressing table. Loranna had sold most of the Challey furnishings, but remained steadfast in keeping her treasured pieces in her bedroom. The folding mahogany handkerchief table, a favorite of Janielle's, along with the exquisite japanned highboy, would require special packing. The blue glass hunting horn atop the mantlepiece she would carry by hand back to Patterson. That piece could never be duplicated.

Janielle sighed, considering the long list in her hand. It would seem easier to leave the larger pieces at Challey. But apparently Ryan didn't want them.

Micah and Irene entered the room, bearing stacks of soft cloths for wrapping. Janielle looked apprehensive.

"No worry, Mis Janielle. Harmon 'n' me will see your things careful to Patterson," Micah drawled reassuringly.

"Masta Ryan asks that you join him for lunch downstairs," Irene announced sourly.

Janielle nodded, moving to the japanned highboy, opening the narrow center drawer. Loranna's satin jewel case still rested in its intimate place. Janielle peeked inside. The diamond brooch and the set of sapphire and diamond wedding rings were inside. She scanned the list and found they were intended for her. But surely Ryan would wish to have these, she thought, closing the case. Satisfied that her task was completed, she left Irene and Micah to arrange the priceless pieces in the large trunk.

Brandon and Ryan were waiting for her in the breakfast room adjacent to the verandah. A charming set of piazza chairs surrounded the new butterfly table. Brandon seated Janielle at the sunny end of the table facing Ryan. The fare was simple but excellently prepared, and she was hungry. She listened attentively to the easy banter between the two men, pondering over their discussion of the blight on the new cotton leaves.

"I have saved the master wing until last," Ryan announced abruptly, causing Brandon to choke on a mouthful.

"The room with the *pond*," Janielle asked, laughing.

"Pond?" Ryan shot a puzzled look at Brandon. "Hell, it's my bathtub." Ryan smiled, buttering a slice of freshly baked bread.

Brandon took the cue, excusing himself to return to the fields. He left the manor somewhat surprised and irritated at Ryan's arrogant air toward Janielle. It troubled him.

Janielle watched Ryan carefully fold his embroidered napkin, waiting for the proper moment to discuss Loranna's jewels.

"Ryan—" she began. "The jewel case in your mother's room contains her diamond brooch and wedding rings. I am certain there was an error on Morris Chapman's list—"

"They are yours, Janielle," Ryan interrupted sharply. "I have no need for them."

She stared down at her plate, weighing his comment, almost wishing he had answered her differently.

"Come, I wish to show you the *pond*." Ryan smiled down at her, lifting her to her feet.

She hesitated at the foot of the stairs. "Ryan, I don't think this is proper." She spoke softly, gazing at him and thinking of the upstairs room where they had first made love.

"I don't intend to have a bath," he said, "only to show you the room." He paused, waiting for her to decide. His ice-blue eyes were suddenly stormy.

"I won't touch you, Janielle—unless you wish it."

She studied him, noting how incredibly handsome he looked in his velvet coat of slate blue. "I will see the room,

72

then I must return to Patterson. Your invitation disrupted my chores for the day."

She accepted Ryan's arm, moving in a dreamlike walk up the curving stairway. His closeness was strong and comforting, almost a completely natural thing. She felt she had moved this way with him before, close beside him.

He threw open the doors to the master wing, watching her expression of wild delight. Shades of scarlet, vermilion, violet, ebony and soft chalky white burst in a kaleidoscope of color, creating an untamed effect. She sank into a purple velvet wing chair, her feet caressing the thick ivory carpet, her wide eyes attempting to absorb the wildness of the hues.

"You do approve," Ryan asked mockingly, pulling her again to her feet.

"How in heaven's name did you *choose* such colors?" she gasped.

He smiled smugly, leading her to the shuttered inner room. The elegant long marble tub lay sunken in the floor, its tiny gold dolphins spraying a thin trickle of water from their yawning mouths. Janielle was speechless. She stood staring down at the marble square while Ryan walked away, returning with two wine goblets, filled with her favorite claret.

This was his room, his perfect exciting room. So like him, so completely unexpected. She lifted her glass, her wide violet eyes glowing with approval as she smiled up at him.

"It is breathtaking, Ryan," she said.

"It is what I desire for now." He spoke quietly, sipping his wine.

She strolled back into the bedchamber, her fingertips caressing the ornate Ribband back chair near the window. The late afternoon sunlight was streaming through the filmy inner draperies. Her eyes swept the view of the Challey land. The giant live oaks across the

73

approach cast a wide row of stately shadows pointing to the wide steps of the manor.

"Ryan—" she spoke dreamily—"how did you manage to place the envelope with the feathers under my pillow?"

Ryan laughed softly. "I borrowed the dove's feathers to make wings and fly to your side," he teased, his blue eyes twinkling.

"But there were so many guests in the manor," she insisted. She felt his warm breath against her neck.

"Enough questions," he said softly. "Come, I'll see you home."

"It has been a lovely day, Ryan." She leaned back against him, savoring the nearness of the moment, wishing there would never be an end.

"Challey needs a mistress, Janielle," he breathed against her white-gold hair.

Instantly she was in his arms. His mouth closed over hers, demanding, exploring, as his fingers worked to loosen her gown. She arched against him, feeling the urgency of her need and his. He lifted her to the bed, easing himself over her, his mouth searing her throat, her breasts, her flat belly.

"Now, Ryan," she breathed against his cheek, feeling his smooth entry begin to pulse inside her. They moved in gentle unison, sharing and giving all, climbing to a surging summit of exploding tremors. Drained of their passion, they lay back breathless, exhausted.

Ryan's large hand caressed her cheek. "No tears this time?" he asked huskily.

"No tears," Janielle replied softly.

chapter 10

Brandon Ord wiped the sweat from his face, grateful for the slight wind blowing downriver. The slaty haze of the morning sky hung listlessly in the air, stifling and unseasonably warm for so near the holidays. The breeze stirred the tiny cotton plants at his feet as he reached for his water cask. He drank deeply, gradually stilling the angry quiver that rankled in his belly.

Reaching again for the hoe, he chopped methodically at the pig weeds near the furrow. He had come very close to blows with the arrogant young master of Challey this morning during one of their heated arguments over the condition of the fields. It had required supreme control to restrain himself when Ryan had flung the purse full of shillings at him, scoffing at his worth as overseer of Challey. Brandon had stormed from the library, leaving his wages behind.

His aristocratic upbringing clashed with his current label as hired man, stirring the flames of his envy and resentment toward Ryan. Deverel had touched a sensitive nerve today, and Brandon vowed that one day the challenge would be fair met.

The north section of Challey land would yield an abundant cotton crop; he had seen to that. It was as though the land were his, and through his toil, his yield.

He tilted his straw field hat back on his head, scanning the warm December sky. The grayish haze was mixed with an acrid smell of wandering smoke that stung his eyes and nose. Fredericks, the Patterson overseer, surely wouldn't call for a burn today on the Patterson-Challey easement. He lifted his head into the wind. He smelled woodsmoke, not a grass burn. Probably some dead timber near the river, Brandon reasoned, resuming his chopping.

The sorrel, tethered near the rise, was wildly pawing the ground, snorting into the wind. He watched the restless horse, sensing a growing uneasiness in the heavy air.

He turned toward the direction of the forked road. Then he saw it—black spirals of billowing smoke were rising from the oak grove near the fork. The fire was on Challey soil! He flung the hoe aside and ran for his horse.

Janielle stirred from her dreams, wakened by the erratic clanging of the landing bell at the jetty. She burrowed deeper into the pillows, trying to escape the jarring sound. She dreaded rising from bed these mornings to face the wooziness and nausea that assailed her. She must, today, send Minna to the slave woman who kept potions for queasiness. She rolled over on her side, her irritation growing with each swing of the bell.

There was no one due from upriver this morning. Her father was traveling to McClellanville for Christmas with the Mallens and she planned to join him in a few days. Who could be at that rope? Angrily, she tossed the covers back, steadying herself as she sat up on the side of the bed. The dizziness quickly passed and she hurried to her corner window, scanned the bend of the Santee but saw nothing. Jebba's small son, Eliah, was jerking wildly at the bell rope.

Janielle flung open her window, calling across the lawn to him. The clanging drowned her voice. Eliah must be having one of those 'devil fits" that Minna was forever talking about. Why hadn't someone fetched him away from the jetty? Where were the field masters, and why the bell this morning?

Suddenly Janielle began to tremble. The landing bell was also sounded for alarms along the river land. One other day, a few years back, the Patterson landing bell had warned of a British invasion at Santee Point. But the war was long over now.

Janielle tasted smoke in the hazy morning air and the acrid film stung her eyes. Could Brandon possibly be firing the river brush near Dancer's Creek? The valley lay swallowed in rising black billows that drifted slowly down river. The smoke furls widened near the fork road at the Challey line.

Janielle grasped the window ledge, her heart pounding. Challey! Challey was ablaze!

Grabbing her wrapper and fastening it hurriedly as she flew down the stairs and out onto the porch, she encountered Minna, twisting and grabbing at her starched apron, her eyes huge with fear.

"No, Mis Janielle, yo' come back here! Yo' pappy skin you for dis!" Minna wailed as Janielle rushed by her.

Janielle ran along the lawn path to the stables, darting through the jumbled activity in the wagon yard. Field hands, carrying wooden buckets and coils of rope, were clambering into the waiting wagons. Fredericks was shouting orders above the din, while the signal for help continued to toll.

Janielle spotted Tom Fredericks' bay tied to the gatepost. She mounted full stride, kicking the horse into a swift gallop. She heard voices calling after her from the wagon yard as she flew across the approach. The dark earth unrolled beneath the flying hooves. Flashes of sunlight dappled the road ahead as she galloped through the Challey lantern posts.

"Ryan, Ryan," she sobbed, brushing at the tears that streamed down her face.

The bay swerved unexpectedly at the Challey approach, nearly flinging her sideways from the saddle. She gripped his mane, straining to see through the smoky cloud ahead.

All was chaos. She reigned up at the wagon line, dismounting and shoving her way through the throngs of field hands, passing dripping buckets to and from the water barrels in the wagons.

Voracious tongues of orange flame were ravaging Challey manor, belching swollen black masses of swirling smoke high into the air. Janielle stumbled, tripping over a blanket-covered mound near the verandah. Sickened, she stood staring down at the covered remains.

"Mis Janielle! Over here!" Irene's anguished voice called across the approach to her.

Janielle raised her eyes, fanning at the smoke that surrounded her. "Irene! Where is Ryan?" she shouted.

"No use, Mis Janielle," Irene sobbed, clutching Janielle's arm. "Dey is all inside."

"Who is inside?" Janielle rasped.

Irene pointed to the smoke-blackened columns. Harmon was crawling dazedly from the flaming front portal, collapsing against the pilaster. Two field hands edged forward, grabbing his feet, jerking him to safety as a sheet of crackling sparks fell from an upstairs window.

Suddenly the library window exploded from the intense heat, sending a volley of tiny glass particles across the smoldering porch. Janielle threw her arms across her face, retreating with the others back across the approach. Incoherent shouts, wails, screams and sobbing filled her ears.

Where were Ryan and Brandon? A shuddering creak resounded from the upper timbers. Janielle looked up, horrified, as the blazing upper floor gave way and the marble bathtub tumbled to a splintering crash on the hard ground below.

Stunned, she continued to stare at the charred,

smoldering pieces. A hush had fallen over the gathering. Buckets were slowed, then held rigidly in the hands of the black field workers. The desperate frenzy had gradually receded as the last hope of saving Challey ended.

Janielle turned disbelieving eyes toward the blazing shell of Challey manor. Brandon came staggering through the crackling threshold, faltering, then rolling helplessly forward with the weight he carried on his shoulder. He fell, unconscious, just short of a safe distance from the advancing, licking flames that surrounded the entranceway.

The wind shifted, separating the smoke layers long enough for Janielle to see Micah crawling along the side of the verandah, attempting to reach the doorway from the west side of the flaming timbers. His rumpled red hat was singed and blood streamed from a gash over his eye.

Without warning, the west frame of the manor collapsed, settling in a shuddering holocaust, tossing long black sticks of charred timber across the granite steps.

Janielle could wait no longer. She edged forward, shielding her face from the searing heat, oblivious to the burning stone under her bare feet. She had to reach Ryan. She fell across Brandon, tugging and yanking at his large, inert frame. He opened his eyes, staring at her with a wild, glazed look.

"Brandon, hurry, you must get out," Janielle choked.

Micah shoved Janielle aside, grasping Brandon about the waist. Brandon roused himself, clutching at Micah and motioning behind him. Brandon got to his knees, reaching back into the flaming doorway. He heaved with supreme effort and was finally able to jerk Ryan through the collapsing entranceway.

A wild cheer rose from the waiting field hands, dissipating the shock that had held them. Many strong arms bent to lift and carry, moments before the fiery door timbers caved in. Janielle caught only a swift glimpse of Ryan's face. Blood was streaming from a deep cut across his head. His leg was twisted at a grotesque angle under him. Micah heaved him across his shoulders and disappeared with him across the smoke-filled approach.

Janielle tried to follow, tried to call after him, but her body refused to respond. She looked wildly about, unable to see or breathe through the suffocating smoke. She was reaching deeper and deeper, gasping for breath. Finally she pitched forward across the steps, screaming a silent sound as the sea of black oblivion swallowed her.

Sometime later she struggled toward consciousness. She needed to swallow but couldn't. Sensing the imaginary tongues of devouring flames engulfing her, she moistened her lips, vainly trying to scream. She only whimpered.

"Easy, Janielle. You inhaled too much smoke." Brandon's soothing voice broke through the waves of unconsciousness. Hot tears coursed down her cheeks. Her eyes were so swollen she couldn't force them open. She reached out blindly toward Brandon and felt his strong arms fold about her, his coarse shirt grate against her face. The word Ryan formed on her parched lips.

Brandon stroked her hair, lifting the cold rim of a water cup to her lips. "Ryan is in the next room. Evan Reed will be here soon to tend him. A portion of the stairway fell on him and we fear his leg is broken. But by a miracle, we are all alive."

Janielle accepted his quiet words, finally able to blink her eyes open. His smile flashed down at her.

"Micah told me of your heroism." Brandon grinned, his dark eyes twinkling.

Janielle tried to move her feet, wincing at the pain.

"I put an ointment on your feet," Brandon said. "The burn is not severe, but it may cause discomfort for awhile. I sent word to Patterson Woods that you are safe and will remain here at my cottage until you are recovered from the smoke vapors."

Janielle nodded, drifting again to sleep. She wakened later as a wave of nausea clutched her. Through clouded eyes she thought she saw a Yemassee Indian hunkering near the door. She squeezed her eyes closed, hearing heavy boots across the plank porch. Dazedly, she fought the hand that raised her head, forcing a semisweet liquid into her mouth. Then a cool soothing hand bathed her face and she slept again.

When she woke the afternoon light had faded from the small window above her cot. She attempted to rise, struggling against the tight woolen blanket that secured her. She stirred beneath the cover, realizing she was naked. "God," she moaned. "Who has undressed me?"

An agonized scream broke the stillness inside the cottage. Then another, beginning in a low groan, reaching a hideous crescendo that shattered the room. Angry voices uttered incoherent curses. The tortured scream broke again, weaker than before. Then, finally, blissful silence.

Janielle retched over the side of the cot. She had to escape the unnamed horrors occurring in the next room. The cot was spinning as she groped slowly along the edge, fighting for her equilibrium. Her eyes focused on two men emerging from the inner room, wiping the sweat from their faces.

Brandon strode to the table, lighting a small candle lantern. A perplexed frown rode his handsome face. He glanced quickly over at Janielle, who huddled pitifully on the edge of the cot.

"Easy, honey," he cautioned, moving across the room.

Janielle's violet eyes welled with tears. "I heard someone screaming," she said, clutching at Brandon's arm. In all the chaotic nightmare of the fire and what had followed, only Brandon's strength seemed real. She grasped his large hand, holding it tightly against her cheek.

The other man in the shadows moved close, staring

down at her with hard gray eyes. He was tall and slender, his light brown hair tossed and unruly. Seasoned lines near his mouth and eyes spoke of weathering sun and high seas. He was scowling.

"Janielle." Brandon spoke quietly. "This gentleman is Sir Evan Reed."

The name meant nothing to her. His manner was surly and unapproachable. She turned her tear-streaked face into the pillow.

"It is unfortunate that you wakened before we finished setting Ryan's leg," Evan Reed remarked coldly.

Brandon pulled a splatback chair near the cot, sighing wearily as he sat down. "Ryan's outcries were more the result of being restrained, than the positioning of his leg bone," Brandon explained, taking Janielle's slender hand in his. "Are you hungry?" he added softly.

Janielle nodded against the pillow, avoiding Evan Reed's harsh gray eyes.

Brandon stretched his legs. "I'll ready a meal for us. All you have taken today is the dram Evan gave you when he arrived."

"Who is he?" Janielle whispered to Brandon.

Brandon laughed, glancing up at Evan. "You frighten young ladies with your infernal scowl, Sir Evan."

"Consider yourself fortunate, milady, that your attempts at heroics did not place you in a grave." Evan Reed spoke sternly.

"Challey—" Janielle choked— "is it—

"Challey was ravaged, Janielle. All was lost. Ryan will recover, though he is still unconscious from his head wound. The fire trapped him upstairs and a timber fell across him," Brandon related sadly.

"Brandon," Janielle breathed, "there was a savage near the door, or was it part of my delirium?"

"The Yemassee is my friend Itoo," Evan Reed snapped. "His skill with herbs and potions has proved valuable to me. He accompanies me when I travel." Evan stepped

82

close to her, placing a practiced hand across her forehead. He peered into her wide violet eyes, then slowly straightened.

"Fetch the lass some clothing and see how steady she is," he snarled at Brandon.

Brandon grinned, seeing Janielle's astonished expression. "Your nightdress was singed to tatters. Irene brought some things to the cottage for you. If you feel strong enough, I'll call her to help you dress." His voice was comforting.

Evan Reed stalked from the cottage. Brandon stepped out on the small porch, calling to Irene. Janielle wavered unsteadily on her feet, wrapping the soft blanket about her, wondering why she trembled so.

Irene, dabbing at her dark eyes, served a silent supper. Janielle toyed with her food, scarcely able to swallow. Everything tasted like smoke to her. Brandon's face was tired and drawn. Evan Reed ate sparingly, glancing occasionally across the table at Janielle. The bitterness of the day hung heavily over the gathering.

The door to the inner room where Ryan lay remained tightly closed. When Irene had cleared the serving dishes away the men strolled outside with their pipes. Janielle sat on the narrow cot, attempting to sort out the hideous events of the day. Her feet were raw but the ointment Brandon had used seemed to soothe them. Her eyes wandered to the closed door to Ryan's room.

Slowly she rose from the cot and stepped softly across the room. She reached for the latch to open the door.

Suddenly a long arm stretched across the doorway, blocking her entry. "I advise, Miss Patterson, that you be patient until morning." Evan Reed spoke curtly. "Mr. Deverel is tended by Itoo and Micah, and is scarcely in need of your company."

"I only wished to see him for a moment," Janielle replied lamely.

83

Brandon pushed the cottage door open, laboring with an armful of fresh logs for the fire. Janielle retreated back to her cot, not wishing to argue with both of them over seeing Ryan. Evan Reed guarded the door, watching sullenly as Janielle slipped back beneath the covers.

Finally he strode over to her, roughly pulling the woolen blanket over her. He reached for a cup of water on the small table beside the cot, expertly mixing a small packet of grayish powder into it. He lifted the cup to her mouth, his slaty eyes holding hers.

"This potion will help you sleep," he said in his crisp British accent. He waited while Janielle swallowed the murky liquid, wrinkling her nose at the bitter taste. "I advise you to remain abed for the next few days. You are far too thin," he added solemnly, his gray eyes roaming her slender body.

Janielle watched as he donned his cloak and stepped out into the night. Brandon stood at the hearth, staring vacantly into the crackling, sputtering flames.

Slowly he turned to Janielle. "Today we watched fire destroy a creation of beauty, and tonight, we seek fire's warmth." His voice was soft with emotion.

Janielle was silent for a moment, erasing the picture of the fire from her mind. "Brandon, tell me about Evan Reed," she said simply.

Brandon leaned wearily against the mantlepiece. "Evan is, or was, a British surgeon, commissioned by the Queen. He tended her minister before his naval commission. Now he lives at Pine Bluff with old Itoo. I know little else, save the fact that he is a notably competent surgeon." he finished dryly.

"You saved Ryan's life today, Brandon. He would thank you if he could." Janielle's voice choked.

Brandon moved over to her cot. "I will sleep near the fire, Janielle. There may be activity through the cottage tonight, but don't be alarmed. No one will harm you. Good night," he whispered tiredly, reaching down to tuck the covers about her. He waited until she closed her violet eyes, her long lashes fanning across her cheeks.

He tossed his blanket on the floor near the hearth, dazedly watching the leaping flames at play. Tomorrow he would look out across the approach and find Challey gone.

chapter 11

Evan Reed deftly angled the scalpel along his jaw, scraping the beard stubble from his face. His bleary eyes ached from the black rum he had consumed the night before. Itoo squatted near the door, his face impassive, watching as Evan rinsed his face in the flowered shaving bowl.

Smoke vapor hung thickly in the air, still rising from the smoldering ruins of Challey manor. Evan coughed as he straightened, then dried his face with a cloth. He glanced across at Ryan Deverel, anticipating some faint movement. He had ceased the drugging a few hours earlier, after closing Ryan's head wound with palmetto fiber carefully fashioned by Itoo.

Evan strode over to Ryan, lifting the eyelid and gazing deeply into the dilated blue pupil. He scowled, muttering a few Yemassee phrases to Itoo. Itoo nodded, rose quickly and left the cottage.

Evan slipped into his worn crimson coat, casting a worried look back at his patient. It had been two days since the fire that destroyed Challey manor and Ryan Deverel had yet to regain awareness. Evan stepped into the middle room, inhaling the inviting breakfast smells of pork and Ashley rice bread. Irene busied herself at Brandon's small cooking stove, lost in her own thoughts.

She raised a dismal face to Evan. "Masta Brandon, he et already. He tole me to tell you he was ridin' out to the cotton plants."

Evan poured a cup of coffee, ladling thick cream into his cup. How these Americans abided the offensive brew, he'd never understand. It was barely passable even if diluted with cream and honey.

Janielle slept soundly in her cot across the room. He watched her gentle breaths, her slim fingers occasionally twitching in her dreams. The sleeping draught that Itoo had mixed was potent and she would probably sleep most of the day. Irene shuffled over to the table, refilling Evan's cup.

"Masta Brandon tole me to say 'Merry Christmas,'" she said tearfully.

Evan nodded, gathering the rice bread in a napkin, fitting it in his pocket. He downed his coffee, feeling an aching bitterness rising within him again. Last Christmas Eve he had been at McClellanville with Kaylee Mallen in his arms. He kicked the chair aside, storming from the cottage. He remembered the flask of Jamaica rum he had in his saddle pouch.

Janielle painfully opened her eyes to the bright sunlight. She tasted smoke in the air, and a moment of vivid horror ensued. Worriedly she glanced about the empty cottage. Usually Brandon was close by. She called his name softly, listening intently but hearing only the clucking sounds of the chickens in the side yard near her window.

She tested her steadiness, feeling only a slight twinge of nausea. The sleeping powder that Evan Reed had given her made her feel lightheaded. She slipped into her fleece stockings, wrapping the woolen blanket around her, trembling even in the warmth of the cabin.

A deep moan came from Ryan's room. She hesitated, waiting to see who would appear. Something fell to the floor in his room and she jumped. Could all of them have left him alone? She edged toward the door, remembering her fearful encounter the night before with Evan Reed. She lifted the latch and peered inside. No one was about.

Ryan's left leg was propped inside a trough, secured by heavy leather strappings. The pungent smell of medicinal herbs and a plaster that reeked of brackish river water brought on a gush of nausea. She eased inside the door, sickened by what confronted her.

The covers were heaped on the floor beside the bed. Ryan lay naked, drenched in sweat. A hideous gash sliced his head from the crown to the middle of his forehead. Bits of suture bristled along the surface of the wound. His face was ashen, his mouth moving in silent agony.

Janielle braced herself against the chair, determined not to faint. She bent to dab a cloth in the pitcher beside the bed. At least she could bathe his fevered face.

As the cool cloth touched his forehead, he began to thrash about. His hand jerked the cloth away, knocking Janielle aside. Her knees gave way and she crashed against the bed table. The reservoir of unshed tears broke and she lay sobbing beside Ryan's bed, hating herself for her weakness.

Evan Reed appeared in the doorway, breathless and scowling furiously. Brandon was close behind him.

"By God—" Evan swore, reaching to lift Janielle to her feet. "Take her out of here!" he shouted.

Brandon picked Janielle up in his arms, carrying her through the cottage and outside. Itoo passed them hurriedly, holding a snakeskin medicine pouch under his arm. Janielle buried her face in Brandon's shoulder, weeping abandonedly. Brandon stalked toward the oak grove, his wide mouth set in a grim line. He slowed his stride near the sweet gum thicket, seeing that Janielle was able to control her violent sobbing. He smiled down at her.

"I hate Evan Reed," she choked, wiping at her tears.

She swayed slightly as Brandon set her on her feet. Brandon smelled of sweat and horseflesh. She noticed that his brown hair was singed along the side. She winced, thinking of her selfishness.

"Today is Christmas Eve, Janielle." Brandon's tired eyes twinkled while his arm steadied her.

"I hate Christmas! I hate the fire that destroyed Challey! But mostly I hate that pompous Evan Reed!"

Brandon shook his head scoldingly. "Evan Reed undoubtedly saved Ryan's life. The head gash was nearly fatal."

Janielle thoughtfully studied his stern expression. She sighed, seating herself on an upturned log. Brandon removed his riding coat, placing it about her slim shoulders. She shivered in the brisk air.

"There was a letter from your father this morning. You were asleep when the rider came." Brandon spoke softly. He lifted the letter from his shirt pocket and handed it to her.

Janielle opened the envelope, feeling guilty that she had not once thought of her father the last few days. Hurriedly she read the lines, then crumpled the parchment.

Brandon looked suprised as she tossed the letter aside.

"He merely sends regrets over the loss of Challey and offers our home to Ryan or any of the others who care to stay there," she commented indifferently. "He expresses gratitude for your care of his only daughter and wishes us all a Merry Christmas."

"And Johnathan?" Brandon asked guardedly.

"Johnathan will not be able to sail from London in time for the holidays," Janielle replied vacantly.

"Is it the news of Johnathan that distresses you?"

"Everything today distresses me. Seeing Ryan that way—" she felt a tear trickle down her cheek.

"It is Christmas Eve, Janielle. I feel obligated to have some celebration for the Challey servants and slaves,

89

despite the fire," Brandon said determinedly.

"I fail to see the necessity," she replied sullenly.

"Itoo and I spotted a pine upriver. I think we will cut it and bring it to the cottage for the Yule tree. Perhaps you could find some ornaments to grace it. Some preparations were accomplished before the fire. Harmon's family has already made some gifts for the black children. Irene seemed willing to provide some treats from the kitchen. Do you feel strong enough to help?" Brandon's even gaze held hers.

Janielle felt a vague flutter of excitement. There was a subtle intimacy about being alone with Brandon in the sundrenched sweet gum grove. He was virile and constant in his maturity and they shared a possessive love for Challey that only the two of them understood.

The sadness and shock of the last few days dissipated in the realization that it was indeed Christmas Eve.

Janielle finished tying the last red bow on the outstretched pine bough, while Brandon towered above her on a chair, carefully lighting the few candles placed in sconces and clamped to the hastily decorated tree. Despite the sparseness of ornaments, she and Irene had managed to sew and piece together what remnants of ribbon they could gather from the slave quarters. Tiny dolls of yarn and stuffing had been made for the few slave children. Irene had complained over the lack of cooking pots but produced a tray of sweetmeats and the traditional Challey plum pudding.

Evan Reed had remained sullen throughout the day, casting thunderous looks about at the frenzied preparations. Janielle chose to ignore him, swishing by him in Jenny Walters' borrowed dress. Itoo had woven colorful garlands from bits of leather and rope to adorn the mantlepiece. Shortly before dusk the unpredictable Yemassee had rolled an enormous Yule log into the hearth, much to everyone's amazement.

The crisp December night boasted a full moon, illumining the sky in a chalky glow. A scattering of tinsely stars flickered above the oak grove. An excited procession moved quickly from the slave quarters through the splashes of moonlight, winding their way toward the beckoning candle in the window of Brandon's cottage.

Brandon held the door wide as the polished, eager faces appeared in the doorway. Harmon Walters stretched his hand accordion, breaking into the strains of a familiar Yule carol. Brandon led the children around the tree, delighted at the glowing, wonder-filled expressions on the young faces. Each child was given a small gift fashioned from the scraps Irene and Janielle had found. Pudgy fingers reached forward hesitatingly as Brandon passed the gifts.

Harmon was playing a lively rigadoon and Brandon grabbed Janielle, whirling her around the floor. The children clasped hands, skipping gleefully about in wild disorder. Irene passed among them, offering each sweetmeats and frosted jumble.

Evan Reed stalked to the door of Ryan's room, flinging it open. He scowled at the noisy gathering.

Brandon paused, watching Evan. "There's syllabub on the sideboard, Evan. Fetch a cup for everyone," he shouted across the room.

Evan's harsh expression softened. He made his way to the sideboard, selecting the cups and ladling the thick mixture into them. A tiny yarn ball rolled across the top of his scuffed boot. He bent to retrieve it, placing it gently in the small outstretched hand. Grateful dark eyes smiled up at him, and reluctantly he smiled back.

Janielle caught the simple exchange, inwardly pleased. Evan was almost handsome when he smiled. She relaxed, seeing the bitterness leave his face. This Christmas Eve she would remember happily, after all. There were no glittering chandeliers, no satin or velvet ball gowns, no long banquet table groaning with sumptuous Yuletide fare, yet in its simple way this night touched her deeply. If only Ryan were awake to see it!

Evan Reed motioned to Brandon, muttering to him in low tones. Brandon nodded agreeably, moving to the doorway. He reached for the basket near the door, distributing a cask of molasses, a pouch of tobacco and a bolt of cloth to each adult slave. This had long been a tradition at Challey at Christmastime, and he had used coin from his own wages for the extra purchases.

Evan Reed rigidly watched the thankful expressions on the faces of the Challey slaves as they passed by Brandon. Finally he shrugged disgustedly and stormed from the cottage.

The children hastily gathered their treasured gifts, scurrying to follow their families out the door.

"Merry Christmas, suh." Micah spoke quietly, accepting his gift.

"Are you to sit the first or the second watch over Ryan?" Brandon asked.

"I's spendin' a little time with my woman, then I be back," Micah replied.

Janielle and Brandon stood staring after him, watching him cover the worn path down to the slave shacks. Brandon closed the door, leaning wearily against it.

"A fine Christmas Eve, Janielle. Even Evan Reed was pleasured in his way," Brandon said.

Janielle sniffed, making him laugh. "I seriously think that he has never enjoyed anything," she commented.

Catching a movement from Ryan's room, Brandon swung about. Quickly he moved to the doorway, staring down at Ryan.

"Janielle! Fetch Evan! Ryan is awake," he called to her over his shoulder.

Janielle snuggled deeper beneath her covers. The radiance of the shifting moonlight bathed the room in a luminous glow. She felt around her neck for the gold locket that Brandon had placed there a few hours earlier, asking her to accept his Christmas gift. He had explained that the locket was all that remained of his family's heirlooms and he wished her to have it.

For a moment Janielle had been too stirred with emotion to reply. "It should be for someone special," she had replied tearfully at last.

"The gesture speaks for itself."

Janielle trembled. Brandon was arousing feelings within her that she refused to face. Her thoughts turned furiously to Evan Reed, who had earlier come marching through Ryan's doorway at her call, expressing obvious displeasure at the interruption.

Seeing Ryan's eyes open, glazed and vacant, had brought a sigh of relief from Reed. He moved quickly to Ryan, watching for a further reaction.

"Can you speak?" he had asked.

Ryan had rasped something unintelligible before lapsing back into slumber.

Evan Reed straightened, facing Janielle and Brandon, a trace of a smile on his mouth. "It appears Mr. Deverel will recover. My fears for the loss of his facilities were unfounded. He should improve quickly now. The shock that held him has dispelled." Reed moved through the door. "I bid you a Merry Christmas," he said brusquely, and left the cottage.

Janielle clenched her fists, feeling an unexplainable fury toward the arrogant British surgeon. It almost reminded her of her reaction to Ryan's cold, dominant manner when he had first arrived at Challey. She softened, thinking again of Ryan. He would recover now. His leg would mend and then, perhaps—thoughts of Brandon stirred her again. Sleep was futile.

The hour was late, she knew. Micah had already slipped into the cottage to stay with Ryan until dawn. She had not taken her sleeping draught tonight and her thoughts were churning. She sat up on the cot, resting her chin on the window sill, watching the shadowy streaks of moonlight play through the oak trees. The ground outside glowed with an eerie white pallor.

The sudden urge to run through the moonlit night overwhelmed her. Sleep was lost, so perhaps a walk would help. She snatched Brandon's cloak from the hook near the door, quietly easing through the threshold and out onto the porch.

The cold air made her gasp. The lamps below the path to the slave quarters had long been extinguished. The stark light from the full moon chased at her shadow as she ran to the coppice of live oaks. She felt free again, a wildness taking her as she danced from tree to tree. Breathlessly she leaned against the weathered bark of a twisted oak tree.

The crunch of a brittle twig sounded behind her. She jerked around instinctively. A tall figure emerged from the trees, pulling her roughly to him. Her long hair tangled in the buttons of his coat. She could hear his ragged breathing against her ear.

"No!" she cried. "Leave me alone." A warm, demanding mouth found hers, moving slowly, expertly. His hands loosened their hard grip, moving caressingly along her spine.

She struggled helplessly, realizing she was no match for his strength.

The forceful arms gradually released her. "It is not wise for you to be out in the night alone, Janielle. I'll take you back now."

She gasped, recognizing Brandon's soft drawl. "Brandon, why?" she asked incredulously.

"Because I wanted to hold you, Janielle. Because I understand your reason for escaping out into the moonlight. You want me, Janielle, just as I desire you. But until you come to me willingly, I can wait."

"But, you should have—" she faltered.

"I will never hurt you, or allow anyone else to,"

Brandon said fiercely, lifting her into his arms and carrying her to the cottage.

He nudged the door open with his knee and moved toward her cot. Janielle revelled in the silent strength of his presence. Perhaps it was the circumstances of the last few days, the forced intimacy of confinement, the Christmas Eve celebration, the rum cup she had drunk. "No," she confessed to herself, "it's Brandon. Simply that." Strange that she should feel so guiltless.

"Now, moonlight princess, stay put for the remainder of the night," he chided teasingly. "You have had a full day."

"Brandon, Merry Christmas." Janielle spoke softly.

"I cannot trust myself to kiss you again, Janielle," Brandon said, straightening.

Drowsily, she heard him go to the sideboard, clinking the cup as he poured a drink. She listened for awhile to his restless footsteps, and eventually she slept.

chapter 12

Morris Chapman stood silently surveying the charred rubble before him. The Challey pilasters and smoke-blackened granite steps sprawled bleakly in the dawn light, reminiscent of an ancient Greek ruin. He clutched at the collar of his greatcoat, pulling it closer about his neck, fighting the chilling tremor that shook him.

"Loranna, gone. Now Challey, too," he said, kicking at the loose dirt clods in the approach. He lowered his head reverently, pondering the most effective method of achieving his mission at Challey today.

His session yesterday with John Patterson had left him deeply disturbed. If what his friend had said were true, he could waste no time. John Patterson's appraisal of the matter of Janielle's obsession with Challey was over-whelming.

John Patterson had drawn Morris into the problem while they sat in the library at Patterson Woods. "I have been selected to the statesman committee to negotiate an appropriate site for our new capital in Columbia," Patterson had remarked casually.

Morris cringed at the troubling news. "So it is to be?"

"For a certainty, in time. Consent has been approved," John Patterson said resignedly. "And were you aware that work on the Santee canal will proceed within the year?"

"I will have to remove my offices to Columbia, or have two." Morris spoke distractedly, still weighing the impact of the first statement.

"There are many causes for concern these days, Morris. I used to believe that once this nasty business with the British was concluded, it would put an end to pressing troubles." John Patterson settled in a wing chair facing Morris, sipping his glass of usquebaugh.

"What did you achieve during your lengthy stay in Charleston?" Morris asked solemnly.

"I brought a new plantation manager and his family back to Patterson. He's a tobacco man from Virginia. He claims to have knowledge of a bright leaf strain that he says will produce on the land. And he suggests a new fire cure method."

"You know we are too near the coast for good tobacco. I wonder at his reliability." Morris suppressed a yawn.

"Mallen found him, but Mallen is so damn involved with his shipyards, he couldn't use him."

"Harrelson should stay with his planting," Morris said, recalling the talk of the Mallen shipyards as a long-standing joke among the Coast Merchants.

A heavy silence followed the diversive conversation as Morris waited to hear the real cause for the hurried summons from his friend. He knew John Patterson too well to believe that his visit here was for the sake of casual banter.

John Patterson frowned dismally, sloshing the whiskey in his glass. He swallowed the last of it. "There is a matter in which I require your aid." Patterson spoke reluctantly.

"Business or family?" Morris inquired, edging forward in his chair.

"You were aware that Challey was destroyed by fire?" John Patterson paused, seeing Morris nod his head. "Janielle suffered the poison of smoke vapors and remained at Brandon Ord's cottage while Evan Reed

97

tended her. I brought her home a few weeks ago and insisted that Ryan Deverel be brought here too until he mends. Evan Reed felt it would slow down his progress, and advised against it. That savage who shadows Reed has Ryan trussed in some foul-smelling vise that is appalling." Patterson shrugged disgustedly.

"I fail to see where that concerns you, John."

"Janielle has not been in a normal state since her return. She continues to ride to Challey each day, returning at dusk in a state of exhaustion. I forbade her to go there for awhile, but she became so apathetic I relented. She seems to feel a responsibility for Challey and the men there. I, frankly, cannot understand it."

"What did you devise to change the situation?" Morris asked.

"I propose to get her away from Challey completely. Janielle is young and should be in the social swim in Charleston while she awaits Johnathan's return. She has been a puzzle to me since her mother's death. I ask that you speak to her." John Patterson regarded his friend intently.

Morris rested his chin in his hand, pondering the problem that Patterson had presented. "Has Janielle recovered from the smoke poison?"

"Evan Reed is mostly concerned about her frailness."

"Johnathan is in Paris. Perhaps she could be persuaded to join him. Aurora and Kaylee Mallen could accompany her and the arrangements could be made within the week. But first she must agree to go." Morris spoke intensely.

"That would suffice. A change would cure her frailness, I am convinced. There appears a breach between us that I cannot compass. She is my sole heir and will be wealthy for the remainder of her life. I am regretful over the year she spent with Loranna Deverel at Challey. It seems she formed a strong fondness for Challey during that time. I would wish she felt the same affection for her own land."

Morris frowned down at his whiskey glass. He disguised the irksome stirrings he felt. Nonchalantly he inquired, "How is young Deverel?"

"His mood is foul, his leg is mending slowly. He acquired a hideous scar across his head during the fire. I like the lad, and admire his spirit. God knows the boy has endured a bitter life," John Patterson remarked solemnly.

Morris' thoughts leaped back to the image of young Ryan, standing forlornly on the wide steps of Challey manor, awaiting rescue from a drunken father intent on whipping him to death. He shuddered at the recall.

"I will journey to Challey at dawn and see Ryan and Brandon Ord. I believe it best to speak with Janielle when she is away from Patterson Wood," Morris concluded.

John Patterson rose slowly, gripping the arm of the chair for support. He smiled gratefully at Morris. "I shall be profoundly relieved when Janielle and Johnathan are wed."

"So shall I. However, I feel that the matter must be corrected. Janielle is dear to me, and obviously there is a sense of duty that she feels toward Challey. We must adjust her sentiment as best we can, for your sake as well as Johnathan's." His eyes roamed to the clock on the mantlepiece, wishing the hours would speed until dawn.

Morris left the site of the great house, leading his horse down the path to the acreage behind the orchards, where Brandon Ord's cottage stood. He forced himself into a moderate cheerfulness which he scarcely felt. He would have to confront Janielle and attempt to persuade her to follow through with her father's plans for her.

The overseer's cottage was barely recognizable from its former state. A new coat of whitewash covered the old clapboards, the boxwood shrubs were neatly trimmed along the porch, and a row of flowerpots, blooming with vivid geraniums and hyacinths, sat along the porch railing. Smoke climbed lazily from the brick chimney, mingling with the bluish mist from the river. The scent of hickory wood hovered in the morning air. The scene was reminiscent of the tidy English farm cottage near the Inns of Court where Morris had attended school. A pang of longing shot through him, remembering the unfilled hopes of the past. His eyes blurred with emotion as he rapped on Brandon's door.

Evan Reed swung the door wide, glowering at Morris. He stretched forbiddingly across the doorway.

Morris met his unwelcome expression with calm eyes. "I am Morris Chapman, from Charleston."

After a moment Evan Reed stepped aside. "Enter, sir." He spoke crisply.

Morris recognized Janielle's soft voice from the other room.

"Who's there, Evan?" she called out. Her face appeared in the doorway, breaking into a surprised expression when she beheld Morris. She hurried across the room to him.

"Lovely dear," Morris said, embracing her. She seemed childlike in her frailness, her violet eyes filling her small face. Her thin wrists seemed too fragile to hold the heavy bound book she carried. Morris churned with bitterness at the situation, well understanding John Patterson's concern for his only daughter.

A deep voice resounded from the inner room. "Janielle! Who the hell is it?"

Morris gasped angrily, as Janielle calmly led him toward the room. "Ryan is in a fitful mood this morning. He often is before breakfast." Janielle smiled apologetically. She edged the plank door open, allowing Morris to enter.

"Good God, Morris. I thought it was Itoo, returning

with another of his beastly smelling ointments," Ryan said.

Morris' anger faded as he stood staring at Ryan Deverel. The handsome face was gaunt, the wide shoulders and chest, as he sat leaning on one elbow, revealed severe leanness. The red of his healing wound creased his forehead from his brow to the center of his skull. His even white teeth flashed a weary smile at Morris as he extended his hand.

Morris swallowed hard. "Good to find you mending, Ryan." He smiled weakly.

"A difficult patient," Evan Reed commented coldly from the open door.

"Spoken as my kind surgeon," Ryan remarked, wincing when he moved his leg. Instantly Janielle was at his side.

Morris had not missed the tender exchange. "So that's the way of things," he reflected silently. He watched Janielle's adoring eyes on Ryan while she helped him resettle.

Brandon slammed the door, walking with loud strides across the bare floor. He strode into Ryan's small room, a wide smile on his rugged face. "I wondered whose mount was at the rail," he said, shaking Morris' outstretched hand. "Welcome to our humble home. Janielle has the place nearly fit for habitation now." He smiled, his gaze resting hungrily on Janielle.

Morris caught the trade of sheltered glances between Janielle and Brandon. "So there is more than one attraction here. I had best summon Johnathan home at once," he thought worriedly.

Irene bustled into the room, carrying Ryan's breakfast tray. The aroma of cured ham and chicory coffee floated across the room. The men shuffled out to the breakfast table where Irene had spread an inviting meal. Morris idly wondered where the provision for food was coming from.

He glanced back at Ryan, seeing him catch Janielle's hand.

"Breakfast in here with me," he ordered arrogantly. Janielle nodded ·obediently, watching the men seat themselves around the table.

Evan was anxious for news from Charleston. Morris related amusing stories about the remaining Tories in Charleston being dragged to the water pumps and doused, ignoring Evan Reed's disdain. The discussion fell to the new methods of dealing with the swarming turkey buzzards plaguing the Charleston wharf markets.

Brandon cast uneasy glances toward Ryan's room, finally rising from the table, taking his plate with him.

"You join the others, Janielle," Brandon said softly, entering the room. "I need to speak with Ryan."

Janielle wore a puzzled expression as she left the room. Evan Reed looked up expectantly when she moved to the table. He rose from his chair and seated her near him. She smiled graciously up at him, disregarding his stern look.

"The shrimp pie is particularly satisfying," Morris commented, refilling his plate.

Evan Reed ladled hominy and the thick shrimp pie onto a plate for Janielle, setting it firmly in front of her. His hard look at her insisted that she eat.

Janielle lifted her fork, fighting a rising wave of nausea. The smells from the steaming plate choked her. Mumbling an excuse, she fled out the door.

Evan Reed clenched his fists, rising to follow her, but Morris Chapman restrained him. "I also am concerned about Janielle's frail health. Her father and I are seeking a cause." He spoke solemnly.

"I am uncertain at this time," Evan remarked stiffly. "She spurns all my efforts to help her."

Brandon walked across to the gathering, interrupting their conversation. "Gentlemen, I must be about my labors. 'Twas an honor to· have you visit us, Mr.

102

Chapman. Ryan will wish to discuss some pressing matters with you before he tires." Brandon opened the door, looking out at the threatening clouds.

"The day will yield rain, I predict," he said, trying to make his departure seem casual. He had seen Janielle hurry from the cottage and he was anxious to find her.

"I am relieved that Ryan employs a good overseer." Morris spoke blandly. "His losses at Challey were severe, but his life was spared. He can rebuild."

Brandon nodded agreeably, clamping his field hat on his head. He swung along the path toward the site of Challey manor, trying to determine which direction Janielle had chosen. Her horse was still tied at the stable, so she was afoot.

As he neared the spring house, sounds of violent retching, followed by muffled sobs, reached his ears. He edged the heavy door open and found Janielle pitifully slumped across an overturned butter churn. He waited until her new wave of retching subsided before approaching her.

"Janielle, let me help you," he whispered, as she twisted away.

"Let me be, Brandon," she said, hiding her face from him.

"Let me fetch Evan. He has medicines—"

"No," Janielle sobbed, reaching for him.

Brandon untied his neck scarf and dipped it into the trickling spring. He bathed her tear-streaked face, holding her gently against him. Her thin arms tightened around him.

"Come, Janielle, I'll take you to the cottage and you can rest."

"No, Brandon, please. I can't go back there. Morris and my father are scheming against me. They make plans for me that I cannot fulfill. There are always questions upon questions." She began to weep again.

A low rumble of thunder swept the air. Janielle shivered. "You cannot remain here in the spring house," Brandon replied.

"Help me, Brandon. Take me somewhere for awhile, away from their prying eyes. After I rest I agree to do whatever you say."

Brandon studied her thoughtfully, a perplexed frown creasing his forehead. Her violet eyes pleaded with him. "I have been using the flood shack off the fork road. It is primitive, but dry and warm. I can send Micah ahead with food and blankets. Can you ride if I hold you?" Brandon asked worriedly.

Janielle nodded gratefully, her eyes never leaving him.

"I will instruct Micah to tell the others you have returned home. With the storm approaching, Morris Chapman will probably elect to stay overnight at the cottage. Your father knows you are safe here. Micah knows I use the flood shack, so there will be no cause for concern. I wish you to stay perfectly still until I return with my horse. I question the wisdom of this, Janielle, but if it is what you wish—" Brandon hesitated before leaving her.

"It is what I wish." Janielle spoke quietly, allowing him to slip her arms into his field coat and wrap it snugly about her.

"I won't be long, I promise," he said reassuringly.

Brandon held Janielle firmly about the waist as the horse paced the distance to the secluded flood shack. He bent his head to nuzzle her fragrant hair as she nestled against him. The storm clouds had lowered into the valley, bringing light splatters of rain. He saw the unloaded wagon near the shack and estimated that Micah had left only moments before them. Smoke was drifting slowly from the stove chimney. The fire would warm Janielle and she could rest throughout the day.

He did not regret the unplanned opportunity to be

alone with her. There had been few moments alone together since the Christmas Eve he had found her in the oak grove. His resentment toward Ryan had grown daily since the fire at Challey manor. He understood Ryan's helplessness, but he could not forgive his foul treatment of Janielle. A plan had been formulating in his mind since the morning of the fire and soon he hoped to accomplish it.

"I am weary, Brandon. Are we near the place?" Janielle asked, blinking open her eyes.

"We are there, milady," Brandon said, swinging down from the saddle. He reached for her, setting her gently on her feet. She tottered against him, unable to stand. He swept her up into his arms and carried her into the shack, shielding her face from the raindrops.

Micah had hastily set everything inside. The ticking on the rope bed was fresh and piles of warm blankets had been stacked on top. Brandon was glad he had put new panes in the windows and replaced the old shingles on the roof. The shack was clean and tight.

He sat Janielle near the hearth. A hard crack of thunder crashed down on the shack, shaking the foundation. Janielle reached quickly for Brandon's hand, relaxing tiredly against the chair.

"Let me spread the blankets and place you abed. You need to sleep. Do you think you could manage some warm broth, or milk?" Brandon asked, searching through the basket that Micah had left.

"Thank you, Brandon, for bringing me here. There are so many demands, and I am so weary." Janielle spoke softly.

"We are all gravely concerned for your health, Janielle. Evan told me you refused to discuss your illness with him. In time I shall expect you to be honest with me."

"Yes, Brandon, in time," she replied dazedly, closing her eyes.

A resounding boom of thunder brought a fresh deluge

pitting against the windows of the flood shack. Rivulets of water chased across the smooth glass above her head. Janielle struggled to see above the high layer of blankets on top of her. Her eyes searched the room. She was alone. A gust of wind shoved against the door, swinging it open on its rusty hinges.

"Oh," Janielle moaned, "why did Brandon leave me here?" The damp air blew across the room, the mist hissing in the crackling fire. She rose feebly from the bed, moving slowly toward the door. The room blurred crazily and she reached for the smooth stones along the fireplace. She opened her eyes to find Brandon leaning over her.

"I was only gone a few minutes. The bay horse spooks in a thunderstorm," he said quietly.

"I believed you had left me here alone," Janielle whimpered as he lifted her in his arms.

He laid her gently on the rope bed, pulling the blankets over her. Instinctively she reached for his hand, kissing the hard lean knuckles. Tears brimmed her eyes, while Brandon bent over her, lowering his mouth to hers. She listened to his quickened breathing as he softly kissed her. She moaned as he touched her wet lashes with his fingertip, closing her eyes.

It was a time of exquisite tenderness, an unhurried longing. Janielle relaxed as Brandon's large hands moved to the buttons on her bodice. His moist mouth touched her throat, her shoulders, moving downward between her breasts. His fingers trembled as he unfastened his clothes and pushed out of them. His bare chest pressed against her as his hands roamed the length of her body. Slowly she sat up, helping him remove her gown. He slipped the dress quickly over her head as he had done the day of the fire. Her small body seemed very fragile, delicate to his touch.

She lay completely naked under his gaze. His heavy breath caught in his throat. She responded wholly to him at this moment. Her nipples were ripe, swollen, awaiting his mouth. He would take her, but softly, gently. They had both known this time would come and he chose to savor its fullness.

"Brandon," Janielle murmured. "Help me, love me—"

"Yes, dearest, I will. I fear to hurt you," Brandon whispered.

"Love me, Brandon—please," Janielle's mouth sought his.

He guided her hand to him, demanding that she know him. She flinched, but he drew her back to him, gently but insistently. He ached for release, easing his weight on her. He sensed her readiness, pressing deeply, gently within her.

Janielle felt the warm rush opening wider, crushing her in its invasion. Suddenly she opened her eyes, startled to see Brandon's dark eyes penetrating hers.

"Do I pain you, Janielle?" he whispered hoarsely against her throat.

"No, Brandon," she breathed, her voice lost in the shadows.

Gently they merged, the motion gradually giving way to a sudden upsurge, moving swiftly in a fusion of exploding passion. Brandon held her during her tremors, then sought his own furious path of release. He gripped her roughly to him, forgetting his pledge of mildness.

"God—Janielle," he moaned, at the moment of abandon.

After awhile, he raised above her, searching her face to reassure himself that he had not harmed her. Breathlessly he moved on his side, drawing her into his arms. He smiled knowingly, seeing the glowing satisfaction in her violet eyes. Together they watched the raindrops forming and separating as they coursed down the windowpane.

"Brandon," she whispered, "could we stay here forever, away from the rest of the world?"

"Only if we were wed." He laughed softly.

She was silent at his reply, remembering the troubling

thoughts she had pushed aside since seeing Morris Chapman.

"You make a man weak and hungry, Janielle," he said, moving to sit on the edge of the bed.

"I offer no apology." She spoke softly, her fingers traveling the ridge of his wide shoulders.

Brandon turned to her, the gentleness gone from his face, replaced by a fierce hunger in his smoldering eyes. His hand strayed caressingly across her full breasts.

"Tonight, my love," he breathed, "none is needed."

chapter 13

Ryan hurriedly scanned the lading sheets from the *Waverly*'s last voyage, his eyes narrowing as he reviewed the profit column where Wyler had marked the parchment with careful letters. The sweet and white potatoes, rice and indigo had marketed favorably. The tobacco, loaded at Norfolk, had carried slight gain. Crates of rotted fruit had been cast overboard before docking, increasing the losses. The sea island cotton showed poorly on the profit report. He paused, running his index finger across the line of credit balances against his Coast Merchant account.

"Damnation," he swore, blaming his sea master for the unprofitable voyage. The rivalry between the British merchants in Charleston and the colonial commission agents was sorely favoring the English. The cargoes must have been bartered before they ever reached port, Ryan surmised. Since his recent losses at Challey, he had counted heavily on Wyler's voyage. It would be months before Challey crops could be harvested for ready cargo for the *Waverly*.

He had spent recklessly at Challey, restoring the manor, despite Brandon's glum warnings, and payment for that debt would absorb his remaining gold account at

Coast Merchants. Bitterly he faced the gnawing realization that he was deeply in debt.

Gingerly he touched the healing scar across his forehead. His leg still pained him the greater part of the day, but he refused dependency on the packets of white powder that Evan Reed had left with him. Better the pain than a mind befogged with dullness, he reasoned.

Ryan pulled himself upright on the side of the bed, painfully swinging his leg to the floor.

"Irene!" he shouted, waiting irritably as she scurried to the door.

"Yes suh, Master Ryan," Irene said breathlessly, stooping to retrieve the papers that Ryan had scattered on the floor.

"Leave the papers where they fell," he thundered. "Where is Janielle?"

"She ain't rode over yet," Irene replied worriedly. "But I can fetch yo' tea and pork side."

"I am wearied of food, and more wearied of being an invalid. I intend to stand today, then walk out of this room," Ryan bellowed. "Fetch my clothes!"

Irene clutched nervously at her apron. "Masta' Reed, he say—" she began.

"To hell with them all! They are not ones to advise while I lie here depending on the strength of others! Fetch Micah or Brandon!" Ryan raged.

Irene fled the room, her eyes wide with fright. Ryan braced himself for the overwhelming pain that came when he put pressure on his knitting leg. Itoo had fashioned a pair of long walking canes, thick and sturdy to support his large frame. Leather straps had been secured to hold them about his wrists to prevent them from slipping from his hands. His few attempts at using them had produced only pain and frustration. But today he could endure it. He could brook no further delay.

Perspiration stood in beads across Ryan's forehead. He brushed his arm across his face, steadying himself for

110

what he must attempt. The overpowering smell of Itoo's herbs on the casing about his leg caused him to retch.

"I hope to God my leg won't reek of those damn herbs for the rest of my life," he grumbled, reaching to the window and pushing it wide. The fragrant morning scent of dew-wet grass mingled with the hyacinths that Janielle had planted after Christmas. The day spoke of promise, as Ryan inhaled the fresh sweet air.

He pulled his shirt from the back of the chair, working his long arms into it. He fastened the buttons along the front, thinking idly that usually Janielle performed this routine task for him. The gesture always initiated a gentle caress, a feather touch behind the neck, a fingertip across his wide chest, invariably ending with his kissing her.

Janielle seemed withdrawn these last few days, he recalled. Her smile was forced and she seemed even thinner than before. Only her breasts remained full and ripe as they strained at her bodice.

"God, I crave a woman's comfort," Ryan groaned, his head throbbing like a galley drum. He reached down, fastening the braided leather strapping securely about the leg splint. He reassured himself with Evan's comment concerning Itoo's peculiar treatment for broken limbs, adding that the bones knitted fast and evenly with his method.

Micah broke through the doorway, his huge eyes wide when he saw Ryan's intention to walk.

"Oh, Masta' Ryan, I dunno," he wailed. "Mr. Reed, he say—"

"Help me up," Ryan snapped. He grimaced as the sharp pain swept him.

"Yo' gotta put yo' body weight on de good leg and swing de other," Micah said, setting the canes under Ryan's arms.

"These goddamn poles are flimsy as chopsticks," Ryan muttered as his leg took the weight. He edged a few steps, then paused to rest. Sweat was pouring down his face.

"Yo' is doin' good, Masta' Ryan." Micah spoke in a choked tone.

Irene stood against the door, her hand clasped across her wide mouth.

"Good day, Irene," Ryan called recklessly, faltering between steps. The pain was agonizing as he labored determinedly toward the front door.

Clearing the threshold, he watched Janielle and Brandon walking slowly along the path from the wagon shed, their hands entwined, their eyes shining with happiness. As they strolled along the footpath toward the cottage, Brandon brushed a light kiss on Janielle's cheek. She smiled up at him, the bright sunlight glinting in her white-gold hair.

Ryan grew rigid. It took only seconds for the impact of the scene he witnessed to fully grasp him.

"Son of a bitch," he swore softly as Brandon and Janielle approached the steps leading up to the cottage. A cold resolve gripped him.

Micah reappeared, bearing a chair. Ryan waved him away.

"I will stand, it is too difficult to rise again," he snarled.

Janielle stopped abruptly, stunned to see Ryan's large frame standing in the doorway. The smoldering fury in his eyes alarmed her.

"Ryan! By God," Brandon shouted.

"You are late in arriving today, Janielle." Ryan's tone was deadly. "I was forced to dress myself."

"Father left for Charleston this morning and I waited with him at the jetty," Janielle replied guardedly, sensing his changed mood since yesterday.

Brandon glanced uncertainly at Janielle, who was reaching for a chair for Ryan.

"I've been through that with Micah," Ryan snapped. "I prefer to stand."

"I'll fetch tea and we can have it out here on the porch," Janielle said worriedly, watching his strained expression.

112

"Brandon needs to be about the tasks for which he is being paid." Ryan spoke coldly.

"The peach blossoms will be out soon," Brandon commented. "When you are able, we'll tour the orchards. Evan said you were not to—" Brandon hesitated, seeing the harsh look in Ryan's ice-blue eyes. He turned to leave.

"Will you be back for lunch?" Janielle called after him.

"Brandon can eat with the field hands today." Ryan spoke sarcastically as Brandon walked away.

Janielle spun to face him. "That is unkind, Ryan."

"There are many things in this life that are unkind, madam," he retorted.

Brandon cast a hurried backward look at Janielle, standing slim and frail in the shadow of Ryan's towering frame. "Soon," he thought, "I'll tell Ryan of my intention to marry Janielle, with or without her father's permission. To hell with Johnathan Chapman. She doesn't love him." Thus he reasoned, thinking of the night he and Janielle had spent at the flood shack. Still, he felt somewhat uncertain of her affection for him, though she continued to cling to him, to need him. "I'll wait until Ryan's mood improves," he decided, mounting his bay, "if that day ever comes."

Ryan slumped against the doorway, allowing Micah to help him back inside the cottage. Ryan's face showed deep signs of fatigue.

"Der is time, Masta' Ryan." Micah spoke softly as Ryan leaned against him.

"I'll rest on the cot," Ryan said, feeling unable to make the distance back to his room. He uttered a sharp cry of pain as Micah eased him onto the cot. He lay with his eyes closed until the pain subsided.

"I'll be goin' to de wagons, now. Pull de bell at the spring house if you needs me," Micah said, clamping the tattered red hat on his head.

Janielle strolled over to the stove, pouring the hot water into the teapot. Irene had gone to the Harmons' shack with her wash basket piled high. Janielle's heart was light, despite Ryan's foul mood. Seeing Brandon waiting for her at the road had lifted her spirits. They had not been together since the stormswept day at the flood shack. She blushed, remembering her fervent response to Brandon's ardent lovemaking. Soon she would tell him about Ryan. But first she had to confront Ryan with what he must be told.

She had struggled through a restless night, searching for the proper way to approach him. She had delayed until he was stronger, but now she could postpone it no longer.

She filled the teacups, remembering Ryan's preference for a twist of lemon and a drop of honey. Her hand trembled as she carried the cup across the room to him.

"Your tea, Ryan," she said softly.

His hand swung upward, deliberately knocking the cup from her hand. Janielle drew back, stunned.

"You fickle bitch!" He spat the words at her. "A common slut, tumbling in the backwoods with the overseer."

"You are overwrought, Ryan!"

"By God, I believed you different. A sweet virgin, lying in my arms while I—"

"Hush, Ryan," Janielle pleaded, covering her ears.

"And what of your bethrothed, dear Johnathan? Who shall inform him on his wedding night that his virgin bride has been deflowered by the men at Challey?" Ryan taunted cruelly.

"No, Ryan. Enough, please." Janielle sobbed openly.

He laughed caustically. "What would the illustrious statesman Sir John Patterson say of his whorish daughter who no longer needs to protect her virtue?"

Janielle could not answer. She hid her face in her hands. She turned to leave, but Ryan grasped her arm roughly.

His ice-blue eyes bore into her. "First with me here at

Challey, then in your father's own library. I am curious where you dallied with Brandon. Perhaps, Evan Reed also tasted your flower during one of his rare spaces of sobriety—or was he still too enamored with Kaylee Mallen to give you a bedding?" Ryan twisted her frail arm.

"The pain in your leg is making you mad," Janielle managed between sobs.

"I can boast of being the first, of that only I am certain," he shouted. "Bitches! All women are scheming bitches!"

He pulled himself upright on the edge of the cot, reaching for his walking canes. "Your tears begging forgiveness are wasted on me, madam. I have no feeling for a woman's tears."

Janielle bent to help him with his canes. "Ryan, I tried to—"

"Yes, my dear. You tried, but fell quite short of the mark. In bed you are useless, a mere appeasement hardly worth the effort. It is a *chore* to make love to you!"

Janielle could not cope with the cruel barbs pouring from Ryan's tongue. He stood swaying above her, his face white and drawn with anger. She reached out to touch him in one last attempt to soothe him.

Ryan jerked away. "Get out of my sight," he stormed, shoving her aside.

Her voice was low. "Ryan, please listen for a moment. There is something you must know."

"There is nothing you could tell me that I *wish* to know," he replied bitterly. "Be gone, now!"

Janielle stumbled back to the door, clutching at the porch railing. She gasped for breath, running blindly toward the oak thicket. She fell once, then gathered herself up and hurried on, haunted by Ryan's imaginery pursuit.

Near the thicket, two of the Challey slaves chopped at the tangled underbrush. They looked up, astonished, as

115

Janielle seized and mounted one of the unharnassed plow horses, kicking the mare into a frenzied gallop. The aged horse, unaccustomed to a hard pace, balked, then bolted forward, flinging the loose turf with her hooves as she ran.

Janielle could not guide the mare without a bridle, but it no longer mattered as long as the horse continued its gallop away from Challey. The horse crashed through heavy undergrowth, the thick briars leaving deep scratches on Janielle's arms and hands. She hardly felt their thorns. Her only thought was to escape herself and Ryan.

The mare labored under the fast gait, her sides heaving with exertion. Suddenly the horse stumbled over a moss-covered outcropping of stones, pitching Janielle forward over its long neck. Janielle braced herself for the contact, meeting the hard ground with a cold impact. Faintly she heard the mare lumbering away as a black oblivion engulfed her.

Afternoon shafts of sunlight filtering through the tall trees above her wove an eerie spiderweb of rays, stringing their tinsely beams from the leafy branches. Dizzily, Janielle focused on the shifting rays, attempting to make the loosened ends converge. She began to count the wispy beams.

"One, two—no, there are five. Where is one?" Her mind reeled and she closed her eyes.

"How long have I lain here?" she wondered. "Must get home." Where was home? At Challey? No, not there any more, never there any more.

Her mind jarred back to childhood, with a vision of herself sitting primly near her father in her taffeta Sunday dress. He had promised her a candy lick if she didn't fidget through the sermon.

"Can't stay here," she moaned, trying to rise. She managed to sit up, then fell back onto the ground.

Her head pained furiously. "Am I dying, I wonder? Is

this what it feels like to die?" The realization that she was alone and helpless washed over her and she began to weep.

"So alone, always alone," she cried out loud. "Father loved Margaret and mother, but not me, never me. God, I'm afraid to die here alone."

After awhile she became calm. She edged along the floor of the clearing, lost to any sense of direction. A sharp pain inside her began to pulse in rhythmic waves, causing her to gasp. She rubbed her hand across her skirt, horrified to find blood seeping from within her.

She inched across the damp turf, seeing ahead the overgrown path to the flood shack. A glimmer of hope swept through her. Blood coursed down her legs and soaked her riding skirt. The relentless pain surged stronger. Finally she lay quietly, unable to move.

She closed her eyes blissfully. "It is finished," she thought calmly. "All over at last." She welcomed the comforting darkness that beckoned her.

Micah and Brandon found Janielle in the late afternoon as they searched the road. One of the Challey slaves had summoned Brandon after witnessing Janielle's wild flight. The aged field horse, lame and near death, had wandered to Dancer's Creek, and Brandon and Micah had searched the creek path for hours. Now Micah rode at full speed to summon Evan Reed.

Brandon, alarmed at the obvious loss of blood, folded her in tight wrappings. Her breathing was faint and labored.

"Janielle," he whispered, trying to rouse her.

He carried her inside the flood shack, wondering what could have prompted her to ride a half-lame field horse into the dense thicket. His worried thoughts about Evan Reed's sober state were crowded aside by his indecision as to whether to return to Challey with her. The jarring ride might worsen her injuries. He elected to wait for Evan

Reed's arrival at the flood shack. He cursed himself for not having returned to the cottage for the noon repast, despite Ryan's orders. He had tried to question Ryan as to Janielle's whereabouts, only to discover that Ryan had swallowed a full packet of the white powders that Evan Reed had left for him. His senses were dulled and his replies incoherent.

Janielle moaned slightly. Her paleness was more pronounced, her mouth tinged with a bluish hue. Brandon felt a moment of panic.

"Janielle, try to hold on. Evan will be here soon," he breathed.

Her eyes fluttered open. "Ryan?" she whispered.

Brandon sat back, stunned. "No, Janielle," he said quietly.

She moistened her lips, moving painfully in the rope bed.

"Ryan, please, let me tell you about your—" Her voice drifted away as she closed her eyes again.

Brandon was still, gazing down at her. The truth slowly gripped him. In the space near the ebbing of life, the truth will out. There could be no doubt; Ryan Deverel had won again. He slipped his hand from under hers, returning to the small window to resume his vigil.

chapter 14

The field wagon lurched into the ruts along the road, making Ryan grit his teeth in pain. Every circle of the wheel had proved agonizing despite Harmon's careful maneuvers to avoid unnecessary jostling. The wagon was padded with heavy canvas and Ryan's leg was braced securely in a leather splint. Ryan experienced a moment of regret as the wagon creaked through the Challey lantern posts marking the old Devereaux divide.

"Master Ryan," Harmon called, leaning back from the high wagon seat. "You are certain the barge from upriver will be at Patterson landing this morning?"

"Yes, Harmon, I'm sure," Ryan reassured him again. The lad had expressed initial excitement, followed by reluctance in agreeing to accompany Ryan to Charleston. Harmon had never ventured far from the uplands before coming to Challey, and the Santee was as near the sea as he had ever journeyed.

Ryan reviewed his plans of the last few days. His losses on the *Waverly*'s last voyage had been severe. He reasoned that the Coast Merchants' warehouses would be full of unshipped cargo, due to the British Order of Council barring Americans from trading with the British West Indies. The Charleston Chamber was attempting to reopen trade with France and Holland, and Thomas

Jefferson had lent his assistance to the efforts. With bulging warehouses, bidding would be low. Ryan intended to stock his cargo from monies advanced by Morris Chapman, using the Challey land as security against losses. The *Waverly* could sail at once after the repairs that Wyler indicated were completed.

Europe was now crying for raw materials from the colonies. He would bid heavily on the fur stock as he had the previous year, leaving the sea island cotton in short cargo. He would insist on loading the *Waverly*'s hold to capacity, above Wyler's objections. Perhaps he could make the voyage with Wyler and auction his cargo himself.

Harmon pulled at the wheel brake, lessening the fast descent down the knoll to the causeway. The wagon lumbered to a halt and Harmon tied the reins securely about the brake. He peered nervously at Ryan as he reached to drop the back loader.

"You still reckon to go downriver, suh?" Harmon asked intently.

"I do. I am going to Charleston," Ryan replied determinedly, swinging his leg down from the wagon. Harmon propped the canes for him, and Ryan eased into position with them.

Surprisingly, the last few days he had managed to master their use to some degree, finding his movements slow but firm. Harmon grabbed the two valises, pausing to stare at the wide Santee.

Ryan laughed softly. "Your journey will be rewarded, Harmon. I assured your mother of your safe return after you have had your fill of rum and wenches in Charleston."

Harmon blushed openly, hurrying ahead to watch for the river barge that would take them to Santee Point. Ryan paused at the jetty, leaning his large frame against the railing. His leg ached miserably and he felt suddenly weak from the mild exertion. He hoped that Carey had received his message and would have his quarters at

Linden in readiness. The cost of maintaining a mistress was great, and how to ease himself of this expense had troubled him. He had decided to wait until he was secured in Charleston before facing the problem.

It would be easy at this juncture to drop into an abyss of regret and self-pity and return to Challey. He heard the loud hail from the polers on the river barge as they swept the bend of the Santee. Harmon pulled at the landing bell, signaling the barge master to stop for passengers. Ryan straightened as the long, low barge swung into view.

Instinctively he looked up the causeway to the bluff, where Patterson manor sparkled in the brilliant sunlight like an awesome Greek temple, built for all worshipers to behold. Ryan felt a surge of envy, recalling the night of the winter feast, John Patterson's quiet air of aristocracy, his rich, influential friends. The Santee sweep seemed accursed with the power of Patterson Woods.

Filled with raging determination, Ryan limped painfully to the edge of the jetty.

Brandon Ord witnessed Ryan's departure from the Patterson jetty with a vacuum of emotion. From his vantage point at Janielle's corner window, he had caught Ryan's lingering look at Patterson manor. Brandon's eyes continued to follow the low barge as the polers eased into the sluggish current, gathering motion as the barge swung into midstream. Ryan had left a destructive imprint on Challey, regardless of what his intentions might have been.

The gnawing hostility he felt toward Ryan Deverel was surfacing again as he reread the document that Micah had delivered to him at Patterson Woods.

To James Brandon Ord:
  LETTER OF ADVISEMENT: Witnessed by barrister Morris Chapman, drawn and sealed by legal court and signed by my hand.

Regarding state of overseer wages at Challey Plantation.

I hereby assign in your name, 1000 acres of choice Challey land, the profits of which shall remain solely your own. The overseer cottage with furnishings, four horses of your preference, two wagons, and the Challey carriage are reassigned in your name.

The above granted in lieu of wages until I advance my earnings. At such time I shall renew your wages, though the foregoing provisions shall stand.

Ryan Paul Deveral
Challey Plantation
March 3, 1786

Brandon folded the parchment as John Patterson and Evan Reed entered Janielle's room, their faces lighted with smiles.

"Good day, Brandon. Jedda tells me you breakfasted early." John Patterson spoke warmly. Patterson wore a fashionable gray frock coat with a high-standing fall collar, buttoned over a vertically-striped waistcoat of armozeen. His starched white wig was drawn into the voguish Ramillies queue at the nape of his neck. He embodied the genteel distinction of his class, even in the atmosphere in his country home.

"I wished to see Janielle before I left for Challey, but she has been sleeping," Brandon said, motioning toward her bed.

Evan Reed strode briskly over to Janielle, resting his hand across the velvet backboard. He smiled down at her, taking her small hand in his.

"Janielle—" he said softly.

"Minna tells me she enjoyed a robust meal last night," John Patterson commented, unaware of Brandon's jealous glance in Evan's direction.

Minna had brushed and curled Janielle's long white-gold hair, leaving it to fall in casual ringlets about her face. She was dressed in a delicate English nightgown, trimmed with Valenciennes lace flounces at the neck and elbows. She stretched languorously, opening her violet eyes slowly to the sea of faces gazing down at her. Evan Reed placed his large hand across her forehead, then gently moved it to rest on her abdomen.

"Any pain, Janielle?" he asked when she squirmed.

"I am not fully awake enough to know." She flashed a teasing look at him.

Evan straightened, turning to the others. "You see how she rejects my endeavors to serve her," he said, his expression growing stern again. "I must return to Pine Bluff today, gentlemen. I should ask a few words in private with Janielle before I dismiss her as my patient."

"That is rude, Evan," she scolded laughingly.

"Nevertheless, I insist," Evan stated firmly, clasping his hands behind his back.

John Patterson moved toward the door. "Come, Brandon," he urged quietly.

Brandon reluctantly followed the elder statesman to the door, sending a warning look in Evan's direction.

"We shall be outside, Janielle," Brandon snapped, "should Evan need reminding that he is not tending sailors aboard a British vessel."

Janielle shifted uneasily as Brandon closed the bedroom door.

"Whatever ails Brandon, today?" she asked curiously.

Evan smiled knowingly down at her. "Brandon has become unduly possessive since he found you that day in such a severe dilemma. He fears to let you away from his sight. He has plagued me with questions and advice since our arrival here."

"Brandon has suffered immensely on all counts," Janielle replied wistfully.

She glanced at Evan, noticing the embossed umber

123

frockcoat with New Market waistcoat that he wore. His brown hair had been cropped and swept back from the forehead and temples. He bore slight resemblance to her first impression of him. Evan was, indeed, a handsome Englishman.

He caught her appraising glance. "A gift from your father," he remarked, smoothing his hand across the soft fabric. "He has paid me well for tending you."

Janielle was silent, waiting for the questions that she knew Evan would inevitably ask. There appeared to be no polite way of escape. She could scarcely order him from the room.

Evan leaned upon the bedpost, staring down at her.

"I am a surgeon, Janielle, not a midwife," he said quietly.

His words stung her. She looked down at the ribbon streamers on her gown. "I know, Evan," she whispered.

"You also know you lost the child," he said evenly.

The silence was long, broken only by his deep sigh. He moved around the bed, seating himself on the edge near her.

"Sometimes, Janielle, there are hidden complications in these unexpected matters," he said softly. "The next time it may be difficult—"

Janielle touched a fingertip to his mouth, quieting him. Her violet eyes welled with tears. "I beg you not to condemn me, Evan." She swallowed hard.

He straightened, standing tall beside her. "I am no judge of another man's doing. I wish you well. Good day, Janielle." He bowed gallantly. Slowly he buttoned his frock coat, watching her with calm eyes. Then he moved quickly through the door without glancing back.

Janielle stared at the closed door, shaken by his pointed words. The relief of knowing the cause of her illness was gone, lay shadowed in a deep sense of loss. How different she had thought the experience would be.

Evan was bound by professional oath to keep silence about her former condition, but what of Brandon? Did he know?

She brushed away the collecting tears as Minna bustled into the room, carrying a heaping breakfast tray. They would all forget, in time, she consoled herself.

Brandon glanced at his reflection in the ornate gold leaf mirror, as he chose a chair near the parlor window. He fidgeted with his riding crop, anxious to be on his way to Challey. It appeared that John Patterson had chosen this time to expound his opinions on the political future of the Carolinas.

"You see, Brandon, it is imperative that our delegation make its mark in Philadelphia. Charles Pickney, John and Edward Rutledge, Pierce Butler and I must stress the southern interests. Our views on slavery are hostile to northern economic matters. The rice and indigo markets in Georgia and the Carolinas must be guarded by Constitutional guarantees. Benjamin Franklin has recommended that these interest documents be prepared in unanimous fashion before their presentation to the Congress." John Patterson's eloquent voice echoed through the spacious room.

"I understand that President Washington has offered Thomas Pickney a minister's appointment to London when his governorship term expires," Brandon commented.

"And, that, too, for our southern cause," John Patterson agreed. "Charles informs me the appointment is to secure American commercial rights and compensation for 25,000 slaves taken away in '82."

Brandon shifted in his chair, listening for Evan Reed's footfalls coming down the hall. He wanted to see Janielle again before he rode to Challey.

"It would appear, sir, that these weighty matters will

require a great portion of your time be spent away from Patterson Woods," Brandon said, tapping his quirt against his thigh.

"It would seem, in truth, that I must put the plantation entirely in the hands of a competent overseer. Janielle cannot perform the enormous task, nor should she."

Brandon felt a prickle of apprehension as John Patterson's hard gaze held his.

"It is my thought to offer the position to you, Brandon."

Brandon stared incredulously at the elder statesman. "I am honored, sir," he said hoarsely, thinking of Ryan's document in his coat.

"I understand your attachment to the Challey land. However, Challey is in death throes. Evan Ryan Deverel's attempts at restoration ended in failure. He is heavily indebted and Challey will eventually have to be auctioned." John Patterson spoke dryly.

Brandon could not agree. The fields were progressing and expectations for the cotton harvest and his own fields of experimental tobacco yield were promising. He had envisioned flooding the choice acres that Ryan had deeded him and planting rice along the riverland. Challey soil was superior to most in the Santee sweep.

"Ryan Deverel has deeded me a thousand acres of Challey land. I intend to farm it," Brandon said evenly.

"A pittance!" John Patterson bellowed. "You may name your own wage as my overseer," John Patterson's eyes narrowed. "I have not dismissed from memory your care of Janielle during the fire at Challey, nor your rescue of her in the woods. But for you, she would not be recovering in her room upstairs. Nor do I doubt your value as an overseer. The gesture has a twofold purpose."

"Like a constitutional proposal," Brandon thought wearily, rising to leave.

Aloud, he said, "I shall give the matter reasonable consideration and give you a decision within the week."

He smiled warmly. "Now I shall bid Janielle good day and be on to Challey."

Brandon left the parlor hurriedly, having made his decision even before John Patterson had finished speaking.

Janielle brushed her long, white-gold hair with a gentle motion, letting Brandon's gaze rest hungrily upon her. She reveled in the devastating effect her actions had on him. That effect was easily read in his smoldering dark eyes.

"You were in my room at dawn," she accused teasingly.

Brandon turned away, gazing out the window at the wide bend of the Santee. "I watched your slumber, as I have done on many occasions." His voice was husky.

"Evan says I can be about tomorrow, though he cautioned against mounting spirited horses."

Brandon's large hand gripped the window ledge, indicating his sudden surge of anger. He spun to face Janielle.

"Why in God's name did you ride a horse into the thicket? That poor beast hadn't run in years! You know how to ride—what demon possessed you to such foolishness?" he demanded angrily.

Janielle held his furious gaze, a slow smile breaking across her face. "Are you annoyed with me, Brandon?" she asked innocently.

"I am raging, Janielle!" he thundered. "Must someone ever be at your side to protect you from yourself?"

"It need not be you," she retorted arrogantly.

"I didn't come to quarrel." Brandon spoke crisply. "I'm riding to Challey and wished to bid you farewell."

Janielle lifted her violet eyes, surprised at his sudden change of tone. "But surely, Father spoke to you about a position at Patterson Woods," she said quietly.

"He did. I will inform him that I decline his kind offer. My place is at Challey."

127

"That's nonsense, Brandon. Ryan never esteemed your worth."

Brandon bristled at the sound of Ryan's name. He thought fleetingly of telling her about Ryan's departure for Charleston, then decided against it.

"It is enough that I realize my own worth, Janielle."

Janielle trembled, seeing a side of Brandon that he had never disclosed before, a brooding ruthlessness that frightened her.

"Hold me, Brandon," she whispered softly, reaching her arms up to him.

"I choose to remain a safe distance from you, Janielle. I cannot afford the luxury of your fickle whims."

Janielle stared unbelievingly at him. So Brandon not only suspected, he knew. He knew about Ryan; there was no need to tell him. The rest, she prayed, if he knew, he wouldn't voice.

"You are cruel, Brandon. The day at the flood shack, you spoke of—"

"I recall what I said to you, without being reminded," Brandon interrupted harshly, gazing down at her. She looked immeasurably pampered, in her elegant canopied bed, her white-gold hair shining with platinum streaks, her wide violet eyes full of astonishment. He was near to relenting.

"Brandon," Janielle said softly, "if we could begin—"

"No, my love. Our paths separate at this junction in life. You chose long before the time of our affection. I will not risk another deception. I love deeply, Janielle, and could not abide the shallow pretense you offer."

Janielle stared quietly down at her folded hands. Tears brimmed her eyes. Brandon's strength and affection had sustained her through the ordeal of the fire, Ryan's recovery and the loss of her unborn child. She had never realized until this moment how much she relied on him.

"I will take my leave now, Janielle," he said quietly, his face impassive.

"Brandon?" she called after him, as he strode swiftly to the door. He left her without a backward glance.

Her eyes blurred with spilling tears. How complicated her life had become since the day Ryan Deverel arrived at Challey. She wanted to hate him, hate all men, but she couldn't call forth the emotion.

After awhile, she lifted her eyes to the closed door, willing Brandon to return.

"I did care, Brandon." She spoke softly to the empty room.

part two
CHARLESTON

chapter 15

Charleston was rapidly approaching a new pinnacle of importance in the flourishing independent nation. Strengthened by Constitutional ratification protecting the state from foreigners and debtors, rather than only from the North, the city's already teeming wealth paralleled her prominence. The decade was birthing the most opulent class of merchants, the most lucrative trade channels, along with its greatest number of master artisans. Charleston homes were filled with the most exquisite furnishings of the times. The city wallowed in the luxurious afterglow of its unique founding.

Morris Chapman lolled in his leather chair, entertained by Ryan's furious riffling among the cargo duns stacked on his massive desk. His clapboard office near Bay Street wharf brimmed with activity as he accepted the new surge of legal duties, restoring confiscated British property back into the hands of its patriot landowners.

"I would presume it to be your first chore of the day to locate my lost accounts," Ryan fumed, searching through another stack.

"I told you before that Wyler McGee has your cargo purchase accounts," Morris Chapman commented dryly.

"That Scottish bastard! If he were not such a good sea master, I'd—"

Morris stretched in his chair. "I sent Benjamin to fetch him."

"Good of you, sir barrister," Ryan snarled. "That enormous cargo must be counted and loaded. Sail is set for Friday. And how in God's name did you talk me out of sailing with the *Waverly*?"

"Your mending leg convinced you," Morris said solemnly. "You can scarce manage on even ground. How would you hobble on a wet deck?"

Ryan settled back in the desk chair, running his large hand through his newly cropped dark hair. He felt spent after the last few days of selecting cargo for the *Waverly*'s voyage. Morris had arranged a position for him within the Coast Merchants' exchange, offering him a generous stipend until the profits from the voyage could sustain him again.

Ryan had seethed with turmoil since his exhausting river trip from Challey. He had consulted a German surgeon in Charleston, who pronounced his broken limb knitting remarkably well and graduated him to a more sophisticated pair of walking canes. Though the wide scar across his forehead was obviously defined, his dark hair was covering the length of it across his skull. He found himself wincing less often at his reflection in the glass.

Carey, his young mistress at Linden, presented yet another problem. Carey had insisted on joining him in his quarters that Morris Chapman had secured for him at the Sea Hawk near the dock, but he had not wished it. He needed no additional complications at this critical juncture in his life. Soon the mounting expense of keeping the cottage at Linden would have to be relinquished. Each shilling had to be tallied.

Benjamin burst into the office, startled to see Ryan seated at the barrister's desk. He was breathless.

"I found Master McGee, sir, but—" he faltered.

Morris waited curiously, while Benjamin floundered with his message. In time the lad would gain poise.

"You told him the import of my summons," he asked patiently.

"I did, sir. Master Wyler said to inform you he was—ah—*fishing*," Benjamin said sheepishly.

"*Fishing*?" The two men voiced incredulously, breaking into wild chuckles. The unpredictable Scotsman would most likely be indulging in his favorite diversion for the remainder of the day. Ryan admired Wyler's independence, attributing the cause to his long years of bachelorhood. Wyler's love for the sea had replaced his need for the confinements of marriage and children.

"Aye, sir. But Mistress Chapman is on her way here, her footman advised me." Benjamin spoke hurriedly.

Morris' face fell as he heard Benjamin's words, remembering the dinner invitation at the Mallens' new home on the bay. Editha was beset with viewing the restored La Pueblita por la Bahia that Harrelson Mallen had purchased.

All too soon he heard the familiar clicking of her Kampskatcha slippers along the dock planking. "I shall seek to pass another evening in tippling," he thought miserably as Editha entered the office.

"Morris!" her shrill voice accosted him.

"I was preparing to leave, my dear. Benjamin brought news that we could not conclude our reports today," Morris said tiredly, rising from his chair. He motioned toward Ryan.

"You recall Ryan Deverel of Challey," he offered stiffly.

Ryan bowed elegantly on one leg, reaching for Editha Chapman's plump hand.

"Indeed, indeed," Editha muttered irritably, her eyes critically raking Ryan. "I hope you are recovered, Master Deverel."

"Somewhat, madam," Ryan replied smoothly, cringing at the waspish tone of her voice.

A slow flush spread across Editha Chapman's chubby

face as she met Ryan's ice-blue eyes. This young man had caused many tongues to waggle in Charleston. Viewing him closely, she understood why. Instantly she dismissed the seductive thoughts that were presenting themselves. She had never approved of him even as a boy, and now his ruthless manhood disturbed her.

She turned sharply to Morris. "Why must you forever delay? We are due at the Mallens' within the hour!"

Morris glanced resignedly at Ryan, who returned a knowing smile. "Damn me if the lad isn't perceptive," Morris thought fleetingly. Suddenly a solution to the evening's ennui occurred to him.

"A moment, my dear," he said gently, taking Editha's arm. "Master Deverel has only recently returned to the city, and would delight in accompanying us to the Mallens' soirée. Aurora relishes entertaining the younger set. What say you, dear?" Morris asked lightly.

Editha Chapman was aghast. Morris had chosen an awkward moment to present such a proposal. It was unthinkable that the Mallens would wish to include guests outside their rigid social range. Ryan Deverel's reputation, his questionable parentage, his absence from the rolls of Coast Merchant oligarchy, would scarcely endear him to the Mallens. Yet, she recalled, John Patterson had included him in his Thanksgiving repast. She wrestled with the decision that Morris had pressed upon her.

"Perhaps Master Deverel has other plans for the evening," she said pointedly.

"Nothing that cannot be altered," Ryan replied tersely, thinking guiltily of Carey, who waited for him at Linden.

"Fine, fine." Morris smiled approvingly. "Our carriage will call at the Sea Hawk at seven on the clock," he said hastily, before Editha could voice further objections.

Morris handed the ivory-head walking canes to Ryan as Editha Chapman flounced through the doorway, her ample hips leaving a wake of swishing silk behind her.

Morris grinned at Ryan, who regarded him dubiously as he followed him across the room.

La Pueblita por la Bahia was built on land once occupied by the exploring expeditions of Lucas Vasquez de Ayllon, as they chartered their way to the mouth of the Peedee River. The house's unique design was purportedly the work of one of the later descendants of de Ayllon. Its thick walls and fortresslike plan consistently recalled the simplicity and servicability of its functional Spanish design. Wide gates opened along the smooth azure tiles, laid symmetrically along the walk to the inner patio, where a towering marble fountain rose prominently in the center. For this special night, torchlight flickered across the silvery spills, cascading over the lips of the curved marble structure, spewing a fine mist into the warm night air.

Aurora Mallen stood near the wide iron gates, graciously greeting the arriving guests as they stopped to stare at the majestic lighted fountain. Owning this home gave her a great sense of affluence among her influential friends, and she fairly gloried in the result of Harrelson's shrewd manipulations in obtaining the property.

The Chapmans had arrived, walking slowly to adjust their pace to the slower one of their guest. As they moved closer into the light, Aurora recognized the tall young man with them. He did appear different in an almost sinister way, though his ice-blue eyes and flashing smile drew attention away from the vivid scar across his forehead. He would be a novelty among the austere guests at the soirée.

She noted his immaculate attire, the deep scarlet dinner coat, the ruffled shirt with stiff cape collar, his double-breasted New Market waistcoat and fashionable oval knee buckles on his white breeches. His blue morocco shoes boasted of oblong buckles set with Bristol stones. Aurora Mallen quickened with the sight of him.

His appearance was most attractive. She moved forward to greet the Chapmans.

"Morris," Aurora breathed, brushing his cheek with a light kiss. She reached out to hug Editha Chapman. "Welcome to La Pueblita por la Bahia," she said in her faltering Spanish. "I see you have brought us another guest," she remarked sweetly, smiling up at Ryan.

"Ryan is staying in Charleston for awhile and I assumed you would be pleased to have him attend tonight," Morris stated authoritatively as Editha disappeared into a familiar cluster of guests.

"Why yes, of course," Aurora said uncertainly. "And are you quite recovered from your accident, Mr. Deverel?"

"Entirely, madam," Ryan replied teasingly.

Morris reached to the tray held at his elbow, lifting two glasses of champagne. He handed one to Ryan and quickly drained his own. He turned as Harrelson Mallen sauntered briskly up to them, a startled expression on his face when he saw Ryan.

"Well," Harrelson Mallen drawled, "good to see you about, Mr. Deverel."

"It is an honor, sir, to be invited to your home, although the invitation came from the Chapmans," Ryan offered smoothly.

"Next time it will come directly from me," Harrelson Mallen replied, impressed with Ryan's resourcefulness in an awkward situation.

"Damn regretful about the loss of Challey manor," Harrelson Mallen continued. "I understand that John Patterson is introducing a new bright leaf tobacco strain into the river land. It might bear investigating," he advised, studying Ryan's fashionable attire.

"I shall inform my overseer." Ryan spoke respectfully, though he and Brandon had already discussed the possibility of using a few acres for experimentation with the new tobacco leaf.

"Ryan is currently occupied with his shipping interests," Morris supplied, thinking of Harrelson's obsession with the new Mallen shipyards north of the city.

"Good man," Harrelson Mallen remarked. "The gentlemen here tonight are endorsing the advent of my new shipyard. I hope to boast of the finest ropewalk and merchant repair class outside of England." Solicitous of Ryan's labored steps, he steered him to a group of guests.

Morris Chapman regarded Ryan from a distance, feeling a sense of pride at Ryan's impeccable manners and confident attitude. This particular assemblage would put to trial his polished conversation.

Ryan acknowledged introductions to William Loughton Smith and his father-in-law, Ralph Izard, a resident of Goose Creek, who held vital interests in the Santee Canal Company. Ryan conversed intently with James Simons, the naval officer in command of Charleston port. Morris observed that the austere gentleman smiled wryly at one of Ryan's comments. Isaac Huger, the Georgetown rice planter, joined in a discussion concerning the shipment of rice and indigo to the French West Indies. Morris moved slowly away from the group, confident that Ryan could hold his own in this prestigious group, whose families had been established prior to the Revolution.

A sudden flutter of excitement spread among the guests as Kaylee Mallen and her escort arrived. The young French army officer at her side, wearing the honor ribbons of King Louis XVI, was resplendent in his full dress uniform and gleaming French top boots. He bowed attentively to the lady guests, his dark eyes flashing as Kaylee introduced him.

Kaylee's emerald eyes swept the clustered guests, pausing to rest on the towering gentleman near the garden. A faint smile grazed her mouth. Her Rutland gown of the *Open Robe haute couture* was of lettuce green satin, fastened at the side of her slim waist with a diamond brooch instead of the customary buckle. She opened her fan, nervously watching the garden, cloaking her annoyance as Ryan Deverel moved into the shadow of the patio wall, oblivious to her impressive entrance.

Ryan hobbled to the far end of the secluded garden, relieved at the brief respite during the flurry of Kaylee's arrival. His leg ached interminably, and the hastily consumed champagne, swilled on an an empty stomach, made him drowsy. He regretted his curious acceptance of the Chapmans' invitation, finding his stamina still lacking for a strenuous social *assemblee*.

Dinner was being announced above the din of chatter and feigned laughter, the aroma of highly spiced Spanish foods slowly wafting across the garden. Past the point of hunger, Ryan eased into a large wicker chair, stretching his aching leg into a relaxed position. The low strum of guitar chords, husky and bold in its tones, was amazingly soothing. He closed his eyes, his thoughts drifting back to Challey—the swerve of the road, the spring house, his library shelves bulging with selected volumes, the low, sunken marble tub. The gnawing ache in his belly surfaced again.

"Master Deverel." A soft feminine voice beckoned him from his poignant wanderings.

Ryan opened his eyes, staring into pools of deep blue, matching the hue of his own.

"I am at a loss, madam." Ryan spoke softly, struggling to his feet.

"I doubt you are ever at a loss, sir. I inquired as to your name, and have cause to wonder if we are related." She smiled down at him.

Ryan stood erect, finding himself but a few inches taller than the statuesque lady before him. Her skin was a tawny gold, her blonde hair, streaked by the sun, was swept away from her face, secured by a large gold comb at the back of her head. One long, shimmering tress trailed her shoulder.

"My name is Caroline Coswelle," she said evenly.

Ryan bristled at the sound of the loathsome Coswelle name. His bitterness was difficult to disguise. "A pleasure, Miss Coswelle," he said stiffly.

"It is Lady Coswelle, sir. I am wed to your late stepfather's brother, Lord Robert. Is it likely that we are distantly related?" She smiled teasingly.

"I extremely doubt that possibility, madam. However—"

"My mother is distant cousin to Aurora Mallen, which explains my presence here tonight. I am not certain how you and I could be joined, but Aurora said—"

"Everyone is remotely related to Aurora Mallen," Ryan said, his expression softening. He was mildly intrigued with Caroline Coswelle's challenging beauty.

"Do you intend to invite me to share dinner in your company?" Caroline asked brazenly.

Ryan ran his large hand through his hair, baffled for an instant by her pointed manner. Her clipped British accent held an aristocratic tinge, yet it was most improper for a lady of refinement to offer the suggestion.

"I shall be honored," he replied gallantly, placing his canes so he could walk the distance to the banquet tables.

Caroline took his arm. "It is spoken that you deal wickedly with women, sir. Is it the truth?"

Ryan swallowed his astonishment. Without replying, his gaze raked her thoroughly, giving her the answer she sought. His eyes lingered at the full swell of her breasts, straining against the bodice of her violet satin gown. The invitation lay open to him in her clear blue eyes.

They approached the long banquet table, laden with mounds of soft-folded thin Spanish breads, stuffed with spiced meats, swimming in a red thick sauce. Hesitatingly, they filled their plates with the unfamiliar food, then retreated to a quiet corner of the patio.

"When can you learn if we are perhaps related?"

Caroline asked, spreading the snowy white linen napkin across her lap.

"I can tell you tomorrow, madam," Ryan answered distantly.

"In England, I am called Lady Coswelle," Caroline gently corrected.

Ryan nodded. "And how is his Lordship Philip Coswelle?" he sneered.

"Your stepfather succumbed to plague last year," Caroline replied flatly. "I know of his unfortunate marriage to your mother. I also know he returned to England during the exile with a goodly sum of Deverel gold," she added.

"I see," Ryan remarked thoughtfully, watching the torchlight glint across her golden hair. Caroline glanced across the patio where Kaylee Mallen stood, surrounded by a bevy of young male admirers. Their eyes locked in glaring dislike.

The musicians, seated near the fountain, poised their instruments awaiting the downstroke of the maestro's baton. The strains of a saraband *majestueux* filled the garden. Idly, Ryan wondered what had become of the cithara, now fashionably labeled by the Spaniards a guitar.

The couples were moving to the slow triple-beat rhythm of the saraband, the sharp rap of their heels echoing on the smooth azure tiles of the patio. Ryan squirmed restlessly in his chair, cursing the leg that kept him from joining the dancers. He scowled at Caroline, who was watching Kaylee and her French officer sweep across the patio.

Suddenly, Kaylee pivoted, leaving the dancers and turning in Ryan's direction. She threaded among the couples, with the anxious Frenchman close behind her rustling skirts.

Ryan instinctively reached for his canes as she

139

approached, struggling hurriedly to get to his feet.

Kaylee's flashing green eyes softened as she moved close to him. "Good evening, Master Deverel."

"Mistress Mallen," Ryan acknowledged, bowing shortly.

"You appear to be hedging the other guests," Kaylee taunted, casting a scorching glance at Caroline Coswelle.

"My apologies, Kaylee." Ryan spoke familiarly. "I appear to be at a slight disadvantage with the saraband tonight."

Kaylee studied him in amused silence, a slow smile edging across her full mouth. "I will have him," she thought determinedly, feeling the wild attraction again.

"May I present Jean Robere La Bonte, special emissary of King Louis XVI to the Carolinas," Kaylee said impressively.

The handsome French officer made the official royal bow of acknowledgment, his eyes moving swiftly to Caroline.

"Lady Caroline Coswelle," Ryan indicated, turning his attention to her.

"Indeed a pleasure," Jean Robere attempted in heavily accented English.

"Really, Jean! We cannot always understand you," Kaylee said impatiently. "Perhaps you should find your translator."

"How odd to send an emissary who speaks so little English," Caroline remarked softly to Ryan, realizing that Jean Robere understood little of what she said.

"That may be the reason he was chosen."

Jean Robere smiled agreeably at what they were saying, his eyes devouring Caroline Coswelle.

"Tell me, Ryan," Kaylee said sharply, "will you remain in Charleston for awhile? There are many galas planned with the opening of the theater. The Rutledges are entertaining tomorrow evening. I am certain that an

140

invitation can be arranged for you. The Governor's Ball is next week, you know."

Caroline tapped her fan impatiently. "If you will excuse me," she said in a frosty tone, turning to leave.

"Perhaps Jean Robere could show you the gardens," Kaylee offered sarcastically.

"I have already seen them many times over," Caroline replied haughtily. Her steady blue eyes held Ryan's. "Master Deverel, you will supply the information I requested?"

"I shall see to it tomorrow, as promised, Lady Coswelle." Ryan smiled into her eyes.

"Adieu, Monsieur," Jean Robere said in an embarrassed tone, following Lady Caroline into the thinning crowds.

Ryan laughed softly as the two disappeared from view. "That was quite a display, Kaylee," he chided, "but your tactics could use some refinement."

"What would you know of refinement?" Kaylee flung the words at him. "That bitch, her Ladyship Coswelle, she's no lady."

"Neither are you."

"Why do you always try to make me feel inadequate, Ryan?"

"It is not my intention," he replied softly.

"My mother thinks you are incredibly handsome, even with your wicked scar." Kaylee smiled, her mood lifting.

"And what are your thoughts?"

Kaylee moved closer to him, her green eyes smoldering. "I want you to escort me to the Rutledges' formal dinner tomorrow evening," she said quietly.

"What of your French officer? I hear the Frenchmen are quite adept in the company of young ladies," Ryan teased.

"He isn't—he doesn't—" she stammered.

"Doesn't what, Kaylee?" Ryan said. "Speak perfect

141

English?" He was enjoying himself. The arrogant, unattainable Kaylee Mallen was losing ground in her attack, in spite of using all her feminine weapons to gain a victory for the night.

Ryan eased back into his chair. She stood above him in her gown of orange silk, beautifully laced with green velvet bows. The torchlight caught at her diamond brooch and earrings, playing across their brilliance.

"I cannot dance with you, Kaylee. Seek another partner," Ryan said tiredly.

"Then you refuse to escort me?" She asked incredulousy.

"Why is it important to you?"

"Because you cannot—" She stopped suddenly.

"Ah, my lovely Kaylee. You cannot abide a man who doesn't fall at your dainty feet," Ryan mocked.

Kaylee looked down at her feet, as Morris Chapman came striding across the patio.

"I have hunted you down at last," Morris bellowed, his voice heavy with drink. "We are taking our leave now." He bowed awkwardly to Kaylee. "A fine evening, Kaylee. We shall share company again tomorrow evening at the Rutledges, I am informed. Your father has arranged for all of us to ride in the barouche, and there is space for Master Deverel," he added, his eyes twinkling with mirth as they met Ryan's.

"It would appear I have been outmaneuvered this evening," Ryan said harshly.

Kaylee smiled knowingly up at him, her eyes bright green pools of light. "You might find it enjoyable, Ryan," she said softly.

Morris watched the interchange with a practiced eye. What a pair these two would make! He felt a keen sense of accomplishment as he walked along behind them. "Kaylee has finally met her match," he chuckled contentedly to himself.

At the gate, Ryan paused to bid the Mallens farewell,

thanking them for the fine dinner. He lavishly commented on La Pueblita por la Bahia, obviously intrigued with its colorful history. Harrelson Mallen talked at length about his latest prize, and finally Morris tugged at Ryan's arm to hurry him.

"You are welcome here at any time," Harrelson Mallen said, casting a sidelong glance at his beautiful daughter.

Kaylee clung to Ryan's arm as he neared the carriage. She stood on tiptoe to whisper in his ear.

"Until the morrow, Ryan," she said softly, brushing his cheek lightly with her mouth. The shocked onlookers turned away, gasping.

Ryan savored the moment, playing on Kaylee's bold advances. Gently he lifted her hand to his mouth, kissing her fingertips.

"I shall be waiting," he said longingly. Calmly, he turned and climbed into the carriage.

Morris Chapman settled beside him in the carriage seat, ignoring the disapproving glare from his wife's face. The carriage wheels began to roll, closing fast the distance to the King's Highway.

"Damnation," Ryan swore under his breath, hearing Morris Chapman's muffled chuckles.

chapter 16

Bands of shifting crimson and gold slashed across the eastern sky. Beads of dawn mist clung to the mullioned windowpanes of the gable room where Ryan slept. He stretched blissfully, casually lifting a long, sun-streaked tress that trailed his wide shoulder, gently smoothing it to keep the tickle from his nose.

Caroline lay on her side, her tawny, naked back pressed against his side. He sighed, his fingers tracing a circling pattern along the length of her golden body. Lady Caroline possessed a depth of maturity he sought in lovemaking, totally satiating his frequent arousals.

Yesterday's quarrel with Carey, laced with harsh, biting words, had convinced him that his *affaire* with her was at an end. After the Governor's Ball tonight he would go to Linden and close the house. He had no further use for a jealous, viper-tongued mistress, regardless of the young graceful body that had once intrigued him.

Caroline stirred, sleepily propping herself up on an elbow. She gazed drowsily down at Ryan.

"Good morning, my love," she murmured, snuggling into his arms.

"Ah, Lady Caroline, you please me enormously," Ryan whispered against her golden hair.

Caroline raised herself slightly, her full breasts probing

gently against his wide chest. His slim fingers grasped her shoulders, pulling the silken cones to his mouth. He felt the surge of arousement ripple through her as he began.

"Again, Ryan?" she said.

"Always, again." Ryan spoke hoarsely, his hands moving downward.

She responded instantly to his swollen demand, spreading herself across him as her fingers caught in his tousled hair. Her hand guided expertly, effortlessly, and Ryan felt engulfed in her. She moved carefully, hesitatingly, until he was frantic for release. Their motions were pressed, then delayed, their timing perfectly keyed to each other's response. Caroline gasped at his pulsing burst, then lay quietly on him, momentarily drained of strength. Ryan reached for her face, holding it above him.

"I have some revenge on the Coswelle name." Ryan laughed softly.

"You were aghast at my arrival here last night." Caroline sighed, rolling onto her side.

"It is rare when a great lady visits my humble quarters," he breathed, teasingly.

"Your message said we were not related by blood, only by choice," Caroline reminded him, rolling her long blonde hair into a chignon.

"So you came by choice, so heavily disguised that even I did not recognize the tall dark woman knocking on my door. I hope to God you weren't seen," Ryan said solemnly.

"Your scar looks brutal," Caroline remarked distractedly.

"What of your husband, Lord Robert?" Ryan's eyes were curious.

"He stays on that infernal island in Raleigh Bay, when he isn't in England," Caroline replied indifferently.

"And how does he consider his beautiful, unfaithful lady?" Ryan inquired tauntingly.

"It is getting light, Ryan. I must leave," Caroline said guardedly, avoiding his piercing blue eyes. She reached to pull the woven coverlet across her. Angrily, Ryan snatched it aside, leaving her breathless and naked under his scorching gaze.

"I will not play games, Caroline," he snapped.

Caroline bent forward, kissing him hungrily. "You are every woman's desire, Ryan," she breathed against his neck.

Ryan shook her stubbornly. "Caroline, I am committed for this evening, but tomorrow—"

"I must go now, before full light. I will come to you whenever you desire," she said softly, lowering her eyes. "I suppose you are escorting Kaylee to the Governor's Ball."

"Yes, I am," Ryan admitted reluctantly. "After tonight, I shall set an end to this social circus I have been indulging in," he added determinedly.

"I should caution you about your silly virgin," Caroline said haughtily. "You waste your talents, Ryan."

"I have wasted nothing yet, Lady Caroline," Ryan said.

"Nevertheless, she—"

Ryan caught her face between his large hands and kissed her soundly.

"Do I hear a note of jealousy, my love?" Ryan laughed softly, releasing her.

"You flatter yourself, sir," Caroline retorted angrily, reaching for her gown. She dressed hurriedly, wrapping the long, dark cloak about her and placing the thick veil across her face. Ryan stared lazily at her from the bed as she turned to leave.

"A fine evening's romp, my lady," he called jeeringly after her as the heavy door slammed shut.

The afternoon ordeal with Maurice, his French tailor, did little to improve Ryan's sullen mood. Maurice was ecstatic over the completion of Ryan's finely tailored formal attire, but Ryan could share little of his enthusiasm. Despairingly, Maurice threw the needle aside, refusing to sew another stitch of gold braid to the white velvet coat.

Ryan grumbled about the tedious fitting but finally acquiesced to the chore, and Maurice cheerfully resumed his sewing.

"I see you are about with only one cane now," Maurice commented guardedly.

"Yes, I shall be whirling the entire ballroom tonight," Ryan remarked sarcastically.

"Ah, you see, Monsieur Ryan. *Dernier cri*, yes?" Maurice exclaimed, raking his eyes critically over Ryan. "Magnifique!"

"Whatever the hell that means," Ryan snarled, glancing at his tall reflection in the standing mirror. The chalky white velvet coat with a finely embroidered plum satin waistcoat and matching white pantaloons would set a fashion standard in advance of its time. He decided at that moment to wear the carefully crafted Hussar buskins instead of the leather court shoes.

He cast a sidelong look at the pained expression on Maurice's face. Relenting, he allowed, "It is expert work, Maurice. Come below and we'll share a turn in the tavern."

Maurice nodded feebly, gathering his accessories while Ryan doffed his formal clothes for his casual double-breasted waistcoat. Ryan left off his cravat and strode to the door.

"Such a handsome man," Maurice reflected thoughtfully, "but such an unhappy one." He half remembered the rumors that had caught his ears. Master Deverel was the constant escort of the beautiful Mallen heiress, seen frequently at the Charleston galas. "Perhaps she is the cause," Maurice concluded, following Ryan down the winding stairs to the tavern below.

Ryan sat stiffly erect in the red plush carriage seat, staring intently across at Kaylee. Her court dress of cream satin, the petticoat spilling with festoons and bouquets of green satin roses, shimmered in the fading dusk. Her small, perfectly shaped breasts pushed upward eagerly from the curving sweep of her bodice. She fussed with the folds of her wide satin skirt against the lurch of the red barouche.

"God, she is the most extraordinarily beautiful girl I have ever beheld," Ryan judged, studying her closely. She possessed an exquisite form of beauty that seemed impossible for man to create.

Aurora Mallen chatted vivaciously over the prospect of seeing her prestigious friends from the uplands again. Harrelson Mallen, tapping his silver-knobbed cane at intervals against the carriage floor, nodded attentively as his wife prattled on.

"Gracious! Look at the procession." Aurora pointed ahead excitedly as the Mallen carriage swung into the boulevard leading to the governor's mansion. Quickly she reached to Kaylee's hair, affixing a diamond clip that had worked loose.

"There," she breathed, obviously overjoyed with her daughter's breathtaking appearance.

"You fuss overmuch, Mother," Kaylee scolded, shifting in the velvet seat.

Ryan mentally retreated, thinking drearily of the long evening that stretched ahead. Thoughts of Challey had persistently plagued him throughout the afternoon. He closed his eyes, leaning his head against the tufted backrest of the carriage seat.

Impressions of the green-swept valley, the long oak groves, the flowering magnolia tree outside the library window at Challey, flashed before him. He felt a tug of conscience at the clear image of Janielle's face, the undisguised hurt written in her large violet eyes.

148

"Ryan? Ryan!" Kaylee's voice shattered his reverie. He flicked open his eyes to see the carriage halted beneath the long yellow canopy, waiting for its occupants to alight. He smiled broadly at Kaylee as the footman pulled at the carriage door. Kaylee returned his smile, her green eyes flashing a look of glowing satisfaction.

Janielle and Evan Reed dipped, bowing agreeably as they traced the familiar movements of the minuet. The gradually fading strains fell to silence as the musicians rustled their parchments, preparing for the next waltz. Janielle glanced across the ballroom to the reception row where Governor Thomas Pickney and Lady Pickney were receiving the unending flow of dignified guests. Her violet eyes rested on a tall slender man dressed entirely in subtle white, the unusual cut of his attire marking his broad shoulders and lean hips. He leaned on a gleaming blackthorn cane, as he waited near the end of the crowded line. For an instant he appeared to be alone, but as she watched, Janielle caught a glimpse of the dark-haired girl clinging to his arm.

Her legs felt suddenly weak and trembly as she recognized Kaylee on Ryan's arm. So the smatterings of rumor that had burdened her ears at Editha Chapman's afternoon tea were true, she thought despairingly.

"Why Kaylee?" she agonized, turning to Evan with a labored smile.

Kaylee was leading Ryan across the polished ballroom floor, being momentarily detained by one of her entourage of suitors, who was enticing her onto the dance floor. Ryan bent his dark head as Kaylee whispered in his ear, nodding and laughing softly as she whirled away in the arms of a wide-eyed young gallant.

Evan had scouted the crowds, spotting Ryan near the edge of the dancers. He led Janielle, picking his way through the throngs of conversing guests gathered on the

149

glazed oak floors. Ryan raised his head, pausing as he recognized Evan moving toward him, a wide smile breaking on his handsome face.

"By God, Evan!" Ryan shouted above the din. "Despite your bumbling efforts, I can walk!"

Evan buckled with laughter, reaching Ryan's side and clasping his hand. "How in God's name did you arrange an invitation here tonight?" he teased.

"The better question would be, 'how did a besotted Tory get by the Governor's guards,'" Ryan joked, brightened at seeing his old friend.

"Janielle reformed me." Evan spoke lightly, reaching behind him and pulling Janielle close.

Ryan's expression sobered as Janielle stood clear, Evan's long arm encircling her small waist.

"You know our lovely lady," Evan said elegantly, unaware of the existing strain.

Ryan recovered first, his blue eyes sweeping Janielle in his familiar manner. "A pleasure, Mistress Patterson," he said stiffly.

Janielle swallowed, hoping the words she uttered would carry forth. "I am pleased to see you well, Ryan," she managed.

Ryan's eyes regarded her quizzically while she shrank back against Evan.

"The champagne trays are this way," Evan announced, motioning toward the terrace. "Shall we imbibe?" he asked, already threading his way across the congested room.

Ryan followed at a distance, allowing his eyes to caress Janielle's trim backside. He felt some unexplainable ache as he watched her drift through the throngs. A soft hand caught at his arm. He turned casually to see Lady Caroline Coswelle's blue eyes regarding him warmly.

"Lady Caroline," Ryan mocked gallantly, as his mouth grazed her fingertips. The smoldering invitation in her eyes bespoke of the night before when they were entwined in passion.

"May I present my husband, Lord Robert," she said steadily.

Lord Robert, his rotund build straining under the evening's demands, bowed slightly, his face red and perspiring.

"An honor, Sir Robert." Ryan spoke tersely, concealing a smug grin.

"So you are the young Deverel whelp," Lord Robert wheezed.

Ryan, preferring to ingore his insinuation, stole a wicked glance at Lady Caroline. "I am Ryan Paul Deverel, heir of Challey," he stated arrogantly.

"Lord Robert and I would enjoy viewing the Challey land," Caroline offered smoothly, sensing Ryan's irritation.

"There is nothing remaining other than the land," Ryan replied coldly. He turned to leave. "A pleasure, my Lord Robert, and *his* most beautiful Lady Caroline," he said distantly. He bowed shortly, walking slowly away, a twisted smile on his face.

Nearing the French doors that led to the terrace, the sound of loud angry voices drifted into the room. Ryan hurried forward, seeing Evan Reed surrounded by a circle of hot-tempered patriots flinging abrasive words. He caught the phrase, "Loyalist bastard," as he joined the fringes of the group.

Evan was on treacherous ground. Prejudices still ran rampant, though the war was officially over. Evan's clipped British accent and outrageous remarks were provoking the colonials, inflamed by drink, and the dispute was fast gathering force. Ryan raked the ballroom for a glimpse of John Patterson or Morris Chapman, who could diplomatically intervene and disperse the crowd. They were nowhere about.

Suddenly Evan's arm lashed out, his fist striking the jaw of a stout antagonist, sending him sprawling across the room. Evan swung from the other side, catching a fat, long-jowled man square on the nose. The group moved in on Evan.

Ryan stepped into the crowd, caught in the melee of flailing arms.

"Rutting English bastard," Ryan heard the face say before his shoulder was grabbed. He dodged to miss an oncoming fist, then reeled to find another opponent crashing down on him. He met the leering face with his large fist, downing him in one sweep. He accepted the next foe with enthusiasm, faintly aware of the screaming and shattering of glass in the background.

Evan moved close to him, his face streaming blood. Two of the Governor's aides had joined the battle, but Ryan showed no preference. He hit dirty like he had learned at Brocksburg when he was the smallest boy in the ward. Evan grinned before another fist pounded into his belly, his face going white. He slumped against Ryan.

Ryan felt multiple arms grappling at him, jerking at the ripping cloth of his coat. Then the governor's order intervened, shouting at the patriots, separating the crowd, snatching Evan roughly to his feet and hustling Ryan out the door to the grounds outside.

The guards moved forward, barring the shocked guests from following. The music timidly began again. Ryan caught the horrified expressions on the faces of John Patterson and Harrelson Mallen as three of the governor's order gripped him.

Through battered lips, Evan quipped lamely, "I believe, sir, your leg is mended."

"God, Evan," Ryan rasped, amid loud orders being barked at them from behind. He jerked his hand free to wipe at the smeared blood, his own or another's. He saw Janielle collapsed on a wide marble bench near the steps, her face glistening with tears. He winked at her as he was unceremoniously whisked aside. They approached a group of dignified statesmen, heatedly discussing the events they presumed had provoked the incident.

Ryan distinguished the eloquent tone of Morris Chapman's parley as Governor Pickney and his aides conversed in low tones. One of the young aides, an undisguised expression of admiration on his face, politely handed Ryan his sleek black cane. The guard commander reluctantly permitted Ryan to take the cane, scowling as Ryan leaned his weight on it, easing the now throbbing pain in his leg.

Governor Pickney approached Ryan, a grim expression on his furrowed face. Morris Chapman shot Ryan a quick look of caution.

"Your name," the Governor commanded, glowering.

"Ryan Paul Deverel, sir." He spoke alertly, holding the Governor's steely eyes.

Governor Pickney shifted his gaze to Evan Reed, standing calmly, dabbing at the trickle of blood spilling from his mouth.

"And you," he said shortly, giving Evan the same hard look.

"Evan Curtiss Reed, sir, former commissioned surgeon, Her Majesty's Royal Navy, assigned to the *Dover*," Evan replied smoothly.

"Later a foul prison ship, I am reminded," Governor Pickney remarked, frowning and speaking quietly to Morris Chapman.

The governor touched his starched wig, feeling the Perruques "naissante" in place. Abruptly he turned to Ryan.

"Morris Chapman and John Patterson have spoken in your behalf," he said harshly. "I am inclined to value their judgment. That, in concurrence with the fact that your grandfather, Roland Alexis Devereaux, and my own grandfather, sailed to the Carolinas together, override my decision to place you both in the gaol. It is regretful that

153

you two apparent gentlemen chose to dishonor this night with a brawl."

Ryan drew himself to his full height, his ice-blue eyes flickering with anger. "A word, Governor Pickney, if you will allow," he said evenly. The governor and his orderlies paused, waiting.

"It is my conviction that the uneasy pact existing between us new Americans and our former British enemies be resolved. Evan Reed, a British subject, has elected to remain in the low country to gain service as a physician in this land. Let it be known that he has administered to both Englishmen and American patriots, of which I am one. Therefore, tonight, when my friend was vastly outnumbered by a company of bitter citizens, I came to his aid. My apologies, Governor, for disrupting your evening."

A long silence fell across the gathering as Ryan turned to Evan, exchanging meaningful glances. The governor stood thoughtfully absorbing the impact of Ryan's words. Finally he spoke.

"Well expressed, Master Deverel," he allowed, studying the handsome man who stood tall before him. "Though I wonder at the sincerity of your words. As a reprimand to your actions tonight, I must order you to leave the governor's grounds immediately. Good night, gentlemen," Governor Pickney said sternly as his aides escorted him across the well-manicured lawn.

Harrelson Mallen and John Patterson approached Evan Reed and Ryan, securing them by the arms, ushering them to the waiting Mallen carriage.

"We have decided it advisable that you both come to La Pueblita por la Bahia for the night, until this affair quiets," Harrelson Mallen said gravely. "It is well protected in the event of further confrontations with that hot-headed group from the uplands."

They agreed accordingly, following the Mallen footmen across the broad expanse of lawn leading to the governor's boulevard. Ryan was forced to slow his pace, his mending leg paining him severely. He turned to John Patterson.

"What of the women?" he asked.

"Morris Chapman will see them securely home," John Patterson replied, amazed at Ryan's consideration.

Evan Reed marched across the lawn as though in British regiment formation, stopping only briefly to murmur something to Janielle, who waited by the gate to the approach. When Ryan caught up to him he moved hurriedly on through, glancing over his shoulder to insure that Ryan followed.

Janielle turned to leave, delaying as Ryan limped to the gate. She stood quietly, drinking in the countenance of the tall man who approached her.

Ryan lifted his dark head defiantly, as she had seen him do many times before. The blood-smeared shreds of his formal coat tossed in his stride. He closed the distance to her.

"The evening has proved interesting after all," he quipped, lowering his head to her.

"Are you all right, Ryan?" she asked, biting her lower lip.

"Entirely, though your concern touches me, Janielle," he said softly, noting the effect of the bright moonlight playing across her shimmering hair.

Janielle felt the closeness of the moment, her body aching for his embrace, wishing that time would halt and his nearness would swallow her.

"Good night, Janielle," he breathed, his fingertips lightly brushing her arm as he stepped through the gate.

chapter 17

Darkening billows rode the crest above the sunken meadow where the "campagne foire," brazenly spread its gaudy splash of dazzling colors. Medieval pennants flying above the gaily flamboyant stalls beckoned invitingly to the throngs that swarmed its circular paths. The humid day spoke promisingly of an evening shower as the sun faded behind the errant cloud covers.

Ryan grasped Kaylee's arm tightly as unruly gangs of hardened sailors milled through the aimless crowds, often jostling an unsuspecting onlooker and walking away with a purseful of shillings. He had experienced doubts about escorting Kaylee to the spring fair, but her insistence, and her father's approval, had won over Ryan's reservation. Besides, he thought, it was a relief to be free of the confining walls of La Pueblita por la Bahia.

Evan Reed had ridden to Pine Bluff early in the day under heavy escort provided by the governor. Ryan had elected to return to Linden on the morrow, since the assemblage from the uplands was returning to Columbia. Much controversy had ensued from the dispute at the Governor's Ball, and Evan Reed and Ryan had appeared heroes to some, enemies to others. The governor had endorsed the statement that Ryan had presented, asking the citizens to bear the conflicts gently, as the new country settled into its hard-fought independence.

Ryan motioned to the display stall where two shaggy ponies stood in miniature. At first glance he thought them an animal freak, but on closer inspection he saw they were pefectly proportioned and appeared sturdy. His curiosity piqued, he pulled Kaylee with him into the pen, calling to the slovenly lad who leaned against the postern.

"What can you tell me about these beasts?" Ryan asked.

"Eh, sir, she's a shaggy mount from the Shetland Islands of northern Scotland. Has to be sturdy, sir, due to her homeland. They be for sale, sir, if you've a mind to." The sandy-haired lad spoke with a slur.

"For what coin?" Ryan asked, as the lad frowned, folding his arms across his chest. He eyed Ryan's prosperous appearance and ventured on a heavy profit.

"Twenty shillings, sir."

"Twenty shillings for the pair, and it's done," Ryan said flatly. "Do you know the place of La Pueblita por la Bahia?"

The boy shook his head slowly, indicating that he did not.

"The Spanish fortress north of the bay," Ryan explained.

"Eh, that one. Yes sir, I know of it," the lad replied, obviously relieved.

"Deliver the pair, with this note from me," Ryan instructed, reaching for the quill and stand on the low table. "The purchase paper—let me see it," he ordered.

Kaylee tugged at his arm. "Why are you purchasing these freaks? They are too small to ride," she said lazily.

"Not for children," Ryan retorted, surprised at his own statement. Turning again to the lad, he said sternly, "See that the beasts are well fed and watered, and take care in their travel." He counted the twenty coins, signing his name on the ownership parchment.

"How is the lady called?" Ryan asked, pointing to the tiny mare that stood innocently watching him.

"We call her Flower, sir," the lad replied, hoping for approval from the tall gentleman who regarded him closely. Ryan strode over to the small horse and stroked her dark muzzle. He raised an arm over her mate and the tiny stallion jerked away in fear.

"Be at ease, man." Ryan spoke reassuringly. "I have purchased your lady as well."

Kaylee stamped her foot impatiently, as Ryan surveyed his purchase. The vision of Brandon's surprised expression when the pair arrived at Challey brought a huge smile to his face.

"I want to visit the ribbon stall," Kaylee demanded arrogantly, clutching at Ryan's sleeve. He cast a backward look at the tiny horses as he allowed Kaylee to draw him across the path to the colorful ribbon stall. Strands of shimmering ribbons dangled listlessly in the humid air, their hues intertwining and tangling as a whiff of air stirred them. Kaylee swept enthusiastically through the rows, gathering a handful, under the watchful eye of the dowdy woman who displayed her treasure of ribbons. Kaylee brought them to Ryan, holding them to his gaze for approval.

"Do you require so many, Kaylee?" he asked, scowling his displeasure.

"Father buys me as many as I wish," she retorted haughtily.

Ryan felt a prickle of irritation as Kaylee turned to select another few velvet bands, adding them to the collection he held in his large hand. He stood mutely, gazing down at the mass of brightly colored ribbons in his grasp.

"How can you balk at my choice after buying those miserable freaks over there in the pen?" Kaylee taunted.

Ryan stood in indecision as anger welled forth in him.

"Hurry and pay the coin. I am thirsty," she said

158

flippantly, turning to admire her reflection in the long cracked glass.

"Kaylee!" Ryan spoke her name with such force that Kaylee spun against the glass, sending it shattering against the hard ground. Her green eyes bespoke of terror as she faced him.

"Hear me well, Kaylee. I do no woman's bidding," Ryan said firmly and clearly, turning on his heel.

Kaylee stood frozen, gaping at his broad back as he disappeared into the crowd. She fumbled in her leather drawstring purse for sufficient coin to pay for her purchase. The haggard ribbon woman watched in amusement as the elegant lady failed to produce the adequate exchange. Kaylee flung the ribbons defiantly at her and dashed along the circular walk, searching for Ryan.

She found him at the brewer's cart, his broad shoulders bent over the rough hewn table, waiting for the ale to be served. Kaylee brushed against his arm, ignoring the fury in his eyes. He downed the ale, motioning to the brewmaster for another. As he raised the pewter mug to his mouth, Kaylee intercepted the movement, sipping daintily from the rim, wrinkling her nose at the taste of the stiff ale. Ryan regarded her warily. He noted that she carried no ribbons and smiled inwardly, thinking of how seldom Kaylee Mallen was ever denied anything.

The cool frothy ale relaxed Ryan's ire, but he realized the afternoon was lost to enjoyment. He shucked his coat in the moist, sullen air, noticing that the pennants above the stall stirred only slightly in the oppressive air. He detected the faint scent of oncoming rain as his eyes raked the somber skies. He finished his ale, ordering a flask to carry with him. He took Kaylee's arm and guided her through the swarm of onlookers, oblivious to her protests.

"Where are we going?" Kaylee asked worriedly.

"Home!" Ryan snapped.

"But the carriage won't arrive for us until the seventh hour," she argued.

"Then we will walk," he asserted.

"That's madness!" Kaylee stormed.

"No, my dear child. Madness is being confined within your father's ivory walls and portraying the fop for his daughter's whims," Ryan replied sharply.

"You are spoiling my day," she pouted.

"I shall spoil your lovely derriere in a moment," he threatened as he jerked her along the entrance path.

Calculating the shortest span across the meadow to meet the principal road to the left Charleston fork, Ryan estimated they could reach the bayside bridge in an hour. His leg felt stiff and the mild exercise seemed to relieve it. The slight breeze had shifted and playfully rustled the long grass flourishing in the neighboring hollow. Kaylee stumbled along behind him, her soft leather slippers misstepping on the uneven tufts of meadow grass.

Ryan studied the skies again, gauging their progress to be well in advance of the evening storm. He scanned the wooded area they were approaching, looking for possible refuge should the wind shift westwardly. He paused to await Kaylee's faltering gait, feeling a twinge of sympathy as she carefully lifted her billowing skirts and struggled up the incline. He moved forward as she reached him, stopping abruptly as Kaylee ptiched forward, losing her balance and sprawling clumsily at his feet. She raised on her elbows, her beautiful face smudged with dirt, mixing with tears of rage that streamed down her cheeks.

Ryan knelt beside her, pulling off his neck scarf and gently dabbing at the dirt on her face.

"I loathe you, Ryan Deverel," she snapped, pushing his hand away.

Ryan pulled her roughly to her feet and continued down the winding path to the copse of oak trees, threading his way through the tendrils of silvery moss that moved restlessly with his passing. The sky had lowered and the breeze now blew stiffly through the towering ancient oaks.

"Ryan, wait," Kaylee gasped breathlessly as he paused and turned. "We have passed this way already. See, your boot marks," she said, pointing to the ground, where the soft imprints lay in the dark earth. Ryan studied the black sky for some sign of sun, but in the dense grove the fading light obscured any trace of sunbeams. His sense of direction rarely failed him, so Kaylee's words went unheeded. He proceeded quickly through the length of the copse, venturing out into another heavily wooded area.

A small brook played across a narrow outcropping of rocks at the edge of the underbrush, and Ryan stopped, staring upward at the stream's source. He reaffirmed that his westwardly direction was correct, then glanced backward as Kaylee scurried to reach him.

"Can we rest a bit, Ryan? I'm so thirsty and weary," she pleaded.

He motioned to a flat gray rock at the curve of the brook, and Kaylee collapsed gratefully, no longer caring about her mussed appearance. The hem of her yellow lawn gown was in shreds, with mud and grass stains clinging to its front. She trembled in the cooling gust of air as she cupped her hand to drink from the brook. A warble from a low-hanging branch caught her attention and she raised her eyes as the bluebird flew angrily away. She discovered Ryan staring fixedly at her.

"My father will be furious with you," she said sternly.

Ryan shrugged, caring little what Harrelson Mallen felt or thought. Seeing Kaylee in such disarray temporarily jolted him. "I suppose I am the first man to see her thus," he mused. Something primitive touched him as he watched her bend to drink from the trickling brook. He reached into his coat pocket and pulled the cork from the flask and drank deeply. Kaylee sat back on her heels, shivering in the cooling breeze. She glanced nervously up at the scowling sky, then turned her gaze on Ryan.

"I am frightened, Ryan. The storm will break soon and we are miles from shelter."

He regarded her thoughtfully, wondering at the sincerity of her apprehension. He rose slowly and moved close to her, placing his coat about her shoulders, drawing it tightly across her breasts and closing the top button. Kaylee's green eyes flashed a look of astonishment as he finished.

A low echoing grumble of thunder broke the stillness and the first tiny splatters of rain touched his face as he lifted her to her feet. Tears began welling in her green eyes and her long dark lashes glistened against her cheeks. Ryan raised her chin with his slim finger and looked deeply into her eyes. She returned an imploring gaze as he slowly tilted her face up to him.

Hungrily, Ryan crushed her to him, brushing her tears aside with a gentle hand. Her breasts pressed hard against him as his coat fell away from her shoulders. The droplets of rain pelted against his back as he held her close. His large hand tangled in her long dark hair as he lowered his head to kiss her.

Suddenly he stiffened, feeling an inkling of warning edge along his spine. The faintest metallic sound reached his ears while he loosened his hold on Kaylee. He put a finger to his lips as she opened her mouth to speak. He detected no other movement except the moaning wind as it cruised the hollow. Cautiously, he turned to peer at the oak grove behind them, his ears straining for the sound to repeat. Reaching down to the ground, he retrieved his coat, placing it snugly around Kaylee's shoulders. He cursed for neglecting to bring a weapon, remembering that his British dragoon pistol lay on the Mallen carriage seat. He carried only the flat gold knife that had been a gift from Morris Chapman.

"What is it, Ryan?" Kaylee whispered as they moved forward through the dense foliage.

"We should see the left fork from that knoll," he said shortly, pointing to the rise and ignoring her concern.

As Ryan stepped through the heavy undergrowth, the unmistakeable sound of clinking metal pierced the air. This time its rattle was definite. Ryan reached for his knife, pulling Kaylee tightly against him. A loud clap of thunder brought her flying into his arms, and the downpour fully descended upon them. He took a step, then halted as the repeated clatter of heavy chains drew his attention back to the brook. This time the sound was accompanied by a soft agonized moan. Ryan frantically wiped at the rain beating at his eyes, scanning the direction of the sound.

"No, Ryan, let's go on," Kaylee begged pulling at his hand.

He cautiously backtracked to the brook, entering the thicket, where his eyes rested on an extended clump of willow reeds near the marsh. He motioned for Kaylee to wait near the brook as he ventured forward. He heard no sound other than the sloshing rhythm of his boots as he moved into the mire.

A prickle of readiness stirred in his belly as he reached the marsh. A dart of color caught his eye and he leaned over, swiftly parting the willow grass. He straightened suddenly, shuddering with revulsion at the sight before him.

The giant black man lay half submerged in the stagnant backwash water that lapped against his body. His massive chest was stripped bare of flesh, with a recent branding burn of fragmented tissue forming a distorted "R," marking his muscular shoulder. The remains of boots cut to fit his mammoth feet were strapped to each foot. Ryan glanced at the boot heels, which explained the tracks Kaylee had noticed in the oak grove. Wide coils of chain, such as Ryan used aboard the *Waverly*, bound the man's wrists and ankles, with a leaden link connecting to the thick iron collar surrounding the slave's neck. The raw flesh at his ankles oozed with festering above the leather boot parings. The man's face expressed untold agony as he lay staring blankly up at Ryan.

Ryan moved cautiously, leaning toward the man to determine if the slave still breathed. "Jesus," he swore, as he considered the mutilated giant that sprawled below him. A sudden movement caught him unaware, as the giant black swerved to one side, hauling at the weighty chains, emitting a tortured cry.

"Easy, man," Ryan breathed, recovering his balance. He put forth his hand hesitatingly and touched the black man's shoulder. The slave gaped in terror at Ryan, his eyes crazed with fear, as Ryan moved aside. Droplets of rain plopped into the mire, expanding in swollen bubbles near Ryan's feet.

He strode back through the bog, calling to Kaylee to join him. She picked her way across the soggy ground, hurrying to reach him. She grasped at Ryan, burying her face in his chest. Softly he stroked her hair, brushing it away from her damp face.

"Listen, carefully, Kaylee," he said quietly. "There is a runaway black in the marsh. He is badly hurt. I want you to wait here while I tend him." He moved his mouth against her cheek. "I need a hairpin," he said, his fingers searching her hair for one of proper length.

"Leave him, Ryan. We must get to the bridge before dark. Please," Kaylee whimpered. She watched incredulously as Ryan slipped her hairpins into his pocket.

"What are you going to do, Ryan? I want to see," she demanded.

"Kaylee," Ryan said sternly, shaking her. "I doubt that you have ever encountered such a gruesome sight. I can't have you swooning on me. Wait here as I told you," he snapped.

She stifled a sob as she watched Ryan move back into the marsh. When he reached the black giant, sounds of an unintelligible dialect poured from the man's lips. Ryan deftly turned the leg chain until the key lock appeared. The odor from the festering flesh caused him to recoil. The slave rolled his eyes, the saliva dribbling from his huge mouth as he continued his babblings.

"God Almighty," Ryan swore, as the slippery lock escaped his fingers. "You must be still, man, while I work with this lock; it's rusted."

He inserted the heavy end of Kaylee's hairpin into the key position. "They must have thought you a Goliath, to truss you in such a manner. Rest assured, my hungry years at Brocksburg forced me to learn the art of opening locked pantry doors," Ryan said lightly, seeing the expression of fear fade on the black man's face as he realized Ryan's intention to free him.

Ryan began the work on the right leg set, feeling the inner catch more swiftly this time. This done, he gently pulled at the length across the man's pulpy chest, careful not to drag the links along the raw flesh. He fished in his pocket, bringing forth the flask of ale, lifting the slave's head so he could drink from it.

"'Twill ease your agony some," he said as the giant black man swallowed the ale and lay back into the mire.

Ryan lifted the hand irons, appalled at their width and weight. "I shall remove these, and you are free," he said, realizing that his words were not understood. He reached for another hairpin as the first one snapped inside the lock. A look of despair flashed across the black man's face as Ryan fumbled with the iron cuffs.

"No, man, I know what I'm about," Ryan said. The bands snapped apart and he flung them disgustedly into the sluggish water, sending a startled thrush flapping away in frantic flight. A surge of admiration swept him as the huge man struggled to his knees. The giant groaned as his ankles bore his full weight.

Ryan spun quickly as Kaylee neared the marsh. Before he could warn her away, she caught sight of the enormous man. Her terrorized scream ripped the laden air.

Ryan made the distance through the brackish loam, attempting to reach her before she fainted. Barely in time, he swept her into his arms.

"Kaylee, will you never learn to do as you're told?" Ryan spoke gently against her closed eyelids. The wind stirred the wet leaves against his feet as he turned with her in his arms to see if the giant black followed.

The slave had disappeared, without a sound. Ryan scanned the brook and the marsh but saw nothing. He carried Kaylee toward the shelter of the woods, noticing a speckled thrush circle the bog and land gently on the waving reeds.

"You and the black man are both free," Ryan silently rejoiced, as he laid Kaylee on the soft grass. He remembered an emigrant's cabin near the overgrown road and decided to take Kaylee there until the rain stopped. The land looked vastly changed since he and Johnathan had ridden the meadow in search of grouse. The bayside bridge lay less than a mile from the cabin, the bridge nearing La Pueblita por la Bahia from the north. The sky was an angry black as he attempted to rouse Kaylee from her swoon. He brushed her hair back from her face, chaffing her wrists vigorously, and forcing ale into her mouth.

Kaylee struggled against him, sputtering as the ale filled her mouth. Dazedly she opened her green eyes. She moaned, and began to sob uncontrollably as Ryan pulled her into his arms.

"Hush now, Kaylee. We're almost to the bridge. Perhaps I underestimated your endurance," he said softly. "There is a cabin over on the knoll where we can rest. Do you think you can make the distance?"

She nodded weakly. "That—that huge black—" she sobbed.

"He has gone on his way. I freed him; he won't harm us."

"But, I never saw—" Kaylee whimpered.

166

"I know, Kaylee. A true giant," Ryan agreed, helping her to her feet.

Slowly, they walked to the abandoned cabin, Ryan's arm about Kaylee's waist, supporting her on her unsteady legs. The cabin remained intact, despite its years of disrepair. A broken chair and a rickety table stood in the center of the small room, with a broken rope bed stretching across the corner of the far wall. Smooth polished stones, once attached to the fireplace, lay near the door. A small cache of firewood spilled near a rusted iron stove. Oilskin flaps hung at the two windows, shutting out the stiff wind that blew across the hollow. Ryan glanced about the room, satisfied that it would suffice until the storm eased.

"I am going over the knoll to scout the bridge, Kaylee. Try to rest, it's a good walk yet," Ryan said, setting a flint to the tinder. The dry, dusty wood caught at the sparks, sending a crackling warmth spreading into the small room. Ryan pulled the chair near the fire, setting the trembling Kaylee gently down. He laid his coat near the stone hearth to dry.

"Now, Kaylee, sit here until I return," he ordered sternly. "I'll be quick."

He slipped the gold pocket watch from its chain inside his waistcoat, noting the hour of five approaching. "Enough daylight to reach La Pueblita por la Bahia," he estimated, "once we cross the bridge." He climbed the narrow trail over the rise, stopping short of his destination and staring in disbelief at the landscape. The bridge was gone. Its remains were leveled in the lapping tide water that inundated the ravine.

"Goddamn," Ryan swore as his eyes encompassed the view. "The work on the Santee waterway—they started at the lowest point," he reasoned silently. They would have to double back to the principal road to Charleston, and it would be dusk by then. Kaylee could never do the distance this afternoon. Ryan cursed his earlier irrational behavior and his decision to walk back. By now the Mallens would be sending the carriage for them, and failure to find them at the fair would result in panic. Ryan shrugged in his usual manner. "It appears as though Kaylee and I will spend the night in the hollow," he thought resignedly, surveying again the destroyed bridge.

Kaylee sat huddled in the chair were he had left her. She seemed numb with cold and shock, not even glancing up as he came through the door.

"I'm a reasonable fisherman, Kaylee. Are you hungry?" Ryan asked jokingly.

"My father will kill you," she uttered viciously, her green eyes flashing fire.

"I doubt that." Ryan laughed, shucking his shirt and spreading it to the fire.

"How far is it to the bridge?" Kaylee asked sarcastically.

"There is no bridge," he replied calmly.

Her eyes widened as she stared up at him. Ryan reached for his flask, taking a heavy swallow of ale. He offered it to Kaylee, watching her grimace as the ale burned her throat.

"It would seem that we are destined to stay the night here," he said smoothly. "I am going fishing, Kaylee. There are catfish and blue bass in the brook. See if you can find a pot for cooking," he said over his shoulder as he left through the door. Kaylee stared dumbfounded after him, hearing his low whistle as he crossed the hollow back to the brook.

The rain had ceased and only a low wind rustled the oil flaps at the cabin windows. The smell of smoked fish filled the small room. Kaylee and Ryan sat on the extended hearth, silhouetted by the shadow from the candle stub that sat on the tottering table. They ate from the same crockery, scrubbed heavily with sand and fresh water from the brook. Kaylee wore only her chemise and lawn underskirt. Her gown lay drying across the only chair.

"The fish really is delicious," she said happily, delicately picking the small bones from the bass fillet. "How do you know about fishing, Ryan?"

"My Scottish captain, Wyler McGee, taught me the use of a river cane and stout thread. And, of course, a lively worm."

"I've never spent the night in the wilds," she said simply.

"Johnathan Chapman and I spent many nights, hunting in this hollow. But the bridge was there then. I honestly was not aware that the canal work was proceeding so rapidly. I apologize, Kaylee," Ryan said quietly.

Kaylee watched the red glow of the fire dance across his dark handsome face. His brooding blue eyes gazed intently into the leaping flames. She felt her blood racing.

"Ryan," Kaylee whispered, "do you remember the day at the flood shack at Challey?"

"I remember everything about Challey," he replied wistfully, drinking the last of his ale.

"If I wanted you to kiss me now, would you?"

Ryan turned, his eyes resting hungrily on her. "I am a man of strong desires, Kaylee. Don't tempt me," he said intensely.

She moved close to him, her small hands caressing the length of his shoulders. Her fingers inched up along his neck, smoothing the crisp waves of dark hair that grew near his hairline. Ryan grew tense as he felt her touch.

He spoke into the fire. "I caution you, Kaylee."

Her silken arms slipped about his lean waist as she pressed her face into his wide muscular back. Ryan reached down and covered her hands with his, slowly moving to her face. His hand slid to his belt and he began loosening the lacing on his breeches.

"You were warned, Kaylee," he breathed, his mouth crashing down on hers. Primitive fire surged through his veins, fanned by the wildness of the day. He felt slightly drunk, and Kaylee's face seemed blurred as he devoured her mouth, his tongue exploring the depths of her softness. His hands moved quickly to unhook her chemise, pushing it away from her body. A tremor shook her as his warm hands cupped her firm breasts, then slid lower to caress her. She gasped as Ryan's fingers played across her hips.

"Ryan, don't," she murmured.

Ryan reached for his coat, tossing it on the floor. He grabbed Kaylee and pushed her down on the coat, tumbling on top of her as she tried to shove him away. His mouth trapped her and slowly she relaxed under his questing hands. His stiff manhood pressed hard against her bare thigh.

"By God, Kaylee. You have teased enough," he said harshly. "Now, tonight, it is ended."

Kaylee opened her wild eyes, realizing the moment was upon her. A scream tore from her throat as he thrust into her. He moved forcefully within her, then waited while her body recovered from his entry. Unexpectedly, she began tearing and clawing at his back, her long nails raking him. Sobbing, her mouth searched again for his.

Ryan eased his ruthless attack, kissing her softly, murmuring against her hair. "Easy, love, the pain will diminish."

Kaylee quieted under his kisses, adjusting to the probing, expanding, splintering penetration that filled her. Ryan moved gently now within her, holding her hips close to him, encouraging her motions to blend with his. He surged in a rolling sweep, deeper and swifter as he neared his release. He clutched Kaylee tightly to him, spilling his store of passion.

After awhile, he lifted his weight from her, resting on his elbows while he smiled down at her. "I did caution you, Kaylee."

"Yes, Ryan, you did." She spoke dreamily as he bent to

kiss her. She was drowsy in his arms, snuggling her head against his shoulder.

Ryan eased nearer the fire, pulling her with him. In the few moments before slumber took him, he thought again of Challey, the ravaging fire, the long recovery, and lastly, softly of Janielle. He visualized her wide violet eyes, her white-gold hair shimmering in the moonlight as she stood in the governor's garden. He felt Kaylee stir against him, and he pulled his coat over her shoulders. "It would seem to be my season for virgins," he thought, as he closed his eyes.

chapter 18

With his fingertip, Morris Chapman traced the raised bluish veins on the back of his hand, concentrating, examining a familiar element of himself. Too many years of serving British courts had conditioned him to the rages of emotion, but, today, he fretted. Tiny pearl raindrops dribbled down the palmetto frond outside the open window, coursing downward in a steady path, shedding themselves like teardrops from the human eye.

John Patterson, his back turned, his hands webbed neatly behind him, was skittish, apprehensive. Harrelson Mallen, his face still a shade of crimson, paced the thick Turkish carpet, his silver-knobbed cane stabbing at furious intervals. Morris noticed that Harrelson's laboriously tended peruke, with fox-ear cluster, had dropped, stringing about his ears. The room still smelled of wig powder. Feeling a new rise of bitterness, he waited while the monarch of La Pueblita por la Bahia prepared to administer his justice.

Double doors to the study opened slightly, admitting a Mallen house servant, bowing respectfully, "Master Deverel is outside," he said hollowly.

Morris felt a prickle slide along his neck. Ryan entered calmly, impeccably attired in a muted green waistcoat with pointed lapels of gold, his gleaming black top boots rimmed with a wide matching band of the same gold. Morris sensed the envy Ryan provoked. Ryan moved gracefully across the room, despite a slight limp.

"A good day, Master Deverel." Harrelson Mallen drawled the words slowly.

"Gentlemen," Ryan returned, bowing slightly to the group.

Mallen's cane struck the cherrywood desk, his puffy face a new shade of scarlet. "Your actions of yesterday, Master Deverel, no longer qualify you as a gentleman," he blurted.

Morris winced at the stunned silence, knowing Ryan's sensitivity on this point. Harrelson Mallen had fired his first volley close to the mark.

"What is it you seek, an apology?" Ryan retorted.

"You delivered my daughter home safely, with one exception," he accused, his eyes wild.

"And that exception," Ryan countered.

"Her virtue, Master Deverel," Mallen spat.

Ryan held a rigid stance, only a flicker of surprise crossing his dark face. The corners of his mouth set in a firm line.

Morris ground his fist into his thigh. Accuse, condemn and sentence; it was always the same, he thought tiredly. Mallen was leaning forward, unwavering in his attack.

"Your alley cat morals are well known about Charleston, Master Deverel. I had hoped since you joined the company of gentlemen and accepted their hospitality, that some reform was possible for you. Kaylee related the entirety of events of the past day to her mother, who presented them to me. You must understand that since the loss of Kaylee's brothers during the epidemic, she has been our only treasure. As befitting a gentleman, since you have violated her honor you will be expected to comply with the rules."

Ryan was incredulous. "Is *this* the purpose of this urgent meeting?"

John Patterson interceded. "You must realize, Master Deverel, that your recent actions at the Governor's Ball caused controversy that was unbecoming to those who had accepted you into their homes. We stood with you on that matter. However, this, today, is a different affair."

"You stood with me only because it was politically advantageous," Ryan said sharply.

"Nevertheless, you flaunted our good will," John Patterson returned angrily.

Ryan confronted Morris Chapman. "And have I flaunted your good will, sir barrister?" he asked sarcastically.

"Ryan, there is a serious aspect to this conflict, as you will discover," Morris said resignedly.

"My intense dislike for you at this moment, due to your irresponsible behavior of yesterday, has forced me to ask the opinions of my friends. If left to myself for judgment in this matter, I should most probably destroy you," Harrelson Mallen rasped.

"You cannot destroy me," Ryan replied evenly.

"There are many paths to destruction, and I am certain that you have walked most of them." Mallen was livid with fury.

"Gentlemen!" Morris shouted, gaining his feet. "Likes and dislikes are of no importance if this matter is to be resolved today. We are present to discuss the solution to the events of the past hours. State your conditions, Harrelson," he ordered.

Ryan leveled his stormy eyes at Mallen. "Conditions? I am not on trial here. These parlor antics that you and your opinionated friends have employed are not worthy of my time. I bid you good day, gentlemen." He shrugged disgustedly, turning to go.

"You will find the door bolted and guarded, Master Deverel." Harrelson Mallen's voice was flat.

"Very well, sir." Ryan turned calmly. "Since you choose your method in this order, state your terms."

Mallen readied to fire his second volley, directly on target. "Today you will announce your intention to marry Kaylee. The banns will be posted, the vows exchanged within the month."

A dense silence filled the room as Ryan felt the collision of forces against him. He waited, allowing the impact of the moment to subside. Finally, he spoke.

"Should I refuse your demand?"

"Then there are certain ruinous things that will confront you."

"It puzzles me, sir, that you no longer consider me in a class with gentlemen, yet you require me at this moment to act like one. Why should you force marriage with an unwilling bridegroom?" Ryan's voice was caustic.

"Merely a matter of honor," Harrelson Mallen answered venomously.

John Patterson retreated to a leather wing chair, settling tiredly into it. Morris eased back into his chair, watching the continuing drizzle outside the window. "Perhaps Ryan deserves this," his sense of justice argued silently. "He should not have dallied with Kaylee." Yet the queasiness in his belly reminded him that Ryan's life was being wrenched, twisted, by this ugly scene. Suddenly the resemblance of Ryan to his mother, Loranna Deverel, overpowered him. The same slate-blue eyes, the same determined mouth. Saddened, sick, Morris turned his face away.

Ryan's even voice broke the stillness. "Explain the 'ruinous things,' sir."

Smugly, Harrelson Mallen reached across the desk, lifting a stack of neatly tied documents. He handed the top one to Ryan.

"As you see, these are procurements of your debt accounts with Coast Merchants. It is obvious that you are banking heavily on future cargo profits, extending beyond the time of usual payment on your postings. As you are aware, John Patterson and I own the Coast

Merchants association, and it is due to our—ah—generosity that some overextended accounts are carried. We have reviewed your losses at Challey, and, even with its sale, there is not sufficient funding for you to repay your immediate debt in full. We have learned that profit proceeds on the *Waverly* are still being paid to the Crown."

Harrelson Mallen leafed through the stack, finding one parchment that lighted his face. "This one is a bill from your tailor, which is considerable. And this one, the rents on your Linden property—shall I continue, Master Deverel?"

"So it is your intention to call for full reimbursement at this hour?" Ryan demanded.

"Should I be called on to do so, it will raze you financially," Harrelson Mallen stated coldly.

Ryan shrugged his broad shoulders, giving him time for moment's thought. Kaylee had maneuvered extremely well, trapping him. He had vastly underestimated her intentions. Fleetingly, he recalled Lady Caroline's warning about this "silly virgin." Reasoning out the conditions, he was left with small choice. He would lose Challey but could retain the *Waverly*. Wyler could make four voyages a year to outside markets, and two would pay the account if the markets were steep. He shrugged inwardly, thinking of the small return on Wyler's last voyage. Harrelson Mallen had proved very thorough.

"It is not my plan to deal you an injustice," Mallen continued blandly. "I might even consider, as a wedding gift, cancelling your debt with Coast Merchants—with John's permission, of course. Morris informs me you have expert skill with merchant accounting, and have some talent for design and building. I have need of these qualities in someone to task my new shipyards. With a proper decision, I could offer you a position of this nature. Your reputation might, in time, be restored." Harrelson Mallen's face was sour.

"You are most generous, sir," Ryan sneered.

"I can accept the man Kaylee chooses," Mallen added boastfully.

Ryan felt a tingle of unleashed anger ease along his neck. Being thus subjected to the terms of forced marriage to a plutocrat's daughter or reduced to a pauperous state gave him little choice. He glanced down at his dark hands, the nails trimmed, smooth, white. Even roughened with rigging work aboard the *Waverly*, his hands were the hands of a gentleman. The vision of beggarly hands, grimed, filthy, diseased, crossed his mind. And, nagging, lurking, in the deeper corners of his mind, he could not stand the loss of Challey.

He turned flinty eyes to Harrelson Mallen. "It appears I have only one wise choice to consider," he said quietly.

"And, that is, Master Deverel?" Mallen's eyes narrowed.

"I shall take your daughter in wedlock," Ryan gritted.

A visible look of relief crossed Mallen's perspiring face as he glanced nervously about, seeking approval from the others. Morris Chapman wore a mask of disgust, his face still turned to the window. John Patterson sprang to his feet, walking briskly over to the sideboard, reaching for a bottle of Harrelson Mallen's treasured collection.

"A drink, gentlemen, for gentlemen," he offered with dignity, lifting his glass in toast. Morris Chapman shook his head in refusal while Mallen mopped his flushed face with his black silk handkerchief.

Impassively, Ryan surveyed the revolting scene. "I believe the matter is attended," he said curtly. "I leave the arrangements to your discretion. Good day, *gentlemen*," he sneered, crossing the room.

Harrelson Mallen scurried after him. "I doubt that you shall ever have cause to regret this day," he remarked hurriedly.

"I regret it already, sir," Ryan countered, stalking out of the room.

177

Kaylee paced in her upstairs room, never venturing far from the scrolled-iron window overlooking the patio gate. The last visit downstairs had yielded little report. Her father's footmen were still standing on either side of the library door. She could hear nothing of the activity inside the closed room. The patio was deserted, only the pair of peacocks paraded near the entrance.

"Enough," she decided, glancing hurriedly at her reflection in the mirror, adjusting a stray curl that had slipped its ribbon. Quietly, she moved along the tiled hallway, down the servants' stairs, out into the patio gardens.

Congratulating herself on a carefully executed plan, she felt confident of the outcome. Ryan would never part with Challey, she reasoned over again in her mind, there was too much longing in his eyes when he spoke of it. Nor would he part with his merchantman, which filled his purse. She believed her perceptive judgment of him to be correct. "I will have him," she repeated to herself; she wanted him. Never had any man treated her in such ruthless fashion. He had denied her everything. Even in their lovemaking, there was a part of him she could not own. But as his wife—that was another matter.

Black ornate gates swung apart as Ryan moved between them. "Yes, I have him," Kaylee thought, seeing the menacing look on his dark face. The skirt of her green-sprigged tea gown brushed the smooth marble of the fountain as she ran to intercept him.

"Ryan! Wait!" she gasped.

Angrily, he faced her, his eyes blazing, yet cold, deadly.

"I am in no mood for you, Kaylee," he snapped.

Hot tears sprang to her green eyes. He looked even more handsome today, his square jaw firmly set, his dark hair falling across the livid scar on his forehead. His wide mouth was a hard fine line, but it was his eyes, always his eyes, that held her.

"I—I love you, Ryan," she breathed.

He shrugged furiously, brushing away her hand.

"So, you agreed," she murmured softly.

"By all that is holy, Kaylee, this I vow. Your trickery will gain you no part of me." Ryan's blue eyes bored into hers.

"I intend to have all of you, Ryan. You will be my husband," she replied arrogantly.

Ryan's hand lashed out, locking in her dark hair. His other hand came up fast, reaching to her bodice, jerking roughly at the sheer fabric until it gave. Cruelly, he snapped her head backward finding her mouth, bruising, twisting her mouth against his. His brutal hands found her breasts, closing harshly over them, hurting her.

Wildly, Kaylee began to struggle. Clawing his face with her nails, biting at his mouth until their blood mingled, twisting, hurting, still his attack continued. Roughly he lifted her in his arms, carrying her to the summer porch at the end of the garden. He flung her across the bench, shredding her gown from her in one savage wrench. His long fingers worked the brace buttons on his breeches.

"No, Ryan, please," Kaylee pleaded, "not this way."

His body smothered her. Without preliminaries, he thrust himself into her, covering her mouth with his hand when she screamed. He moved unmercifully, driving, plunging within her, caring nothing for the pain he gave. Violent release shattered him after a few moments and he withdrew quickly. Kaylee's tears had soaked his neck and shirt. He leaned over her, his ice-blue eyes glaring down at her tear-streaked face.

"Look at me, Kaylee," he commanded.

Kaylee shook uncontrollably. "Why, Ryan? Why?" she moaned.

"I have just given you your wedding night," he answered harshly, rolling away from her.

Kaylee lay stunned, staring up at the sullen sky, refusing to meet his eyes.

Ryan was buttoning his breeches. "I have agreed to wed you, Kaylee. You may consider this our final consummation, for I shall never touch you again." He hooked his wide belt about his lean waist. Without a backward glance he stepped through the archway and out into the garden.

Wyler McGee stretched his tired legs across the weathered dock bench, gazing out across the harbor. The last of the London cargo had been unloaded, the crew was "hogging" the *Waverly*. Wyler scraped his boot against the slime and barnacles that lay near the bench, produced by the previous effort of the "hogger."

"Damn me, sea creatures," Wyler swore. "Why ye choose to carry yerselves agin us, I canna' fathom." He must tell Ryan about replacing the iron bolts in the hull below the water line with new copper grippings to stop the corrosion from the iron and salt water.

The rhythmic drag of the "hogger" sang across the deserted docks. Unloading cargo and making repairs to the ship were dreary chores in the spitting drizzle. "Damn me, agin, if the skies are not always full when me be in Charleston port," Wyler thought. He thought of his bottle of usquebach in the ship's cabin. He rose slowly from the bench, his head jerking at the sound of carriage wheels on the dock planking. The carriage moved toward the *Waverly*'s moor. Idly, Wyler stroked his red beard, wondering.

He watched Ryan alight from the carriage, striding across the wharf to the *Waverly*'s dock bridge. Ryan's shoulders were set in a hard square, his deliberate gait told Wyler that the younger master was enraged. He caught the marks of livid claw scratches across Ryan's face.

Ryan was near enough to hail. "Me God, man, did ye finally bed an unwilling bitch?" Wyler roared with laughter.

Ryan turned, shooting him a devastating glare from cold eyes, which Wyler chose to ignore.

"I'll sleep aboard the *Waverly* tonight, Captain McGee. Should anyone inquire for me, you have not seen me, understood?" Ryan snapped.

Wyler scratched at his full beard, trying to suppress his mirth.

"Would be me guess, her husband is seekin' for ye."

Ryan spun away from the dock bridge, squarely facing him.

"I have just raped my bride-to-be, so that should indicate my mood," Ryan snarled.

"By all that is holy, man—" Wyler sputtered.

"Tell the shipwright to cease his 'hogging' and bring me two bottles of your usquebach," Ryan ordered from the deck. He stepped below into the narrow passageway, walking to the captain's quarters at the end of the ship. The salt air and familiar scents inside the French frigate brought some relief to his flailed nerves. The *Waverly* rocked easily in its moorings, occasionally emitting a churlish groan from its ancient timbers.

Ryan strode to his small desk beneath the ornate embrasure, gazing out at the greenish-gray sea. The events of the day had taken their toll. He turned as Wyler entered the cabin, two bottles of his beloved Scottish rye riding his arm.

Wyler studied Ryan's pensive expression as he poured two pewter mugs full of the fiery brew. " 'Twill ease you, man," Wyler offered.

Ryan drained his mug, loosening his cravat, tossing it aside. Wyler slumped into the wide chair by the berth, waiting for Ryan to uncoil.

Wyler swilled the liquid in his mug. "And which lass this time?" he asked dryly.

Ryan braced after a long pull with the usquebach. "They are all nameless, faceless bitches," he said bitterly.

Wyler shook his head, knowing Ryan's reputation with women. "Is she with child?" he asked.

"Not unless it gained hold yesterday or today," Ryan answered indifferently.

"Hell, me man. Then, why the wedding?" Wyler pressed, spreading his muscular arms across the back of his chair.

Ryan spoke quietly of the events of the past two days, pausing as Wyler spewed obscenities of every description at close intervals.

"I canna' believe the good man, Morris Chapman, had a hand in the scheme," Wyler commented when Ryan had finished the story.

"I couldn't find a way to outwit them," Ryan confessed angrily.

"Me surprise at findin' that dandy, Mallen, with the balls to tackle ye, is considerable," Wyler said, his words slurring with drink. "'Tis rumored she's a pretty lass, son. It could be worse."

"What in God's name could be worse than a loveless marriage?" Ryan groaned.

"I dinna' know, lad. Aye, but there's a plenty of that sort," Wyler remarked slowly.

Sometime later, Wyler hung the ship lantern near the berth and tossed a woolen blanket over Ryan. He stumbled across the cabin, making his way up the dim passageway, reeling as he stepped onto the main deck. He breathed deeply of the salt night air, feeling thankful that his own troublesome problems were small by comparison.

chapter 19

Janielle plucked away the withered brown gardenia, tugging the bloom free of its fragrant bush. She spent more and more time these days in the secluded greenhouse set apart from the rest of Patterson manor. Lifting a newly potted lantana, flourishing with dainty pink flowers, she inhaled the drift of red jasmine trailing near the latticed doorway.

Essence of red jasmine made her think of Ryan. Always. The night of the Governor's Ball, gentle blue eyes that caressed her. She recalled her last day in Charleston, bribing Jedda to drive her to the harbor, insisting on a closer look at the *Waverly* from the pier, obsessed with need to see some part of where Ryan had been.

The three-masted French frigate dipped gently into the current at its moorings, the soft slap of the greenish ripples stroking her large red hull. The round tuck stern boasted of a new jib boom and spiritsail topsail, extending from the bowsprit. A tattered British flag still hung from the jib boom, overlapping the shredded French flag that indicated the proud frigate had been captured on high seas. Idly, she wondered why the new flag of the States of America had not been hoisted.

Traveling the river barge back to Patterson Landing, she had casually asked her father how Ryan had acquired the *Waverly*. Her father had seemed reluctant to discuss Ryan, but commented that Morris Chapman first held the *Waverly* as payment from the Crown for barrister's services. The ship had been badly damaged in sea battle, towed to Boston harbor by the British man-o-war, the *Britannia*. Morris assigned the ship to Ryan, reconditioning it for a cargo vessel. The Crown had reassessed another levy on the former warship, leaving Ryan to absorb the added debt.

The *Waverly* carried only ten guns, cannon, culverin, sakers, and minions, none fit for sea war. Forsaking her former image for the more sedate one of a merchantman, John Patterson had mentioned how fortunate Ryan had been to secure a competent Scottish sea master while he learned the ways of ships and sea.

How she had craved to set foot aboard Ryan's ship! Her heart pounding heavily in her breast, she had calmly instructed Jedda to drive away from the pier, though she felt she left a part of herself with Ryan and his ship.

Startled at the tolling of the landing bell, she quickly replaced the watering vessel, remembering it was Tuesday, and the lumber barge was due with a supply of fresh timber for the new slave quarters. Her father had ridden upriver early in the morning, leaving her to sign for the delivery.

"A good day, Mistress Patterson," Dester Bowles called to her, securing the ropes on his long clumsy barge. Dester had been poling freight upriver for as many years as she could remember. His disfigured mouth had always held her curiosity, but never would she dare to ask him about it.

"Your new grandson, has he been named?" Janielle called across the jetty.

"Aye, that he has. Another Dester Bowles." Dester's mouth twisted in a grotesque smile. He reached across to her, handing her the mail packet.

"I'll send the servants down with your rum," Janielle promised, climbing the causeway.

"Obliged, Mistress Patterson," Dester called after her.

Janielle paused along the caseway, opening Johnathan's letter.

> *Beloved Janielle:*
>
> *I have adventures to tell you of my travels to China that will last our lifetime. I am bringing gifts from the Orient that I believe will please you.*
>
> *I regret my long absence from you and the postponement of our marriage. Know you are close in my heart. I shall return to the Carolinas by early autumn.*
>
> *Always your love,*
> *Johnathan*

Janielle slipped the letter back into its stained folder, mildly intrigued with the fact that it had come from such a great distance. Her eyes fell upon two identical envelopes bearing the Mallen seal. One carried Brandon's name and the other was inscribed with her father's name and her own in smaller lettering. Quickly she opened the flap, pulled the elaborately engraved parchment from its inner casing, her eyes widening as she skimmed the lines.

> *"Your honorable presence is requested at the wedding bonds of Kaylee Suzanne, daughter of Harrelson Mallen and wife, of McClellanville, South Carolina, to Ryan Paul Deverel, of Challey Plantation, on this, our Lord's day of—"*

Janielle felt a sinking sickness in her belly, then anger overcame her as she continued to stare at the words before her. How had Kaylee snared Ryan? Ryan was not a type for her. Kaylee was barely eighteen, scarcely old enough to cope with Ryan's mood swings, merely a child at love. Had she and Ryan done what Ryan was expert at? "Like he did with me," she tortured herself. No, Kaylee would never permit it before wedlock. But Ryan was dominant, maybe he had persuaded her.

"Stop!" she screamed silently, running the rest of the distance up the causeway, hot tears stinging her eyes. She would ride, get away for awhile, lose herself in the land, drown herself—something.

She was still gripping Brandon's mail parcel in her hand. She had not seen him since that awful morning when he had said farewell to her. And she had not crossed Challey land since the day she had bolted from Ryan.

She decided to ride to Challey and deliver Brandon's packet instead of waiting for Micah to fetch it as he usually did. Besides, she could watch Brandon's reaction to Ryan's forthcoming marriage to Kaylee. Maybe he would offer some sort of solace. At least she could talk to him about it.

Passing the huge mound of charred rubble that was once Challey manor, Janielle noted that the burned magnolia tree, growing near what once was the library window, had sprouted new leafings, the forsythia hedges along the granite steps had managed a few sparse yellow blooms.

The fruit in the orchards had been picked, the furrows neatly weeded. The land was orderly, well-tended under Brandon's watchful eye. His overseer's cottage had a new coat of whitewash with crisp fresh curtains hanging from the tiny paned windows.

She dismounted, tying the reins to a new carved birch railing. The red geraniums she so carefully nurtured during Ryan's convalescence were nudging each other for space inside the gleaming white pots.

A crumpled note was tacked to the smooth pine door

of the cottage. She unfastened it, smoothing it, reading Brandon's wide scrawl.

"Micah, set the men to pump today. I am at the north field. B."

Edging the door open, Janielle felt a ripple of disappointment. She had wanted to see Brandon today. Intending to only glance about inside the cottage before riding back to Patterson Woods, she strolled about the neat cheerful room, fighting needles of poignant memories.

She had been foolishly in love with Ryan Deverel, allowing him to use her, taunt her, and finally discard her. And Brandon had waited, comforting her, even loving her with a tender intensity the day at the flood shack.

Nothing had been right in her life since Ryan came to Challey. Suddenly his face came clearly into view, the arrogant set of his mouth, the brooding ice-blue eyes.

How seldom she thought of Johnathan. It was difficult to form his features in her memory. They were blurred, fragmented. She shuddered, thinking of Johnathan's caress, his naked body touching hers.

Quickly she moved to the door, clicking it shut behind her. The midday heat was stifling. Dabbing at the beading moisture on her face and neck, the stickiness between her breasts, she mounted her sorrel, riding leisurely along the road to Dancer's Creek. On impulse she guided the horse north toward the natural waterfall near the spread of the Santee. A cool splash in the silken waters would restore her, soothe her trembling. She would forget Ryan, Brandon, all that was past. Somehow.

The waterfall tumbled lazily over oblong, pock-ridden rocks, brimming into the azure pool below. Wavelets lapped softly against the lush bank. She shrugged out of her green and white sprigged lawn dress, rolling her pantalets high above her knees.

Janielle flinched as a bulging-eyed river frog belched

his displeasure of her intrusion. She waded into the cool oozing mud near the bank, then splashed into the center of the pool below the waterfall. She drifted, dreamed, her long white-gold hair floating in the clear water.

So, she had loved him. Been naive in believing he returned her love and intended to wed her. Ryan was possessive, wiser in the complicated ways of love. He was restless, deceptive and outright charming. And now, he was to wed Kaylee. How? How had Kaylee trapped him?

Swimming back under the waterfall, her ears caught a beckoning whinney from the creek road. Her sorrel snorted, pawing the ground near the bank. Maybe Brandon, or Micah, was riding the upper path. Hurriedly, she swam to the bank. She didn't want to be in the water when whoever it was approached.

Janielle stepped onto the sand bar, squeezing the water from her dripping hair. She would slip into her gown and ride the back path behind the waterfall. Suddenly she didn't want to confront anyone.

Her gown had fallen from the branches where she had laid it. Carefully she lifted it from the ground, brushing away the clinging wheat grass and dried moss. She shivered with cold, wishing she had brought something to dry herself with.

Swiftly she turned, hearing a crackle in the brush behind her. Ryan stood in the small clearing, a fawn-colored hunting coat slung over one shoulder, his horse moving forward, lowering his head to drink from the pool.

If he was surprised to find her here, he cloaked it well. His mouth was set in a bitter fold, his eyes cold and distant. He appeared leaner, harder than she remembered.

"I—I thought you were in Charleston," Janielle said awkwardly, clutching her gown to her.

Ryan studied her for a moment, a restless smile easing

across his mouth. "I needed a space of serenity," he replied quietly.

Janielle slipped the gown over her head, stretching her arms into the full sleeves, hurriedly buttoning the bodice. She shook her head, tossing her damp hair behind her shoulders.

"Does Brandon know you are about?" she asked, working her feet into her shoes.

"We have been hunting pheasant since dawn," Ryan said tiredly. He moved closer to help her mount. His hand brushed her arm, sending a tremor through her.

She raised her eyes, searching his face. She had to know. "Is Kaylee with you?" she asked brokenly.

Ryan's eyes flashed with anger. "No, she is not," he snapped.

"I should think she would wish—" Janielle let the other words fade.

Ryan turned away from her, moving to the edge of the pool. He reached down, gathering a stone in his hand, hurling it into the deep azure center. He stood gazing at the spreading circlet of ripples until the pool was still again.

"Come here, Janielle," he said harshly, without turning around.

Hesitantly, Janielle moved to stand beside him. Ryan reached out his hand, taking hers.

"There has been a heavy matter concerning me, Janielle, since I left Challey. The day I spoke to you in jealous anger, I have had cause to regret. Brandon informed me you suffered as a result."

Janielle reeled. How much had Brandon told him? She prayed he didn't know everything. It would only cause strain between them now. Looking into his cool, beseeching eyes, she still felt an incredible hunger for him, despite the control she was exhibiting.

"Will Kaylee content you as a wife?" she asked evenly.

Ryan let her hand fall from his. His voice was hard. "I cannot say, Janielle."

The warm afternoon breeze stirred the lush foliage around them; shafts of glittering sunlight spilled across the pool, setting it to a golden shimmer.

Janielle brushed aside a wisp of her white-gold hair that had caught at the corner of her mouth. Ryan was watching her. Her throat was dry. She had prayed, dreamed of being with Ryan again, and now as he stood beside her on this quiet, golden afternoon, she felt at a loss.

"Johnathan should return in the autumn. Have you plans to wed?" Ryan asked.

"Y—yes." Janielle swallowed. She had nothing to lose. "Do you love Kaylee?" she asked boldly.

Ryan wheeled, facing hers, gripping her by the shoulders. "Love? How in God's name would I know of love? A mother who spurned me, a drunken man I knew to be my father, beating me with his riding whip until blood ran down my legs, disclaiming me, calling me a bastard's spawn. Schoolmasters with empty eyes and frozen hearts—women who warmed under my caresses, offering only appeasement—Tell me, how *could* I know of love?"

Janielle gasped as he drew her to him, his mouth warm against her neck. "I know of but one way to love." He spoke hoarsely against her hair.

Soon his demanding mouth was moving on her, seeking, devouring. Instinctively, she responded, feeling a rushing glow of surrender engulf her. Moments of incredible tenderness, even drowning passion would follow. Then Ryan would be gone again.

"No, Ryan," she said determinedly, breaking free of his arms.

"Must we play the master and parlor wench again?" Ryan said angrily.

"You shall not take me today without force," Janielle snapped.

"I am equal to that if you wish it that way."

"I do not wish it at all! You belong to Kaylee!" Janielle felt the sting of hot tears pricking her eyes.

"She may take my name, but I will never belong to her or any woman."

They spun around as heavy footfalls crunched through the brush behind them. Janielle wiped tears from her check, watching Brandon ride toward them. She wondered how much he had overheard; his calm expression told her nothing.

Casually, Brandon dismounted, leading his horse to the edge of the pool.

He glanced across at them. "Irene will be pleased with the brace of pheasants." He spoke lightly.

Ryan moved to the trunk of a sassafras tree, retrieving his musket. He holstered it in his saddle pouch and swung into the saddle, giving Janielle a long bitter look.

"You should have someone accompany you when you choose to go wading," he said caustically, turning his horse into the path to the road.

Janielle watched the rhythmic swish of the horse's tail as he moved into the thick foliage. She heard the echo of his hooves on the soft earth above the bank as Ryan rode away.

Her heart was thudding heavily in her breast. She hadn't noticed when Brandon had come to stand beside her.

"What brings you to Challey, Janielle?" he asked softly.

"I—I came to see you," she replied hollowly. "It became so warm in the cottage, I—" she faltered, glancing away from Brandon's penetrating eyes.

"Do you still wish to stay?" Brandon breathed, moving closer to her.

"Ryan is to wed Kaylee," she blurted out.

Brandon threw back his head, laughing a throaty laugh.

"Ah, Janielle. Revenge is honey, poison to the soul."

"What do you mean?" she asked furiously.

"Ryan is to become partner in the Mallen shipyards and Harrelson Mallen is giving La Pueblita por la Bahia to him and Kaylee as wedding bounty. Ryan will become a member of Coast Merchants. Could a man seek more?"

Janielle chewed at her lower lip. Had Ryan needed the money so badly? And prestige was never so important to him before.

"But, he—he doesn't love Kaylee," she stammered.

Brandon led her to her horse, cupping his hands for her foot. She mounted, fitting her knee around the horn.

Brandon looked wistfully at her. "You should remember, with Ryan, love never enters into it," he said evenly.

He moved to his own horse, swinging into the saddle. He pulled his field hat down over his sun-bronzed forehead, waiting to follow Janielle down the overgrown path.

chapter 20

Evan Reed pushed his way across the crowded dock, relieved to part company from an ailing Harrelson Mallen. Evan had arrived at La Pueblita por la Bahia at noonday to treat the wealthy merchant for a case of gout. Smearing yellow bark mixture on the inflamed foot had brought shrieks of outrage from Aurora Mallen.

Evan smiled wickedly. Itoo's peculiar treatments were primitive, but effective. He recalled the foul-smelling poultice Itoo had kept for weeks on Ryan Deverel's broken leg. Thankful that his medical shipment aboard the *Devonshire* would inspire a more refined practice of medicine, Evan was still grateful for the knowledge of Yemassee potions.

Exchanging the favor of the ride for agreeing to meet Johnathan Chapman on his return from London made Evan furious. Harrelson Mallen complained of his gout, Morris Chapman was in Columbia with one of General Washington's chief aides. They asked that a "suitable representative" greet the prestigious barrister's son aboard the *Devonshire*. The task had fallen to Evan.

His eyes swept the harbor, spotting the massive, soiled sails of the awesome British brigantine. No time for a short dram of rum. The *Devonshire* plowed into the tide current with a good press of canvas, her square mizzenmast and mainmast sails furling in from full blow. She was running in, gradually shortening sail.

Sight of the British warship caused a deep stirring in his breast, remembering how proudly he had once served aboard a "ship of the line." The crew gathered about the capstan, laboring with the heavy coiled rope, bringing sail in up to wind. The drummer aboard the *Devonshire* began his roll as the giant anchor plunged into the harbor.

The majestic brigantine dipped into the landing block, the crew in stiff British Navy formation for its disembarkment. Evan watched in silent salute as the familiar orders were called. At last the dock bridge was lowered, the crashing drum roll diminished. Passengers were gathered on deck, shuffling about as the wide bridge was secured to the deck of the *Devonshire*.

Evan strode to the edge of the bridge, scanning the crowded deck above him. He knew when he saw Johnathan Chapman. The handsome golden-haired gentleman wore a rakish cloak of crimson, his white breeches and gleaming light jackboots clearly marking his status. His smile was white against the deep tan of his face.

"He stands almost as tall as Ryan," Evan thought fleetingly, waiting for Johnathan to make the distance down to the pier.

Evan stepped forward. "Johnathan Chapman." He spoke firmly.

"You are correct. And who am I addressing?" Johnathan asked formally.

"Evan Reed, sir. Your father was detained in Columbia and Harrelson Mallen is incapacitated. Therefore the *honor* fell to me," Evan replied sardonically.

Johnathan Chapman eyed the unkempt colonial suspiciously. The man reeked of sweat and sour rum. Johnathan wriggled his nose distastefully.

"Have you a carriage?" he asked.

"Harrelson Mallen awaits above the docks in his red barouche. It was his intention to transport you to La

Pueblita por la Bahia to wait for your father's return."

Johnathan frowned. This was hardly the reception he had expected after a year's absence. "Has he news of my mother?" he asked pointedly.

"She remains in McClellanville suffering from vapors," Evan said.

"I was expecting a young lady to be waiting at dockside," Johnathan said, glancing about the bustling wharf.

"Janielle is at Patterson Woods. It is doubtful that she knows of your return." Evan spoke distractedly.

"How have you knowledge of Janielle?" Johnathan demanded.

"That, sir, is a long tale." Evan laughed shortly. "Should you wish to accompany Sir Mallen now?"

"I think not. I carry papers that must be secured at Coast Merchants before I leave the dock. I wish to stay in Charleston for a day or so, anyway. Inform Mr. Mallen that I shall join him later. I bid you good day," Johnathan said curtly, dismissing Evan.

Evan bristled. He had disliked Johnathan Chapman at first glance.

"I will not be returning with Harrelson Mallen. My medical supplies from the *Devonshire* are yet to be unloaded. You may make your own arrangements with Mr. Mallen," Evan snapped, turning to leave.

Johnathan caught at his arm. "My curiosity overwhelms me. You seem to know considerable about my family and their friends. How have you come to know Harrelson Mallen?"

"I treat him," Evan replied arrogantly.

"You mentioned medical supplies. You are a physician of sorts, then?" Johnathan asked incredulously.

"I am a British surgeon," Evan said, squaring his shoulders.

"And now a colonial surgeon, I would suppose." Johnathan grinned, noting Evan's attire.

Evan hailed a dockman, slipping a coin in the dirty palm, charging him with a message to deliver to Harrelson Mallen.

"Tell the gentleman in the red barouche that he will have no passengers returning with him this afternoon." He glanced sidelong at Johnathan. "Do you wish to add to the message?"

Johnathan shook his head, intrigued with the style of this caustic Englishman. They watched as the dockman made his way through the throngs up to the road along the dock.

"I am in need of a good meal and some strong American ale," Johnathan said lightly. "Would you care to join with me while we await the unloading?"

Evan didn't. His intense dislike for this man was growing. He started to walk away, then he stopped. "I frequent an inn called the Sea Hawk. Their fare is decent and I have a friend who lodges there. Should you be inclined to supply the coin, I shall join you," Evan said mockingly.

"Done," Johnathan said, falling into a step with him. They walked in silence for a few steps.

"I noticed that the *Waverly* is in harbor. The ship belongs to a schoolmate of mine," Johnathan commented, glancing back toward the harbor.

"Our friend seems to be the same man," Evan said dryly. "The *Waverly* belongs to Ryan Deverel."

Johnathan raised a brow at Evan. "How have you come to know Ryan?"

"I mended his leg and his head when Challey burned," Evan shouted above the buzzing din along the pier.

Johnathan wheeled in front of Evan. "Did I hear you say that Challey burned?"

"I did. You have been abroad for many months. There is much you have to learn of," Evan said, pushing Johnathan aside.

Astonished, Johnathan followed him through the broad door of the Sea Hawk, threading his way among the rough tables in the dim interior. Evan was bellowing for mugs of ale.

The harassed innkeeper set them down gruffly before them, wiping his greasy hands on a leather apron. Evan grinned at the flustered expression on the old man's face.

"The mutton last week was rancid," Evan called after him ignoring the scalding look the innkeeper returned. He took a long drink from his mug.

"Ryan gives the old goat a few rounds when he stays here and the old man favors him," Evan remarked, watching Johnathan lift a gold snuff box from inside this frock coat. Daintily, Jonathan set the mixture to his nostril.

Evan sat through the sneezing procedure, filled with disgust. The golden-haired gentleman, the son of a fine, hard-working barrister who had gained the respect of both the British and the colonials in Carolina, had none of his father's qualities.

Johnathan sipped at the froth on his ale.

"Tell me about Challey," he said, while the meal was served.

"I arrived only to see the burning rubble and the gore that followed. Ryan was caught upstairs in the blaze. Janielle was overcome with smoke vapors. Brandon Ord and I cared for them," Evan said, leveling his gaze at Johnathan.

Johnathan's mouth fell open. "Janielle, is she well?" he asked brokenly.

"She danced quite well with me at the Governor's Ball," Evan replied, his words slurring with the effect of ale. He found himself enjoying Johnathan Chapman's discomfort.

"Janielle and I have been bethrothed for a year and plan to wed soon," Johnathan remarked haughtily.

197

Evan threw back his head and laughed. "You are a bit late for the wedding," he retorted, watching the shocked expression on Johnathan's face.

"Explain yourself," Johnathan demanded, rising to his feet.

"You should have wed Janielle before you sailed. Before she lost the child she carried."

Johnathan paled, sitting down weakly on the carved bench. His hand trembled as he held the mug to his mouth, swallowing the full amount. After a long silence, his eyes met Evan's.

"You tended her," he asked quietly.

"I did," Evan replied.

"Did she state the child was mine?" Johnathan asked pointedly.

"She merely asked that no one be told. I watched her suffer losing her seed, while you cavorted about on the high seas, caring little that she was left unprotected. You knew the consequences of your union," Evan snarled, motioning to the innkeeper for another round of ale.

"I have a fondness for Janielle," Evan continued, "and, if she should accept me, I would wed her this moment."

Johnathan paused, collecting the jumbled thoughts that spun inside his head. Evan Reed was drunk. Perhaps the story was a fabrication. But something about it nagged at him.

"Did Janielle spend a great deal of her time at Challey after Loranna Deverel's death?" Johnathan asked softly.

"How in hell would I know," Evan snarled, the mellow effect of the ale giving way to wrath.

Johnathan stroked his chin, watching as Evan Reed refilled his mug. His eyes narrowed.

"The overseer, Brandon Ord—has he remained at Challey?" Johnathan probed.

Evan swayed, placing his elbows on the rough table.

"Brandon is a good man, a good friend to Ryan," he drawled. "He took care of Janielle, treated her like a spoiled child. She cared only that Ryan was mending. The first time she saw him after the fire, she fainted from shock. After she was stronger, she still came every day to Challey to care for him. With Ryan's foul temper, that took an angel of sorts," Evan mumbled.

Suddenly Johnathan had his answer. He knew Ryan Deverel very, very well—knew his recounted success with women. He recalled the uneasiness he had felt the night of the Thanksgiving feast at Patterson Woods. Ryan had probably taken her before that night.

"God damn, what a fool I've been," he swore under his breath. A strange sense of calm settled over him as he rose to leave. The niggling rivalry he had always felt toward Ryan Deverel had at last come to confrontation.

He glanced down at Evan Reed, filled with loathing at the sight of the drunken British fool. Perhaps there was truth to what he had said; perhaps not. He intended to find out.

"I shall retire to my offices now, Mr. Reed," Johnathan said, flipping a gold piece on its side.

Evan stared dumbly at the spinning coin. Johnathan's words were lost to him.

Johnathan slammed the door to the inner office, bolting it against interruption. The Coast Merchants' offices hummed with activity as the cargoes from the *Devonshire* arrived. He unhooked the money belt from his waist, clipping away the heavy leather stitching along the fold. The gold notes were folded neatly inside velvet pouches. He counted the notes from the Merchant Bank of London, storing them in the iron wall box, setting his key to the lock.

The door to his father's office upstairs was slightly ajar. Benjamin was inside, filing the ledgers in the pine chest. He looked up, startled, as Johnathan stormed into the office.

"Uh, Mister Johnathan, sir—welcome home," he

gasped. "Your voyage—was it profitable?"

"Until I docked," Johnathan snapped. "I am interested in knowing the whereabouts of Ryan Deverel."

Benjamin smiled. Ryan had become a popular figure on the docks since Harrelson Mallen had opened a new office there.

"Mr. Deverel keeps to the new building of Mallen shipyards," he stammered.

"Where are they?" Johnathan demanded angrily.

"At the far end of the north pier. I can beckon a carriage for you," Benjamin replied, his voice quavering.

Johnathan strode to the walnut cabinet where his father kept his whiskey store. His thoughts were racing wildly. A slow smile crossed his face as his eyes focused on the concealed drawer of the cabinet. He reached for a glass, splashing a heavy amount of whiskey into it. He drank it slowly, savoring it.

Finally he turned to Benjamin. "When do you expect my father?"

"The coach from the uplands arrives before nightfall," Benjamin replied uneasily.

"I have writing to do. That will be all, Benjamin," Johnathan said curtly, turning his back on the flustered lad.

Johnathan breathed heavily, hearing the outer door click. He pulled the cork from a second bottle. He didn't bother to pour the wiskey into a glass.

The clamoring in his belly was stilling. He walked over to the walnut cabinet, his fingers groping, searching for the tiny spring above the drawer. It gave. The drawer slid quietly open.

His eyes glowed. The small velvet case that held the Kentucky flintlock pistol was still there. He opened the lid, lifting the smooth hand gun from its velvet groove. He counted three lead balls inside it. The small ram stick, firing wad and vial of powder were still intact.

His eyes were fuzzy as he fumbled in his coat for his

French watch. Stuffing the pistol inside his belt, he reeled to the door, his steps uncertain as he descended the narrow, creaking stairs outside the building. He was anxious to find Ryan Deverel.

Small circlets of light twinkled about the harbor as the ship lanterns atop the high masts blinked into the gathering darkness. Hawkers along the wharf had closed their stalls for the day. Heavy scents of fish, rotted fruit and smoking torches mingled with the salty taste from the sea.

Ryan leaned out across his open window, inhaling the night salt breeze, idly watching droves of sailors picking their way along the docks, seeking a place of solace for the night. His gaze swept the east harbor where the *Waverly* snuggled into its moorings, the furled topgallant sails starkly silhouetted against the pinkish glow of the sinking sun.

Kaylee would be waiting for him, beautifully gowned, eager for another long evening spent in a sea of unfamiliar faces as the prenuptial invitations continued. Outwardly he appeared to be faithful to his role, attentive and considerate to his bride-to-be. But alone with her, the coldness and indifference remained. It was at best only an arrangement.

Ryan shrugged. He began to set his desk in order, carefully rolling the crisp parchments and securing them. He glanced over one of them, studying the detailed sketch he had drawn. Shipbuilding was new to him, but he would learn.

He reached for his new Spencer coat, drawing his long arms into the sleeves. Kaylee had chosen the coat for him and for awhile he had refused to wear it. The feeling of being kept by a woman smothered him. Damn her and her money, anyway! If it weren't for Challey—

Ryan wheeled as the door was kicked open, its wide planks vibrating against the wall. Johnathan Chapman weaved menacingly in the doorway, his arms grasping the sides for support.

"You bloody bastard," Johnathan hissed.

Ryan stepped back. "I assume your recent voyage was a disaster," he said, gathering his scrolls beneath his arm.

Johnathan advanced, his face dark with fury. "It wasn't enough you raped every goddamn bitch in Carolina, you had to bed her!"

Ryan cast him a hard look. "It appears, friend Johnathan, that you are beyond your reason."

"It took awhile to fit the pieces together with that drunken fool, Evan Reed, goading me," Johnathan rasped.

Ryan met his piercing gaze with cold eyes. "Hold, Johnathan! Your drunken ravings are wasted on me."

"Wasted?" Johnathan sneered. "'Twas you who wasted your spurting seed on Janielle! She lost your unborn child! The bastard child of a bloody, whore-spawned bastard!" Johnathan spat.

Ryan lunged at him, gripping his coat collar, their faces close.

"You drunken fop," Ryan snarled, tightening his hold on Johnathan. "Explain."

"Evan Reed can explain if you're alive to hear it," Johnathan gasped, spinning away, shoving Ryan against the desk.

Ryan's look was deadly as he straightened. He shook his head. "I know nothing of a child I supposedly fathered."

Johnathan braced himself against the wall, waving the pistol in his hand. He slowly cocked the flintlock hammer, steadying the gun.

"The weapon is primed, Ryan," he said, attempting to stand free from the wall.

"You are drunk, Johnathan, and will benefit Janielle little hanging from a rope."

"Janielle is spoiled for me by your use," Johnathan

202

snapped. "All decent men in the Carolinas will thank me for what I am about to do."

Ryan whirled away from Johnathan's range, grasping at the pistol in his hand. The impact set off the charge.

Ryan reeled as the lead ball struck his chest. First the shock, then a searing pain. His eyes clouded, his belly was swimming.

Johnathan fumbled with the hot barrel, ramming, reloading the smoking pistol, leveling it again at Ryan.

Ryan fought to hold consciousness as savage pain tore through his chest, spreading to his arm. A trickle of blood dripped from his knuckles. Faintly he heard the familiar click of the cock set.

He spun in a second, catching Johnathan about the waist, charging him, knocking him into the wall. His blood smeared Johnathan's face as he grasped him about the throat.

Johnathan kicked at him, grabbing, twisting at Ryan's bleeding arm. They fell, rolling across the floor, grappling and lunging for the pistol that lay near the desk. Ryan's fist crashed into Johnathan's face, the soft nose bones crunching beneath his blow.

Ryan struggled to his knees, kicking Johnathan away from him. Johnathan moaned, clutching his bleeding face. He moved swiftly, grabbing Ryan's ankle. Ryan swerved, bringing his boot heel down hard on Johnathan's outstretched hand.

Ryan was beyond control now. The pain enraged him. He pulled himself up to the desk, leaning against it, watching Johnathan strain to rise.

"You fool," Ryan gasped. "No woman is worth a man's life."

Johnathan's eyes were wild. He groped for the pistol.

"There was never a time when I didn't despise you," he hissed. "When Father brought you to McClellanville I hated you. I'll see you finished yet." He plunged at Ryan.

Ryan backed away, grabbing the desk chair, raising it

203

above his head. Blood was everywhere. He could smell it, his eyes were full of it. Johnathan was out of focus.

"Ryan! For God's sake, Ryan, no!" Morris Chapman was shouting from the doorway, his voice horror stricken.

Johnathan was a red blur at his feet. His arms relaxed, the chair slid to the floor. He gazed dazedly at Morris.

"Holy God, Ryan! You would have killed your brother," Morris Chapman was sobbing.

Ryan shook himself, clutching at his bleeding arm. Morris was bent over Johnathan, somewhere in the red haze of the room.

"What in God's name are you babbling?" Ryan demanded, slumping against the desk.

Morris Chapman held his face in his hands. Slowly he raised his eyes to Ryan. "What has brought this about this Cain and Abel—brothers killing each other?"

Ryan reached across, pulling Morris Chapman up by the collar.

"What do you mean *brothers*?" he rasped.

Morris Chapman stared unblinkingly at Ryan, tears coursing down his face. His voice choked with pain.

"I am your natural father, Ryan."

"You are *what*?" Ryan stormed.

Morris swallowed hard. "It is true, Ryan. Forgive me, but it is true. Loranna and I, before—"

"Enough!" Ryan shouted, shaking his head in disbelief. "You made a whore of my mother!"

"No, Ryan, it was not like that. There was love between us. She—"

Feebly, Morris touched a hand to Ryan's shoulder. Ryan slapped it away.

"Get the hell away from me, you son of a bitch! I have had enough lies for one day!"

Morris fell back. "You are badly hurt, Ryan. Let me—"

"Your true bastard son lies there on the floor. Tend to

204

him!" Ryan paused a moment, gathering his strength. Then pulled himself erect, making it slowly across the room.

He felt the rush of cool sea air upon his face as he stumbled out into the night.

part three
SCOTLAND

chapter 21

Ryan slumped against the empty warehouse, too weakened to make the distance across the pier. Patterns of wandering green-black swirls swam before his eyes. Easier to rest here, away from faces, voices, lies. Searing numbness spread into his arm and chest. Fingering the wound, staring glassy-eyed down at bloody fingertips, he wondered. Nothing could have prepared him for this day.

Dizzily he watched circlets of red and green mast lights nodding to him from across the harbor. Strangely, his only concern was to be left alone. Sleep through the pain. Forget.

A rough black hand touched his shoulder. Ryan jerked instinctively, forced awake by the jagged pain surging through his chest. A low grunt came from the massive face looming above him.

"Get away, you black bastard," Ryan snarled, pushing at the hulking form. He was slipping down, limp, unconnected to himself. The coiling was rapid, finally stretched free, swallowing him in a pitchy sea of oblivion.

Wyler McGee choked, snoring in fitful slumber. Swearing, he rose from the squatty berth aboard the *Waverly*, stumbling across the second mate's cabin, locating his bottle of usquebach. He fumbled with the stubborn cork, finally setting the bottle to his mouth. He spit the grainy pieces of cork into the chamber pot, wiping his mouth with the back of his hand. He took a long pull from the neck, shuddering as the whiskey fired his belly. He paused midway to his second drink.

Something was amiss. The reddish hair along his neck bristled. He strained, hearing nothing above the rhythmic slap of the current's waves against the *Waverly*'s red hull.

"Likely the sheep in the forehold—should have left 'em in the warehouse pens 'til Friday," he muttered, glancing out the slanted aft deck opener.

Suddenly he heard it. A pitched howl arose from main deck, followed by muffled shouts, scuffling of feet. The stern watch was alerted. Before he could make the distance to the updeck passage, the disturbance was upon him.

"Holy God," Wyler gasped, shrinking from the bizarre form lurking in the cabin way.

The giant black, his shoulders filling the passage, swayed slightly with the burden he carried in his massive arms. His bare, heavily scarred chest was splotched with fresh blood.

Wyler remained motionless, his gaze level, watching the giant black. The crew, armed, gathered near the base of the steps. They retreated when Wyler waved them back. He must proceed carefully.

The massive black man panted, laboring to speak. The words formed a gutteral dialect that Wyler couldn't fathom. In the dimly lighted passage, Wyler tried for a glimpse of the man that the black held in his arms.

Suddenly, without warning, the hulking black advanced on Wyler, his unrecognizable speech more rapid, urgent.

Wyler had one quick look at the unconscious man's face. "Jesus, me man! It be Ryan," he croaked.

Wyler grapsed a belaying pin from the hook, daring the fearsome black to come nearer. "Get to the orlop and fetch the Cuban." Wyler spoke quickly to the second mate, who was hovering near the door.

Wyler circled the black man, sensing no urgent attack. The man's tongue was moving hurriedly with sounds lost to Wyler. A steady dribble of dark blood splattered on the boards at his feet.

After a few minutes the second mate reappeared, bringing with him a slight, dark Spaniard whose eyes bulged with fear when he beheld the sight in the cabin.

Wyler's eyes fastened on the giant black as he spoke across him to the Cuban.

"Enrico, man! This brute speaks a tongue I canna' grasp. Me knows the man he carries. Tell him no harm will abide him, only let me tend the man," Wyler said distinctly.

Enrico, the Cuban, nodded obediently, beginning a discourse into one of the many African dialects he spoke. He had signed aboard the *Waverly* in Wilmington, after Wyler had initially rejected him because of his wiry frame.

"Ye do not stand strong enough, man," Wyler had said gruffly.

"I am strong, el Capitan, and I have no fear of ratlines," Enrico had boasted. "And, señor, I speak native dialects from having served aboard a slaver from Jamaica."

That had convinced Wyler to take him on crew standing, and Wyler was at this moment thanking his own good judgment for having done so.

The glistening giant, sweat coursing down his massive face, remained impassive while Enrico faltered through the dialects. Wyler shifted impatiently, considering rushing him. Moments dragged.

"Christ, man," Wyler swore at Enrico, watching a wolfish smile edge across the black man's face.

Enrico paused, wiping his face with his hands. He scratched at a greasy curl along the nape of his neck. Thoughtfully, his voice slipped into a base tremolo, the gutteral sounds breaking in heaving rhythm.

The huge black man stiffened, listening intently. Slowly he turned to face the Cuban, who was speaking to him in his own language. Their exchange began.

Wyler swung his arms helplessly, finally jamming a fist into his palm. Enrico held up his hand, brushing aside the towering giant, moving close to Wyler.

"Capitan, I have your answers," Enrico said proudly. "The black man comes from the Kalahari Desert, a village, called Kakid. He relates that *su hombre* befriended him when he was chained in the marshes, and he was followed him since that day. Tonight he found him on the north dock, and he does not *comprehende* how he received his wound. He say he watch *el hombre* come to the *buque* and thinks he has *amigos* here. He begs to stay aboard."

Wyler stroked his full red beard, stepping toward the berth, motioning to the black man to bring Ryan.

"Tell the bloody giant to lay him soft," Wyler said to Enrico.

Wyler moved briskly into the passageway. "Wilson! Fetch the pram and secure the Spanish surgeon from the *Cristobal*. He be the nearest help to hand. Fetch clean linen! Move, man!" Wyler bellowed.

The crew scurried up the deck ladder. Wyler turned back inside the cabin, lifting a stack of steamed flannel from his sea chest. Swiftly he tore away the bloodied clots of Ryan's shirt, packing and pressing the flannel into the wound.

"Need to stop the flow," he muttered, his rough calloused hands moving with urgency. "Where is that goddamned Spaniard?"

Signal watch blew softly, indicating a craft starboard. In a while the elegant Spanish barber, dressed in shimmering sea-green satin, appeared in the doorway. Wyler bristled with instant dislike.

Scowling, he said, "Me man here requires your skill. I canna' staunch the blood."

The Spaniard bowed politely, snapping his long fingers for an assistant to bring forth his elaborate case of tools.

Ceremoniously the case was opened, revealing the brassy cutting knives. The surgeon's fingers groped about the wound, fingering its depth. He recoiled when Ryan's blood spurted out unexpectedly, flecking his satin breeches.

"Madre de Dios, su amigo sangras!" The barber straightened, ruffled by the contact. Quickly he shook his dark head.

"Captain, the wound is fatal, for the ball has broken apart within him. See how he bleeds?" his thick accent slurred the English. "I fear he will be lost before dawn," he concluded grimly.

Wyler shot him a hard look. His temper blared forth. "Some goddamn barber you be! Get yer fancy ass from me ship! I'll tend him meself!"

The dark Spaniard stared incredulously at Wyler, glancing over his shoulder at the black giant, lounging in the doorway.

"As you order, senor," he said reservedly, bowing slightly. "However, your friend breathes his last hours."

"Be gone!" Wyler shouted, his fists clenched, watching the Spaniard sweep from the cabin. Damned if he didn't smell perfume on the bastard.

Wyler bent over Ryan, placing a finger beneath Ryan's nostrils. "He breathes thin, Enrico," Wyler sighed.

Ryan stirred, moaning. His eyelids fluttered apart.

Startled, Wyler pressed close. "No, me man. Wyler will not let ye die. But ye must fight for life. Ken ye hear me, lad?"

Ryan's mouth twitched as he caught at Wyler's hand. His words were feeble, not yet a whisper. "Heel—heel to sea, Wyler," he rasped. Struggling for breath, he closed his eyes. "I order it," he gasped, already bridged into unconsciousness.

Wyler felt hot prickles behind his misting eyes. He turned his face aside.

"Ye be daft, man," he breathed aimlessly. "Ye would wish yer wake to be at sea. Me'll not commit yer shroud to the sea. No, man! Not before I try!" He jerked the blanket over Ryan's chest and stomped from the cabin.

The first rosy blushes of dawn roamed the eastern sky as Wyler went above deck. The crew was already about the sailing order given earlier. Wyler had considered the matter of Ryan's last request, aware of the penalties of sailing without harbor clearance. Ryan might not live to know his request was not fulfilled. These were pressing circumstances and harbor officials might be lenient. The cargo and stores were aboard for the regular sailing date next week, and most probably a few hours from the harbor would find the *Waverly* returning. Wyler could depend on the crew's loyalty.

"Before God, I canna' deny the lad his wish," Wyler decided. His eyes swept the ship. Everything was in order as it should be.

The familiar order resounded across the deck.

"Heave short," Wyler boomed.

Methodically, the crew moved about the capstan on the forecastle head, the traveler cable coming in slowly. They hove short with the cable, until only a few fathoms remained to draw in. All sails were loosed.

"Set the tops'ls," Wyler thundered, watching the breeze catch the six topsails on the main and mizzen masts. Always the tingle in his belly when the heavy canvas began to fill.

The *Waverly* nosed into the current. The windlass was manned again and the anchor hove up, held only by a length of cable equal to the depth of sea water.

"Up and down," the second mate shouted, indicating the readiness phase.

"Break her out," Wyler shouted above the wind.

The *Waverly* pivoted with the backed foreyards canting, until she was headed seaward. She eased forward like a bird eager for flight.

"For ye, lad. We heel to sea." Wyler spoke brokenly, staring out at the universe of waiting wave falls.

The anchor would remain cockbilled, should he decide to return to Charleston harbor within the next few hours. Glancing at the new sun crouching on the pastel horizon, he went below.

Startled, Enrico leaped from the wooden bench near Ryan's berth as Wyler entered the cabin. He twitched nervously. "El Capitán, the man cries in his agonies," he stammered.

Wyler nodded indifferently, glancing at the black giant standing by the narrow port slit, watching the sea slip away. The black turned confident eyes on Wyler.

Enrico moved restlessly, following Wyler's movements.

"The black man—we talk more. This name is 'Thrudhah' in his own tongue. He say it is a small bird in their desert. He say his father is king. He tell me about the big man who he call. He say Rión take off his chains when he is hurt, and he not forget."

Irritably Wyler waved him to silence. "Save yer jabber. I need to think," he gritted.

He looked hard at Ryan. The pallor was chalky, no tinge of natural hue. He watched the padding on Ryan's chest fill again. He recalled watching a Norwegian shipwright probe for and pull a shot of cannon from a mate's chest. But how near the man's heart, he had forgotten. A careless slip and it cut life. Waiting, the wound will fester or Ryan will bleed to death. How had the shipwright stopped the bleeding after he took the pieces out? Wyler shook his head, trying to remember. The coal pan. Hell, he did it with the coal pan!

"Enrico!" Wyler bellowed. "It be me plan to take the

ball from his chest. I need 'Thrudhah,' or whatever the hell his name is, to secure him. It must be tight, for his squirmin' will kill him. Fetch Wilson and the shipwright and explain to the black what we do. I no want him attackin' me when I use the knife on Ryan."

"Aye, Capitan," Enrico replied, his eyes wide with terror. "But, me Capitan, *por Dios*, the man is close to death. *Tener medio!*"

"Stay or go, Enrico," Wyler fumed. "It not be a sight for a weakling."

Enrico spoke rapidly to Thrudhah. Fearfully he turned back to Wyler. "He understands, senor—but—"

"God's truth," Wyler swore. "Cease your womanish jibber and be gone! If the lad pulls about, me'll learn the cause of this. *Now, do as I order!*"

The *Waverly*'s cutwater, its hull gripping the water well, split the sea cleanly as a fresh trade wind from the coast puffed its sails. The brilliant sapphire sky held a resplendent late summer sun high at noonday mark. The apprentice shipwright worked unhurriedly, greasing the steering gear, a job he usually did on Saturday morn.

With the sailing advanced a full week, he was doing many in-dock tasks with the *Waverly* under sail. He had moved to a position where he could watch the passageway for the captain. The shattering screams from below had finally ceased. Wilson had remarked that the man below owned the *Waverly*.

Unconcerned with activity above deck, Wyler washed the blood from his roughened hands, splashing handfuls of cool water onto his sweat-drenched face. He leaned across the water pail, sighing tiredly.

The second mate moved to his elbow, proudly handing him the whole of the rounded lead ball, the small pieces neatly fitted together.

"You got them all, sir." Wilson smiled at Wyler.

"By damn, I should ha'," Wyler agreed. "Eh,

shipwright, me thinks I ruined yer pincers," he chuckled, examining the bent angle of the jaws.

"Is of no mind, Captain. I have others," the mate replied.

Wyler leaned against the table, glancing toward the corner of the cabin where Enrico lay sprawled in a dead faint. "Toss some water to him, Wilson. Me warned him it was a bloody go."

The giant black hovered above Ryan, regarding Wyler with questioning eyes. The smell of burning flesh hung heavily in the small cabin.

"When Enrico comes about, he'll explain to you about cauterizing the wound," Wyler said softly to the undiscerning black man. "The coal pan was necessary, though brutal."

Wyler pulled the chair between his legs, facing the berth. Thinking at first there might be two wounds in Ryan's chest, he had probed from two directions. Surprised to find only one spot where the leaden ball from a flintlock hand gun had struck, he still puzzled over the shattering lead after it had borne into the flesh. He could only guess the lead was fragmented with age.

Enrico was sitting up, his dark eyes glazed. Slowly they focused, resting on Wyler. "He lives, señor?"

"He does," Wyler said gruffly. "The bleedin' was furious, but me ha' staunched it with the coal pan."

Enrico retched, remembering what had caused his faint.

Wyler moved to the cabinet, drawing a bottle of usquebach from the lower shelf. He took a long pull, offering the bottle to Enrico. Thoughtfully he gazed down at Ryan, watching the labored breath, ragged but strong.

"Tell your friend Thrush that he sails with us until Ryan comes about. He can decide the man's fate."

Enrico struggled to his feet. "Thrudhah tell me he has had no *comida* for many days. Perhaps the capitan—"

"By God! Do I have to wet nurse every soul aboard this

214

ship! Me has charts to tend!" Wyler growled disgustedly at Enrico. "Feed the waif! Wilson, take first watch over Ryan and advise me of any change in his color! Fetch the mates to scour the blood from the planks!"

Wyler stalked from the cabin, suppressing a smile, a look of triumph on his sea-weathered face.

chapter 22

Four days out into the Atlantic, teasing westerly winds canted to a fresh southwest blow. Shuddering, the *Waverly* leaned into the stiff headwind.

Wyler stood by the helmsman, his experienced eyes watching the canvas overhead. "Keep her clean full, Wilson," he ordered, cupping his hands to his mouth.

"Ready about! Down helm!" Wyler's voice strained above the wind.

Instantly the rudder kicked the ship windward, the spanker hauling clean, free into the wind's eye. The sails on the main and mizzenmast began to fill on the new tack.

"Let go and haul," Wyler shouted, satisfied that the frigate was steadied on her new course by the wind.

Feverishly Ryan pitched in his berth below, jolted from drugged slumber by the sharp veer of the ship shifting windward. Ribbons of light stung his swollen eyes.

"Jesus," he moaned, prying cracked, splitting lips apart. The cold rim of a cup jarred his clenched teeth.

"Aye, drink it all," a light feminine voice soothed from a seemingly great distance.

Ryan felt his head exploding at the scrambled voices that buzzed around him. Weakly he tried to steer himself back into the cool quiet darkness where he felt nothing, but it eluded him. Where in the hell—

"No, and I won't!" Kip McLaughlin stormed at her uncle. "'Twas not me fault that we sailed with no warning! 'Tis a wee one and me'll not have him put below!"

"Ye canna' keep a howlin' pup in here!" Wyler boomed.

"He dinna' howl! He lays at Ryan's feet and is still! Mayhaps he even comforts the *puir* man," Kip retorted angrily.

"Animals stay below!" Wyler thundered, crashing a beefy fist down on the table near Ryan's head.

Ryan's eyes shot open. Wyler's looming figure was blurred above him. Who in holy blazes was he talking to? Ryan blinked up at them, his eyes finally focusing on the slim figure standing beside Wyler.

"Now, Master McGee, we have awakened him," Kip's soft brogue floated across to Ryan.

Hurriedly, Wyler moved about, glaring down at Ryan, a huge grin creasing the cloud of his red beard.

"Damme, rogue," he chuckled. "The lead ball me fished from yer shoulder lies yonder in the dish. 'Twill be livin' ye will!"

Through a film of pain, Ryan caught a keen trace of rose water as Kip McLaughlin edged to the side of the berth. Vibrant copper-streaked tresses swung freely at a toss of her head. Sapphire green eyes glittered down at him. She was glowing pastel made of sunrise and sea.

"'Tis glad I am that ye not be cross like me uncle." Kip smiled, wringing a cloth in the basin. "And ye be a strong man."

Ryan grinned feebly, tensing as the cold cloth touched his face. Kip bent across him, scooping a drowsy puppy up in her arms, cuddling him to her.

"Ye see, he not be troublesome," she murmured.

Wyler scowled at both of them, muttering while he scratched at his beard. "Me niece saw fit to bring 'er pet aboard. 'Tis a scummy mutt that mewls for a teat."

Undaunted, Kip floated to the doorway, giving Wyler

a knowing look. "The wee one stays above." She spoke sweetly, touching a fingertip to her full mouth, blowing a kiss to her uncle as she flounced through the doorway.

Fuming, Wyler slumped heavily on the foot of the berth, disregarding the painful groan that escaped Ryan's lips.

"Hell's breath!" he swore. "Kip was waitin' aboard the *Waverly* while the *Devonshire* readied for sail. In all the ruckus, me forgot her bein' here. She be a spirited lass pampered by 'er parents, 'en spoiled by 'er brothers. Damme, if me don't *ken* the McGee blood flaring in her veins!"

Gradually Wyler calmed, turning his attention to Ryan. "How do ye fare, man?"

Ryan stared up at the swaying, blurred timbers of the cabin, trying to absorb the reality to which he had awakened. The *Waverly*, Wyler, the open sea and a woman aboard. Destinations were unimportant. He was alive.

"Who aimed the ball at ye, lad?" Wyler asked intently, leaning closer.

Wyler's question was hollow in his ears. The drumming in his head threatened to explode. His own voice sounded strange. "Johnathan Chapman," he managed finally.

"Holy God!" Wyler erupted, bolting from the berth. "Me thought ye be friends! The giant *nigra* brought ye aboard, telling he found ye on the north dock. Do ye recall ordering me to sail yer ship from the harbor?"

Ryan nodded incoherently, tumbling toward oblivion. Wyler's voice droned, faded, and was silenced.

Evan Reed slapped frayed reins into the hands of the Patterson stable boy, casting a distrustful glance at the awesome sprawl of Patterson Manor. He had refused the first message from Harrelson Mallen summoning him to treat Kaylee. The second had brought his response.

The events of the last few days were bewildering. News

from the Spanish man-o-war, the *Cristobal*, in Charleston harbor, that a man had been shot aboard the *Waverly*, Ryan's sudden disappearance on the eve of his marriage to Kaylee, and Johnathan Chapman's scurried retreat under guard to McClellanville. And now Kaylee's inevitable hysterics.

Beautiful, treacherous Kaylee, a forgotten bride. By damn, how did she feel being the one rejected? He could almost gloat over the fact, except for the pity he felt for her. Somehow he dreaded the confrontation today, remembering still a stirring desire for her. Kaylee wanted him now—not the throbbing taste of his manhood that he had ached to plunge within her, but the taste of his healing skills—his goddamn services! Christ, he needed a drink.

Janielle opened the wide gilded door, her violet eyes swallowing him. Suddenly he forgot it all. Cuffing the road dust from his faded British officer's coat, fighting a moment of awkwardness over his mussed appearance, he smiled warmly down at her.

"Good day, milady," he breezed.

Janielle flashed a dubious smile, strolling ahead of him into the elaborate receiving hall. She turned slowly, resting a slim hand on his arm.

"They are all upstairs, Evan. Kaylee's screams have ceased, but she is dazed. She needs you," Janielle said quietly.

Evan drew a heavy breath, his thoughts racing. "And I need you," he said silently, watching her trim figure move from him, noting the sloping waist that he could encircle with his hand, the swing of her white-gold hair that shimmered like spun sunlight.

"Have you been well, Janielle?" he asked pointedly.

Janielle turned a lazy smile on him, her violet eyes tinged with softness. "I am not the patient today, Evan."

Buoyed with an arrogant confidence after his encounter with Janielle, Evan met the sea of grave faces awaiting him in Kaylee's chamber. Aurora Mallen remained stiffly erect in her chair by the window, apparently beyond emotion. John Patterson clustered near Harrelson Mallen, his limp hand spread across Mallen's slumped shoulder.

Evan's gaze struck Kaylee's slim figure standing near the French doors, dressed in her wedding gown of billowing sarcenet silk. Intricate silver brocade touched the edges of her filmy gauze veil. Possessively, Kaylee held a wilted bouquet of miniature white tea roses against her pale cheek.

John Patterson moved across the room to Evan, his voice barely a whisper. "She waits for Ryan. She believes she is at Challey."

Battle shock at sea was not unknown to Evan. He had seen stout sailing men reduced to quaking imbeciles under its effects. Their minds could not cope with the untoward gore of battle. Itoo's people, the Yemassee, had a name for it—"moon death." There was a potion among Itoo's peculiar herbs given to the stricken ones. The curing effects were violent but Itoo claimed it "emptied the moon death in the soul."

What in the hell was he thinking? He was no Yemassee medicine god. Most civilized surgeons agreed that a sickness of the mind was incurable. Swiftly he approached Harrelson Mallen.

"What have the physicians in Charleston done for her?" he asked quietly.

Mallen turned despairing swollen eyes up at him. "One wanted to purge her, another to bleed her, a third wanted to set her in ice bags," he rasped brokenly. "Nothing I could agree to."

Evan scowled disapprovingly. "The screaming rages— how long between them?"

"This morning at daybreak was the last one. She neither eats nor sleeps, only stands by the window waiting. She'll not allow anyone to remove the dress,"

Harrelson Mallen added, his voice choking with emotion.

Evan glanced again at Kaylee's willowy shadow. "I have a potion that may release the barrier in her mind. Its effects are somewhat odd, but safe enough. If you agree to its use for your daughter, I must make it clear that the room must be left to myself and the Yemassee who attends me. I will suffer no interruptions."

Shocked silence followed Evan's pronouncement. Evan ignored the gathering murmurs of disagreement, moving close to Kaylee and turning her gently to him. Hollow, vacant eyes stared through him, beyond him.

Mallen crooked a knobby finger at him, motioning him across the room, a disgusting gesture that always made Evan bristle. Foul aristocrats! Even under duress their revolting habits accented their pompous, stupid airs. He turned a defiant back to Mallen, studying the dull glaze in Kaylee's sea-green eyes.

Mallen nudged his elbow. "Do you trust you can make her normal again?" he wheezed nervously.

"The threads of a mind are easily snarled, Mr. Mallen," Evan replied curtly. "Her mind has closed to the reality of what she cannot accept as true. If Ryan were here, perhaps his presence would restore her. Meanwhile, I can administer the Yemassee potion for three days and witness the result. The decision is yours."

Abruptly, he turned aside, feeling the wild need of fresh, sweet air. "I will be downstairs, gentlemen," he said, nodding briefly to them and hurriedly taking his leave.

Janielle lingered in the gracefully latticed belvedere, watching skittish glow worms weave tiny buttons of light through encroaching night shadows. A hushed golden spread across the velvet plush of emerald lawn. Evan would join her soon.

She sighed heavily, relieved to see the full autumn moon bursting above the cedar trees, lighting the long veils of silvery moss that clung to their scruffy branches. She stretched slim arms above her head, lacing slender fingers through her white-gold hair.

Let them think what they will, she thought defiantly. Johnathan had formally ended their long engagement with a message of insincere brevity that had arrived from McClellanville. A wedding she knew would never take place after the morning with Ryan at Challey. Her father's shock of outrage was stifled by Kaylee's pressing illness. Johnathan's timing proved a trifle raw, but what matter? She was free.

Evan's tall figure, silhouetted against the withering golden twilight, was striding toward her. His arrogant presence at Patterson Woods the last few days had charmed away the gravity of Kaylee's madness. Evan remarked little to her bout Kaylee, only to say there were signs of lucidity. Janielle cared little. Broken hearts were not fatal, only uncomfortable.

Breathlessly, Evan dropped down beside her, the aging wicker sofa creaking under his sudden weight. "I should have saddled my mount," he complained wearily. "This spot must be halfway downriver."

Janielle laughed softly, inhaling the heady masculine scent of him. A tingling warmth spread into her breasts, peaking until her nipples drew taut. She caught a sharp breath, startled at her quick desire for a man she had once loathed.

Evan's unguarded, smoky eyes had followed her constantly about the manor during the last few days and there was no mistaking the signs in them.

How would it be with Evan? she wondered. Not bitter hurtful wrenching from her arms afterward, not the poignant rippling of Ryan's brutal love, not the possessive, uncertain tenderness of Brandon's lovemaking. With Evan, she didn't know.

Evan knew. He had explored the intimate caverns of her femininity, touched the core of her arousal, and taken

222

a lifeless mass from her womb. Janielle—on a blurred winter night, violet eyes that penetrated the fortress of his dead emotions. Roughly he had covered her with Brandon's patched coverlet and bolted from the cottage, fleeing the raging emotional storm that threatened his comfortable love grave. A deep grave where his affection for a woman was entombed. He had weathered it—or had he?

"Janielle," he said, touching her face, tilting her chin up to him. Slivers of moonlight flecked her white-gold hair, a cloud of shimmery gossamer that caressed him.

Janielle gently led his warm fingers to her swollen breast. It had been so long—since she had felt a man's strong hands on her body. Evan's mouth was swallowing her, liquid, sweet fire that burned through her, arousing her.

Smoothly, effortlessly, his weight was on her. She lay sweetly open, urging him, hurrying him, the tempo of passion drumming wildly, begging release. Still, the velvet jab of his manhood startled her. In moon-quivering shadows, she looked up at the figure that covered her, filled her.

At that moment she caught herself. "God, what am I doing," she moaned, struggling against the force that joined her tightly to its root. Too late, she was lifting to Evan, reaching farther to catch him until she could expand no further. Savagely, she rode the satiny-crested wave with him, bursting to absorb his spilling fountain until it dissolved within her.

Ryan! Ryan had done this to her, made her aware of an aching wildness, an unleashed craving that defied her senses. Could it be that with any man the demand had to be fulfilled? But only with Ryan could it ever be complete, fully complete.

Evan's arms trembled as he tumbled onto his side, drawing Janielle against him. Janielle was more, much more than he had reckoned. He felt gloriously empty, drained, peacefully free. Johnathan Chapman was a fool.

Tenderly, Evan lowered his mouth, kissing Janielle softly, his hungry fingers still grazing her slackened, silky breasts. In a moment he would be ready for her again.

"Johnathan Chapman is an imbecile," Evan breathed against her throat. He chuckled deep in his chest. "Your pompous betrothed was aghast when I charged him with fathering your child. Forgive me, Janielle, I shouldn't have told him, but the temptation to torment him was overpowering. To leave you without waiting to learn if you conceived—"

Janielle bolted upright, shaking loose from Evan's arms, tossing her head wildly to clear it. No, no, she couldn't have heard right! Why, before God, did men always ruin the precious moments after lovemaking with their hideous words!

Furiously, she caught at her bodice, grasping it closed. "You told Johnathan that I carried his child?" she repeated bitterly. "Small wonder he was shocked. He believed me a virgin."

Evan released a sharp gasp. Roughly he reached for her, pulling her to him. "What did you say, Janielle?" he demanded.

Janielle flung her head wildly about, a low bitter laugh easing from her throat. "You are the fool, Evan."

"Christ, Janielle—I don't—" he stammered.

"Johnathan knew nothing of a child," she gritted. "The child was Ryan's."

Evan scrambled to his feet, catching at her arm. "I have no reason to regret what I did, Janielle. Nor do I care whose seed you carried. That lies in the past. It is tonight, now, this moment that I regard." Gently, he bent his head to kiss her.

Achingly, Janielle savored him, tasted the scent of him, drawn to the sharp-sweet tenderness he gave her. At this moment some of the pain locked inside her escaped.

"Marry me, Janielle," Evan breathed, holding her to him.

Janielle glanced up at the glittering sprinkle of stars strewn across the blue-black heavens. Her eyes trailed the moon, now a golden orb over the Santee. Still Ryan. Always Ryan.

Aboard the *Waverly*, Ryan eased onto his good side, his eyes watching dancing slivers of moonlight perform a macabre spectacle above the berth. The ship locked into a steady roll, dispelling the shadowy moonbeams above him, bringing a quiet vision of white-gold hair, haunting violet eyes and softness. Always softness when Janielle challenged his thoughts. She felt very close at this moment. Cool jasmine fragrance drifted over him, her fragrance. Briefly he sampled the gentleness before sleep overtook him.

chapter 23

"Sail! Yon!" Wilson shouted from his perch atop the mainmast, pointing his arm to the eastern horizon.

Cruising the horizon line, the *Santissima Trinidad* plowed heavily through the seas, her one hundred and thirty guns mounted arrogantly along her gangways. Veering into the trade path, the majestic Spanish man-o-war presented her royal colors, the wine-red crosses stamped on the sails bulging under full canvas.

Below deck, Ryan heard Wyler's orders to furl the British flag and send the tattered French colors aloft on a second traveler. The green Coast Merchants' flag whipped atop the job boom, identifying the *Waverly* as an American merchantman.

Ryan chuckled at Wyler's *ruse de guerre*. "That should certainly confound the Spanish *almirante*," he thought, "hopefully enough that they will not chance to board." Weakly, he leaned against the slanted port opening, watching the awesome *Santissima* loom nearer broadside.

Cautiously, the man-o-war hovered at gun range, shadowing the *Waverly*. Ryan tensed, waiting for the bow shot signal. Minutes pulled by. Then, apparently satisfied, the *Santissima* stretched full into the southerly wind, rocking the *Waverly* in her wave pattern.

Wyler stomped down the passageway and entered the cabin, wiping beading sweat from his face. "Now that be a ship, lad: Did ye see her width?"

"I saw her at closer range in Martinique when I was outrunning a French brigantine," Ryan commented dryly, rubbing a damp towel along his starkly protruding ribs.

"Me thinks me *ruse de guerre* confused her," Wyler said.

"Perhaps," Ryan agreed, "though her first admiral, Aguilar, and I have shared the gaming tables and wenches at Marie Cecile's in New Orleans," he added. "In fact, I still carry some of his king's doubloons."

Wyler scratched nervously at his red beard. "So that's why he dinna' fire at the *Waverly*."

"Not this time, but with Spaniards, who's to know?"

"Nah—we could ha' outrun her under half-sail," Wyler boasted.

"Not if she lowered her culverin flackers at us. The *Santissima* as always undercanvassed and overgunned and grains to leeward. A schooner could take her but for the range she carries."

"Ye sound like a piratin' man again," Wyler said. "Yer Carolina letter of marque from the general will do ye little good now that the war is over."

"I own a respectable merchantman now." Ryan laughed bitterly. "Or did."

"And ye still have stolen British gold ridin' yer pockets," Wyler snarled.

"What gold I have left is in Charleston," Ryan retorted, "and most of it helped us win the war."

Wyler stamped his foot angrily. "Ye not be even a fit pirate captain any more! Ye be more a rattle of tall bones!"

Ryan winced, pulling a soft woolen shirt over the healing burn left from the coal pan that Wyler had used. "I am branded like a Challey slave, only lower and

227

larger," he seethed, casting a fiery glance at Wyler.

"That be me thanks!" Wyler shouted, springing to his feet.

Suddenly Ryan threw back his head and laughed. "It will give my women another scar to intrigue them on a cold wintry night."

Wyler fought a smile. "Damme, lad, I ha' thought ye'd had yer fill of womanly woes."

Ryan edged back onto the berth, sighing wearily. "In truth, Wyler, I have. Enrico tells me we've been at sea for twenty-nine days. What port do we take? London?"

Wyler shifted uncomfortably. "That be a matter me wish to discuss with ye, lad. Ye're mendin', but only fair. Ye need strong meat and fresh fruits to fatten ye. 'Tis me thought to take ye to Scotland. Me kin will welcome ye and see ye fit again."

Ryan shook his head. "No, Wyler. We sail where I say and I go where I choose."

"And where do that be, lad? We carry full cargo and need to unload her. Another week will see us short of food hold. Could be the Royal Admiralty Court will be seekin' for ye in London like before. And ye hardly be sound enough to match wits with 'em now."

Ryan folded his long arms across his chest, pondering the truth in Wyler's words. He was indeed weary of struggle. Ceaseless nightmares of the fire at Challey, the searing gunshot from Johnathan Chapman's pistol, the painful realization of his ties to the barrister, Morris Chapman—Janielle—Kaylee, tormenting jumbled visions that pounded at him, draining him.

"What say ye, lad?" Wyler asked finally.

"The North Sea is a damnable place," Ryan grumbled.

"Aye, perhaps. But Crail is sweetness," Wyler said. "Ye'll like the McLaughlins. Me know it."

At this moment," Ryan growled, "I like no one and no place." When he glanced up again, Wyler was gone.

Late October sun dappled slaty gray waves lapping the shoreline of Crail harbor. From the foredeck of the *Waverly* Ryan gazed at the Fifeshire houses lining the harbor, built solidly of fitted harled stone, most with Dutch influence of crow-stepped gables and pantile roofs. Polished cobblestone streets, worn glassy smooth by North Sea gales, wandered the length of the port.

"Aye, see, Ryan? There be Crail!" Kip McLaughlin smiled, nudging him excitedly. Her reddish curls were brushed neatly about her face, her liquid green eyes flashing with happiness as she met Ryan's sullen gaze.

Ryan choked back a biting comment, still angered over Wyler's decision to sail to Scotland.

"Ye'll be content here. I know ye will," Kip murmured, leaning toward him.

"So I am informed," he said sarcastically, gripping the wide varnished rail on deckside.

A modest carriage rumbled along the cobblestones to the docking moor, disturbing the softly quiet afternoon of unhurried activity on the pier. Ryan noticed only a few small fishing boats piled high with lobster traps.

Two young men bounded from the carriage, waving at the ship, cupping their hands to their mouths. The heavy Scottish slur of one of the voices reached across the water.

"Ho, Wyler!" We spotted yer sail a mile off point! Have ye Kip aboard?"

"Aye, Blake!" Wyler shouted back, watching the *Waverly*'s anchor plunge into the harbor shallows. Slowly the dock bridge swung against the cobblestone landing block.

The two Scotsmen raced along the bridge, leaping the final distance to the *Waverly*'s foredeck. Both reached instantly for Kip.

Ryan watched disjointedly as Wyler clapped the men on the back, glancing away as Kip showered kisses on both of them. His legs ached with the strain of standing and the damnable weakness that plagued him was threatening again. He leaned heavily against the rail, steadying himself.

"What in God's name does a giant be doin' aboard?" Cameron McLaughlin gasped, staring up at Thrush.

"He be makin' a fine sailor," Wyler roared, sobering as he caught the ashen pallor or Ryan's gaunt face. Swiftly he made a space through the gathering.

"Cameron! Blake! Give me a help here—Deverel be ill," Wyler said hurriedly, moving up deck. "Tell Rowena that he's to be put abed at Hawksmoor and tended. Me'll be about when the *Waverly* is in berth."

Wyler moved beside Ryan, taking his arm. "Ryan, lad, these gentlemen be Kip's brothers. They'll be takin' ye—"

Wyler's words were lost on Ryan, who had quietly collapsed against the rail.

Hawksmoor, Fifeshire, the home of Ramsay McLaughlin, retained the prestige of being one of the oldest dwellings in northern Scotland. Set in vivid green background, the majestic walls of the sixteenth century dwelling, harled and splashed a silvery-pearl hue, exhibited angle and staircase turrets jutting forward from the incline of the house, displaying an unusual type of corbelling—a stone version of the jettying of half-timbered houses. James Smith, master mason from Glasgow, was responsible for the wrought-iron appointments and stone piers surmounted by classical sculptured urns. Fields of white and yellow daffodils surrounded the wide approach to Hawksmoor, nodding drowsily to the skipping winds from the North Sea.

Ryan listened discontentedly to the soft wailing of the wind straining against the sturdy window of Hawksmoor manor, comforted to see the first splashes of daybreak. Jerking the plaid Tartan blanket closer around his chest, he watched the naked maytree outside his window shivering in the morning wind. He had slept the better of two full days, waking only to relieve himself and swallow the mouthfuls of hot, tangy broth that were offered to him.

Damn if he hadn't felt better aboard the *Waverly*. As soon as he was stronger, he'd leave Hawksmoor, on foot if necessary.

He glanced up as Kip McLaughlin slipped quietly through the doorway, carrying a steaming breakfast tray. Unexpectedly, Ryan felt ravenously hungry. He ran a hand across his heavy beard, wishing for a bath before breakfast.

"Today, ye eat," Kip announced, smiling as she set the tray on his bedside table. She drew the cloth aside and lifted the silver covers from the plates. Bannocks were swimming in hot, thick butter, A dish of warm raspberries floated in thick cream. And tea—expertly brewed, English tea.

Deftly, Kip tucked a white linen napkin across his chest, her green eyes twinkling with merriment.

"'Twas never we ha' a guest at Hawksmoor who stayed abed so much and who looked like the devil's spawn of a morning," she teased as Ryan raised up on his elbows.

"So, I am a guest? I thought I was a frail invalid." Ryan smiled up at her.

"No, invalids be old and rickety, and ye not be either," Kip breezed, tossing her copper-streaked hair over her shoulder. She strolled to the window, carelessly arranging a bowl of fresh cut flowers.

"Do ye like the hunt?" she asked, gazing out at the timid sunlight.

"Yes, if your mounts aren't frozen with the cold."

"It not be cold yet—the autumn is still about," Kip replied, slowly regarding Ryan while he sipped his tea. "Be it true ye were shot in a quarrel over a woman?"

Ryan choked on his tea. Goddamn Wyler! He swore silently, shoving aside his tray. Wyler's usquebach had undoubtedly loosened his bold Scottish tongue and by now all the McLaughlins had probably heard the story. When Wyler returned from uncargoing the *Waverly*, he would assume command again and Wyler could seek a new captaincy.

He scowled darkly at Kip. "You may take the tray out, *now!*"

Kip floated easily across the room. "Don't be cross, Ryan. Ye raved in yer pain aboard ship while I tended ye, and the lady's name—ye kept—"

"I do not wish to be reminded," Ryan snapped. "I do wish a hot bath and *privacy*."

"Cameron wished me to ask if ye play chess. He thought ye'd like some diversion from sleep," Kip said warmly, ignoring the furious expression on Ryan's face.

"If he is a master opponent, yes. Otherwise, no," Ryan said sullenly.

"Ye dinna' answer me first question." Kip spoke dreamily. "Was she very beautiful?"

Ryan lunged for her, gripping her small hands in his.

"Kip," he said fiercely, "you have much to learn of the ways of love. Until you do—"

"Ah, but ye will teach me," Kip murmured, her mouth close to his. "And Blake be havin' some worsted for ye that his tailor is bringing for a fittin' today. Ye be taller than Blake, but there be a full bolt, and maybe enough for a kilt like Wyler's. And even ye may like some leggins from Argyll," Kip said, rushing the words before she burst into laughter. Carelessly her reddish tresses spilled across Ryan's shoulder.

Ryan threw up his hands, forcing a smile. "You make it difficult to stay angry, Kip," he said softly.

"Ye canna' ever be angry with me," Kip said, suddenly frowning at him. "I dinna' like yer beard, Ryan Paul Deverel." Impulsively, she bent to kiss him, springing back when he moved.

Ryan laughed. "Haven't you kissed a man with a beard before?"

232

"Me only kissed Rua Bothwell, and he not be enough man yet—well—he doesn't have—" Kip faltered.

Chuckling to himself, Ryan reached for her hand, planting a light kiss in her upturned palm.

"Now be off, little one, so I can bathe and dress for the day. Tell Cameron to bring the board and we shall play," Ryan said, shoving her off the bed.

Reluctantly, Kip obeyed. She paused as she reached the door, turning back. "Was she more beautiful than I be?" she asked softly, her sea-green eyes leveling at Ryan for an instant before she disappeared through the doorway, not waiting for his reply.

Ryan tossed aside the woolen coverlet, his gaze traveling angrily around the room. The marble fireplace in the center was a study in elegance, adorned with two perfectly sculptured likenesses of Ceres on each side of the hearth. A thick Tartan plaid rug, layered in blueblack and subtle green, the clan distinction of the McLaughlins, stretched the length of the floor. Chair coverings and a Queen Anne settee were splashed with the same plaid. The room smelled wildly of new heather and white lilacs.

Impatiently, Ryan combed his dark fingers through his rumpled hair, at war with the heady scent of Scottish heather and the plain fact that he was penniless, indulging in the warm hospitality of Ramsay McLaughlin.

Ramsay McLaughlin was Scottish gentry, a renowned counterpart of Edinburgh's *legal intelligensia*. Retired now, his days were spent in writing tedious reforms and philosophies. His sons, Blake and Cameron, had assumed charge of the vast McLaughlin holdings under the bespectacled watchfulness of their father.

Kip had been the unexpected child of Ramsay and Rowena McLaughlin's later years and it was immediately clear that she reigned at Hawksmoor.

Kip was refreshing. Bluntly honest, a keen fast wit with a wild, rebellious vein that no one had bothered to tame. And for all her sixteen years, she was beautiful, the soft, firm curves of her womanhood nearing full bloom.

Ryan shrugged into a heavy robe, strolling lazily to the long window that faced north from Hawksmoor. Tufts of chilled, withered grass blended stiffly to the wind. Lowland woods stretched northward into craggy slopes, wending their way to the rise where the tumbled ruins of Hepburn tower house, once a refuge for James II, defiantly stood. Scotland was a defiant land—the medieval fortresses, scattered across the land, attested to that. And proud, like the McLaughlins, whose many battles had finally claimed Hawksmoor for their own. But one could be proud when wealthy. Like John Patterson and Morris Chapman.

Ryan shuddered suddenly as the biting edge of memory sliced through him. Wealthy one day he would be, he vowed determinedly. Whatever measures were needed, whoever was trampled in his forward path, from this time on, somehow it would come to be.

> "Aft hae I rove by bonnie Carlene
> To see the woodbine twine.
> And ilka bird sang o' it s love,
> And sae did I o'mine."

Kip's lilting voice broke with a rush of laughter as she dodged Cameron's teasing fist. Her brother, bristling with the onslaught of her mischievous prattle, had finally lost patience with her incessant baiting.

"Be God, Kip! Me'll have no more of yer annoyance about Carlene," Cameron seethed.

Kip wriggled closer to Ryan, oblivious of the disapproving looks from her brothers. "Ye be a stuffy lout," Kip said defensively, tossing her copper-streaked curls over her shoulder.

Ryan shifted Kip's body a space from him, reaching for his leather packet under the seat. Suddenly the carriage swung, jolting hard against a road stone, nearly unseating him.

Righting himself, Ryan opened the leather packet, leaning across to Cameron. Carefully he untied the parchment and spread it across his knees.

"Here Cameron," he said, pointing to a line circled on the sketch. "Lord Bothwell should place the loch bridge between these sites. Otherwise the bog will sink the shores."

Intently, Cameron studied the expertly drawn sketch, fighting the swaying of the carriage. "Aye, Ryan—but Lord Bothwell will need convincing. Me told ye he prefers stone bridges."

"And the rock he used sunk into the bogs," Ryan remarked.

"Carlene Bothwell needs no convincing," Kip interrupted tartly, "or she not be marryin' the likes of Cameron."

Ryan smiled at Cameron's indulgent smile. The last few weeks at Hawksmoor had conditioned him to the sharp banter exchanged between Kip and her older brothers. Cameron had, indeed, proved a formidable chess opponent and their afternoon games had become ritual. Their conversations, in wandering, had arrived at the point of Ryan's interest in design. Cameron had produced the necessary quills, instruments and French parchment and Ryan had set to work. The training earned during the dreary years at Brocksburg, tolerating Master Dodd's foul habits in order to excel, had resulted in an acceptable talent for construction design. At a show of his work, Ramsay McLaughlin had immediately ordered new tenant cottages at Hawksmoor, and a granary near the loch.

Cameron had arranged the meeting today at Lord Bothwell's retreat near Ceres. Ryan had agreed to study the sites where Lord Bothwell had attempted three bridges at various locations on his estate near the Eden River, all of them faltering within a short time. Ryan felt confident he could name the problem. The depression that had lingered since his arrival at Crail was finally lifting as the late night hours found him at his desk, pondering the answer to why the bridges had failed. Often the scraping of his quill against the rigid parchment lasted until dawn.

The carriage lumbered across Archbishop Sharp's Bridge, where a strange enchantment engulfed the landscape. The scattering of low houses, some of them adorned with robust heraldic devises of a sixteenth century artist, seemed to belong to another time, another land.

Kip, weary of teasing her older brother, rested her head on Ryan's shoulder, curling her slim fingers around his arm.

"Care ye to hear the legend of Archbishop Sharp's Bridge?" she asked dreamily.

Cameron and Blake McLaughlin groaned in unison.

"Perhaps later, little one," Ryan laughed as the carriage slowed near the road to Lord Bothwell's retreat.

Lord Bothwell leaned across the wide table, following Ryan's hand as he carefully described his sketches for the proposed loch bridge. Ryan eased his hip onto the table, bracing his other leg against the floor.

"I can take samples of the loam substance and test for a sound shore laying," Ryan concluded.

"Well and done, lad!" Lord Bothwell thundered, studying Ryan with a practiced eye. "If your bridge be sturdy within the year, I'll see ye well paid."

Cameron McLaughlin heaved a sigh of relief. Ryan had proceeded well, impressing Lord Bothwell with explanations that were concise and honest. Inwardly, he felt pleased with himself for judging well the tall American his uncle had brought to Hawksmoor.

Fascinated, Carlene Bothwell watched Ryan's lean, sun-darkened fingers roll the parchment into a tight cone. A curious ripple of desire swept through her. How would it feel to be caressed by those strong hands? she wondered. Kip McLaughlin had floated over to Ryan, resting her hand on Ryan's arm.

Annoyed at Kip's flagrant flirtation, Carlene tapped her foot impatiently. "Why isn't Kip out climbing the glens with Rua?" she seethed silently.

Lord Bothwell led his guests into a long banquet hall, lined on each side by mullioned windows. A collection of Scottish targes and Italian tapestries decorated the fitted stone walls. Ryan half expected a Scottish warlord to be seated at the table.

"How do ye like our Scotland?" Lord Bothwell asked Ryan, peering sharply over the rim of his crystal chalice.

"The defiance of your land intrigues me," Ryan said simply.

"Your own country has recently fought a battle of defiance against our old enemy," Lord Bothwell said. "What was your part in the struggle?"

"My struggle was at sea, sir," Ryan replied tersely.

Bowls of Scottish *haggis*, still swimming in sheep's stomach, thick spalebone stew and bashed neeps were offered to him. Politely, Ryan refused.

"Your ship, the one Wyler commands," Lord Bothwell continued, "has it seen battle?"

"French and British, and American privateering engagements, sir," Ryan said evenly, his gaze locking on Carlene Bothwell's sensuous breasts.

Carlene Bothwell was making full judgment of Ryan Deverel. Standing well above the other men, Ryan Deverel was incredibly handsome even in his gauntness. She puzzled over the long scar across the dark forehead. The tip of a knife, or perhaps a dueling sword? She blushed suddenly, remembering the hungry look in his ice-blue eyes as they raked over her during the introductions. And when he raised her fingertips to his mouth, she had trembled. He was looking at her in the same way now across the table.

"Ryan's ship be a beauty, Lord Bothwell," Cameron was saying lightly. "She has a red hull and flies all but our own Scottish flag."

Ryan shifted uneasily under Carlene Bothwell's hot gaze. Cameron had better wed her soon. The bitch was in heat. Impulsively, Ryan shoved his plate aside, turning to Kip.

"I would like to view Archbishop Sharp's Bridge before we return," he said shortly, ignoring the surprised glances from the other guests. "With your leave, gentlemen, and milady Bothwell." Bowing slightly, he lifted a startled Kip from her chair and led her from the room.

The wooded glen of Dura Den maintained a dreamlike atmosphere, rare in the bracing climate of the eastern Scottish coast. Ryan tugged his blue hill jacket closer about him as he walked beside Kip.

"Me used to stroll here with Rua Bothwell," Kip said playfully, pulling Ryan toward the slow running stream.

"Is this the place where he kissed you?" Ryan asked teasingly.

Kip's mood shifted suddenly. "Ye do make sport of me, Ryan."

"No, little one." Ryan smiled gently, placing his hands on her narrow waist.

Kip stamped her foot angrily. "Me not be a 'little one,' Ryan Deverel! Me be sixteen and a full woman! Ken ye not see?"

"I see." Ryan spoke guardedly, bending to plant a light kiss on her nose. Suddenly, Kip stood on tiptoe, reaching up to him, locking her arms about his neck. Her eager mouth sought his, warmly moist, awaiting instruction.

She was fragrant like morning heather, mingled with fresh innocence, warm, yielding against him. Ryan's hand tangled in her flaming copper tresses, pressing her to him. Demanding, fierce desire surged through him as his fingers wandered to the ribbons on her bodice. The grained ribbon slid loose between his fingers.

Suddenly Ryan stiffened, pushing her away. "We had best be returning," he said curtly.

Smoldering green eyes, swimming with passion, gazed bewilderedly up at him. "Ye do care for me. I know it," Kip breathed brokenly.

"I cannot," Ryan said quietly.

"Tell me, how can ye 'cannot,'" Kip demanded tearfully.

Ryan pulled her gently to him. "I cannot take you here in the woods, Kip—nor be the first man to possess you. A younger man, someone to cherish you—a Scotsman. It would be wrong."

"Wrong? When me wishes it with all me heart? When me ha' seen ye each day in every circumstance and find no fault? When me uncle and all me family has approved ye? No, Ryan—'tis ye who are wrong!"

"This is not the time." Ryan spoke firmly.

"Then, when we are wed?" Kip asked hesitantly, brushing furious tears aside.

Ryan swallowed the words that were on his tongue. How simple it would be to give Kip the answer she sought. A hasty flash of Janielle's face blanketed his thoughts, blurring until it faded.

"You have much to learn of love," Ryan said finally, stretching out his hand to her. Gently he entwined his fingers with hers as they strolled back down the path to Lord Bothwell's dwelling, each engaged in a private struggle with their tightly coiled emotions.

chapter 24

Ryan scraped at the stubborn limestone clay hugging his top boots. The pair he had purchased in Edinburgh were showing the effects of many weeks spent at the bridge site on the Eden. The work was resuming after the first thaw and Ryan was relieved to be spending more time out near the loch.

The chilling winter storms had subsided at last and only a thin sparkling crust of ice lingered about the edge of the loch. The shores were being raised by a select company of Lord Bothwell's tenants with James Smith, the master craftsman from Glasgow, sending Ryan a skilled assemblage of his men. The drumlin near the isthmus was being leveled to support the left framework where the shores would sink into the strand line of red sandstone.

"So, it's been settin' on peat flat," Lord Bothwell boomed when Ryan informed him of his findings.

"The loam from the forest bed could not support it," Ryan affirmed. "The limestone and sandstone gravelings from the glacial drift should hold it."

"Aye, lad. Ye be a fine one." Lord Bothwell smiled, clapping Ryan on the back as they stood overlooking the sloping bank of the Eden.

Ryan kicked loose the remaining clay from the heel of

his boot, thinking disgustedly of Carlene Bothwell. She had appeared at Hawksmoor on a rainswept day while the McLaughlins were at St. Andrews. Ryan had been alone sifting the loam samples into labeled boxes. When advised the McLaughlins were away, Carlene had asked to see Ryan Deverel.

Hastily, Ryan unrolled his shirt sleeves, fastening the lace cuffs about his wrists. He reached for his blue hill jacket as Carlene entered the small office set aside for Ryan's use.

"It is rare when all the McLaughlins are away." Carlene smiled, taking one hand from her fur muff, offering it to Ryan.

"They should be returning soon," Ryan offered politely, adjusting the collar of his coat.

"Cameron is still in Edinburgh, is he not?" Carlene's eyes conveyed a seductive glint.

"Shall we go into the main room?" Ryan asked, skimming Carlene's narrow figure.

"I prefer it in here. It's cozier," she said openly. "My father is extremely pleased with the work you are doing on his loch bridge," she added smoothly.

A sheet of rain slammed against the thick windowpane, sending a chilling draft across the room. Ryan reached for cedar logs, tossing them recklessly into the fire.

"Scotland is damn cold," he said, straightening. "Is there nothing about it that is warm?" He smiled into Carlene's eyes.

"Aye, the women are warm," Carlene purred, moving close to him. "Do ye plan to stay in Scotland?" she asked softly.

"For a time, yes," Ryan replied thoughtfully, recalling that Wyler would be sailing the *Waverly* in within the month. The cargo profits had rallied well in London and Wyler had returned to the Carolinas.

"I have seen little of you since High Yule," she said, warming her hand against Ryan's shoulder.

"That is as it should be." He spoke reservedly.

"I think not. Cameron and I are not man and wife, yet." Carlene's hand slid around Ryan's neck, her dark eyes fastening hard to his. She lifted her chin. "I had a purpose for coming here today. I knew the McLaughlins were at St. Andrews."

Ryan was becoming unbearably warm in the close room. The scant light filtering through the only window held the room in soft shadows. He had not had a woman in many months, and Carlene was here, her reason apparent. Ryan fought the rising swell as she touched him, molding herself against him.

"Carlene, I," he breathed hoarsely, as she began kissing him.

"Don't feel guilty over Cameron. I do not love him," she rasped, catching his tongue between her teeth. She helped his fingers, hurrying him.

He took her harshly, violently, on the fur rug before the sputtering hearth. He released his tightly coiled passion in a burst of welcome agony as Carlene dug her nails into his back. She gasped, drawing him deeper. And he was content to have a woman, any woman.

"Ah," she sighed brokenly, as Ryan withdrew. "I *knew* ye were not dallying with Kip McLaughlin."

Cold rage swept over him. He tangled his long fingers in her hair, enraged, erect, ready for her again. "You bitch," he murmured, pulling her to him. Neither of them heard the soft click of the door as it eased shut.

Kip sat curled in the side chair near the fireplace, her sparkling green eyes following Ryan as he moved to the walnut wardrobe. He reached for his favorite woolen hill jacket, a tone of blue that matched his eyes. A soft leather collar and cuffs accented the carefully woven coat he usually wore. Kip was startled to see him replace it, selecting another heavier coat of deep crimson.

"Me thought ye'd wear the blue one tonight," Kip said softly, gliding across the floor to where Ryan stood before the standing mirror.

"Don't you know it is not proper for a young lady to watch a gentleman dress for dinner?" Ryan scolded, as Kip stood on tiptoe smoothing his collar. He was thinking irritably of his blue hill jacket with staghorn buttons which reeked of Carlene Bothwell's heavy perfume.

"Me can't be a lady when ye're about," Kip teased, fondling the buttons of his coat.

Ryan turned at a light tap on the door. Cameron McLaughlin edged into the doorway, flashing a withering look at Kip.

"Uh, Ryan," Cameron said hesitatingly. "There be a man to see ye."

"At this hour?" Ryan said. "I hope to God the bridge hasn't sunk. Who is it?"

"I dinna' know. He be a stranger and will speak only to ye," Cameron said.

Ryan was perplexed, striding down the long hall of Hawksmoor. He felt a familiar twinge of anticipation rankle in his belly as he neared the Waiting Hall. The McLaughlins knew everyone in Fifeshire and rarely a stranger appeared at their door.

The tall man was silhouetted in the graying shadows of early winter dusk, his coat disheveled and travel stained. The man turned slowly at the echo of Ryan's boots.

Ryan found himself staring into the unyielding eyes of Evan Reed.

"Holy God, Evan," Ryan rasped. Evan was hollow-eyed, his beard unkempt, his British naval coat sagging on his lean frame. Still his bearing was arrogant as he spoke.

"Well, Ryan Deverel—" His tone was caustic. His critical appraisal of Ryan was comparably severe. The beard hid Ryan's handsome face, and he, too, was gaunt. Ryan's once twinkling eyes were cold and distant.

"How did you—what brings you—" Ryan faltered.

"To Scotland?" Evan interrupted with a twinge of sarcasm.

"Hell yes, Evan. I didn't expect anyone—" Ryan paused, a deep frown creasing his face.

"We were friends once, Ryan—and there are certain matters that you should be informed of. I came to—" Evan groped for words.

"Easy, man," Ryan said softly. "Later, after dinner, we'll talk. I'll explain to the McLaughlins while you have a bath and fresh clothes." His voice was firm as he extended his hand.

"Jesus, Ryan." Evan's voice trembled. "You look like hell."

Tight-lipped, Brandon Ord inserted the ornate key into the massive door of El Roble plantation, casting a sidelong glance at Janielle as she waited beside him. The day had been long coming, and finally, with John Patterson's influence, Chalmer Pierce had agreed to sell his plantation home to the newly prosperous Challey overseer.

While the key ground slowly inside the lock, Brandon fidgeted, impatiently thrusting the door open. He paused, allowing Janielle to precede him. The curved frame of the fanlighted doorway cast a flash of brilliant sunlight across the gleaming red cedar floors, dazzling their eyes.

Brandon fished in his coat pocket. "Here is a list of the items that stay with the manor." His hand trembled as he gave it to Janielle.

Janielle ran her hand along the smooth plaster work in the hallway. "Mr. Pierce was a strange man, almost eccentric. Few have visited this home," she said quietly as she and Brandon explored the silent rooms.

In the back parlor was a backgammon table and a wall-high bookcase containing seventy-three volumes. A pike and broadsword leaned against a lower shelf.

"You'll never want for books to read." Janielle smiled as her eyes swept the towering bookcase.

"There are other things I had in mind." Brandon laughed wickedly, his arms encircling Janielle's narrow waist.

"Look, Brandon, the list says there is a red morocco hair mattress in one of the bedrooms, and a coach in the stables valued at one thousand pounds." She shuffled the lists.

"Which would you prefer to see first?" Brandon asked, nuzzling her white-gold hair.

A faded miniature family portrait caught her eye. She lifted it from the table, studying it closely. "Why do you suppose Chalmer Pierce would leave such a treasure behind?" she questioned.

"You remarked he was eccentric," Brandon said casually, grasping the heavy broadsword between his hands.

"Now, Lady Janielle, I am a knight fit to defend your honor," Brandon teased, catching her and drawing her against him.

Janielle felt a prick at his choice of words. She had accompanied Brandon today to share his happiness with the acquisition of El Roble plantation. The prime acreage Ryan had deeded him had thrived with bright leaf tobacco, the entire yield sold to a Virginia tobacco merchant. Brandon's English grandfather had willed his entire Liverpool estate to him, with Morris Chapman delivering the sterling pounds himself. Challey would be in need of a new overseer.

"I'll fetch the food hamper and we can dine in the ballroom upstairs," Brandon said lazily, "though we may have to strain a bit to hear the music."

Janielle laughed softly, watching him swagger down the sunlit hallway. His light brown hair held a whisper of silver now, his alert dark eyes revealed a glow of confidence. She noticed it often as his bold gaze raked hungrily across her.

She strolled to the wide window, glancing out into the small courtyard, where every shade of green was evident. The beautiful ivy, glittering with varnish, delicately veined, wandered to the high walls of the piazza. El Roble was a fitting home for an esteemed gentleman, and Janielle was happy for Brandon. His mood toward her had heightened from protective concern to playful lust. They spoke sparingly of Ryan.

"Which room do you prefer?" Brandon asked impishly, swinging the hamper, climbing the stairs to the ballroom.

A rush of remembrance flooded through her as Brandon repeated the question Ryan had asked of her as he had shown her the newly appointed room at Challey. For an instant she saw his face clearly, tilting, mocking, the cold arrogant eyes holding her. The ache in her heart welled again.

"I haven't seen the stables yet," she replied teasingly, ignoring the strained look on Brandon's face.

Irene had prepared a lavish cold repast, particularly satisfying on the warm spring day. Brandon pulled the cork from a full bottle of Madeira, deftly filling the crystal goblet for Janielle.

"A toast to my new home," Brandon said, lifting his glass.

Janielle swallowed hard, the tears brimming her wide violet eyes. Ryan had said that at Challey. Dear God, was there no end to this torment? Ryan was here, everywhere.

Brandon looked harshly at her level glass. "What distresses you, Janielle?" His voice was cold.

"Did you know Evan Reed has gone to England?" she blurted out.

"And *that* makes you weep?" Brandon asked disgustedly.

"No, I—" her voice choked on a sob.

Brandon stood, lifting Janielle to her feet, folding her in his arms. "Next he'll be saying that El Roble needs a mistress." Janielle sighed, swaying against him.

"Evan proposed marriage to you, did he not?" Brandon said against her hair.

Tears coursed freely now. "Yes, Brandon, he did," she murmured.

"Evan requires a certain type of woman, just as I do," he said, his large hand trailing the smallness of her back. She stiffened.

"I wish to return home, Brandon."

"No!" his voice boomed, echoing in the cavernous ballroom. Jerking her against him, finding her mouth, bruising, exploring fiercely, his large hands cupped her breasts.

"I'll make you forget him, by God I will." His warm mouth, tinged with wine, sought her breasts.

Janielle gasped, frightened. Never had she seen Brandon so inflamed. "Please, Brandon," she gasped through his wandering, scorching kisses.

He let her go, abruptly stunned by his own actions. Lifting her slim hands to his mouth, he kissed each palm, tenderly, quietly. He gazed calmly into her bewildered eyes.

"Forgive me, Janielle. I want you."

They left the ballroom, strolling through spacious hallways leading to the portico. At the front door, Brandon paused.

"I brought you here today to ask you to wed," he said. "I can provide well for you now and I have never ceased to desire you."

Janielle leaned into the doorway, feeling faint. The proposal was coming from the wrong face, the wrong mouth. Ryan! God, Ryan, what shall I do?

The voice was continuing. "If you agree, I shall speak to your father this evening. I know I can make you happy, Janielle."

"Oh, Brandon. There is—"

"There is or was another man in your heart. I know that, Janielle. It is of no importance to me."

"And what of me," Janielle thought despairingly. "Am I to be passed along from one man to another? It is important to me whose children I bear, whose arms I crave—"

Aloud, she managed, "Give me time, Brandon."

"I plan to give a ball by early summer when the house is finished to my taste. We will announce our wedding bonds then. I do not hold to long engagements. I told you once, I would wait until you came to me willingly. And the day at the flood shack you were more than willing. You will be again. All these months I have not forgotten, Janielle, even though—"

"Even though I carried Ryan's child," she gritted.

"Yes," Brandon stormed. "Lying, rutting bastard!"

"You would always remember and so would I," she said turning away. Brandon trailed her to the carriage in silence.

Kip flew down the winding stairway, Pippin close at her heels, her wild red tresses a mass of swirling color behind her. Colliding with Evan on the landing, she burst into rippling laughter.

"Don't you ever walk anywhere?" Evan scowled, gaining his breath.

"Me not be old and rickety like you," she taunted, while Evan leaned into the bannister.

"What is your haste this cold Scottish morning?" he wheezed.

"Me be hearing that Ryan went to Crail. There's news the *Waverly* is in London," she said, her eyes glittering.

"Ryan left an hour ago," Evan teased, still frowning. It was all too obvious that Ryan had captured the heart of this feisty Scottish lass. He thought of the elaborate sketches of the new Challey manor that he had seen on Ryan's desk last night, and he wondered.

Ryan had changed. Their long exchange had revealed very little of the former man. When told that Morris Chapman had paid Ryan's account at Coast Merchants, Ryan merely shrugged. Even the mention of Kaylee Mallen brought no response. Ryan had smiled when Evan related that his Shetland mare at Challey had foaled. He told him of Brandon's success with the bright leaf tobacco and of the healthy inheritance Brandon had received from his English grandfather. Ryan had casually flipped through a stack of sketches, rolling one neatly, tying it with a band of leather.

"I am surprised you didn't bring that stinking heathen, Itoo, along," Ryan joked, forcing a change in the conversation.

Evan scoffed laughingly. "Itoo would be frozen hard in this damnable weather."

Evan recounted that Johnathan Chapman had sailed for Paris, planning to reside there permanently, noting that Ryan's fist clenched, whitening his knuckles. But his face remained impassive. Evan was puzzled.

"Will Ryan be returning soon?" Kip asked pointedly, her lilting Scottish brogue resounding down the long stairway.

"As you know, pretty lass, Ryan is unpredictable," Evan commented dryly. Seeing the joyous expression her pert, young face, how could he tell her that Ryan had gone to Crail to inquire about passage to London? The *Waverly* was in port there.

"They be opening the bridge today at Bothwell Loch and Ryan promised he'd take me with him." Kip's disappointment was apparent.

"Then he will," Evan said reassuringly.

Ryan had spent hours explaining to him about the loch bridge, oblivious to Evan's disinterest. Ryan was enormously proud of his work, commenting that Lord Bothwell had rewarded him generously.

"The work brought me back to some semblance of

normality," Ryan had concluded, setting his sketches aside.

"Wyler performed a skilled task," Evan remarked, referring to Ryan's chest wound.

"I owe him my life," Ryan said seriously.

"What are your plans now?" Evan had asked solemnly, waiting for a ready moment to disclose the purpose of his travel to Hawksmoor.

"I have none." Ryan shrugged indifferently.

Evan shifted in the tartan plaid chair, pouring another glassful of usquebach. "I think, Ryan, it is time you returned to Carolina." Evan's tone was direct.

Ryan spun in his chair, glowering at him. *This* had brought a response. "Why?" His tone was guarded. Evan could fence now, he had Ryan's attention.

"There's Challey," Evan suggested easily.

"It can be sold," Ryan snapped.

Evan saved his winning thrust, waiting while Ryan silently raged at him. The one careful name he had avoided eased out.

"There's Janielle." He said her name softly, watching the flicker in Ryan's stormy eyes.

After an endless silence, Ryan spoke, his voice harsh. "You sailed across the ocean to bring me this slip of news." Ryan's laugh was brittle. "That I am the father of her child, the one she lost. You are too late, Evan. I already know."

Evan was undaunted. "I have asked Janielle to wed," he said evenly.

Ryan stood up wearily, his eyes angry, dark, as they raked Evan. The scar across his forehead became pronounced. He downed his fiery usquebach.

"I pray she agreed," he tossed at Evan, storming out the door.

Evan smiled knowingly. His mission to Scotland was accomplished.

Kip McLaughlin bounded on down the stairs, her burnished curls trailing her trim back. Evan's smile twisted sadly, watching her. Another one, he thought, as she disappeared down the hall.

chapter 25

Ryan carefully knotted the muslin cravat, tucking the lacy edges inside his Newmarket waistcoat. Countless times he had performed the simple chore, but on this dreaded morning his long fingers had seemed clumsy. He had avoided breakfasting with the McLaughlins, requesting that a service tray be brought to his room.

Steam from the brewing kettle clouded the mirror in front of him. Resignedly, he circled the clinging moisture away, still filled with an odd sense of melancholy. Flint-blue eyes flickered back at him in the clear glare from the mirror. It was difficult to meet their gaze.

He should be with Lord Bothwell in Midlothian today, viewing the castle ruin of Chrichton Castle, home of the fifth Earl of Bothwell. The journey across the Firth of Forth to Edinburgh and on to Tyne Water had been arranged before Evan Reed's sudden visit to Hawksmoor.

He should have sent Evan on to London to join Wyler for the about voyage to Charleston. And he should have ordered a new hill jacket of the vibrant blue and green tartan plaid worn by the McLaughlins.

Nervously, Ryan breathed on his stiff fingers, warming them against his mouth. He should have done these things. The events since Evan's arrival had unfurled too rapidly. There was no more time to weigh his decision. Right or wrong, he had chosen.

Keening sounds of Kip's racking sobs had remained with him throughout the night, knifing through him, calling forth a fathom of emotion he did not realize he possessed. There had been no gentle way of telling her of his decision.

"No, Ryan! Ye canna' leave! Ye have made a new life in Scotland. 'Tis foolishness to tear open yer wounds from the past," Kip had cried openly.

He had held her trembling body close, smoothing the coppery locks of her windblown hair. They had met near the Bothwell Loch where the maytrees were in creamy bloom, shining with a chilly glitter on the twisted branches.

"If I could spare your hurt, Kip—"

"Me onc't sought to spare yer pain aboard the *Waverly* after Wyler used the coal pan, but I could na'. 'Twas a fierce struggle for ye, Ryan. Now ye are mended and free, yet return to the scene of yer miseries. I canna' fathom it, Ryan. I canna'!"

Ryan held her tighter, stilling her quaking. "Hush, love," he murmured gently against her hair, while a million thorns of conscience pricked him.

The thorns were still at work, their nettles piercing the deeper layers of his soul as he fastened the wide leather straps across his sea trunk.

The *Waverly* rode at anchor, head to wind, her red hull swallowing the gentle waves of Crail harbor. Her main and mizzen had been trimmed and the foreyards braced on other tack. The familiar sight of the *Waverly* riding the swells beyond the harbor wall brought an ache to Ryan's tight throat.

Evan Reed rested his hand on Ryan's shoulder. "Look to sea! Wyler is lowering the long boat," he said tremulously, fighting the fierce hammering of his own heart.

Cameron McLaughlin came to stand beside Ryan, the red leather case with Ryan's sketches and drawing instruments clutched under his arm.

"'Tis a sad day for the McLaughlin clan, Ryan. We ha' spared a hope that ye would—" Cameron's voice broke.

Ryan turned swiftly, striding over to the carriage where Rowena and Ramsay McLaughlin waited. He leaned inside the carriage door, clasping the elder McLaughlin's hand.

"It has been an honor, sir, unequaled, to be a guest in your home."

Ramsay McLaughlin cleared his throat, his deep green eyes resting on Ryan.

"Lad, should ye ever wish to return to Hawksmoor, 'twill be yer home," he said hoarsely.

Blake McLaughlin climbed down from the high carriage seat and busied himself with adjusting a lead harness that needed no adjustment. His eyes caught the *Waverly*'s long boat hurdling the waves near the harbor mouth. His throat was dry as he watched Ryan mount the path to the stone wall surrounding the harbor watch fortress above the sea wall. Kip was up there alone, her gaze fixed on the *Waverly*'s sails. Quickly he turned his face away.

Ryan stood quietly beside Kip, watching the sea wind play through her copper-streaked hair. She held her Lunardi hat in her small hand, its soft straw brim whipping and folding in the stiff breeze. The long silence caught at them.

"Me knows about Carlene Bothwell," Kip said finally.

Ryan was still, watching Wyler shore the long boat, cringing when the curved timbers scraped the stone pier. Wyler never could dock a small craft. Enrico, the Cuban, glanced up, waving to him and pointing to Thrush, the enormous black, as he clamored over the side, hauling anchor ropes around the dock post.

Suddenly, Ryan's heart began to pound wildly inside his chest. He felt neatly sliced apart.

"Ye need not suffer that me'll say a word to Cameron. He will learn enough of her someday," Kip was saying, but the words were falling short of their mark. "I learnt by hearing the servants' prattle. They watched while ye and Carlene—"

Ryan stiffened, turning sharply to Kip. "It no longer matters, Kip. None of it. I am returning to Challey to amend a wrong."

"While ye continue to wrong others," Kip remarked coldly.

Ryan gripped her by the shoulders. "Hear me well, Kip McLaughlin. I will face the consequences of my choices. These last moments with you now are all I can offer you. I'll state no regret or bumbling apologies."

Kip lifted misting green eyes to him. "'Tis no matter the others, Ryan. I can forgive ye. I can wait for yer return to Scotland. I can—"

"No, my innocent love," Ryan breathed, wiping her silken tears away with a gentle fingertip, his mouth brushing her cheek, lingering softly for an eternal moment.

"Ask no more of me, Kip," he said brokenly, pulling away from her.

In an instant he was gone, threading his way down the steep path to the harbor wall, where Wyler waited with the long boat.

El Roble plantation blazoned with light from a thousand glowing candles, spreading their radiance through the warm summer twilight. Doormen in splendid plum velvet frock coats and starched silver-streaked wiglets held flickering torchlights around the curved approach way. Seated musicians in the Moorish gallery above the wide portico played for the guests being lavishly entertained in the adjoining upstairs ballroom.

Brandon Ord had mastered every detail of the night, sparing no expense, insuring that his first successful ball at El Roble would long be remembered in the Santee sweep. John Patterson had influenced the Charleston Coast Merchants into attendance, bringing his own entourage of distinguished statesmen to El Roble. Brandon's engagement and forthcoming marriage to Janielle would be announced before midnight.

Brandon lounged against the verandah pillar, biting the bitter end of a cheroot, the leaf grown on his own land at Challey. His dark eyes swept the setting before him.

Janielle wore the violet satin ballgown he had bought for her at Mademoiselle Yvette's Vanity in Charleston. The gold locket he had given her that long past Christmas Eve at Challey was now encrusted solidly with diamonds and hung delicately about her slender neck. He patted the pocket of his ebony velvet waistcoat, feeling the bulge of her ring case. The massive diamond set in fire opals should please her.

For a moment he frowned, flicking a cigar ash on the polished tile floor. His goddamn floor; he could grind out the cigar with his heel and leave it for the slaves to clean. He was absolute master of El Roble and was about to take a wife.

Meticulously he had followed the formalities to the letter. Even John Patterson, who had given his consent to the marriage, was visibly impressed with the future home of his daughter. Throughout the day Brandon had been plagued with an air of uneasiness, which had disappeared somewhat after his third whiskey. Nothing must go amiss this night. There was still Janielle to conquer.

Janielle was docile now, almost agreeable, allowing him to make most of her decisions. Brandon hadn't wondered if he loved her. She was essential to his plans.

And he had waited a long time for this night. At the thought of Janielle lying naked in his arms, he felt a gathering bulge in his groin. Janielle would give him sons. He would keep her breeding until the memory of Ryan Deverel was lost to her.

Impatiently, Brandon ground out his cheroot, moving quickly across the ballroom and gathering Janielle in his arms for a waltz.

Ryan tethered his mount to the porch pilaster of El Roble, shrugging away the restraining hand of the curt footman.

"Only gentlemum with de invitation go inside," the servant drawled threateningly.

"Stand wide!" Ryan stormed, his large hand grazing the butt of Cameron McLaughlin's Scottish flick pistol. The footman fell back, giving space for Ryan to pass. Ryan's mood was testy after the brutal ride from Patterson landing, where he had extracted from Jedda the news of Janielle's engagement ball at El Roble.

Ryan knew the location of the former home of Chalmer Pierce. It was a good two hours' ride from Patterson Woods on the road winding upriver on the North Santee sweep. Ryan had scoffed at the impressive news that Brandon Ord, the former Challey overseer, had renamed the site El Roble.

Arrogantly Ryan stalked up the marble steps, cuffing the dust from his blue hill jacket. Hurriedly he ran a hand through his windblown hair. Hardly the picture of a gentleman, he thought absently, stamping the powdery dust from his English top boots. His presence tonight would be a shock to her, to all of them, but his reason couldn't wait.

Morris Chapman saw Ryan first, instantly recognizing his handsome natural son, the child conceived in the depths of his honest love for Loranna Deverel. The excruciating recall of the night Johnathan had shot Ryan, his own intervention that acknowledged he was Ryan's

257

father, suddenly shattered his control. Morris turned aside, shrinking into the shadows of a dimmed hallway. Ryan would have to seek him out. The memory was still too raw.

Ryan wasn't looking for the usual familiar faces. In the throngs that clustered the glittering ballroom, he sought only one face, hers. A wave of unrest preceded him, the stunned guests separating as he strode determinedly across the showy red cedar floor. Tonight he was an intruder among former friends, and he didn't care.

Standing near the musicians' gallery, Janielle turned slowly at the unwelcome hush that had fallen on the ballroom. Somehow she knew before she even turned around.

For a wavering instant she reeled. Ryan's appearance was noticeably rugged, with his full beard, the rough cut of his Scottish hill jacket, his English top boots with silver rowels. His face was dark, deeply tanned by sea winds and harsh sun. Only the unrelenting slate-blue eyes that devoured her were the same. Ryan Deverel was here, this moment, and never had he been more handsome.

White even teeth flashed against his dark face, the bitter lines easing as his eyes caressed her. Nervously, Janielle glanced around for Brandon. Hadn't he mentioned that he was going to the wine cellar for a twenty vintage claret for their engagement toast? But that had been some time back, and still Brandon hadn't returned.

The musicians had keyed again amid the nervous quiet, the selection easing into a French polonaise. The guests hung back, uncertain as to what would follow. No one approached Ryan.

"I ask a dance, milady," Ryan said brazenly, with a tinge of Scottish brogue as the metallic clink of his rowels scraped the highly polished floor.

He swept her into his arms, holding her too close, inhaling the well-remembered jasmine fragrance of her. Janielle melted against him, letting him crush her, letting the smell of river musk and horseflesh, the cool strength of his hands, the virile warmth of his body take her. She was in his arms, floating to him in his world.

The heady dream was suddenly shattered as Janielle was jerked roughly from Ryan's arms. Brandon, his face drawn and angry, separated them.

"You chose an inopportune night, Ryan," he said caustically.

"I know of many such nights," Ryan replied shortly, his gaze flickering over Brandon. His former overseer had softened with the rich planter's image.

John Patterson had stepped forward, his eyes blazing with anger. "I would ask your departure, at once, Deverel. Your untimely appearance on this special evening is unwelcome and uninvited. Brandon and Janielle intend to—"

"Their intentions do not concern me," Ryan snapped back.

John Patterson was trying to keep the rage from his voice. "You cannot march in here, playing the role of a Scottish overlord, and expect—" John Patterson's words faltered as he met Ryan's cold penetrating eyes.

"We could approach this from a gentleman's manner," Ryan sneered, remembering the bitter afternoon in Harrelson Mallen's library at La Pueblita por la Bahia. "A method where men's lives are twisted to meet the reigning gentlemen's rules, compulsive marriages, and pistols aimed by gentlemen's sons. This night, however, I prefer my own rules."

From the corner of his eye Ryan had caught the summoning motion that Brandon had attempted to conceal, calling the purple-clad footmen to intervene. He tensed, allowing a flutter of a moment to pass. They were closing in.

Suddenly his arm lashed out, gripping Janielle about the waist, drawing her against him. The flick pistol was in his hand, aiming steadily at Brandon.

"I am taking Janielle with me," he gritted, taking a step back.

"Has she no say in her fate?" John Patterson hissed at him.

Ryan wavered for an instant, realizing that Janielle had said nothing to him since he arrived. It was too late. His plan had clicked into position, her decision was unimportant.

"Before God, Ryan!" Brandon breathed hotly. "I will kill you!"

"The planter's portrait had corrupted you, Brandon," Ryan said coldly. "Our roles are reversed."

Blindly, Brandon lunged at him, grappling at his arm until the butt of the flick pistol crashed down on his skull. Janielle shuddered as Brandon slid to the floor at her feet.

Panther quick, Ryan was moving along the wall, still gripping her firmly against him. They were down the stairs and out into the approach. He was lifting her with him into the saddle and spurring hard. The gelding broke free into a full gallop, skirting the dark trees along the road.

Janielle gasped as Ryan pulled her roughly against his chest, his arms crossed around her. Janielle's head no longer felt attached to her body. Sudden fear for her own safety pummeled at her. The cold shock of seeing Ryan again and her own recklessness in handling the situation now frightened her. She was not riding with the Ryan Deverel she knew. This man was a stranger. But Brandon would follow, the wardens would find them. They would hang Ryan.

Ryan's breath was warm against her neck. He spurred the gelding cruelly, not allowing any break in the stretched rhythm. The horse thundered down the night-black road to the river fork, veering sharply when Ryan jerked the reins toward the cay.

A patch of moonlight between the water oaks loomed ahead. A beckoning whinney, short, muffled, then silent, reached across the glittering sandbar. Ryan slowed the gelding, circling the outstretched knees of the oaks. A frightened wood ibis, startled from his night's nesting, cawed out at them. Ryan pulled taut, waiting.

The hulking shadow of a giant spread eerily across the narrow cay, partly concealing the smaller form that cowered behind him. Ryan walked the horse across the cay toward them.

Janielle shrank back against Ryan, feeling tension ease from him. He dismounted in a flash, sweeping her to the ground. She swayed against the heaving horse, her fingers tangling in his coarse mane. The horse seemed, for now, her last grip on reality. No farther, she vowed, no farther, would she go with this madman.

"Rión—" a thick voice came from the darkness. "*Ees* ready as El Capitán says."

Ryan strode across the oozing sandbar, returning with three horses. The towering giant followed.

"You may ride single or with me," Ryan said evenly, pulling Janielle's arm free.

"I am not going with you, Ryan."

Behind them, the giant black had swung into his saddle, edging toward Ryan's steaming horse.

"The tide, Rión," the smaller man whispered. "We must make the tide."

Ryan was moving away from her. He spoke hurriedly to the two men. His steps were heavy as he returned to her side.

"After tonight, there will be no safe place for me on land, Janielle," Ryan said quietly. "I am taking you to sea."

Janielle felt her legs crumble, her slim body sliding down the horse. Strong arms caught her before the swallowing blackness came.

With Janielle cradled in his arms, the sound of slapping waves parting in the cutwater's path, the soft crackle of Thrush's straining muscles at the oars, Ryan could relax.

The *Waverly* was anchored in the shallows off Santee Point. Wyler had followed his orders carefully, and Thrush and Enrico had been waiting at the appointed spot.

Janielle stirred against him, moaning softly. The *Waverly*'s mast lights glimmered on the blackened sea through the chilly mist of dawn.

part four
RUM CAY

chapter 26

The sea wind beating the strained canvas overhead, salt spume whipping, stinging across her pale face, Janielle stood on the *Waverly*'s main deck, her legs wobbly, but her stomach finally quieted. So ill death would have been a blessing, she had never expected to survive the onslaught of seasickness during the last few days. Mountainous waves, swelling, falling monotonously, had tortured her mercilessly.

Brief spaces Ryan spent with her, his form blurred, her face turned away from him in the narrow berth, loathing herself and him. Anything to halt the relentless motion. Then Wyler's calloused, freckled hand on her burning face, his easy, "Hold, lass, 'twill ease," while he urged a honey-whiskey mixture into her chalky mouth.

She leaned into the main mast, steadying herself, staring ahead while the *Waverly* galloped into the eternal horizon of green. The yellow-muddy waters of the Santee seemed a trickle of memory in comparison. All her life she had lived near confined waters, winding to the sea, but never had she imagined such a universe of immense waters. In the freedom of the sea she could almost forget. Almost.

The impact of seeing Ryan again, Brandon lying bloodied at her feet, the desperate flight to the cay off

Santee Point, the endless pull of the longboat heading out to open sea, had brought her to this moment. She wanted to go home now, even if it meant marrying Brandon. She had finally compromised herself into caring a little for Brandon, though the solid numbness she felt inside hadn't altered. Had Ryan appeared in a different manner, courted her respectfully, shucked his acquired, barbaric Scottish traits, perhaps she could— No, she couldn't. Ryan was changed. The slim, gentle fiber was gone completely from him.

Janielle smiled reassuringly to herself. She had caught the dark, disapproving glances that Wyler shot at Ryan. And once she had heard fragments of their heated quarrel.

"Be God, man! Did ye leave yer brains in yon apple barrel? Ye tole me we'd be takin' the lass to Charleston for ye to wed, not friskin' her away in the night, even bloodyin' her intended. And her a statesman's bairn! There'll be a wager, now, on yer dense head. Mayhaps even the Continental fleet will give ye chase. Ye be no better 'n a scoundrel," Wyler had bellowed.

"This is my ship, Wyler! You'll not question my decisions," Ryan stormed back.

"Me'll have no part in a bloody kidnap! Me'll hold no captaincy under a blackguard's command!"

"I intend to wed with her," Ryan had shouted.

"Be God, man! Some likely! She looks at ye like a crawlin' viper. I see no love in her eyes for ye!"

"That will change!" Ryan countered, his voice fading into the pitch of the wind as they moved up deck.

Janielle bent forward, grasping the water-stained hem of her violet ballgown. Her silver embroidered slippers with saucy Italian heels were ruined beyond repair. Now she reasoned that a portion of her seasickness was actually homesickness. At the suggestion, her belly began to churn again.

"Señorita," Enrico, the Cuban, called softly behind her. "Señor Rión sends a cup of tea up deck to ease your *mal de mer*." An anxious smile flashed across his dark weathered face.

Janielle turned, accepting the clattering cup and saucer. The Cuban wore a reasonably clean over-shirt of bold stripes, a lone earring glistening in his ear. He stroked his beard nervously.

"The lady, she is better today, no?"

"Yes, thank you." Janielle tossed the words into the rising wind.

Enrico glanced upward at the strained topgallants, swollen in the southwest bluster. A worried look swept his face.

"El Capitán say we may have to veer ship and brail in if the wind grows." Enrico's eyes were large in his small face. "El Capitán spilt oakum in the water to make a slick path for the *Waverly*." Enrico flashed another uncertain smile.

Janielle tried to avoid watching the heaving waves, still distrustful of her stomach's calm. She managed to sip at the tea, which was surprisingly well brewed and hot. She had no idea what the Cuban had meant about the ship.

"Does he fear bad weather?" she asked indifferently.

"Ah, no, señorita. El Capitán fears nothing," Enrico said.

"Where is your companion, the huge black man?" she asked.

"Ah, my friend Thrush, he is about his chores. He does the work of *seis* men."

Janielle turned her head away in a bored fashion, catching hurried movements across the deck. Several of the mates had assumed positions under the masts. Two climbed into the shrouds, oblivious to the pitching motion of the ship, making their way upward to the weather clews. Janielle watched their climb, her neck aching as they moved to the dipping top masts. Straining to see into the dizzying heights brought it on again. She swayed unsteadily.

Enrico grasped her slim arm firmly. As though he had appeared from thin air, Ryan was beside her, scooping her up in his arms. Janielle locked her arms about his neck, feeling the solid, warm strength of his body.

"The sea is pitching today, Janielle," he said quietly, carrying her below to the captain's quarters.

"It pitches the same below," Janielle retorted caustically.

Ryan was silent, carrying her down the passageway. Opening the small door with his shoulder, he dodged the low swinging oil lamp, placing her gently on the rolling berth. Slowly he straightened, looking down at her, his eyes unreadable.

"Would be best if you stayed in the cabin until the squall that Wyler predicts is over," he said vacantly.

Janielle sprung to her feet, grasping at the berth rail.

"I hate it down here! The air is close and foul, and—there is little to do!"

Ryan frowned, his large hand stroking his beard.

"I hadn't time to bring ladies' delights aboard," he snapped.

Still scowling, he edged across to Wyler's sea trunk, flipping it open, sorting through it. Gathering a wadded bundle from it, he flung them at Janielle.

"Here, madam, mend these, if you can hold a needle steady!"

Janielle caught the clothing with both hands, her violet eyes widening with shock as a pink silk pelisse fell from the bundle. Her fingers traveled across the delicate fabric, her eyes holding Ryan's.

"Whose is this, Ryan?" she asked coldly.

His gaze fixed upon Kip McLaughlin's silk cloak.

"It belonged to Wyler's niece," he snarled.

"Was *she* aboard the *Waverly*?" Janielle asked incredulously.

"For a time, yes."

"With you?" Janielle demanded.

"You misunderstand, Janielle. It was—"

"As I once tried to explain my presence at Challey, before you raped me!"

"Then, by God, do a parlor wench's bidding! Mend sailor's clothes, scour the foul-smelling cabin! I care not!"

"Perhaps I should wear the silk pelisse to remind you of happier times," she taunted angrily.

Ryan closed the distance between them in one stride, gripping her roughly by the shoulders. His large hand traced the outline of her face, forming a fist that tilted her chin up to him.

"Perhaps I made a wrong judgment," he said quietly, drawing her to him, breathing the still fresh fragrance of her white-gold hair.

Janielle was rigid in his arms. "Take me home, Ryan."

His arms fell away. "I cannot, Janielle."

"But we can't sail forever. Is there not some port near where we can go, where I can send word, and father or Bran—" She froze.

Ryan's mouth set in a hard, stubborn line. "I have duties above. I advise you to amuse yourself in some way until the bluster is over." Turning on his heel, he stalked from the cabin.

The cabin door groaned shut behind him. Ryan climbed the rocking steps into the passageway to the main deck. A full blast of gale-driven wind caught at him, knocking him sideways into the shrouds.

"Up helm," Wyler barked above the wind, intending to wear ship, his own rough hands shoving the spokes of the wheel.

"Stand by to square the crojack yard," Wyler bellowed.

Ryan struggled to his feet, making his way up deck, glancing upward at the tacks being run off before the wind. He hoped the wind currents wouldn't circle before the *Waverly* could be brought into wind again. The menacing darkness hovering above was lowering, dropping the first sprinkles of a hard squall.

"I dinna' like the looping of the wind," Wyler scowled, nodding to Ryan. "'Tis a foretaste of hurricane."

Ryan thought of the hurricane in his own tumbling thoughts. Damn her, anyway! Janielle was a vexation, a blend of sulking, raging, apathetic womanhood, making him curse himself for ever having left Scotland to return to her. He was still baffled over his reaction to Evan Reed's sham persuasion. Somehow he couldn't abide the thought of Janielle's marrying anyone else. Or so he had reasoned. Now, he doubted. Damn those violet eyes that tore at him!

"How many days to Caicos Passage?" Ryan shouted to Wyler.

"Yesterday, I'd ha' said two. If we be headin' into a hurricane drift, we may be blown to Honduras," Wyler said, watching the sails fill on starboard tack.

"She's shifting again," Ryan yelled before the *Waverly* rolled, setting the decks awash.

"Damme, the gasket ha' fouled on the weather clew," Wyler swore, ordering Wilson aloft on a weather side shroud. "Lower topgallant is fouled," he muttered to Ryan, steadying the helm.

Ryan voiced aloud a decision he had just made.

"We'll put ashore at Grand Caicos Island. Enrico knows a family there with a villa they rent. I'll take Janielle there and find a minister."

"Aye, if the lass and the storm are willin'." Wyler spoke thoughtfully, his keen eyes on Wilson's form at the wire foot rope. "'Twould be me guess, lad, both ye and yer ship are in for a hard run."

Janielle huddled on the rocking berth, so frightened and cold her seasickness had vanished. The cabin was shrouded in darkness, the heaving sea washing endless whitecaps against the shuttered porthole. The giant sea had gone mad, lashing, biting, companioning with frenzied winds, throwing the forces of their power to devour all that ventured into their midst.

Biting her lip until it was numb, choking back stinging tears when Ryan had stormed from the cabin, she wished he'd come to her now. She wouldn't flail at him, try to hurt him. She knew of his countless women before her and most probably after. Like Kaylee, or the captain's niece, or whoever. She just hadn't reckoned on his taking them aboard his ship. The *Waverly* had seemed a sacred place to her. Obviously, to Ryan, it was not.

He had mentioned nothing of his plans for her, only left her to guess. The only time he had touched her was to help her through one of her heaving bouts, when he had spoken tenderly to her, stroking her hair, holding her to him.

In her foggy recall of that night, she had thought he'd mumbled something about his son, their son, but she couldn't tap it, couldn't be sure. Since that night, he'd been aloof, sending others with messages, asking about her welfare. Until today, when they had both exploded.

The ship and the endless sea did strange things to one. The close confinement, constantly unsteady footing, nerves always taut with some degree of fear, grated at one's senses. Ashore there are diversions, at sea there are few.

Enrico tapped lightly on the door, poking his dark head inside the crack.

"Señorita, *por favor*, Señor Rión *pregunta*, uh, asks, that I breeng you some *comida*. The galley fire must soon be put out with the storm." He stepped lightly into the darkened cabin, carrying a tray covered with yellow-white linen, his oilskin glistening with raindrops.

Wincing, Janielle glanced at another helping of bully beef for her stomach to wrestle with. But the coffee smelled good.

"Is the storm worsening?" she asked softly, watching

269

Enrico raise the greasy wick in the oil lantern.

"Beautiful señorita should not sit alone in darkness," Enrico crooned, watching the reddish light flicker across her white-gold hair.

"I am a favored prisoner," Janielle gritted, adding a measure of sugar to her coffee.

"Ah, no, señorita. I hear what Rión say to El Capitán. We sail to a place—"

Enrico's words cut short as the *Waverly* shuddered, heaving first right, then left, into the wind, slamming Janielle into the berth. The lantern swung frantically in a wild circle. Enrico sat up, holding his bleeding nose, mumbling broken Spanish. Janielle edged across the berth to help him, but he waved her away.

The *Waverly* was throwing, plunging, when a sharp crack rent the air, a thundering crash of timbers echoing above deck. Shouts and screams were swathed in the howling wind.

Enrico crossed himself in holy sign, his black eyes huge, his forehead beaded with sweat. Water was trickling under the cabin door.

"Above hands," the dreaded command echoed through the flooded passageway. The cabin door gave way under a crushing wave of sea water.

The second mate sloshed into the cabin, pulling his soaked oilskin about him.

"The lady is to come with me," he rasped, reaching for Janielle's hand. He passed a yellow oilskin across to her, waiting while she shrugged into it.

"Wh—what has happened?" Janielle stammered.

"The mainmast has cracked and the topsails and gallants are fouled. The *Waverly* is swamping, miss," the second mate replied flatly.

"Aii-ee," Enrico cried, rolling his huge eyes.

"Will we sink?" Janielle whispered, wading through the cabin door.

The second mate did not answer, only gripped her arm firmly, leading her up the seeping passage way of the crippled ship.

The overset decks were awash with relentless waves. Cautiously they picked their way across the wreckage of the splintered mast, the tangle of shredded canvas. Sea and sky met in a frothing cauldron where Janielle could find no horizon.

Drenched and cold, she shivered into the mass of wet oilskins clustered about the small forecastle. Enrico closed the door against the maddened sea. She stepped inside the stifling room.

"Cut away yon mizzenmast and 'fore," Wyler thundered above the gale. Drenched mates leaned into the wind, carrying axes, hurrying to the masts. The mizzenmast toppled first, the foremast following it into the raging swells.

With one crashing stroke, Thrush felled the bowsprit. The *Waverly* shook violently, righting herself.

"The tiller broke short in the rudder head, Captain!" Wilson shouted across to Wyler.

"Christ, me man! Set to the pumps," Wyler bellowed from atop the stump of the mainmast.

The *Waverly* was rocking into the wind, laboring to stay above the churning sea. Bolts of blue lightning shocked the sea beyond the *Waverly*'s cutwater. Janielle gasped at the smack of thunder that rolled across the rising waves. Salt tears mixed with pelting rain on her face as she turned, realizing she was lashed into the ropes of the forecastle.

"Chain pump choked, sir," a voice called from the hatchway near her.

"She be too pressed," Wyler shouted back. "Clear a passage to the well! There be seven feet in the keelson!"

"Spare pump in the fish room is working," Wilson reported.

"Bail with buckets before she swims!" Wyler blared, scanning the laden sky.

Janielle reached a salt-crusted hand to her raw face. How many hours had the *Waverly* breasted the hurricane? The horizon shadowed a faint light. Twilight, or daybreak?

"Take heart, senorita, the ship will not founder." Enrico spoke softly, turning to face her.

The ship hurdled another gigantic wave, filling the deck with foaming, lacy whitecaps, clearing the cutters from their moorings. Janielle choked on the spewing sea water, wiping again at the stinging salt in her eyes. When she could see plainly again, she raised her face.

Ryan loomed before her. For an instant he hesitated, then, gathering her into his arms, he was kissing her hair, her neck. His warm mouth sought hers, locking her into a space of secure tenderness.

She clung to him long after he had moved his mouth away.

"Wh—where have you been?" she whispered against his cheek.

"Everywhere, love. You forget, it is *my* ship." Ryan smiled down at her.

"Will we—are we going to—" Janielle began.

"Wyler says the gale is easing. The *Waverly* will swim until daybreak. With the chain pumps and bailing, and a fresh blow from westwardly to propel us out of the hurricane's track, we will hold." He spoke calmly, turning to leave.

"Ryan, there is something I wish you to know," Janielle said, catching at his arm.

"Not now, Janielle. Later perhaps, when the lull is upon us. I must return below. When the cabin is safe for you I'll send someone to fetch you."

Janielle watched him climb across the scuttle into the hold. The *Waverly*'s naked deck glistened in the murky early light. It was enough for now.

chapter 27

The jangle of chain pumps echoed through the flooded passageway below decks. "Still she gains! Heavy lee!" Wilson shouted down from the quarter deck.

"By God, me knows she lays too much along," Wyler swore, sloshing updeck through standing sea water.

Ryan perched on the quarter deck railing, watching choppy waves stroke the *Waverly*'s stern. Wearily he leaned an arm on his knee. Wyler moved beside him, staring up at a clearing sky.

"God, me man, we be blessed! If we can move afloat into the northeast trades, we may scrape Little Bahama Bank."

"With no masts and a crippled rudder, it is a miracle she lasted this long in the swells." Ryan spoke quietly.

"Her iron work is good! Me saw to that! She ha' been in ugly seas 'afore. Remember, lad, she ha' bested a heavy sea battle with a British man-o-war," Wyler said loudly, grabbing one of Ryan's hands, studying the raw, bloodied palm.

"Ye should have cook attend yer hands," he muttered. "Ye been too long at the pump."

Ryan laughed suddenly, causing Wyler to start. "The last time I saw cook he was swimming about his quarters grabbing at his tools as they floated by him."

Wyler frowned, seeing little humor in Ryan's words. "Where be yer lass?" he asked, squinting into the appearing sunlight.

"Asleep on a soggy berth in the mate's cabin. Enrico found a tin of dry herring and crackers in the orlop and saw her fed."

Wyler shook his head disapprovingly. " 'Twas a wrong ye did, lad. She dinna want to come aboard and she might ha' perished in the gale."

"We all might have perished, and may yet," Ryan retorted hotly.

"Aye, but methinks yer ship will swim to land." Wyler squeezed water from his captain's coat. Deep, weary lines puckered his ruddy face. "Time to relieve at the pumps. The mates weary fast, with the close air and no fresh water."

"There's a rum keg in my cabin," Ryan commented, jerking his soaked shirt over his head.

Wyler smiled a long smile. "By God, Ryan! Me men may be thirsty, but yer rum will freshen them. Mayhaps me'll drink it all."

Ryan's half smile faded. He pointed suddenly across the quarter deck to starboard. Wyler saw it, too.

The vessel was bearing down on them like a meteor. She was a rakish, two-topsail schooner with a long swivel amidship and one mounted on the foremast. The vessel was painted dead black, even to the reaches of her flush deck. She flew no flag. She was approaching at extraordinary speed.

Wyler scratched worriedly at his beard. "I dinna like it, Ryan. I smell trouble."

"We'll run our distress flag if I can find it below," Ryan said, scrambling to his feet.

"No, lad," Wyler cautioned. "They ha' already seen our distress."

"Pirates, then," Ryan said, answering his own question.

"Mayhap. Ye best find any dry arms on board and alert the mates. Keep half pumping and send the rest updeck. We be vulnerable so they won't hurry to board us. Fetch Thrush to stay with yer lass, have Enrico explain the danger to him. 'Twould be wise they not be knowin' a woman is aboard." Wyler's orders were calm, deliberate, though he wore a concerned scowl on his face.

Ryan crossed the deck in long strides, casting a sidelong look at the swift schooner bearing down on them. He should have insisted the *Waverly* remain armed as she had been when he sailed her. They would have blasted the marauders out of the water.

Janielle was snuggled into the berth, asleep under a length of shredded canvas. Ryan stared down at her, feeling a sharp twinge of regret. Two years of their lives wasted, and now perhaps more, even if they survived the newest threat moving across the sea toward them.

"Janielle," he called softly, savoring the sharp-sweet jasmine fragrance that still clung to her white-gold hair.

She stirred only slightly. Ryan leaned across her, gathering her in his arms. Ever so slowly, she opened her wide violet eyes.

"Ryan, wh—what?"

He touched a finger to her lips. "Listen to me, Janielle. There is little time. An unnamed vessel is stalking us from the southwest. She flies no flag and the *Waverly* is without arms or sail to outmaneuver her. There may be danger. You are to remain in here with Thrush and Enrico until I come for you. You are not to come above deck. Do you understand?"

Janielle watched Ryan's brooding eyes, a deeper blue now with a sparkle of fierce warning. She wanted to speak but he hushed her words with his warm mouth. A gentle kiss, even a fragile one, that spoke faintly of tenderness. She was still lost in that kiss, her eyes closed, when he released her.

"We were to anchor on the morrow, Janielle. I had a

275

place for you at Caicos Island."

When she opened her eyes again, he was gone.

Mead Bennington signaled his bosun to fire the Long Tom across the crippled merchantman's bow. He leveled his glass to his eye, watching the red hull dip into the churning, weather-ravaged sea. The merchantman appeared French in design, a broken ship with her masts gone, swamping low in the swollen waters. Adjusting his glass brought the worn gold lettering along her bowsprit into focus. The *Waverly*.

Impatiently he shook his blond head. The frigate was swimming, a fractured vessel, taking water rapidly, hardly worth the effort of salvage. It was not his nature to concern himself with rescue. Still, there might be some small gain aboard, if only the crewmen's supplies.

As he studied the frigate, something struck a chord of memory. The *Waverly* had once seen battle, but her gun ports were now empty. No flag flying, but then there were no masts. She was pulling toward the trades and there was a possibility she'd make the Bahama Bank. But, no, after he'd ravaged her, she would be scuttled.

"No signal, sir," the bosun reported.

"How in hell can she signal? Her deck is stripped bare!" Bennington thundered.

"There's crew aboard," Indee, the Portuguese second mate, commented, massaging a furry hand across his greasy belly.

"A gentle challenge," Bennington muttered, fastening his sword belt around his waist. "Hoist our blood flag! Ready to board!"

The *Copperhead* closed in fast on the disabled merchantman, trimming her canvas, the well-seasoned pirate crew glittering in readiness.

Mead Bennington, beads of battle sweat glistening across his brow, climbed into the lower shrouds. He signaled for the longboat to be lowered.

"Yield or die!" he bellowed across the narrow span of water separating the ships.

Ryan watched the arrogant pirate captain with a twinge of recall. "I know the bastard from someplace, Wyler," Ryan muttered.

"Bloody vermin resemble them bloody selves," Wyler stormed.

"We may be able to negotiate," Ryan remarked coldly as the first longboat carrying the pirate crew drew alongside.

"Na' likely!" Wyler scowled, giving the first wavedown of his hand. On the upwave his best marksmen would fire at the pirates with the only three dry muskets on board.

"You can't shoot them all, there are too many," Ryan said evenly.

"Mayhap, but the ruse may cause them to waver and decide a naked merchantman na' worth the risk."

Suddenly Wyler swept his hand wide up, signaling the volley to begin.

Startled screams of pain tore through the longboat. Mutely, Ryan watched the grisly spectacle, indifferent to the slaughter. Wyler had caught the pirates unaware.

Wilson and his men reloaded, firing a second volley at Wyler's command. Still there was no answering fire from the *Copperhead*.

The tawny-haired captain appeared again in the low deck rigging. Ryan had a clear flash of the man. His eyes narrowed; then he remembered.

Without warning, the port-side culverin on the *Copperhead* belched its scattering of lead, finding its mark in the *Waverly*'s weakened timbers. A long gash erupted along the main deck. A second culverin smoked, followed by a barrage of small-arm fire. The pirates were attacking wildly from broadside, endangering their own ship.

Ryan lay close along the deck, cautiously raising his head to survey the damage. Wilson was sprawled on his back, sightless eyes boring upward at a sky he would never see again. Dazedly, Ryan stared at the dark puddle of blood near his feet. The shipwright next to him had no face left.

Wyler crouched down next to him. "There be two longboats aft," he rasped.

"Yield, Wyler. This is madness." Ryan spoke hollowly.

Wyler stared incredulously at him. "And ye a piratin' man! 'Tis never ye would yield!"

"I never fought pirates from a raft before," Ryan said bitterly.

"Aye," Wyler said thoughtfully. "Well, lad, yield we will, but the rutting bastard captain is mine," Wyler gritted, slapping the carved handle of his thin knife.

After the call for surrender, Mead Bennington stepped aboard the stricken ship, his dark face impassive as his eyes swept the broken bodies strewn across the *Waverly*'s deck.

"Indee!" Bennington shouted. "Set the men to pillage and bring the captain and all survivors before me!"

Indee nodded, running a bloodied hand across his cutlass, wiping the blade clean across the back of a dead crewmate. His mouth hung open, his beetle-black eyes glassy as he licked at the yellowish drool escaping from his lips. The blade of his cutlass prodded at Ryan.

"You are captain?" Indee asked, lisping in his Spanish accent.

"I am the owner of the ship," Ryan replied.

Indee looked puzzled for a moment, then his mouth broke into a toothless smile. Without warning, he brought the flat side of his cutlass down hard across Ryan's back.

Caught off guard, Ryan pitched forward across the slippery deck planking. Slowly he gathered himself up on spread palms, his eyes level with Indee's blood-encrusted boots.

"*Ees* not what I ask, Englishman," the Portuguese sneered, kicking Ryan full in the face.

Furiously, Ryan caught at the swinging boot, spitting blood from his mouth. Off balance, the Portuguese tripped, falling hard against Ryan. Instinctively Ryan reached for the pirate's throat, his fingers gouging deeply into the stubby flesh.

"Ryan Deverel!" The harsh British voice from above him stayed his attack. Swaying, Ryan struggled to his feet, vaguely aware of the throaty gasps from the Portuguese.

His eyes met the yellow-green animal eyes of Mead Bennington. Shaking his head to clear it, he stared incredulously at the tall, flaxen-haired pirate captain.

A twisted smile played across Bennington's mouth.

"So it is to be again that I am the victor!" Bennington taunted. "The scrawny bastard lad of Brocksburg still has lessons to learn!"

Ryan's words felt thick in his mouth. "Bennington—" was all he could manage. "Why in God's name?"

Bennington threw back his head and laughed, a tortured, nerve chilling laugh that tore through the air. "Do you not recall that my hero during our days at Brocksburg was Stede Bonnet?"

Ryan shook his head in disbelief. "Your family was English titled. Your father—"

"As dreary as the gray stone walls that enclosed us in that living tomb they called a 'boy's preparatory,'" Bennington said, watching Indee adjust his loose boot.

"My ship is foundering," Ryan said briefly, studying the detached expression on Bennington's face. "We took a harsh lashing during the hurricane. I ask she be allowed to drift into the Bahama Bank. We'll shore her and—"

"Still the diplomat, eh, bastard Ryan?" Bennington's eyes glowed wolfishly. "As you attempted to talk your way free from the food *I* stole and placed in your coffer.

279

Tell me, when the warden master inflicted your punishment, did you cry with agony?"

Ryan cast him a murderous look. Out of the corner of his eye he saw Wyler approaching, escorted by two heavily armed pirates. Wyler's eyes were glazed, his wide mouth firmly clamped together.

Bennington relaxed, leaning on the railing, folding his arms across his chest. He frowned into the sun.

"State yourself!" he flung at Wyler.

Worriedly, Ryan watched the corded neck muscles throbbing with fury as Wyler fought for control.

"Easy, Wyler," Ryan cautioned, moving into step with him.

The glint of steel flashed before either man could move. Mead Bennington heaved, groaning as the thin blade slashed into his ribs. Wyler ground the point of the blade, twisting it, locking beefy arms about the slender pirate captain.

"No man takes me ship," Wyler gritted.

Ryan heard only the fast metallic swish of movement behind him. Indee, the Portuguese, sliced across the air, laying his cutlass deep into Wyler's neck. Wyler was sliding down Bennington's length, his partially severed head lobbing grotesquely onto his left shoulder.

Stunned, Bennington blinked vacantly at Ryan. Quickly Indee stepped over Wyler's inert form, ripping away Bennington's shirt, jerking roughly at the embedded hilt of Wyler's knife.

"The Scottish bastard conceal it in *hees* groin," Indee hissed, stuffing a cloth into the gaping wound. Mead Bennington, his face ashen, stared down at the blood dripping from his side.

Ryan swallowed the hard lump grained in his throat.

"Before God, Bennington, I will kill you!"

"Ryan!" Janielle's scream from across the deck shattered the air. She jerked free from the two pirates who held her, and rushed into Ryan's arms. Her violet eyes widened with horror when she saw Wyler lying face down in a spreading red pool of his own blood.

Ryan pulled her close, pressing her head into his chest. "Wyler is dead, Janielle. Do not look his way."

Mead Bennington's eyes dulled with pain, flickered over Janielle. "Who are you, madam?" he breathed hoarsely.

"The lady is mine," Ryan snapped.

"Are you wed?" Bennington addressed Janielle.

"We—no—I—" Janielle stammered, feeling Ryan go rigid.

"She is mine," Ryan repeated deliberately.

Suddenly the *Waverly* pitched to port, uttering a shuddering groan from the bowels of her lower timbers. The deck heaved beneath their feet. The pirate crew scrambled toward the side, making ready the longboats.

"Nothing is yours this day," Bennington said viciously. "It would do you well to remember that."

"*Ees* no time to scuttle her, Captain," Indee lisped, shoving Bennington toward the rail.

"Who is left aboard?" Bennington asked hurriedly.

"A giant black we tied in the hold and the crew you see here, Captain."

"Bring the black, I'll sell him in Jamaica. Take half the crew to the *Copperhead*. The others, spread them in longboats and cast them off. Deverel and his lady go with us."

Janielle leaned against Ryan as they moved to the railing. She cast one last look at the naked deck of the *Waverly*. Wyler's body lay near the stump of foremast.

She lifted her eyes to Ryan. "What about Wyler?" she asked softly.

Ryan's face was impassive. "His day and mine will come," he vowed, taking Janielle's arm and lifting her over the portside rail.

chapter 28

Ryan lifted his head, tensing as dreaded footsteps pounded toward the bolted door. Instinctively he tugged at the sluggish chain looping him to the aft hold planking. Days swam together now, broken only by the agonies above deck when Indee, the Portuguese second mate, practiced his expertise at flogging the remaining shreds of flesh from his back.

Morbid anticipation took him after the first five strokes, bidding him welcome the pain. Another five and he soared loose from his own body, winging free into a fathomless nether where he felt nothing until he awakened in the hold of Thrush.

"Rión!" Thrush's deep voice jarred him. Thrush motioned to the door, listening. Faded footsteps gradually echoed down the deep cargo hold. Indee must be tiring of his sport.

Ryan stretched forward on his belly, ignoring Thrush's insistence that he allow the giant black to tend his back. Surprisingly, the poultice that Thrush had mixed with spittle and moldy biscuit crumbs had drawn some of the pain and eased the bleeding.

Mead Bennington's motives were obviously clear. A taste of the lash to ensure authority, a lesson in humiliation to weaken him. And latent revenge for

Wyler's knife wound. But Bennington wanted something from him; otherwise he would have killed him aboard the *Waverly*.

Thrush reached a hand across to him, bending down from the neck collar that secured him to the aft beam. Indee was cautious, knowing that Thrush's strength could easily rip the planking loose and he could free himself. Indee was babbling in the tongue of his people.

"Cease your mutterings," Ryan groaned, "Enrico is not alive to translate and I can't understand your words."

Wildly euphoric with pain, he suddenly laughed out loud, catching Thrush's worried scowl. "No, my black friend," Ryan rasped between gulps of laughter. Fingers of pain shot through him. "I am not mad, only remembering another savage in another land who sought to ease my suffering with his Yemassee poultices."

Thrush craned his massive neck, smiling uncertainly down at Ryan.

"That was at Challey," Ryan resumed his delirious rambling. "My friend Evan was there—no, Evan is not my friend. But for him I should be in Scotland, wed to a flaming-haired lass with eyes the color of liquid emeralds. Aye, and she a comely virgin—do you know of virgins, my black friend? They are troublesome but adoring. Ah, but I have had my fill of them—"

"Rión!" Thrush shouted, breaking his trance.

Ryan slumped belly down on the blood-soaked canvas. Mercifully, he slept.

The pirate schooner *Copperhead* was running full sail before the south wind, under a brilliant azure sky, at a speed Janielle had not believed possible. Thankfully, no one had approached her since she had been locked in the small mate's cabin, save a grizzled, one-armed derelict who brought a platter of food and a bucket of fresh water to her twice a day. Days ago, she had watched Ryan be manacled and taken below decks with Thrush. She had not seen him since.

During the three days aboard the *Copperhead*, Janielle had ample time to think, to plan. Her core felt tight, impenetrable. Not even the hideous flashes of the last scenes aboard the *Waverly* moved her. She would survive by outwitting all of them.

The pirate captain, Mead Bennington, drew her curiosity—a man nearly Ryan's height, with hawklike features, who spoke in gentleman's tongue. Who commanded his men and his ship in a haughty, concise manner. Ryan appeared to have known him before and was wary of him. But Bennington's eyes frightened her; a feverish, amber glitter of cruelty lurked deep in them.

Pirates sought gold, and her father could spare that. Above gold, they sought what? Security? No, they were doomed, hunted men, calloused adventurers. Like Ryan had become since he took her from El Roble. Somehow she must approach Mead Bennington with an offer, one that would see her safely back to Charleston.

When the clawish hand fumbled with the inside bolt of her door, she stiffened. It was worth a try.

The squatty pirate held the tray on the stub of his arm, tipping the greasy broth until it dribbled on the cabin planking. Blackened gums spread into a wolfish grin as he leered at her.

Janielle backed away from the fetid, overpowering stench that clung to him. "Tell your captain that I wish to speak to him," she said in as forceful a voice as she could manage.

Chalcedony eyes, cold ice marbles set in folds of sea-weathered wrinkles, glittered back at her. He gave no indication that he understood her.

"Do you understand English?" Janielle demanded.

The crippled pirate pointed a filthy, stubbed finger at her.

"The *laidy* seeks for a man," he sneered boldly, scratching the rising bulge between his legs.

Janielle shrank against the porthole, glancing wildly about for some way of escape. His rum-dregged breath was hot against her neck.

"The captain, he likes big women to hold him. Me, I like the scrawny sluts where the flesh rides the bone," he hissed, his twisted fingers fondling her soft breast.

Janielle shoved against him with all her strength. When sticky, yellowish drool from his toothless mouth touched her shoulder, she thought she would vomit. Instead, she screamed.

Painfully, Mead Bennington lowered his arm, caressing the stark white bandage that laced his ribs. Fortunately for him, the Scottish captain had been old, and clumsy with the knife. He looked up, frowning as Indee entered the cabin.

"A disturbance, Captain," Indee lisped hurriedly, looking away from the hard yellow eyes that glared at him.

"Meaning what?" Bennington demanded.

"The woman, Captain. Dolph, the cook's mate, tried to mount her, and—"

"Did he succeed?" Bennington smiled, spinning around in his chair.

"I heard her scream and pulled him off before he spurted."

Bennington had drawn his pistol, pointing the barrel directly at the Portuguese's heart. Casually he flicked the firing hammer.

"Perhaps Indee prefers death to obeying my commands," Bennington said, his amber eyes sparkling with deadly jest.

Indee felt trickles of cold sweat coursing down his face. He had watched his captain kill men for less. Heavily, he sunk to his knees, clasping clammy hands together.

"I could not know, Captain," he whimpered.

285

"She was your charge, Indee! I gave orders she was not to be molested. She represents a valuable exchange for me."

"I know, Captain."

Bennington waved his pistol aside. "You and Dolph should swing by the neck from the mast," he said undecidedly. "Throw Dolph in chains until we reach the cay. As for you—"

"I'll take her food to her, Captain," Indee offered hesitantly.

Bennington threw back his head and laughed. "And gag her so her screams are not heard. Someday, Indee, I may give her to you after I am finished with her necessity. Meanwhile, leave her alone!"

Indee nodded obediently, slowly getting to his feet. With the back of his furry arm he wiped away the sweat that coursed down his face.

Bennington still toyed with his pistol. "What of the bastard in the hold?"

"He makes no sound, Captain, when he is flogged."

Bennington spread navigator charts on the table, frowning over them. "We anchor at Rum Cay on the morrow," he said thoughtfully. Half aloud, he continued. "Even at Brocksburg he was disgustingly stubborn." He suddenly brightened, turning to Indee.

"Have him brought to me and lay a full meal out. He can watch me dine."

"But, Captain, the man is—"

"Bloody? Stinking? Starved? All the better! It should whet my appetite." Bennington smiled, his animal eyes glazed with anticipation.

Ryan needed little persuasion when a choked draft of fresh salt air reached his lungs. Even the jaw of his manacle chomping the raw band of wrist flesh went unnoticed. He eyed Indee cautiously. The Portuguese second mate did not carry the braided lash on his belt. Instead, a dull silver Italian foil rapier dangled along his thigh.

Fading daylight caught the last streams of flaming sun, a dazzling crimson orb settling into its watery nest. A gentle salt breeze rippled the tattered shreds of Ryan's breeches as he followed Indee updeck. Blessed moments free of chains, sea spume needling his face, and light—God, yes—light!

Mead Bennington nodded dully as Ryan entered the cabin. He poured a splash of Madeira into his half-filled goblet, raking polished amber eyes over Ryan. A twisted, arrogant smile edged across his mouth.

"How do you fare, bastard Ryan?"

Ryan made a mental lunge, then coiled his rage. Mead Bennington possessed a tinge of lunacy, a style of madness well remembered.

"What answer do you seek?" Ryan asked, outwardly calm.

"A brief one," Bennington snapped.

"No session with your goon's lash today, and no brine water or rancid gruel. Can it be, my introduction to your style of pirate life is concluded?"

"Perhaps," Bennington said, steepling his forefingers. "What do you think of my seamanship?"

"Effective on stricken vessels," Ryan retorted.

Angrily, Ryan grasped the wine flask on the table, pouring a full goblet of Madeira. He tossed it down and refilled, studying Mead Bennington. He maintained an advantage. Bennington needed something from him. Recklessly, he proceeded.

"Where is the girl?" he demanded.

"Safe for now. The rest depends on your actions," Bennington replied coldly.

"Where do we sail?" Ryan asked, feeling the quieting effects of the smooth wine in his empty belly.

Bennington shot him a hard look. "First the conditions," he snarled. "Your services in return for her safe return to the Carolinas."

"Which services?" Ryan sneered. "My back for Indee to play his lash across? Another grime-ridden soul to inhabit your lice-infested hold? I must refuse."

At that moment the cabin door edged open and the cook appeared bearing a tray of steaming food. Succulent chicken, swimming in its own juices, boiled baby carrots and a full loaf of fresh bread was placed on the table.

Ryan swallowed, reeling at the sight of the food. Overpowering hunger assailed him. His last full meal had been aboard the *Waverly*, days ago.

With a roar, Bennington kicked the table with his boot, sending bits of crockery and strewn food flying across the cabin.

"If you wish to eat, bastard, lick it from the planks like a dog!" He was livid, shaking with rage, his voice suddenly breaking into wild, chilling laughter.

Slowly Ryan eased into a chair, determined to hold his resolve against a raving madman. He remembered the methods well. Quietly he retrieved the wine flask and reached for two tin mugs. He poured them full, offering one to Bennington.

Mesmerized for a moment, Bennington stared at the outstretched mug. Nervously he righted his chair, massaging a hand across his forehead. His sagging expression told Ryan that the mood was spent.

"You were speaking of conditions," Ryan reminded him gently.

Still confused, Bennington regarded him vacantly. After a long silence he cleared his throat.

"At Brocksburg the rector praised your skill at building design. Do you still maintain the talent?"

This was scarcely what Ryan had expected. Calmly, he replied, "I have."

"The girl is John Patterson's daughter," Bennington

said shortly. "A port notice issued in Havana claims you abducted her. There is a large purse for your capture, Ryan. Now her freedom depends on your cooperation."

"What are your needs in construction?"

"A dock is to be built into the lagoon at Rum Cay. Also, a land bridge over the cay that will open to me and close to the path of any intruders, providing an escape if it is needed. My force is growing, Ryan. I need loading piers. My colony on the cay is filling with people like myself. People who—"

"Need a king," Ryan remarked curtly.

Bennington glowered at him. "The Continental fleet is deadly and has declared war on the pirates that prey on American ships. They will force you to survive as I have."

Ryan was not concerned with the Continental fleet. "What materials are available?" he asked offhandedly.

"Two merchantmen reluctantly parted with their lumber cargoes, which are stacked on the beach," Bennington quipped, relaxing with the effect of wine.

Ryan shifted in his chair, leaning across the table. "These are my terms, Bennington." He spoke harshly. "I will design your docks and bridges in exchange for the girl's safe passage to Charleston. No ransom, and I accompany her to the harbor, under your guard if you demand it."

"No!" Bennington thundered, getting to his feet, his yellow eyes flaring with anger.

Ryan rose slowly from the table, leveling flint-hard eyes at Bennington. "Call your Portuguese imbecile and return me to the hold!"

Bennington wavered with indecision. He needed Ryan's skill, but the goddamn bastard was drawing an edge. He knew the project was beyond the experience of any of his men. His knuckles whitened against the side of the table.

"You did not list the terms of your freedom," Bennington said caustically.

"I don't recall asking for it," Ryan replied.

"You make a noteworthy pirate, Ryan."

Ryan shrugged indifferently. "A point I usually make with a rapier," he commented evenly. "For now, I require a bath, a trencher of decent food, and salve for my back. The black man in the hold with me is my property. He goes with me. As for the statesman's daughter—"

"Is she your property?" Bennington interrupted slyly, his glazed eyes flickering over the protuberance of Ryan's manhood.

"I wish to see her," Ryan snapped.

"In time, Ryan. Consider your weighty demands approved for now, with the exception of the girl. That would only serve to arouse you and that would not be tolerated. I warn you, Ryan, my generosity can easily be provoked and denied."

Ryan turned aside from the doorway. "When do we port?"

"At midday tomorrow," Bennington replied lightly, allowing his hand to quiver across his swollen groin. Ryan Deverel possessed a sensuality that was unsettling.

Thoughtfully, Bennington watched the broad expanse of Ryan's back disappear down the passageway. The game would rest between plays. Deverel was mistaken. He thought he had won.

chapter 29

White, showy fingers of glittering volcanic sand reached into the sea, the slanted palms on its surface guarding the beach folds with twisted, dangling fronds ever defiant against the cooling tradewinds. Their heights shadowed from the noontide sun, the ageless palms at Rum Cay were in clear view of the port-bound *Copperhead*.

Janielle grasped the shredded remnants of her violet ball gown across her breasts, listening to the brisk orders being shouted above deck. The *Copperhead* had skirted the shoreline, threading its way into a shallow tidewater vein that spilled into a deep inland lagoon.

Sharp, clipped commands from Mead Bennington echoed through the passageway, followed by a heavy crash. Angry sounds now, of the same Spanish tongue that Enrico had spoken. Then silence. The pirates were going ashore.

Janielle rushed to the door, pressing her ear against the varnish-peeled wood. They couldn't leave her on board. She hammered her fist on the door until her knuckles were bruised. Still no one came to release her.

"Is anyone above?" she called wildly, hot tears stinging her eyes. Only the trills from frigate birds hovering in the lush blanket of nightsage beyond the lagoon answered her.

Once Ryan had left her imprisoned at Challey, tied to his bed awaiting his pleasure. The terror that had gripped her then was small in comparison to what threatened her now.

"Please, anyone?" Janielle tried again, almost reassured by the echoes of her own voice. Minutes pulled by, edging to the hour mark. Stubbornly, she settled down to wait. There was little else she could do.

An hour later the deck planking creaked above her and thudded footfalls made their way to the passage steps. The balky latch on the door yielded under a sharp rupture of metal.

Indee, the Portuguese, flung the door wide and stepped inside the cabin. "The captain welcomes you to Rum Cay," he lisped in halting English. He swept a furry arm to his waist, bowing mockingly. "You will accompany me." He smiled wolfishly, the words forming more of a demand than a request.

Janielle hesitated for an instant, wary of his intentions. The well-remembered assault by the repulsive cook's mate caused her to shudder.

Indee re-emphasized his motions. Janielle stiffened her back regally, preceding him through the narrow doorway, conscious of the spreading leer on his face.

Carefully she picked her way across the crumbling, storm-torn boulders that offered a ready land bridge from the deck. Confused, she halted at the edge of the bank. There was no path to follow.

A low grunt came from Indee, indicating his impatience. Meekly, Janielle followed him into a choking tangle of emerald foliage, brushing at the swarms of insects that surrounded her. Once she tripped over a coiling, yellowish smooth vine, nearly falling against Indee. Horrified, she glanced back to see that the mistaken vine had slithered into the undergrowth.

In a few hurried strides, a worn coral path opened into a long sandy clearing. At the far end, roughly constructed pens of bullet wood lined the clearing. Animal pens, Janielle thought reassuringly. But they were not intended for animals. Through the narrow slits, Janielle could see there were men inside. Ryan. Ryan would be somewhere in there.

Janielle clutched at her throat, overwhelmed by the sudden prospect of what lay before her. Even black slaves in the Carolinas were not kept in small cages under a blazing tropical sun. Swallowing the rising bile in her throat, she spun on the Portuguese.

"That is inhumane," she shrieked, her voice trembling.

"*Ees* necessary," Indee muttered, grasping her by the arm and leading her away from the clearing.

They approached a low, heavily thatched building of fitted marl braced with oyster shells. Janielle had never seen such a building before. Island palms, clustered in a tidy circle, shaded the structure from the broiling sun.

Indee rapped twice on the slanted doorway. From inside, Mead Bennington's voice was firm.

"Enter, Indee."

Janielle swept past the Portuguese, anxious for the coolness of the shelter. Once inside the gloomy interior, she felt peculiarly dizzy.

"A chair quickly for the lady," Mead Bennington said, rising from his desk.

Janielle groped for the smooth firmness of the chair beneath her sinking legs, thankful that she hadn't fainted. If she ever needed her strength, it was at this moment.

A cool metal goblet was being placed in her hand and urged to her mouth. She sipped a sweet liquid, unknown to her.

"I sympathize with your distress, milady," a voice sounding very British ebbed at her drowsy senses.

Janielle raised her violet eyes to the voice, seeing the hazy outline of Mead Bennington's golden form stretched across from her. He was stripped to the waist, his blond hair tied behind his head. Her eyes kept returning to the brilliant gold band on his finger, glittering with studded diamonds. She couldn't seem to pull her gaze from it.

Slowly she drank from the goblet, her thirst still unsated. Instantly the goblet was snatched from her and refilled.

"An island variety, milady, laced with papaya," Mead Bennington explained, his voice strangely different.

"China delight," Indee snickered from the corner of the room, quieting when he caught his captain's hard look.

Janielle felt better, almost gloriously so. First she would demand to see Ryan, then she'd demand her freedom. And finally she would demand that the men held in the small pens be released. Her tongue felt weighted when she tried to move it. She waited through a long shudder, steadying herself.

"You appear a gentleman, sir," she began weavingly. "Therefore I demand to see the man who was captured from the *Waverly*. His name is Ryan Deverel." She swallowed hard, determined to proceed.

"I intend to secure my freedom at any cost and his as well. Also, there is a matter of the men penned like animals in the clearing—" her words were fading in her own ears. What was making her so fearless? "It is wholly unjust to treat any human in that fashion."

"I shall note your requests, madam, in time." Bennington spoke calmly.

Janielle sensed a lingering politeness in his words, as though he were waiting for something to happen. Another long tremor shook her and darts of exploding white flashes swam before her eyes. The room was fuzzy and her chair was tipping over. She couldn't hold on. The last sound she heard was the confident laugh that erupted from Mead Bennington's mouth.

Ryan froze, halting the hollowed gourd dipper halfway to his mouth. His eyes narrowed as Thrush wielded the huge ax, raggedly slicing the rounded dock post in two fallen halves. Methodically, Thrush heaved the parted timber into a stack near the water.

Mead Bennington had wasted no time. The Canadian lumber, confiscated from a French cargo hold, had been floated by raft to the far end of the cay. And Ryan and a ragtag crew of disgruntled pirate mates, a few stoic descendents of the Caribs, and some of his own men from the *Waverly*, had been herded across the lagoon, following the rafts to the point of construction.

The enormity of the task, coupled with the added disadvantages that few of the men understood the proper use of the tools or could translate his commands, had further convinced him that Mead Bennington was, indeed, a madman. Only the unquestioning eyes of Carlson, the *Waverly*'s shipwright, had sustained him.

"Can be done, Ryan," Carlson had said dryly, his thick voice tinged with upcountry slur.

"The lumber is green and unsuited for this climate. It needs time to cure. And of time, I have little," Ryan replied sullenly.

"The lagoon narrows near the water fold. And there are joined rocks. 'Twould take a fierce navigator to enter from this side," Carlson had remarked.

"Or a lunatic," Ryan had offered.

Ryan had to admire Bennington's plan to build the dock where it linked to an escape land bridge. A ship anchored here could be away before the enemy could encounter them, providing the pilot knew the narrows. One would have to know the location of the land bridge through the tangles of island growth or become hopelessly lost. In a few more weeks Bennington intended to attempt the passage to this side of the cay. The dock must be finished before that day.

Ryan spread his sand-grained sketches across his lap, reviewing them again. At best the labor kept him from dwelling on other things. Namely, Janielle. Ryan's only contact with Bennington now was through the Portuguese, Indee. He assured Ryan that the American lady was safe and comfortable, awaiting the time the bridge was completed and she could sail for the Carolinas. Ryan had not seen Janielle since the day they had been taken aboard the *Copperhead*.

"The stretches are ready for lashing," Carlson announced, hunkering beside Ryan.

"Only the first ten until we see how they behave," Ryan said offhandedly, his eyes traveling across the narrow stretch of water.

"Once we start across the land, it will be easier," Carlson remarked, wiping his sweating face.

They both got to their feet as Indee approached, carrying a yellowed paper in his hand.

"I *breeng* news from your city to ease your isolation," Indee lisped, handing the water-stained page of the *Charleston Gazette* to Ryan.

Hungrily, Ryan's eyes scanned the print. The Charleston Theater on Savage Green was offering a performance of *The Tragedy of the Earl of Essex*, and a rival theater, City Theater, was being constructed on the west side of Church Street between St. Michel's Alley and Tradd Street. It would open with a benefit performance for the American captives of the Algerines.

He read on. A new race course sponsored by General Charles Pickney, General William Washington, Gerneral William Moultrie, General Jacob Read, William Alson, O'Brien Smith, Gabriel Manigault, Wade Hampton and Edward Fenwick was being organized as the Fourth South Carolina Jockey Club. It promised to be "a display of beautiful women, gallant fellows and elegant equipages."

Ryan threw back his head and laughed, a crazed sound that brought a worried scowl to Thrush's ebony face. A sound repeated from the bowels of the *Copperhead*.

Indee took a step back, unsure of Ryan's behavior. Instinctively he reached for the marlin spike he always carried with him when he journeyed across the cay.

Instantly Ryan sobered. "*Uunashee!*" he thundered at the Caribs who scurried at his work command. "Traba-har!" he shouted at the others. Sullenly, the men turned to their task.

Ryan whirled on Indee. "I am returning with you in the pirogue," he said angrily to the Portuguese.

"B—but the Captain did not say—" Indee lisped, swallowing the saliva that drooled continually from his mouth.

"Either I return with you now or your captain can find another master builder. Carlson can manage until tomorrow. I have business with Bennington."

Indee ran a stubby finger along his coarse, springy beard. His captain's pleasure with the American lady might be interrupted and he would pay dearly for it. Still, Deverel left him no choice. Yet when the captain had given him the paper for Ryan, his eyes had glowed with some secret amusement.

Warily the Portuguese studied the tall, fiercely gaunt man who towered above him. There was a deadly cold determination about the American sea captain that even he, with his expert lash, had been unable to break. Even the strongest men whimpered. Some even begged.

Finally, he nodded to Ryan to follow him. The reckoning between the two captains was certain to come, and soon.

chapter 30

The Dutch schooner *Den Hoorn* rode easy anchor in the secluded shoals off Rum Cay, the most recent victim of Mead Bennington's pillage through the Windward Passage. The cargo of raw sugar, sisal and tobacco was of little importance: it was the schooner itself that Bennington sought.

Indee reported to him that the work on the land bridge and the dock at the lagoon was half completed, though Ryan Deverel had become increasingly testy about the project. He demanded more men, more equipment, more timber and better food for the workers. He was growing impatient. All the better, Bennington reasoned. His plans for Ryan's future at Rum Cay were nearing finality. A few more sessions with the American slut he penetrated nightly, and the plan should lock in place. For one particular session Ryan would be in attendance.

Janielle awakened slowly to the stabbing ribbons of daylight that reached out at her, plucking her eyes from her head. A thin film of sweat glistened on her naked body. She ran her tongue across her swollen lips, trying to recall the last time she had been clothed. Mead Bennington preferred her totally naked.

Reaching for the slender pitcher beside the bed, as she had done every morning for the last few weeks, Janielle drank thirstily of the frothy, peach-colored island drink, the one Indee referred to as "China Delight."

Somehow she would get through this, she told herself. If only she didn't feel so afloat from herself. "I am Janielle Christina Patterson. My home is Patterson Woods, South Carolina," she would repeat endlessly when her senses were so numbed from the peculiar sensations that swept her she had difficulty remembering even that.

She drifted in an experience where everyone smiled but their eyes were not in agreement. The last clear fact in her swampy mind was the stark actuality that she had traded her freedom for Ryan Deverel's life. That she was, in fact, Mead Bennington's whore.

Dreamily, she smiled, recalling that in Charleston such women were referred to as a man's mistress. It sounded coolly polite, even intriguing, that way. There was nothing polite or intriguing to compare with her situation. The rawest moments of Mead Bennington's insatiable rutting had proven to her that she was nothing better than a dockside whore.

Janielle shuddered suddenly, her slim hand shaking as she drained the last of the island brew from the pitcher. The loathsome Manuela would come in soon to replenish it. Manuela had been Bennington's whore before her: he had performed the same perverted acts with the dark-skinned woman that he did with her. She shuddered again, thinking of that.

Bennington had approached her on the morning after their arrival at Rum Cay, when her thoughts were still unexplainably jumbled, her surroundings filtered by continual, downy vagueness. At moments she felt lifted to the highest pinnacle of her being. And in the murky lower depths, she dreamed in a spreading funnel that had no substance.

Through the layers of awareness, Bennington's crisp voice had assaulted her. "It is a truth, madam, that I hold all lives in this colony within my dominance. Those who oppose me die."

Janielle weaved in her chair. "What are your plans for me?" Her voice sounded strangely thin, detached from her.

Bennington laughed dryly. "So you understand," he chuckled. "That saves us time."

"I ask to see the man who was captured with me." Janielle spoke lamely.

"Impossible! He is at the far end of the cay and has been punished for his flagrant disobedience. You could scarce bear to witness his present state."

Janielle's slim fingers clawed at the edge of the chair.

"Wh—what have you done to him?"

"It remains to decide what I shall do *with* him," Bennington said curtly.

Janielle forced the words forward. "My father is John Patterson of South Carolina," she managed. "He will pay ransom for my safe return to Charleston. Please, sir, state what—"

"I know who you are!" Bennington thundered. "And my informants have the collector's mark on Ryan Deverel's head. His life is of no import to me. I shall determine at this moment his importance to you."

Janielle could only gaze stupidly up at him. All the associated patterns of her reasoning were distorted, muddled. Her mouth opened but no words came.

"My proposal is a simple one," Bennington continued, his amber eyes narrowing at her. Slowly he walked over to her, leaning across her, resting his hands on her slim shoulders.

"Ryan Deverel goes free should you decide to remain with me at Rum Cay."

Bennington's words tolled somewhere in Janielle's gnarled thoughts. She shook her head, trying to clear it.

"For how long?" she rasped finally.

300

Bennington's confident laugh slashed the close air. "Until I tire of you, madam."

Janielle righted herself in her chair, wishing her legs would lift her so she could stand to confront him.

"And otherwise?" she breathed.

"Otherwise, your lover will be hung before your eyes."

Janielle could urge forth no emotion. She only knew that salt tears were slipping down her cheeks, dropping gently on her hand.

"Have you ever watched a man hanged?" Bennington taunted. "The tongue swells black after the neck snaps, his last body juices gush—"

"Stop!" Janielle screamed, grinding her fists to her ears. Bennington jerked her hands away, his mouth close to hers.

"Consider well, madam," he snarled.

For a time Janielle sat in rigid silence, her own breath singing loudly in her ears. A fluttery vision of Ryan's face—arrogantly handsome, steel-blue eyes mocking her on the first encounter with him at Challey—jarred through her. Before God, she still loved him.

Bennington had moved to the doorway, motioning for Indee to enter the room. They conversed rapidly in Spanish while Janielle watched with vacant violet eyes. The repulsive dark Portuguese and the tawny pirate captain had a peculiarly unnatural companionship. An inkling of sensuous affection passed between them, causing Janielle to recoil. Indee eyed Janielle with disgust, his purplish tongue licking along his drooling lips.

After Indee had gone, Bennington stood before her, his legs spread wide. Mutely she stared at the delicately hammered buckle of pure silver on his wide belt. Unconsciously her eyes traveled downward.

"Your eyes caress a part of me that is impatient for you," Bennington said almost warmly.

Janielle lifted searching violet eyes to him. "How will

Ryan know that my decision has spared him?" she asked weakly.

"I shall tell him," Bennington lied.

"When?" Janielle spoke wearily.

"When I send for him," Bennington said.

Janielle only nodded. The island climate was making her ill. Dizzily, she reeled against Bennington, pressing her face against his muscled thigh.

"Manuela will prepare a bath for you, madam. I prefer my women clean before I soil them. Tonight your instructions on how to serve me will begin. I expect perfection and will have it."

Janielle accepted the cup of cool liquid that he urged to her lips. The strange mixture tasted amazingly soothing. It was done. Ryan would go free. And later Bennington would release her, too. Shreds of hope stirred in her mind.

The first morning with Bennington had seemed years ago. Janielle stretched her legs to the floor, pulling a thin sheet over her nakedness. After several weeks she bore little resemblance to herself. She was markedly thinner, caring little for food, sleeping through the daylight hours to summon what strength remained for the demanding activities that Bennington required of her all night.

In the beginning he had not been brutal. He had even seemed detached from the act itself. The vulgarities of watching Manuela perform certain movements with her dark, glistening body, the use of her wide, drawing mouth on Bennington, his unnatural responses, had revolted her. But after the first several nights of instruction, that, too, had become part of the blurred, feathery dream.

Bennington was insatiable. Even after she was certain he had achieved, he hadn't. And once, when she felt herself straining over the edge of her own satisfaction, he had suddenly withdrawn from her, shoving her aside.

"I'll tolerate no frozen receptacle for my thrusts!" he stormed, his hand slashing her face. "Goddamn you, bitch! Ever say his name again while I am in you and I'll give you to Indee!" Bennington swore, stalking naked from the room.

Dazed, Janielle touched the swelling bruise on her pale face, little realizing that she had breathed Ryan's name.

Ryan climbed from the pirogue, glancing hurriedly around the clearing. Smoke snaked chokingly from the few remaining cook fires. The island sun, flaming a burnt golden blush, was settling into the sea. For a moment he absorbed the panorama linking him to the feel of the sea.

The tacked topmasts of the *Den Hoorn* were silhouetted against the rosy fire of twilight. Ryan paused to gaze at the schooner. "What ship is it?" he asked Indee.

Indee licked at the spittle on his stubby chin. "A Dutchman," he grumbled irritably.

"Now part of Bennington's fleet," Ryan said half to himself.

"There will be many others," Indee commented gruffly, leading the way across the clearing. He knew Bennington was with the woman and he felt uneasy. His captain might kill him for the interruption, but he had swayed under the cold determination of Ryan Deverel. Then again, Bennington might be angry enough to kill both Deverel and the woman, and he and his captain could resume their former pleasures.

"When was she brought in?" Ryan demanded, motioning toward the schooner.

"A few days back. She is provisioned for sail and attack," Indee said distractedly.

A nagging thought of escape crossed Ryan's mind. He would need a crew, a willing one. If he could manage the release of even twenty of the men from the *Waverly*—

"The captain does not like surprises," Indee lisped, pawing at Ryan's arm.

"My being here will be no surprise to him," Ryan said

dryly, thinking of the sly torment Bennington had passed to him when he gave Indee the page of the *Gazette*. Bennington's ploys were all too obvious.

"Best you wait while I—"

Ryan had tired of the game. "No!" he shouted. "I am no captive here! Bennington and I struck terms."

"Terms?" Indee stared wild-eyed at Ryan's broad back as Ryan moved swiftly toward Bennington's hut.

Ryan hit the warped door planking with a full fist, bolting through the doorway, ready to confront Bennington. He was finished with terms!

Naked, Bennington sprawled on the side of the narrow rope bed, his legs spread wide, his hand resting on the kneeling form before him. A cloud of silvery-spun white-gold hair spilled across Bennington's thighs. Tawny, golden nakedness, beautifully slim, an illusion that coiled and curved to the strange, unheard rhythms of the bizarre union. Janielle. Janielle was—

Bennington moaned, jerking upright. In an instant his pistol rode his hand, his glazed amber eyes leveling coldly at Ryan.

Ryan advanced on him, knocking Janielle aside. Bennington was flash quick on his feet, cocking the firing hammer.

"You force this, bastard!" he spat. "Your woman chose to be my slut!"

Ryan hesitated, restraining his attack. Roughly he jerked Janielle to her feet, sickened by what he saw. His fingers laced in her white-gold hair, forcing her face to him.

"Is this true?" he rasped, shaking Janielle furiously.

Janielle lifted dazed violet eyes to him, her expression uncomprehending, void of emotion. Mutely, she nodded her head.

When Ryan released her, Janielle dropped to the floor, cradling her head in her thin arms. Swallowing the warm

304

bile that welled in his throat, Ryan whirled on Bennington.

"What in Christ's name have you done to her?" he demanded.

"Nothing she did not wish me to do," Bennington snarled, still holding fast grip on his pistol. "Women always choose a better opportunity."

"I came to end our terms, Bennington," Ryan said harshly, ignoring an occasional dry sob that escaped from Janielle's mouth.

"You would wish to return to the sea," Bennington half asked.

"Your land bridge is a simple duty now that the structure has been mapped. The dock is finished. The Caribs and your men can carry the rest. My bargain is met," Ryan gritted angrily.

Without warning, Indee entered the room, his cutlass drawn. His small beetle eyes swept Janielle's inert form and lingered on Bennington's nakedness. A slow, hungry smile edged across his dark face. The captain's plan had succeeded.

Bennington shrugged into his breeches, his pistol held in one hand. "Fetch Manuela to tend the woman," he ordered, moving to the door. Smiling, he turned to Ryan. "I have a gift for you, Deverel," he said, motioning for Ryan to precede him out of the door. Indee hovered close behind Ryan, his eyes never leaving him.

Ryan stepped outside, casting a look over his shoulder at Janielle. She had betrayed him yet again. For now, she deserved her fate. "What is your *gift?*" Ryan asked, his voice raw.

"The loan of the schooner under your own command with Indee as second officer, and a half split of your spoils," Bennington said sharply.

More of Bennington's terms, Ryan thought sullenly, still torn by the scene he had just witnessed. Janielle was an unfaithful bitch, easily swayed by any man. Only this time it was not the Challey overseer or a drunken British surgeon, but a rutting madman, a pirate of the lowest order of sea scum.

"A league of pirate captains," Ryan commented sourly.

"I seek only capable ones," Bennington replied sternly. "Other pirates in these waters have joined forces and sail as fleets, larger ships to plunder, thus larger rewards."

Ryan felt the shifting night breeze ruffle his dark hair. To feel the restive sea beneath his feet again, the salt air blowing free across his face—there was nothing to tie him to the land again. His responsibility for Janielle had ended.

"I will sail your schooner, Bennington," Ryan said evenly, "but understand—I command the ship. That includes the techniques of encounter and the loyalty of your men. I take some of my own crew from the *Waverly* if they elect to sail under pirate flag. I'll brook no interference from you!"

"I will not be cheated of my share!" Bennington charged.

"It is not my design to cheat any man!" Ryan countered. "I will take the schooner out at tide mark and test her run before the wind. My strategy differs from yours and I remind you of that fact."

Bennington smiled slowly. "She's fleet, Ryan, a true prize. I brought her in myself." Bennington glanced down, shifting his feet in the glittering sand. "Your woman—she has proven a disappointment," he offered quietly.

Ryan bristled. "Women are invariably disappointing," he said tersely, turning on his heel and stalking off down the beach.

chapter 31

Evan Reed straightened his broad shoulders, forcing them into the well-rehearsed starchy position befitting a naval officer. His steel-gray eyes were alert, attentive, as he stood before the Rear Admiral of the South Carolina Continental Fleet.

The dour admiral's mood was testy, his voice thorny. "Understand, Reed," Admiral Cunningham stated, "under ordinary Articles of War, this would not be permitted. Your British background decries patriotism for the country you now profess to claim. Were it not for John Patterson's endorsement of your request, coupled with the pressing need of a surgeon for our fleet, I should not have granted you audience."

"I understand, sir," Evan replied crisply.

"It is for this mission alone that you will be sworn. After its completion, you will be replaced," the admiral continued gruffly.

"That has been explained to me, sir. It is only this mission that I feel compelled to join."

The admiral cocked a white eyebrow at Evan. "The six ships will scour the pirate lanes until the senator's daughter is found. In the interim, the pirate lord Ryan Deverel will be pursued and captured. It is a twofold mission."

Evan held his gaze steady, but his hands trembled at his sides. Hopefully, he would be aboard when Janielle was found, when Ryan was taken. What had turned Ryan to flagrant piracy over the last year was beyond his comprehension. And where Janielle was hidden was a puzzle to the federal navies.

"We have had an ounce of luck over the week," Rear Admiral Cunningham continued blandly. "A former crewman of Deverel's ship, the *Waverly*, a chap named Carlson, was pulled aboard a federal vessel near St. Augustine. The man had been tortured and set adrift. Before he died he babbled about a pirate named "Benjamin," or something of the like, and said the name, "Patterson." When questioned about his ship, the man only muttered, 'avenge.' Still, it is the first solid word we have had in the matter in a year's space."

Evan heard his heart drumming in his ears. "How was it determined that the man had sailed with Deverel?" he asked.

"The wretch carried seaman's papers strapped to his chest. Odd occurrence, as though someone were trying to convey a message." The admiral frowned, shuffling through his documents. "You will be assigned to the flagship, *Trinity*. You have taken your American surgeon's oath?"

"I have, sir," Evan replied.

"The fleet is provisioned and ordered for sail on Tuesday. The Vice Admiral will sign your temporary commission. You will be given the rank of ensign."

An unexpected ripple of disappointment swept Evan and he winced at the admiral's words. As a British surgeon aboard the *Dover*, his rank had been elevated and respected. Still, he had fought a hard battle through many closed doors to get this far. The American navy was toughminded and frowned on a former British naval officer who sought favors.

"John Patterson sends his expression of gratitude by

me," Evan said tersely. "The safe return of his daughter may determine an improved state in his failing health."

Rear Admiral Cunningham's face softened. "John Patterson has done much to promote our fleet and is highly revered by the command. I vow the man responsible for this outrage to his daughter will be hung in chains at the entrance of our harbor!"

Evan's face was impassive. "By naval law, sir?"

"By all laws!" The admiral bellowed, as Evan briskly saluted, taking his leave.

The Dutch schooner *Den Hoorn*, rechristened the *Avenger*, skirted the Gulf of Darien, making upshore for Barranquilla, sailing under shortened sail stiffened by a stout east wind.

Ryan, his long body sun-blackened and solidly muscled, had tracked a listing French corvette from Portobello for two days. The corvette was bulgingly overcargoed and taking water, making sluggish sail despite the sudden wind.

The burly Dutch boatswain, Ort der Beer, had elected to sail under pirate flag rather than leave his ship. Ryan's crew of sixty-eight, including Thrush, some survivors of the *Waverly*, and others who had been part of Bennington's scruffy lot, had proved themselves reliable under harsh sea engagements. With the acquisition of Ort der Beer as first mate, Indee no longer sailed with Ryan. That had been a relief. Ryan had almost killed Indee when the Portuguese had questioned a command. And more, it cut the final ties of Bennington's influence on Ryan's crew.

"We take her?" Ort der Beer asked, watching Ryan's face.

"She's hugging too close to land," Ryan said, lowering his seaglass. "Let her show her intent. If she veers northeast, she's probably making for Kingston."

He shrugged, frowning into the spreading sun. The

Avenger would stalk, fall away, then run and tack, turning to bluff a broadside ram. An unexpected maneuver, one that Wyler had known, borrowed, he said, from the days of Roman sail.

Each prize he took required a modification of his maneuvers, depending on winds, the enemy captain's intelligence, and fate itself. But in the majority of engagements his basic strategy was reliable.

Bennington had been truthful about the capability of the Scot-hulled schooner. The *Avenger* was sharp, swift and agile, responding to the accelerated movements like a sloop, necessities in a marauding pirate ship preying on the larger and clumsier "ships of the line."

China tea clippers, whalers and even fishing smacks had been among Ryan's victims when he first stalked the waters of the Greater Antilles, gradually stretching to the larger game of Spanish, British and French merchantmen. In the early throes of fighting his conscience, he had avoided American ships, often allowing them to press him away. Only one, the *Swallow*, out of New Orleans, cargoed with rum and sugar, had he seized, torching the vessel but permitting the crew to escape. And afterward he had drunk himself senseless.

"She points north'ard, Captain," Ort der Beer said in his stunted English.

"Let her lead," Ryan ordered, seating himself on the windlass. There was no hurry. Full sail would catch her before dusk. Somehow he preferred a twilight capture, often pressing a victim into the shoreline shoals before launching attack. It seemed a more fitting time, more tuned to the blackness in his soul.

"She carries nine pounders, sir," Ort remarked.

"With her list, the shot will fall hollow," Ryan said indifferently, his dark finger tracing the braids of rope curled around the windlass.

A few months ago, green and ragged in the role of an aggressive pirate king, he could not fathom the wealth he

310

had accumulated from his pillages. Even during the war with the British, with his mild American privateering under Washington's acknowledgment, he had netted no portion of the sum he now possessed. The vow he had made in Scotland an eternity ago had borne fruit. The rawness lay in a battle with his conscience.

Mead Bennington's pirate colony at Rum Cay was flourishing, but the risks at sea were becoming greater as both he and Bennington were more often recognized in their engagements. Ryan had suggested a new quartering for their operations, but Bennington had refused.

"With a ship at either end of the cay, escape is certain, even if we are sought out. That was the purpose of the land bridge you built across the lagoon," Bennington had argued.

"Escape is never certain," Ryan had countered. "The passage through the lagoon is treacherous and heavy to out. A man-o-war could block the entrance and trap one of us."

"You annoy me, Ryan, with your caution."

Debate with Bennington was useless. He ruled as he thought, with fanatic abandon—lack of weighed reasoning that Ryan could not share.

Ort der Beer nudged Ryan, his deep voice tense. "Best we lay to full and run, Captain."

"Aye," Ryan said heavily. The corvette had spotted them and was veering east toward land. Another battle, another spoil, this one almost elementary. Coiled knots in Ryan's belly were furling, forming a familiar battle core.

Ryan cupped his hands to his mouth. "Ready about! Engage positions!" The battle was on.

Grim faced and weary, Morris Chapman slumped in his wrinkled leather chair, still shaken by the vision of John Patterson's shrunken body. The eloquent statesman, whose honeyed voice had persuaded thousands, was dying. And the last of the Pattersons of Patterson Woods would be buried with him. Only Janielle remained, and it was doubtful that she had survived the sea.

Morris flicked through the neatly stacked documents on his desk, trying to divert his thoughts from the depression that clung to him. If he lingered too long in the abyss of concern he would take to drink again. And before God, he must not. There was still hope. By an unseen law of rightness, somehow, there had to be an answer. His barrister's mind told him so.

Ryan had turned pirate, a loathsome breed that incurred pure hatred from the simplest minds. What had compelled him to turn to a life he himself had once bitterly denounced, even in his privateering days, stating the difference between those who sailed under their country's freedom flag and those who ravaged the seas in common thievery, holding only themselves to gain. There was a pencil line of difference, but Ryan had known it.

Evan Reed had sailed two months ago with the Continental fleet. His search was to find Janielle before her father died. Morris and Evan had discussed the possibility of finding her with Ryan.

"Ryan will know of her whereabouts, I am certain," Evan had said. "If she is alive, she will be close where he is."

"Ryan's plunder has swept the whole of the Caribbean. He shows no preference for the ship of any country," Morris had replied bitterly. "He must be quartered a goodly distance from his attack lanes."

"The Continental fleet is baffled by his unusual patterns, but they *will* find him," Evan had commented thoughtfully.

"He will be hanged," Morris had said, fighting a swell of emotion.

"He will be tried first, sir barrister," Evan added with a hopeful glitter in his smoky eyes.

Morris was jarred suddenly from his musings by the loud riotous commotion on the dock below. A large

312

throng had gathered, their shouting numbers growing. He strolled to the window, catching a glimpse of Benjamin, his assistant, elbowing his way toward the office. Hurriedly, Morris went to intercept him.

"A ghost ship, sir," Benjamin panted, "only she's not!"

Morris glanced across the waterfront where the harbor master's clipper was moving slowly out into the bay.

"The pilot master is going to board her and sail her in," Benjamin heaved breathlessly.

"What is this about?" Morris demanded.

"A French ship, sir, a docker said—a corvette. She's unmanned and laden with gold."

Morris stared at his ruffled assistant, trying to absorb the import of his words. "Has there been no other identification?"

"I overheard the harbor master's crew say she was a gift to the city from the pirate Deverel."

Morris sat down hard on the weathered steps. His ragged breath was meshed in his throat. He could only gawk at Benjamin, who had beat a dead run back down the wharf.

Later in the day, Morris was summoned by the Vice Admiralty's office, who sought his advice on the legalities of condemning the stolen cargo for redistribution to the state's coffer, filtered through the business of Charleston port. Not since 1741 had a similar incident presented itself.

Morris found himself staring down at Ryan's bold penmanship.

> *A prize of the sea for the citizens of Charleston. An offering, gentlemen, with no apology.*
>
> Ryan Deverel

Morris continued to read and reread the same words through misting eyes. Abruptly, the note was snatched from his hand and an initial cargo list replaced it.

800 serons of cocoa
68 chests of silver coin containing 310,000
pieces of eight
Wrought plate, set of church plate
Two-wheeled chaise of silver
Pearls and diamonds upwards of 600 weight
of gold, assorted gold buckles and snuff boxes

> *First of Count*
> *Obediah Firstly,*
> *Harbor Master*

"H—how did the French ship arrive at the harbor, and from where?" Morris managed.

The harbor officials shook their heads in disagreement. "She was sighted and hailed off Edisto, circling the tide currents. Her zigzag pattern caught the pilot master's attention. He feared she'd ram in the harbor," one of them said.

"But someone sailed her this far," Morris argued.

The young lieutenant offered sourly, "A prank, sir—a foul prank!"

Morris raised weary eyes to the sallow youth. "A gift of gold and a ship could scarcely be considered a prank," he said blandly. "It occurs to me that this is a gesture of some sort, and of good intent."

"From a pirate rogue, sir? Hardly! Pirates are notorious for this type of prank! Often it gains them access to blockade a harbor!"

Morris rose from his chair, suddenly bored with the events. This was not the place to argue Ryan's character. His hand rested on the door latch as his glance flickered over the uniformed men.

"I should conclude that the incident is merely the maneuver of an expert sea captain bestowing his boon," Morris said dryly, turning to leave.

chapter 32

The final shoring beam was rammed into position, lifting
the torn hulk of the *Waverly* to hard, dry land. Sodden
timbers groaned heavily as she was braced into the taut
wooden frame, as though resisting her webbed confinement. The *Waverly* would be careened and made secure
again for the sea.

Ryan had sighted her off the leeward shoals of Little
Abaco Island, wallowing grimly to remain afloat. At first
Ryan considered his ship an apparition, part of the
nightmarish crossing from the seaboard where he and Ort
der Beer had sailed the stolen French corvette too close
inland near Charleston harbor.

On the escape run, under full canvas, they had found
themselves enmeshed between two British frigates, both
pressing sail and firing the Long Tom signal across the
Avenger's bow. The *Avenger's* gun ports were dropped
and a round fired from each of the nine pounders, an
unanticipated tactic from a schooner, clearly outgunned
and trapped.

The action had bought time. The sleek schooner,
stiffened under sail, had swiftly moved into the fog bank
off the Florida straits and escaped. Part of Bennington's
crew had attempted mutiny on the inbound voyage,
protesting Ryan's decision to sail the corvette to

Charleston and give the highly valued cargo to the city. Ryan had promptly shot the instigators and thrown the others in chains. There would still be Bennington to contend with when he returned to Rum Cay.

The *Waverly* had been jury-masted and pumped until she could maintain a tow from the *Avenger*. Ryan had wished for Carlson, the *Waverly*'s former shipwright, who had gone berserk one afternoon near the lagoon and attacked Indee with an ax. Bennington had ordered Carlson to hang, but Ryan had intervened during the crushing preliminary torture, and Carlson, only half alive, his seaman's papers tied to him, had been set adrift from the cay in a longboat. At least it was preferable to hanging. Carlson might make it to land.

Ryan circled the *Waverly*'s red hull, raised grotesquely against the cobalt flush of the night sky. Heavy, lazing cloudbanks were drifting toward the cay and the sweet, humid scent of rain breathed across the nightfall tradewinds.

Ryan sighed heavily. The presence of his ship, the *Waverly*, seemed a gnawing reminder. Shadowed memories of Wyler, Scotland, Charleston, even Challey, stalked clearly across his thoughts. Unbidden, painful glimmers of another man in another time, fragmented until they could not be joined or mended.

Ryan walked slowly along the beach to the clearing, lost in the turmoil of his black thoughts. Rum would help as it always did, if he could drink enough. His new maps of the Yucatan Channel were in Bennington's hut. He would need to study them before his next sail, and before he tasted the black rum which he detested.

Bennington, impatient with Ryan's unexplained delay, had taken the *Copperhead* on a short pillage run to Hispaniola, hoping to catch the ivory cargo reportedly being run from British Guiana. He had left word he'd return in two weeks. Meanwhile, the Portuguese, Indee,

316

would be in command of the colony until Ryan returned.

Bennington's hut was swamped in darkness. Had he taken Janielle with him on the *Copperhead*? Ryan wondered as he neared the door. The door yielded under a gentle nudge and Ryan went inside, groping about for a tinder. His fingers located nubby tallow on the table and he fumbled for the nearby candle. As the candle flame heightened, Ryan heard scuffling in the next room, followed by Indee's lisping Spanish.

"Puta! Yankee puta!"

Ryan's hand trembled as he reached for the map case.

"Perra! Chupa, ramera!" Indee's swollen words tangled with his lisp. "Like you do for the captain," he snarled with a grunt.

A heavy thud. Then Janielle's splitting scream, beaten to silence.

Ryan lunged for the door, crashing it open with his foot. In the penciled moonlight, Indee stood over her with his lash coiled, his naked stunted body crawling with animal sweat. Indee spun on Ryan, his lash whistling in the air near Ryan's head.

Furiously, Ryan charged him, grappling at the fetid slick flesh, knocking him to his knees. He kicked the Portuguese full in the groin.

"You filth!" Ryan spat, grabbing the marlinspike that Indee had left near the door.

In a swift brutal thrust the marlinspike ruptured flesh and crackling bone, neatly piercing Indee's heart. Long after Ryan's hand had left the weapon, Indee still twitched in silent, apish death throes.

Ryan stepped over him, kneeling beside Janielle. Gently he lifted her against him, smoothing her white-gold hair from her face. Even in the hollow shadows from the distant candlelight, he could see the purplish welts and dark bruises across her face.

"God, Janielle," Ryan gasped, swallowing the grainy

317

knot in his throat. Janielle felt like a weightless child in his arms. "Even Bennington would not mistreat you so." he murmured.

Janielle's head sagged against his chest. A stifled, choking sob came from her depths. A slim hand clutched at his shirt. "Please," she begged, locking her fingers in the folds of his shirt, "please, no more—"

Ryan felt his guts being clawed from his belly. Delicately beautiful, faithless Janielle had betrayed him, turned her wiles on Bennington, thrown in her lot with the man who could best advance her own schemes. Clever, but her plans had gone awry. She had miscalculated Bennington's maniacal impulses, displeased him, and he must have given her to the Portuguese. She had forgotten that the pirate's code allowed no quarter.

Ryan glanced about the small room for some sign of her clothing. Finally he jerked the bed cover loose and wrapped it about her, scooping her up in his arms. He moved through the door, pausing to blow out the candlewick.

Splotchy moonlight spread along the path to the beach. They encountered only Manuela, who was too drunk and lewdly intent on being mounted by one of Bennington's crewmates, to notice them.

Ryan met Thrush near the *Waverly*'s shoring. The black giant's huge eyes flickered with surprise. "The pirogue," Ryan muttered, motioning with his head. "Fetch the pirogue."

Thrush stomped through the clusters of palm trees, circling back toward the inlet. In a short time he returned, pulling the pirogue across the sand.

The narrow pirogue was built for only two men. Ryan cradled Janielle on his knees while Thrush shoved off from the beach, steering the pirogue along the shadowed shoreline. They would flank the shallows through the passage to the lagoon where the *Avenger* lay at anchor.

Toward dawn when the tropical sky whispered of safron and pearl hues, Ryan stretched wearily beside Janielle, thankful that at last she had been quieted. Throughout the steamy, rain-laden night, alternate bouts of sobbing and broken screams had ravaged her. She begged continually for "bebida papaya," and once in despair Ryan had shaken her violently to hush her cries.

"Goddamnit, Janielle! I can bear no more!" he had shouted. "What you beg for I can't understand!"

"P—please—I need it—" Janielle had moaned, reaching up to him. At his gentlest touch, she would cringe, trembling, and the frenzied weeping would resume. In desperation, Ryan sought out Ort der Beer in his shed near the land bridge.

The Dutchman, clad only in undress muslin drawers, ran a coarse hand through his shock of wiry blond hair, frowning heavily as Ryan described the night's incidents, omitting the depraved scene between Indee and Janielle.

"She cries for some substance to ease her," Ryan said. "Have any of the crewmen mentioned a mixture with papaya?"

Ort der Beer whistled between his gaping teeth. "The men swill their rum allowance on ship, Captain. Here, they perhaps mix snake oil with sea water and call it favorable."

"Go to the encampment and learn what she speaks of," Ryan demanded finally, fearful of leaving Janielle alone for any space of time.

Some time after the midnight watch was sounded, Ort der Beer rapped softly on the door of Ryan's cabin. Ryan scraped the key in the lock, permitting Ort der Beer inside. The Dutchman cast an uneasy glance toward Janielle's limp form. He handed Ryan a gourd filled with liquid.

"The mulatto crone who serves Bennington—a few cards of cured tobacco loosened her tongue," Ort explained hurriedly. "She says Bennington and the Portuguese use it. They gave it to the girl when they

319

brought her to shore." Ort paused, dreading to continue.

Ryan lifted the gourd to his nostrils, inhaling the sharp-nectared tang of papaya. "What is mixed with it?"

Ort avoided the harsh ice-blue eyes that leveled at him. "Eurasian poppy, sir," he said quietly.

"Opium?" Ryan asked incredulously. "Are you certain?"

"The crone showed me the bundle of seeds, sir. She pestles them herself." Ort's eyes traveled beyond Ryan to Janielle. Slowly he shook his head. "Sorry, Captain," he mumbled, edging through the doorway.

Carefully, Ryan sat the gourd on the table, kicking a chair under him. Obviously, Janielle had been drugged from the time she set foot on Rum Cay. That explained her languor, the glazed, hollow expression in her indigo eyes, the reason she never left Bennington's quarters to seek him. The pieces were closing solidly into place. Bennington had made a separate bargain with each of them, stifling any communication between them until his purposes were met.

Bennington had needed his docks and bridge built and a competent captain in league with his piratical ambitions. And Janielle had been the key. At the time, neither he nor Janielle held a measure of choice, each had acted from the vortex of their own motives.

Ryan stretched his long legs, lacing his hands behind his head, mindful of Janielle's soft, uneven breaths. She stirred, curling herself against him. Ryan slung an arm over her, pulling her closer, thinking that tonight it felt good to hold her again.

"Her iron work is good! Me saw to that!" Wyler's strong words hurled at Ryan during the apex of the hurricane floated back to him as he watched the *Waverly* being trimmed out with copper fastenings along her water line. One of the Caribs had elected to mix the pigments of bay, russet and ocher, and paint her distinguished red hull. Canvas had been scarce, but Ort der Beer had found enough in the cargo sheds to splice adequate sail. The *Waverly* was seaworthy again after being a condemned wreck foundering in warm gulf waters.

Within the week, Ryan expected to take her out for a run. Grimly, he thought again of Wyler. The *Waverly* had been his last sea command.

Ryan gathered his work pouch and started for the pirogue. Bennington still delayed in his return to the cay. It seemed a heavy, ominous lull.

Ryan had left Janielle aboard the *Avenger* for the past weeks with Ort der Beer. Der Beer had turned kindly toward Janielle, no longer alarmed at the throes of her withdrawal from the opium drink. He had even bartered for some clothes to fit her and was vastly disappointed when the smallest garments he found swallowed Janielle's tiny frame. Janielle had somehow charmed the gruff, burly Dutchman into an occasional smile, which faded instantly when Ryan's flint-hard gaze warned him off.

The routine of refitting the *Waverly* each day and returning to the *Avenger* at nightfall had unexpectedly fallen into a mellowing habit. Knowing that Janielle waited for him to return each evening was vaguely settling. Yet, Janielle kept a shroud of reserve about her, allowing no words or touch to penetrate her frail veneer. Ryan hadn't pressed her and each night he tossed his pallet on the deck under the hard, knowing glitter of tropical stars. Some nights, when her huge violet eyes drowned him in their depths, and the wild flicker of lantern light played across her white-gold hair, his resolve not to touch her had almost crumbled.

Reminding himself that he was merely her keeper until Bennington returned and she was strong enough to make a clear choice between the pirate captains, he would dutifully clutch his bottle of Jamaican rum under his arm, joining Ort der Beer on deck, oblivious to the transparent pain that lingered in Janielle's misting eyes after he left her.

Throughout the day, Janielle had been wildly fitful, yearning for someone to talk to, or something to distract her from herself. Ort der Beer had left at dawn with Ryan for the beach clearing where the *Waverly* was shored, leaving Thrush aboard the *Avenger* with her. Timidly, Janielle had ventured on deck, nearly blinded by the brilliant suddenness of the splendorous tropical sun. Instinctively she had lifted her drawn, pallid face to its light and the rush of island wind, drinking of their healing fullness.

Thrush was seated at the end of the quarterdeck, patiently, expertly mending sail. Fascinated by the dexterity of his enormous fingers as he wielded the whalebone needle through the stubborn canvas, she had stared unconsciously at him through hooded eyes until, finally, Thrush raised curious dark eyes to her.

"I didn't mean to stare," Janielle mumbled apologetically, glancing away. Well, she decided indifferently, the giant black wouldn't have understood her anyway, and why she was apologizing to a slave was beyond her. But then, so many things she said or did confused her now.

Ryan was the deepest puzzle of all. A tall, sun-darkened, bearded pirate, lithe, square-shouldered, lean in the flanks, and disturbingly masculine, with a newborn killer reflex that terrified her. Ryan had not hesitated to kill Indee, and through the shreds of what she could recall of that night, he had killed without conscience. A cold, clear slice of brutality befitting a pirate lord. Had she not known Ryan Deverel before, no one could have convinced her he was the same man.

In childish gesture, Thrush moved toward her, carrying a small case in his huge outstretched hand. She lifted it from his purplish palm, delighted to see an arrangement of small sewing needles nestled in the velvet groovings.

Suddenly embarrassed, she glanced down at Ort der Beer's roughly woven sea shirt that was tied about her slim waist. Even the simple mind of the giant black had noticed her pitiful attire and offered her the means to remedy it. If she hurried, she could recut it and make some semblance of a gown before Ryan returned.

Worriedly, she chewed at her lower lip, her slim fingers trembling with frustration. At Patterson Woods Minna had always maintained her gowns when an alteration was necessary, and Janielle had fidgeted with impatience while Minna pinned and cut. For a moment Janielle thought the task before her was impossible. Then, determinedly, she went below, encouraged by the tickle of challenge that swept her. She would try, and at least the chore would occupy her time. And perhaps the result would make Ryan take notice of her. She was still a woman concerned with her appearance. A woman with a woman's desires. Tonight, she hoped to prove it.

Ryan dropped his work pouch near the lagoon, shrugging out of his breeches and torn linen shirt. Slowly, he waded into the hushed emerald waters of the lagoon. Blessedly, his restive mood slaked away along with the day's grime and sweat.

Tomorrow the *Waverly* would feel the sea beneath her solid hull again. The last of the ballast had been loaded and when she was eased off the shoring timbers and afloat, the rigging and sails would be strung. Her new masts were of island bullet wood and mahogany. The *Waverly* lacked the sleek line of the Dutch schooner he now commanded, and most probably the *Avenger*'s extraordinary speed, but the stubborn French frigate was his. The *Waverly* was home.

No one was on board the *Avenger* when Ryan approached. For an instant his belly knotted with panic.

No, not Bennington, he would have seen his sail from the north. And Thrush, where in the confounded hell was the black bastard? Thrush had understood his orders not to leave Janielle alone. But if Janielle had wandered off—

"Rión!" Thrush's leaden voice carried to him from the land bridge. The giant black swung a lantern along the path to Ort der Beer's shed, motioning for Ryan to follow him.

In long strides, Ryan was beside him. "Where is she?" he demanded.

Thrush's face was impassive as he moved in the path ahead of Ryan. Ryan could see the firelight beyond the land bridge, and the tantalizing smell of meat roasting on a ground spit trailed the air.

Ort der Beer hunkered near the spit, laboriously basting a wild turkey. Ryan was in no mood for games.

"Where is the girl?" he thundered.

Ort der Beer glanced casually up at Ryan, continuing to roll the spit with one hand. "Thrush trapped the turkey near the sea cave," he muttered finally. "The lady wished—"

"I wished to have it," Janielle spoke softly from the shadows.

Ryan whirled about, his steely ice-blue eyes wild with rage. His gaze flickered over her, softening while he absorbed her. Not since their capture on the *Waverly* had he seen her in a dress. The one she wore now, awkwardly cut from Ort der Beer's huge shirt, clung delicately to her slim defined curves, gathered below the rise of the breasts with tiny narrow stitching. Her white-gold hair, grown even longer, cascaded down her trim back like a wild gossamer cloud. He had forgotten that Janielle was incredibly beautiful.

Thrush was handing him a cup of light rum. He tasted it, then set it aside, his eyes never leaving Janielle. The smooth evening moved dreamlike through the meal, with a scattering of forced conversation between the men. The words seemed mechanical somehow, and Ryan couldn't remember the exact moment when the others moved away, leaving Janielle and him alone.

After awhile, Ryan got to his feet, his dark hand outstretched to Janielle. "Are you strong enough for a walk to the lagoon?" His words sounded stilted in his ears, spoken like some schoolboy.

Janielle raised smoldering violet eyes to him. "I think I am, Ryan," she said quietly.

The lagoon was dappled in swimming shards of moonlight, teased by the veiling storm clouds that streaked the sky. The thicket was alive with rustling sounds of nightfall. Ryan pointed across the lagoon to the roseate flamingos who delicately tucked their cane legs beneath them as they nested for the night. A short-nose batfish surfaced near the bank, its armlike fins searching for a school of minnows.

It was a space of time when creation stretched new and surging, when simple, familiar surroundings glowed in a blush of untainted freshness.

Janielle lost the moment when Ryan's fingers touched her white-gold-hair, when she turned trembling to him, unafraid, willing him to hold her. The sea-meshed taste of him, the naturalness of his moist, scalding mouth on hers, the unbearable ache of remembered desire. Hungrily, she savored him, demanding more.

Warm sand beneath her, cushioning her while Ryan's fevered eager hands searched, wandered over her, his mouth drawing her, releasing, finding at blessed last her taut, swollen breasts. He paused, feasting on their ripeness, taking, taking—until she could no longer bear it.

"God, now, Ryan," she rasped.

Ryan urged her to him, bracing her upward, then his weight was full upon her. Velvet throbbing splitting her wide, thrusting, surging, attacking, then receding, but never leaving her depths.

Janielle let him, pressing tight to hold him, drowning

him in the rippled glove of her deepness. And in a shattering, fusing moment when white-hot swells engulfed her, she burst, taking Ryan with her.

Some time before dawn, Ryan stirred, lifting her up in his arms. The night-washed air was cold against her nakedness.

"Ryan?" she whispered wonderingly, locking her arms about his neck.

"Again, love," he breathed against her throat. "But this time on the ship."

The gentle rocking of the *Avenger* was beneath her again, lullingly familiar, soothing. Ryan's warm hands were moving again, caressing, pausing to explore her nipples, touching, tasting. His mouth trailed lower and Janielle was caught in a ravaging sensation of sweet-sharpening, a closing—no, an opening—that erupted, heightened until she spread willingly into it. Only then did Ryan let her go.

As the raw stretches of chalky dawn filtered into the ship's cabin, Ryan took her again. The fading, indifferent night stars glittered protestingly against oncoming day, then burned dark.

chapter 33

Ryan spotted Bennington's sail bearing due southeast at a clipping eleven knots, flying a captured Union Jack along with the *Copperhead's* own blood flag, a variation of Christopher Moody's dreaded pirate banner. Bennington's strike had been against a British vessel, so Ryan presumed the Spanish ivory cargo had been too heavily escorted for single attack.

The *Waverly* dipped at gentle anchor off the shoals while the standing rigging was knotted and the running rigging spliced. The first of the main topsails and topgallants were already strung. The *Waverly* would be short of canvas until Ryan could purchase the necessary sail in Puerto Plata.

A grumbling commotion spread through the men as they sighted the *Copperhead.* Ort der Beer came up to stand beside Ryan.

"The mates will show with you, Captain," he said apprehensively.

"The crew's loyalty is to the guineas and crusadoes they carry in their pockets," Ryan commented grimly. His privateer crews had been of a different order of men. The scummy band he now commanded would lean to their own betterment. Their allegiance was to their gold. Ryan had known this time was inevitable. When Bennington had spared him after the *Waverly*'s capture, the vow he had made to Wyler and himself had been only a shadow of words. Now, it was a reality.

Ryan preferred to confront Bennington on the pirate's own ground. The *Avenger* was anchored at the far end of the cay, but Janielle was there. Ryan had considered running sail and taking Janielle with him, but he knew Bennington too well. The fanatic pirate king would haunt the sea lanes until he found and killed both of them. This way, at least he stood a fair chance of evening with Bennington. Both pirate crews would honor the duel between their captains until one emerged victorious.

The draining weariness of last night with Janielle vanished as Ryan watched the *Copperhead*'s progress. He had been admittedly insatiable with her, taking her countless times, determined to have his fill of her. The frothing frenzy had left him gloriously spent, still demanding more.

Her glowing violet eyes, shining with fulfillment, caressing him while he dressed to leave her, told him that she, too, claimed more of him.

Words between them were awkward, strained, but their bodies had spoken to each other at last. Neither Bennington's abuse of her nor the Portuguese's acts of flagrant perversion had mattered last night to either of them. They had meshed in bursting welcome and, somehow, with Janielle it was different. As it had been the first time with her at Challey. As it would always be.

Ryan left the *Waverly* and walked back to the clearing. Bennington would come for him in his own time and he would be ready. This time there would be no terms, no quarter given.

Tongues of leaden red flames vaulted from the spreading circlet of campfires, setting a macabre, death-poised stage in the sandy clearing at Rum Cay. The shell-handled cutlass felt weighty, unfamiliar in Ryan's hand after the slim rapier he preferred. Surprisingly, Bennington had not raged at him, but the deadly flicker in his yellowish animal eyes had cautioned Ryan not to underestimate the golden pirate lord.

"A pity, bastard Ryan," Bennington had said earlier. "I do not mourn the loss of my Portuguese second mate, nor the loss of your cold American woman, only the stupidity of your morals!" he said, referring to the French corvette that Ryan had bestowed on the city of Charleston. "I desired a pirate general, and you, Ryan Deverel, possessed much promise. You leave me no alternative but challenge. A waste, Ryan—a pitiable waste!"

"This life was not of my choosing," Ryan reminded him coldly.

"*This* life made you rich," Bennington retorted. "Another loss—for you will not live beyond this night to spend it!"

The battle spoils had already been drawn. The victor would apportion the plunder from the newly seized British brigantine to the separate crews. The bulk of the bounty that he and Bennington had accumulated and converted to British crowns was held to letter of credit at Martinique. Sea chests full of crusadoes and Indian mahurs would be used to garrison the day. Bennington knew of a certainty that Rum Cay was vulnerable to attack, and soon.

The pirate's charter allowed each crewmate a choice whether to remain with the surviving captain, serve his command, or leave the cay voluntarily. And again the weight of gold in their pockets usually persuaded them to stay.

Warily, Bennington rounded, poised, a deadly confident glint in his amber eyes. A steamy film of sweat clung to his dark forehead. Trickles of sweat covered his hand that trembled with the weight of his cutlass. This was routine, a common duel among pirates. He had grown quite proficient at it. The death smell was strong in his flared nostrils. A fake, off-balance slide and a cut clean through. It required only seconds.

Ryan shifted only slightly, his flint-hard eyes anticipating Bennington's exchange. Bennington favored his cutlass hand, inclining his long body to accommodate it. There would not be time for a second decision. The first cut must be fatal. No thrust, no parry—none of the refinements of the rapier.

Boots crunched in the crust of volcanic sand with an occasional twist to steady footing. Suddenly, Bennington swerved left in a half crouch, but Ryan watched his eyes. In a split second Ryan thrust his cutlass point up to Bennington's right and the long blade found its target.

A raw, bellowing roar, one that echoed the Scottish warlords, heaved from Ryan's throat as he plunged the curved blade through. Bennington's eyes rolled back in shock, his mouth a wide circle.

"For Wyler!" Ryan thundered, his hand leaving the quivering blade. Bennington crashed backward into the warm sand, his unseeing amber eyes still registering the shock of surprise.

Janielle tossed restlessly in her berth. The hour was late and still Ryan had not returned. Perhaps the mocking bitterness she had detected in his ice-blue eyes when he left her at daybreak spoke the words left unsaid. Ryan had taken her many times since that first morning at Challey, and never, never had he said he loved her.

Last night at the lagoon when their lust had overtaken them, humbling them throughout the night, Janielle had thought perhaps there was a chance that Ryan had forgiven her, even loved her.

Suddenly, she bolted upright. Forgiven her? Forgiven her for what? For saving his life? For bargaining her body to Bennington to spare him? Ryan should love her,

330

worship her for the sacrifice she had made.

Furiously, she threw the netting back. Damn him, anyway! He was nothing more than an adventurer, a black-hearted, rutting pirate lord—little more than Bennington professed to be. And where was he tonight? With one of the mulatto wenches that pleasured the pirate crews? Last night his hunger for her had been violent, insatiable, kissing her and caressing her in a hundred new ways. And she had yielded totally to him, blushing in her newfound fulfillment. And she had been a fool!

Angrily, she raised the lantern wick, her slim fingers trembling with rage. She would show him, she'd—

Ryan's heavy sea boots pounded down the passageway, matching sounds with the deep thudding of her heart. His wide shoulder crashed against the door and he stood, swaying menacingly in the low doorway, his hand looped over the latch.

His ice-blue eyes were wild, glazed. He was drunk, very, very drunk.

Alarmed, Janielle stepped back from him. "Get out!" she spat.

Ryan's mouth twisted in a cruel, cynical smile. "Get off my own ship?" he sneered. "Hardly, love!"

Weavingly, he advanced on her, edging her back to the berth. Janielle reeled from the smell of black rum and the drenching smell of perfumed woman's sweat that clung to him. Sickened, she clutched at a sheet to cover her nakedness.

Tauntingly, Ryan surveyed her before he ripped the sheet from her hands. "A modest whore, love?"

"You bastard!" Janielle hissed, shoving at him. "You saved me from Indee only to—"

Ryan's hand fastened cruelly in her hair. "I have killed yet again for you this night! I have come to claim my reward, bitch!"

Janielle felt herself sinking with fear as his mouth

covered hers. He was smothering her, choking her. Weakly, she cried against his mouth, "Ryan—listen to me. No, Ryan!"

His fingers were biting into her arms, bruising her. "Tonight, *I* am pirate king of Rum Cay. A full pirate, and you, love, are the king's whore!"

Janielle shook herself free only to be trapped beneath him as he rolled on top of her. Savage fingers tore at her flesh, spreading her roughly open. Blindly, she struck at him, clawing, struggling against his strength.

"You'll never have me after you've been with another woman!" she sobbed furiously as he lowered himself on her.

A sarcastic laugh ripped from his throat. "I have had many women this night, all whores like you!"

Somehow, while he thrust powerfully, mercilessly into her, a primitive animal rutting that ruptured her, giving only pain, she was finally able to float free of him. He could take her countless times again, use her body as he was doing now, but tonight Ryan had severed the last tenuous thread of love she had felt for him. He could never change and neither could she. It was useless to believe otherwise.

And later, when he withdrew from her, still hugely erect and swollen, stumbling drunkenly from the ship's cabin, she was certain.

Evan Reed steadied himself for battle position, feeling the chewing lump in his belly harden with fear. The palm-studded shore line of Rum Cay had been sighted. The three hundred and sixty ton flagship, *Trinity*, had scouted Exuma Sound, splitting forces with her three sister ships at Cat Island. The *Trinity* and her two naval sloops as escort would wage a land assault from the east, while the heavier ship of the line, the *Agnes*, would lead her attack from the west side of the cay.

Rear Admiral Cunningham had chuckled with delight over the information gleaned from the rescued British survivors of Bennington's assault on their vessel. The elusive pirate lord, Deverel, was quartered at Rum Cay. The Continental fleet had tracked him to his lair. The rest would be history.

Evan scowled into the sun, feeling a peculiar sense of loss. "Janielle, I hope to God, if you are alive, you will find a place of safety on the cay until this is over," he prayed silently. "And, Ryan, friend, I wish I had never—"

"Up all hammocks!" the boatswain bellowed. The carpenter and his crews fastened to prepare the plugs and mauls, the gunner with his mates and quarter gunners scurried to examine the cannon batteries and recheck the loads.

Suddenly the drums beat to arms as the boatswain piped, "All hands to quarters!"

The marines drew up in rank and file on the quarter deck, the poop and forecastle. The lashings of the great cannons were cast loose and the tompions withdrawn. The whole artillery above and below were run out at the ports and leveled to point firing range.

Evan assumed his respective position with the *Trinity*'s officers, his body strained for the commander's firing signal. Only a breath remained before the assault on Rum Cay began. Somewhere in the drumming of his ears, it was audible.

"Execute fire!"

The fierce cannonade began and the shudder of the *Trinity*'s guns belching fire was no greater than the rocking tremor that surged through him.

Janielle bolted from Ort der Beer's shed, dazed by the splintering, thundering roar that trembled the sandy ground where she stood. Heavy black brume spread a spiraling film across the lagoon. Angry cannons, rolling in closer sequence now, were devastating Rum Cay. The sharp crackle of swivel guns and small-arms fire echoed their thunder.

Janielle began to run for the *Avenger*. The land bridge was sliding under her feet, its planks twisting, separating from the ground shock. The air was sooty, streaming with falling ash and sand. The trees above the lagoon had started to crinkle with flame. Janielle glanced wildly up at the *Avenger*, her heart sinking. The foremast was aflame!

"Janielle!" Ort der Beer's heavy voice bellowed across the deck. Janielle tripped, sprawling across the rock bridge to the deck. Painfully, she picked herself up, wiping bleeding hands on her skirt, grabbing for Ort der Beer's outstretched hand.

Thrush was hauling the anchor, furiously pacing the capstan.

"A'fore, God, the fleet!" Ort gasped, pulling Janielle to the deck.

Janielle turned wild eyes to him, her nerveless fingers covering her ears. Her words were smothered in a full shock of cannonade. Ort der Beer toppled over, his hand sliding slowly out of hers.

Horrorstruck, Janielle stared fixedly down at the Dutchman who had no face. Somehow she was floating in red, watery blood, a coccoon of eternity where she felt nothing. A flicker of Ryan's arrogant, mocking face reached out to her, and then it too was gone.

"You are positive, Ensign Reed?" Rear Admiral Cunningham asked pointedly.

"I am, sir," Evan replied briskly, leaning over Janielle.

"There are other wounded that require your aid when you have finished with the girl." Cunningham frowned, gazing down at the slim, silver-haired girl who lay on a pallet at his feet. John Patterson's daughter had been found alive aboard the flaming *Avenger*, and the pirate colony at Rum Cay had been demolished. The pirate

Deverel had escaped their trap, had taken sail with the *Waverly* two full days past. But they would find him. It was only a question of time.

Gently, Evan dabbed at the caked blood on Janielle's slim hands, choked by the brutal sight of her. A long, newly healed scar traced her narrow back and shoulder and her silken skin still bore the marks of recent bruises.

Evan had peeled away the charred tatters of her coarse blouse, shaken by her gaunt thinness. Her tangled, white-gold hair fell below her slender hips, wrapping her in its length. Slowly he probed for signs of broken bones, careful not to pain her. Other than being half-starved and suffering from cannon shock she appeared whole, even though almost unrecognizable.

As he turned her on her back, she stirred, an anguished mewling struggling from her throat.

"Hush, Janielle," Evan crooned. "You are safe now. I am taking you home."

Janielle's violet eyes fluttered wildly open at Evan's warm words. They widened, finally focusing on Evan's sun-bronzed face. He gathered her to him, cradling her like a child, stroking her snarled white-gold hair.

Janielle began to tremble, her teeth chattering in her mouth while the tears overtook her.

"Evan." She sobbed his name repeatedly, pulling, clawing at him.

"The Continental fleet attacked the cay, Janielle. But Ryan has escaped," he said hoarsely as if to comfort both of them.

"R—Ryan did this, he—" Janielle choked on the words, burying her face in Evan's broad shoulder.

"Ryan and others," Evan said grimly, drawing Janielle closer.

chapter 34

Stubbornly, Ryan swung the *Waverly*'s helm, attempting to correct her leeward sag. Her slack in stays and a diminished crew of twenty-three, unused to handling the heavier frigate, had convinced Ryan that the ship needed more seasoning before her cargo run to Martinique. Her repairs at Rum Cay were makeshift, but sound enough. The weightier problems would have to be corrected in shipyard by a shipwright's skill with proper refitting equipment.

Still, the *Waverly* responded to helm, though haltingly sluggish with her missing sail. Another trial run was needed to make certain she was seaworthy before he took Janielle to Martinique. There he'd find passage for her to Charleston. She was free to return now, with Bennington dead, and after the drunken night he had spent with her after he'd killed Bennington, he knew she would be eager to go. She hated him, and for good reason, he thought indifferently. He could force her to stay at Rum Cay as his mistress but it would serve no purpose. Even his impatient lust for her had subsided, leaving only a bitter taste of ashes in his mouth. He could choose any one of the hotblooded young mulatto wenches and have a better lay. If he were drunk enough.

Janielle wanted to spear him with her barbed words,

hack at his guts with her goddamn haughty gentility, and impale him with her smoldering violet eyes. Since that first morning at Challey when he had taken her, she someway had penetrated a hidden flaw in his emotional armor, and every time he took her again the armor yielded a little more. The only way to mend it was to discard it.

"Sail, sir—off port," the newly recruited first mate said anxiously, his finger leveling at the fastmoving sail in the distance.

Intently, Ryan studied the sail, his mind working quickly. He had chosen the deserted waters near Little Exuma for his experimental run with the *Waverly* because few ships used the lane, preferring the larger span of Crooked Passage. The *Waverly* was unprepared for sea battle, her ten cannons rusted with sea brine and her jury-rigged sail sluggish. Ryan decided at that moment to make for the Yuma Straits.

"Bring her about!" Ryan ordered, preparing his run. He tossed a glance up at the clear sky overhead. No chance for a swallowing fogbank.

"Another sail, sir," the crewman rasped, taking the shifting helm from Ryan's hard grip.

"She draws leeward, so compensate!" Ryan snarled, hurrying off across the deck.

"Third ship off point, sir!" the gunner called as Ryan passed him.

Ryan froze in his tracks, staring incredulously at the sweeping man-o-war that had crossed the horizon beam. The Stars and Stripes whipped from her jib boom.

"Holy God, Captain!" the helmsman croaked, "the American *flotilla*!"

The *Waverly* stood a small chance of outdistancing their heavy man-o-war, but its accompaniment of swift naval sloops would easily press the *Waverly* to action or to striking her colors. In any event, the sea was suddenly full of American sails.

"Haul up and full!" Ryan shouted, taking the helm

again. He brought her about full by the wind, feeling the reluctant shudder and strain to leeward grip her. He was spending valuable minutes by the maneuver, but the powerful fore and main topsails were beginning to fill on the new course. The *Waverly* surged with new life, her cutwater pointed due southeast.

Across the water, Rear Admiral Cunningham lowered his sea glasses, his face a mask of surprise. "A challenging tactic," he commented sourly, handing his glasses to the lieutenant. "A pity such an exceptional sea captain chose the wrong side."

The lieutenant nodded glumly, watching the *Waverly*'s sails billow before the wind. There was something disturbingly majestic about the old French frigate with her red hull that clutched at him. Her captain knew how to force her sail and even that was impressive. Sad, indeed, that the pirate lord was hopelessly trapped by the closing net of the fleet. He almost wished—

"Run the signal flags to prepare the warning volley," Admiral Cunningham said solemnly, clasping his hands behind his back. He watched the travelers from the escort sloops slowly acknowledge his order.

The naval sloops pressed forward into gun range pursuit, the gun ports of her twelve nine-pound cannon dropping in rapid sequence. The portside sloop crowding the *Waverly* fired the first salvo of bowshot warning.

Defiantly, the *Waverly* veered starboard, hurling into the wind, refusing to respond to the fleet's warning command.

Admiral Cunningham's jaw fell in amazement, while muffled murmurs of surprise passed among the officers. The traveler flag of the sloop requested a second order.

Cunningham's mouth clamped in a hard fold. "Very well, pirate Deverel, since you chose to be a bloody hero, we shall blast you from the water!" He pulled a heavy breath. "Execute fire!"

The *Waverly* sprang forward as though anticipating

the deadly barrage from the sloops. One of the sloops swerved abaft to the *Waverly*'s weather quarter, spreading her grapnels. The second sloop hedged abreast starboard, her cannon mouths leveled. The man-o-war gained steadily from broadside.

"All hands surrender!" came the heavy shout from the deck of the portside sloop.

Ryan's large hands locked on the varnished helm, his mind whirling with Wyler's vow, "No man takes me ship!"

A salvo of hammer shots curried the *Waverly*'s prow. Ryan glanced up at the jury-rigged canvas, its splicing crinkling under wind strain. The pirate crew was stunned, shaken by the overwhelming fire power and awesome force of the sweeping fleet. Some laid down their arms, others stood mutely, watching the crew of the naval sloop ready the grapplers.

Still, the cannon assault had not come. Close enough to see the gunners at their batteries, Ryan pulled a quick look. They wanted him alive.

The grapplers scratched the *Waverly*'s port rail. Ryan released the helm, drawing his dragoon and cutlass. With a roar, he hurled himself among the boarders, slashing his path among them, driven by a savage frenzy that plummeted him into the whipping, metal-biting fray. His head was hammering with the Scottish warlord drum cry, "Faeght 'er die, faeght 'er die, faeght 'er die, but trye!"

In the end, Ryan was trapped. He slumped forward when a musket barrel clubbed him from behind, his mouth still moving with the words of the ancient Scottish battle cry.

Any trial in a Vice Admiralty Court had a sobering effect on the citizens of Charleston, in view of the pirate scourge that had plagued the city in the spring of 1718, when the Nassau pirate, Edward Teach, had brazenly blockaded Charleston harbor. The following November his counterpart, Major Stede Bonnet, was publicly hanged in Charleston after his capture near Cape Fear River. Remembering Samuel Wragg, a member of the Governor's Council, and his four-year-old son who were held as hostages by the infamous pirate brigand until Governor Johnson complied with their demands, the tendency to promptly execute any and all pirates prevailed.

The intervention of the Continental fleet and the successful conclusion of its pirate mission stirred the Charlestonians to patriotic fervor. The gentleman pirate, Deverel, was in chains. His short, incredible career, wherein he had captured and pillaged more than two hundred and fifty vessels of British, French, Spanish, Dutch and Portuguese origin throughout the Caribbean was grimly staggering.

The gift of the French corvette laden with extraordinary cargo that the pirate lord had mysteriously sailed into Charleston harbor remained only dull recall in the minds of most citizens. The confiscated gold had been spent and forgotten.

Morris Chapman remembered the incident well, for it had strengthened his faith in his natural son. Ryan had his reasons for his actions, he was certain now. But the truth had to be laid bare before the Vice Admiralty Court. Otherwise, as Cunningham had vowed, Ryan would be "hung in chains at the harbor entrance." And Ryan had obstinately refused any defense before the court.

At Morris' insistence, Judge Roger Trott had interceded with the naval legal authorities, citing that the pirate lord had once served his country under General Washington's command, using his merchantman, the *Waverly*, to run the British blockade during the War. And Ryan had surrendered the gold claimed from privateering to the federal navy. At Morris' persistent badgering, Judge Trott had requested the Vice Admiralty Board to allow a public trial, reminding Cunningham that Morris Chapman had friends in high stations throughout the state, and the newly formed Continental fleet would have need of future appropriations. John Patterson's daughter had been returned safely to Charleston, though too late to see her father again. It was Deverel's protection of her while she was imprisoned at Rum Cay that made her rescue possible. Balancing the scales of naval opinion against the possible consequences of a loss of revenue for his fleet, Rear Admiral Cunningham begrudgingly conceded.

Next, Morris Chapman approached an incredulous Harrelson Mallen with the reminder that had it not been for Ryan's unconventional framing design of his now-prospering shipyards, he might have shucked the plan, as he had many times before Ryan presented his. After a bitter exchange, wherein Morris was asked to bear in mind that Ryan had, in fact, been responsible for Kaylee's illness when he sailed on their wedding eve, Harrelson Mallen agreed to lend his support for Ryan's acquittal.

A mild victory was Morris' defense of Ryan, for Mallen shipyards built the naval snows and sloops for the Continental Fleet.

Patiently, Evan Reed waited while Janielle struggled for composure. Her slim, trembling fingers were locked around the carriage settling strap in a deathlike vise. Her beautiful face, pale and drawn among the voluminous veiling of her mourning attire, was a mask of anguish. Gently Evan laced his fingers with hers.

"I cannot, Evan. Before God, I cannot," she murmured.

Evan tilted her face up to him, her tortured violet eyes pleading with him.

"Your father was a fair man, and had he lived he would have followed the support of his friends. In his stead, you must attend Ryan's trial. The testimony Morris asked you to give may well save Ryan's life."

"I—I don't want to see him," Janielle whimpered,

clutching at Evan's sleeve.

"I think you do, Janielle."

The outer chamber of the House of Commons was filled to capacity, some citizens trampling one another for a balcony glimpse of the famed pirate lord. Judge Trott, in his somber judicial robes, with two naval judges and Rear Admiral Cunningham, all wigged and wearing the dark official blue of the Continental Navy, were elevated at the judge's box, stirring in bored fashion the documents spread before them.

A deathly hush fell over the crowded courtroom as Judge Trott motioned for silence. "Bring in the prisoner, Ryan Deverel," he ordered dryly.

Double doors creaked while the midshipmen strained at attention. A scattering of awe-filled murmurs flowed among the spectators.

Tall and erect, attired in a royal blue frockcoat with blunt-angle lapels that appeared to crowd his wide shoulders, Ryan walked through the parted doorway, easing into an arrogant swagger that brought a catch to Janielle's tight throat. The harsh, unyielding lines of his sun-darkened face appeared more pronounced without his beard. His slaty steel eyes were unreadable as they flickered briefly over the crowd.

Janielle eased back in her hard chair, relieved yet disappointed. Had Ryan been dragged forth in chains, covered with prison filth, surrounded by cruel, burly jailors, the mercy of the court might have smiled on him. This way it appeared a mockery that Ryan apparently needed no trial.

Morris Chapman walked briskly up to the judge and admirals, opening his brief. He nodded, bowing respectfully to each one, indicating that he was ready to open his defense for the pirate lord, Ryan Deverel.

The trial lasted two full weeks, an unprecedented time

for a trial of its nature. Daily, Morris Chapman produced new documents and witnesses favoring Ryan.

Surprisingly, the *Charleston Gazette* wrote its own account of Ryan's misfortune at the hands of Mead Bennington, implying that the "captured merchantman captain had acted out of honest protection and concern for the late statesman John Patterson's daughter, Janielle."

Morris Chapman knew when the pulse of public sentiment began to surge in favor of Ryan's acquittal. Even Admiral Cunningham had squeezed a more amiable expression.

At one of the last sessions, he reluctantly called Janielle to testify.

Furiously, Ryan jumped to his feet, bristling with rage, his ice-blue eyes piercing Morris. "I forbid this, Morris," he gritted, before he was restrained.

Janielle moved with slim grace to the low box below the judge's bench, her violet eyes avoiding Ryan. Demurely she sat on the narrow chair, her cold hands quiet in her lap.

Morris Chapman approached her with an expression of equanimity on his weary face.

"I ask your forgiveness, Mistress Patterson, for this unbearable moment of recall. It is only to the final charge of abduction for which I seek your honest words."

Ryan shifted in his chair, paling slightly with unleashed rage. Goddamn Morris to hell, he swore silently. The use of any woman's testimony was unwarranted. The sudden thought that Janielle might have wed Johnathan Chapman if it were not for him rankled in his belly. Hanging was almost preferable to the chains of obligation. Especially where Janielle was concerned.

"I ask you, Mistress Patterson, were you taken against your will by the man Deverel and forced aboard his ship?"

The minted torrent of words was lost to Janielle.

Abducted, taken unwillingly, ravaged, raped and humiliated by perverted pirate chieftains, drugged, beaten—yes, all of these! Yes, yes, and yes!

But somehow the wrong word came forth. "No, sir barrister," Janielle breathed—for in her heart, with Ryan had she ever been unwilling?

Later, Evan was taking her arm, steering her gently through the rows of spectators. From somewhere a cackling woman's voice reached out to her. "'Tis a truth, fine lady, me bets the pirate lord lain with you aplenty!" Swimming faces all around her seemed hugely distorted, leering at her, clutching at her gown. Woodenly, she leaned against Evan. She could see the carriage now. Just a few more steps.

The engulfing din of wild response to Ryan's conditional pardon reverberated through the cavernous House of Commons. Ryan roused himself from stony shock as the Vice Admiral pompously read the conditions of pardon. No license for a vessel or captaincy would be granted him for a span of ten years. He was dispossessed of ownership of the *Waverly*, the *Avenger* and the *Copperhead*. The gold held under his credit account at Martinique was to be confiscated and redistributed to the state of South Carolina.

Ryan's mouth set in a harsh, cynical line as the formalities of discharging the trial proceeded, and finally drew to a close. Without a word to anyone, he moved through the crowds as a voluntary path opened for him in the sea of blurred faces.

Later that night while Ryan walked along the mist-slickened docks, drawing salt breath from the immortal, pulsing sea, he wondered why Janielle had lied.

chapter 35

If she closed her eyes and concentrated very hard, Janielle could bring life back into the swarming visions, even halting the one she chose and lingering in it before she let it dissolve. Curled in her father's favorite chair with a glass of her preferred claret, the freshly laid fire crackling contentedly, she could reflect on the languorous mirror of memories.

Ryan's wide muscled back leaning into the rigging, his stark white shirt ruffling, caressing his sweeping shoulders, his steel-blue eyes scanning the storm-weary heavens above the sea—she *had* lived it, she really had.

Evan's jackboots pounded across the polished floor of the formal parlor, in his usual manner of skirting the plush Oriental rugs spread across the center. Evan was uncomfortable at Patterson Manor since their return from Charleston after Ryan's trial, and had told her so.

Janielle was no longer concerned with propriety. Evan and she—it was different with them. Evan demanded nothing from her, and now not even marriage. She needed him, especially now, and he understood the reasons.

Evan smiled down at her, leaning across her to brush her hair with his lips. "It is late, Janielle. Come to bed."

"Awhile longer," she murmured, her dreamy violet eyes lifting to him.

"No, Janielle, lay the memories to rest," Evan said sternly, clasping her hands in his. "I'll not allow—"

Suddenly, Jedda appeared in the doorway, his ebony face showing alarm. "A rider, Mis Janielle. He done come in and say—"

"Janielle!"

Janielle braced herself against the bitter-steel tone of Ryan's harsh voice. Evan stiffened, letting her hands slip from his.

"Either you tell him, Janielle—or I will," Evan said sharply.

Ryan stalked to the library, looming in the doorway, his dark face hushed in the reddish glow from the fire. There was still the rigidly coiled tautness about him as he paused in the doorway, steadying himself as though the deck of the *Waverly* rocked beneath his feet.

"Tell me what?" Ryan demanded.

Evan cast a hard look at Janielle, then met Ryan's unyielding, stormy eyes. The silence stretched between them, ready to shatter into icy particles.

"Get out, Evan!" Ryan ordered firmly.

With deliberate arrogant grace, Evan kissed Janielle lightly on the forehead, taking her wineglass from her frozen fingers and setting it aside.

"No," Janielle mouthed the word as she heard the definite click of the door shut behind Evan.

"I came to hear your reason, madam," Ryan snapped.

"All reason left me at Rum Cay, as you may recall," Janielle said wearily, her violet eyes tracing the glimmery pattern of her satin gown.

"I took you forcibly from El Roble and kept you as my mistress after I killed Bennington. Obligation chokes me, madam."

"A pirate lord can bear no obligation," Janielle said evenly.

Ryan leaned over her, pressing his arms against the back of her chair, caging her between them. "The pirate

346

lord you speak of is dead. He died aboard the *Waverly*, defending his ship."

Janielle's white-gold hair caressed his shoulder as she raised swimming violet eyes to him. He caught the gentle, delicate fragrance of her, the incredible softness of her that invariably shattered him. He bent to kiss her, his mouth moving warm, easy on hers.

Janielle fought the fluttering ache that welled in her throat. The words came forth thin, unnatural. "Please go, Ryan. I wish it." Then somehow she wanted to erase the senseless words.

Ryan straightened, looming tall before her. In a flashing moment he saw Indee, naked and sweating, his whip poised above Janielle, and heard Bennington's raking, perverted laugh as Janielle lay drugged at his feet. If he could kill them again he would welcome the chance.

"Tell me, Janielle," Ryan said slowly, "had you been my wife, would you still have bedded with Mead Bennington?"

Janielle's face contorted with remembered pain, her limpid violet eyes stirring with rage. "No! Before God, no! Not even to spare your life again would I submit to him!"

A flicker of surprise crossed Ryan's face, then settled impassively. "Are you implying that it was payment for my life?"

"Yes, Ryan, it was," Janielle said simply. "After the dock and bridges were completed, Bennington promised to free you."

Angrily, Ryan ground his fist into his palm. "Bennington lied to both of us," he seethed.

Janielle sighed, rising wearily from her chair. Would Ryan never be done with tormenting her? She felt drained of emotion. The same words, the same accusations over and over again.

Ryan touched her with his ice-blue eyes, taking in every detail of her. "I have wondered, Janielle," he said finally, "why our lives have been so hurtfully meshed. When I took you from El Roble, it was not to make you my mistress, but my wife. Wyler said my manner with you was wrong. The hurricane—and—circumstances interfered. Had I asked you—"

"I am with child, Ryan," Janielle said suddenly, unable to bear the painful softness of his words. She would lose him now, but she had had the courage to tell him.

Ryan gripped her slim shoulders, holding her at arm's length, the cold slivers in his startled eyes impaling her. She felt as though she were turning to marble. God—Ryan—don't do this to me—

The crackling of the inevitable words lashed her. "Is the child mine?"

Janielle shook her head unbelievingly, wildly, a long shuddering moan pouring from her mouth. "Yours? Or Bennington's, or Indee's, or perhaps Evan's?" she cried, near hysteria. She gasped for breath. "I will tell you, Ryan! Not Indee's—he never liked—he preferred—" Her voice faltered. "And Bennington, he sailed from the cay and I had my time afterward. And Evan—"

Ryan jerked her to him, shaking her furiously before he gathered her into his arms. "Before God, Janielle—I knew, but I didn't think. Forgive me," he murmured, kissing her gently, tasting the salt-sweet of her tears.

His lips were warm against her face. "Our son was conceived that night at the lagoon. He was formed by our love, Janielle."

Janielle felt herself being lifted by strong arms and swept from the room. For now, she could lay her head in the nest of his broad shoulder, absorbed in his strength. If only for this moment, this night.

She stirred suddenly, her violet eyes widening.

"Where are you—"

"Before I pleasure you, love," Ryan said, "the clergyman who accompanied me from Santee Point should favor our wedding night with his blessing."

"R—Ryan," Janielle stammered incredulously, "I have to prepare. I have no—"

"You will have no need of a gown tonight, love. Tomorrow, when we go to Challey, perhaps—" Ryan smiled wickedly, kissing her again.

BE SWEPT AWAY
ON A TIDE OF PASSION
BY LEISURE'S THRILLING
HISTORICAL ROMANCES!

FOR THE FINEST
IN CONTEMPORARY
WOMEN'S FICTION,
FOLLOW LEISURE'S LEAD

Make the Most of Your Leisure Time
with
LEISURE BOOKS

Please send me the following titles:

Quantity	Book Number	Price
_____	_____	_____
_____	_____	_____
_____	_____	_____
_____	_____	_____
_____	_____	_____

If out of stock on any of the above titles, please send me the alternate title(s) listed below:

_____	_____	_____
_____	_____	_____
_____	_____	_____
_____	_____	_____

Postage & Handling _____

Total Enclosed $ _____

☐ Please send me a free catalog.

NAME _____
(please print)

ADDRESS _____

CITY _____ STATE _____ ZIP _____

Please include $1.00 shipping and handling for the first book ordered and 25¢ for each book thereafter in the same order. All orders are shipped within approximately 4 weeks via postal service book rate. PAYMENT MUST ACCOMPANY ALL ORDERS.*

*Canadian orders must be paid in US dollars payable through a New York banking facility.

Mail coupon to: **Dorchester Publishing Co., Inc.**
6 East 39 Street, Suite 900
New York, NY 10016
Att: ORDER DEPT.